Honor Series

BSC West Book 15

By

L. Ann Marie

Continuation from Nova: Cred BSC book 14

Everyone knows the Blackhawks. Mase is one that stands out loud and clear. He's always up for anything but don't piss him off. Mase heats up the pages and Kateri is his newest target. Blackhawk's have skillz so Kateri may need some help. Will his Brothers help her?

Blackhawk: Heat

Mase is our next installment in the BSC West saga... BSC book 15, Honor Rising Series.

BSC SERIES Books. Best read in order.

Master's Rise
Benga's Rise
Ranger's Rise
Jack: Honor
Falcon: Respect
Mag: Loyalty
Allegory
Endue
Conform
Justice: Tenacity
Ford's Rise
Driver: Grit
Christiansen: City Boy
Nova: Cred
Blackhawk: Heat
Cooper: Gunslinger
Teller: Connect
Maverick: Insight

Copyright

This is a work of fiction. Names, characters, places and incidents are either the product of the author's imagination or used fictitiously and any resemblance to actual persons, living or dead, business establishments, events or locales is entirely coincidental.

All rights reserved.

Blackhawk: Heat Honor Series (BSC Book 15)
By Copyright 2021 © L. Ann Marie
Published by: L. Ann Marie
Jo-Kat Author Services
Cover by Lori Birkett
Cover: BigStock
Edits 3/22

This book contains material protected under International and Federal Copyright Laws and Treaties. Any unauthorized reprint or use of this material is prohibited. No part of this book may be reproduced or transmitted in any form or by any means, electronic or mechanical, including photocopying, recording, or by any information storage and retrieval system without express written permission from L. Ann Marie, the author/publisher. Thank you for respecting the hard work of this author.

Cast of Characters

*Full character lists on the **Book Info** Page of* https://lannmarie.com/book-info

Cort Masters - President of Phoenix Rising (*PR*), President of Phoenix Badass Security Council (BSC West)

Raid - VP of Phoenix Rising

Ranger - SAA of Phoenix Rising

Web - Head IT for BSC West, Phoenix Rising

Banks - Stockbroker, invests for the Phoenix Rising and affiliates *(AR)*

Amos - Accountant, manages money for Phoenix Rising

Falcon Beckett - President of Bravo Rising (*BR*)

Jack Decker - VP of Bravo Rising

Mag Bailey - SAA of Bravo Rising

Justice LaPonte-James-Lightfoot - Lead (One) of Prince Crew, 2nd to Cort in BSC West *(BR)*

Tats - Protector Lead, New Officer *(BR) Alder Security*

Trask McCabe - President of Champion Rising *(CR)*

Jinx Solaita - VP of Champion Rising, BSC West, second to Cort *(CR)*

Beacon - SAA of Champion Rising *(CR)*

Major Christiansen - MC Colorado former President

Brekan Greywolf - President of MC Badass Colorado

Spook Reno - VP MC Badass Colorado

Pauly - SAA Head Security MC Colorado

Jordan Driver - President of Alpha Rising *(AR)*

Brinks Solaita - VP of Alpha Rising *(AR)*

Slade Nova - SAA *(AR)*

Kyler - Protector soon to be VP for a Club *(AR)*

Angel - Protector *(AR)*

Enrique - Officer, Inner Circle *(AR)*

Kristos Christiansen - President of Honor Rising *(HR)*

Mase Blackhawk - VP of Honor Rising

Spano - Protector Lead, Second to Kristos *(HR)*

Seth – SAA of Honor Rising, former Prince *(HR)*

Mal - Ops Control *(HR)*

Donna - Flight Lead Officer *(HR)*

Mary - PA Enforcer *(HR)*

Anvil - Enforcer Champion *(HR)*
Michaels - Protector Lead *(HR)*
Cline - Protector Lead *(HR)*
Nemo - Security Lead *(HR)*
Benny - Prospect *(HR)*
Thyme - Prospect *(HR)*
Ajhil - Rex and Ant Irma's charge
Rex - Cort's Uncle
Ant Irma - Rex's ol' lady
Crow - MC Badass, Native, Mason, deceased
Morris - Jeweler

Ol' ladies/Old ladies

Stella Jackson - Protector, ol'lady of Jordan and Brinks, former Prince *(AR)*
Hannah McCabe - IT Head, ol'lady to Trask, former Prince, *(CR)*
Alexia - Web's ol' lady, ex-FBI, ABSZ IT Lead, Trainer for BSC West
Seren - Cort's ol' lady, Mom to Caelan, trainer *(PR)*
Freedom - Ranger's ol' lady, Trainer/ Enforcer *(PR)*
Leya - Mag's ol' lady, Chocolatier, Ice cream shop owner *(BR)*
AJ - Jack's ol' lady, Mag's sister, Head of IT for Club *(BR)*
Faith - D'Ability house Director, Beacon's ol' lady, Dreng's mom *(CR)*
Carmen LJL - Justice's old lady, Cytogenetic tech for Alder
Télia Ford - Ford's wife, the Ford brothers' sister-in-law. Saber sibling
Natalia Kensington - Kristos' ol' lady, Head of Technology *(HR)*
Kateri Todachine - Graphic designer, old lady to Mase Blackhawk *(HR)*
Mikey- Prince Lead Protector, Nova's ol' lady, daughter of Cade *(AR)*
Harper Greywolf - Doctor MC Badass Colorado, Brekan's ol'lady

Kids

Dreng - Doug, adopted son of Beacon, Faith
Stephan -Tide's son
Daniel - Raid and Lorelei's son
Tyson - Mag and Leya's son
Caelan - Cort and Seren's son
Chenzo - Jack and AJ's son
Cove Blackhawk - Hannah and Trask's son
Beck Qunhôtuq - Hannah and Trask's son

~

Michael - Web's twin, brother to Ford and Garren

Garren - Michael and Web's older brother, Hamp Ford's twin
Parker Nova - Nova's brother *(AR)*

Doctors

Alder Ford - President of the Alpha-Bits *(BSC)*
Doc - Doctor *(PR)*
Statler - Doctor *(HR)*
Bean - PA *(AR)*
Bones - Doctor *(BR)*
Chop - Doctor *(CR)*
Patcher - EMT, PA *(PR)*

From BSC East Clubs

Ben Knight - President of Territories for the Brotherhood of Badass Bikers, (aka MC Badass) Princes of Prophecy and Badass Security Council (aka BSC)
Ricky Callahan - VP of Territories for the BSC, VP of Mass MC Badass and second for Badass Security Council (aka BSC)
Darren LaPonte-James - VP of Princes of Prophecy
Eliza LaPonte-James - Officer, Enforcer Princes of Prophecy
Elizabeth Callahan - MC Mass, Ricky's old lady, Knight's daughter
Jess Knight - Steve Knight's old lady, Ben and Elizabeth's mom
Dakota Lightfoot - Member of Princes of Prophecy, BSC, pilot, Prophet
Jessie LaPonte-James - Member of Princes of Prophecy
Aiyana Baxter - Princes of Prophecy Protector, Doctor, Shaman
Jeremy Blackhawk - MC, Princes of Prophecy and Protectors
Jacob Blackhawk - Princes of Prophecy and Protectors, BSC
Christian Blackhawk - MC, Princes of Prophecy Protector
Brantley Blackhawk - IT Head BSC, Princes of Prophecy
Taylor Blackhawk - Princes of Prophecy
Beth Blackhawk - Taylor's old lady, nurse
Jess Baxter-LaPonte-James-Lightfoot - old lady to Jessie, Dakota, mom to Justice, Aquyà, Destiny
Sheila Jackson - Enforcer, Princes of Prophecy
Jax Jackson - Princes of Prophecy
The Stooges - Steve Knight, Danny LaPonte, Tiny Callahan, *Pres Ben James (honorary)
Brian - Reader Princes of Prophecy

BSC Protector Crew from Princes of Prophecy
Justice LaPonte-James-Lightfoot, Teller Knight, Mucimi Blackhawk - Bravo

Luke Rayne DeSeville, Jeti Callahan, Tucker Brighton - BSC Training in Nevada.
Hannah Blackhawk (McCabe) - Champion Rising
Cayden Callahan, Lukas Callahan - Elan Rising.
Mase Blackhawk, Seth Baxter-LaPonte-James - Honor Rising
Stella Jackson-Driver-Solaita, Kyler Moniz, Aylen Knight, Mikey Nova - Alpha Rising.
Lisa Baxter-Martel, Nash Blackhawk - Phoenix
Chris Blackhawk - MC Badass Colorado

BSC East Protectors
Phoenix, Aquyá, Honor, Destiny, Joshua, Blake, Chance, Putam, Keesog, Riley
Virginia Badass
Andrew, Brandon, Axe, Heath, Zel, Tekah, Luna, Zeke, Oliver, JC, Kutomá, Case
MC Mass
Harley, Colt, Mitchy, Indie, Brenna, Blaze, Sandy, Shona, Ally

Alpha-Bits
As - Akai, Alta, Amal, Aris, Allen, Aaron (O) *(CR)*, Alder, Asa (O), Anton.
Bs - Brody *(CR)*, Brann *(ER)*
Bs - Budgie, Brex *(AR)*
Cs - Claus (F)
Cs - Cai, Chikako, Chang
Ds - Demetri, Darius, Drexel
Es - Eli *(CR)*, Emilio (F)
Es - Elijah, Ezra -
Fs - Franz (short arm), Faber *(CR)*(F)
G - Gregor (backward foot) (F)
Js - Juan, Jose, Jacques
Ls - Locke, Lars
Ms - Marco, Maddox, Mateo, Mario
O - Orion
Ps - Peyton, Pax, Pace, Percy. (O)
Rs - Roman, Radimir, Rostya *(PR)* (Roland died)
Ss - Sohn, Sabur
Island

9 - 2 yr old - Amell, Bryn, Crain, Denz, Etan, Fynn, Geir, Hali, Indra - *(MC)*
Ks - Kier, Kristoff, Kaval, Keon
Ns - Nasr, Nero, Nigel
Ts - Tamas, Trece
V - Vance
Ws - Wavan, Wesley
X - Xavier

Sweden
Ls - Les: Laran, Lasil, Lance, Levon, Ledell
N- Nox
Os – Odell *(AR)*, Oman
Qs – Quincy *(AR)*, Quillon
Rs - Ramell, Runar
Zs – Zale *(AR)*, Zachon

Finland
Ms - Mabon, Maurice, Matteus *(AR)*
N - Nyle
Os - Oscar, Oliver
Q - Quest
Ts - Tomas, Theo
Ws - Wolfgang, Wain

Total Alpha-Bits 143

*(O) = Oriental look to them
*(F)=Falcon took from monastery

BSC West Clubs

Phoenix Rising and Affiliates:
Cort Masters President of Phoenix Rising, President of Badass Security Council West
Raid Benga VP of Phoenix Rising
Ranger Ross SAA of Phoenix Rising
Web IT Head of BSC West Clubs

Trask McCabe President of Champion Rising
Jinx Solaita VP of Champion Rising
Beacon SAA of Champion Rising

Cooper President of Elan Rising
Cayden Moniz VP of Elan Rising
Cecil SAA of Elan Rising

Falcon Beckett President of Bravo Rising
Jack Decker VP of Bravo Rising
Mag Bailey SAA of Bravo Rising
Justice LaPonte-James-Lightfoot BSC 2nd to Cort

Alder President of Alpha-Bits, BSC 2nd to Cort
Asa, Akai VP of Alpha-Bits
Amal SAA of Alpha-Bits

Kristos Christiansen President of Honor Rising
Mase Blackhawk VP of Honor Rising
Seth Baxter-LaPonte-James SAA of Honor Rising

MC Badass Colorado and Affiliates
Brekan Graywolf President of MC Badass Colorado
Spook Reno VP of MC Badass Colorado

Pauly SAA of MC Badass Colorado

Jordan Driver President of Alpha Rising
Brinks Solaita VP of Alpha Rising
Nova SAA of Alpha Rising

Maverick President of Delta Rising
Finn VP of Delta Rising

FYI

I have written of human trafficking many times. I do because it hasn't stopped. A few years ago, I wrote the FBI Series right from the news. Before that, the MC with news from around the world. There were and still are coastal towns and cities in the US that have city officials charged for taking money to let drugs and contraband come into the country. We've all seen the PD issues, mass shootings, mass graves, drugs, dirty politicians, kids being stolen. These are part of our daily reality. I write them because it beats reading about over a half a million people dying within a year from a virus.

My Badass world can't fix that one, okay, maybe Alder, Mitch and Aiyana could but they aren't real. I see what I see and fix what I can when the Brother that can do the fixing is up. LB handled five towns because he could easily. The news had over nine before I gave up on that story. The FBI were all about the crazy shit we see on the news for three seconds. Most of my books take place over a month or two. No problem is fixed that fast even in fiction.

Badass fixes what they can *their* way and I love them for it. I don't get their stories until I start writing them. I don't have a problem writing about a threat that lasts for a year because I live at least half in reality and see issues last for decades.

You could change the news by helping fix the wrongs in the world. Everyone has the chance and choice to be that guy (or girl). Badass would love the help and I bet you'd meet some real Badass Brothers of your own. Write to me if you do!

In the meantime, have fun with Mase and the crazy Brothers.

Call names

CC - Cayden Callahan

Prophet - Mucimi

Warrior - Mase

Zenobia (female warrior) - Aylen Knight

Again, we are hit with too many Pres's's's's, I used Preses because it works for me. I get that it isn't right or recognized as a word. I will claim it with shield, cloak, push and suspend definitions when someone at Webster's adds them to the dictionary.

Mohegan Help

Ayakuhsak - stars
Ayunam - Help
Inskitôp - Indian
Ituksq - sister
Ki - you
Kisuq - Sky
Kuwômôyush - love you
Miy - Give
Muks - Wolf
Muksak - wolf
Muksak - wolves
Nâhsuk - husband
Náhtiák - dogs
Nákum - he she her him
Nekanis - brother
Ni - I Me
Nimskam - fetch
Nu - my
Nuin - my man
Nukumat - easy
Nupômkoki - my world
Òkatuq - Cloud
Pumshá - go along
Quhshâwôk - fear
Qunhôtuq - spear
Tôn - how
Wàpàyu - wind
Wikco - handsome
Yáhsháyôn - my breath

Table of Contents

Copyright

Cast of Characters

BSC West Clubs

FYI

Mohegan Help

Prologue

Chapter One

Chapter Two

Chapter Three

Chapter Four

Chapter Five

Chapter Six

Chapter Seven

Chapter Eight

Chapter Nine

Chapter Ten

Chapter Eleven

Epilogue

Acknowledgments

About the Author

Author contact links

Other books by L. Ann Marie

Reading Order

Prologue

Mase

On the ride to Champion, I stop to pick up Nova. He waits on the side of the highway by Manny. "Brother. Where's Nash?"

I smile at the quick acknowledgement and question. Nova loves what he sees as the underdogs.

"Flying over. He's on-call later. I need to check-in with Manny, give me ten."

He pulls small bungees from his bag and follows me. "I knew you'd want to stop. I got the news for Kristos from Henry, Clip, Helga and Kent. Mikey loves the rounds." He's a good Brother.

"He's making them in Utah and Colorado. The Brother could run for office and win in either state already."

Throwing chin to the Prospect, he smiles. "The banner bungees. Quincy made these. When they get worn ask him for more or see Wrenchy." He drops the anchors and fasteners he pulled out of his pocket into the Prospect's hand.

The Prospect takes the bungees with a smile. "Thanks, Boss. This will work better than the rope."

I wait reading that he's glad we stopped. "Do you need help to put the fasteners on?" It's a five-minute job.

"I've got it, Boss, but thanks." His head shows a man putting in a new kitchen then working on a camper.

I was like that working with my dad, so I get it and throw him chin. We talk to Manny until he gets customers. Life in a food truck keeps him up on the city and general concerns. Since Nova is here, he'll fix what he can and take what he can't back to Jordan.

"What's with the banner net thing?" I ask throwing my leg over.

"It covers the back door so they get air flowing through. When the door is open, supplies go missing. The Prospect caught a kid stealing bread a few days ago. He pointed him to the neighborhood and asked Stella for help." He starts his bike not saying anymore. I read that he's glad Stella is calm and helpful with what the Prospects are bringing her.

I am too. She's like Alder with the quick fixes. Sarah jumps in my head. The ride through the city toward the ABSZ is quiet. Sarah takes that space today. She's an enigma. The woman is so confident in everything, but something strikes me as off with her. Not reading her throws me. I can't read everyone but get nothing from the woman to help me understand her. I met her the first week we were in Honor and have been called to fuck six times. Feeling she's happy isn't telling me anything but she's glad I showed.

I have absolutely no complaints about fuckin' a beautiful woman anyway I want. She's a sub all the way and my need to control loves that I'm not explaining shit while taking that control. I shake my head smiling, that's a joke, she's got all the control. I love that she trusts me enough to let it go and amazed that she wants to please me without knowing much about me. She isn't a talker. The night we met is the longest we've talked. Her bound body with those eyes downcast and a hint of a smile on her lips has me sitting straighter to adjust for my dick.

"You need an ear, Brother?" Nova cuts into my memory before it jumps to what happened next.

I think about keeping Sarah to myself then just throw it out. "I met this woman. She just does it for me. She's Indian but not Mohegan or of Pequot descent." She's fuckin' beautiful in everything. Every move she makes always strikes me as choreographed to fit her small frame, reach and space. I think it's confidence but that feels wrong. I wish I could read her.

"Her being a different Indian matters to you?" He doesn't like that.

We blow by the military guard at ABSZ throwing respect before I answer. "Not at all. Her bone structure is about all the difference I've noticed. She doesn't talk about the tribe or much of anything else lately. I know she's Indian by look and she has this weird confidence like Aiyana. Even before Aiyana knew of the Paleo-American tie, she had this weird presence. Like she knew shit and had no one to prove it to. It just is."

Words from someone else play in his head, *Cort has that greatness about him.* "I know what you mean about Aiyana and that presence. She's important, but it's not in a way I understand. I just feel it. Why isn't your girl talking lately?" He's wondering why I'm not talking to her.

"She calls me and I show. It's always good, but I can't read her. It's been more than a month and that's getting more frequent but she isn't asking for more." I want more.

"Have you told her you want more?"

"You're not a reader?"

He laughs at me. "No. You're not a Brother that would show when summoned if you didn't care." The fuckin' Brother is smart. He thinks I care more than I'm saying and fuckin' for relief isn't my style.

"Yeah. There's something about her that pulled me in the first night we met. She's smart, independent and confident with a grace that's ingrained in her or something."

He laughs. "She's you."

That feels good but wrong. "She's quiet, has a lone-wolf feel about her and all but her presence is tiny. She's aware and watchful of everything like she's soaking the environment in."

He thinks about that and I shield. "That's the draw. The Indian you feel, attention to detail you admire and tiny. You need to protect her?"

Maybe I shouldn't have, but I leave the shield thinking this is what I need. "Until you said it, I didn't see that. There's something to that. We were taught to protect women from young. Not because they're not strong but there's something women have that we don't. We protect the spirit inside them so they stay strong. Prez always said women have a fierceness that covers their heart. That heart is made of the thinnest glass and our job is to make sure we do everything to fix, mend or rebuild that fierceness so we get to see what she can do with that heart. Women are fuckin' amazing with the shit they can do. There's something in Sarah that feels off. Maybe her glass is cracked."

He's quiet for a minute and I know without pulling the shield he's thinking about Mikey. Prez tried to mend her glass. He's so proud of her being here and showing what she can do with that fierceness.

"It sounds like it's time for you to show up and talk to her before you're summoned and talk isn't part of the plan."

"Yeah. I'll do that today. How are Parker and Mikey?"

"Perfect." He makes me smile. "Ben called Mikey for information on the crews or something. She was proud but never said it. Why is he seeing her now?"

None of us would say so I nod glad Prez called her. "Cade didn't want her on a crew but never told her. I think he regretted it later but he never said. Justice wouldn't step in because he'd have to pick up three not just Mikey. With Mucimi, Indie and Prez sending him then us every fuckin' where, he had no time to put up that fight for her. That would have been a fight with Prez, Dakota and Cade. I can't blame him. The other thing is the results from testing. Taylor is going crazy with Teams now that they split the Clubs and crews up. The board works now and everyone is excited up there. Justice and Teller ran the crew house from when Justice was twelve and Teller ten. Being young was tough when he was going against Prez, his dads and every fuckin' adult that threw advice at him because he was young and thought different. Prez always listens to Justice but has Clubs counting on him so he doesn't always act on it. Fundamentals of the testing falls on Princes. Mikey is a Prince with a mended heart and Badass shining through."

"We're all one to all of you, aren't we?"

I pull the shield to see what he means. "Yeah. Badass ties us together."

We turn into Champion before he says anything else. "I think Cort was shocked because Ben has no problem admitting he didn't know how the board worked. They've had it for years and are just using it now." He's proud of Mikey for getting the Clubs working better. They all see Prez as more and they were all shocked.

I smile at that and shield again. "When Jeremy came up with the testing, he was going through shit with Jacob and Aubrey. He checked out for a while. Trying to get him going back or even explaining something he's already done isn't easy. There's too much he sees happening now. He's learned to focus himself but it's not as easy for him as Mucimi, so a hundred other things have his attention. Prez is the same as Cort, you, me or even Alder. We're just Brothers trying to be the best we can and help show our communities how to be the best them."

He nods shutting his bike off at Jinx's. "Is that why Alder talks worse when he's busy?"

Fuckin' smart. "Yeah. Knight is like that too. Getting information is tough and reading them isn't easy. Readers, even like Prez, Christian, Justice and Teller don't see everything because they can read. The Prophets don't see everything either. We're just men with different abilities than yours, Brother."

He nods watching my eyes. "We didn't grow up in that world. It's easier than before but we still see greatness from the originals that always floors us. It's good to get the reminder that we're all the same."

I slap his back and turn toward the bike coming through the gate. Nash is happy he made it, the Brother is going to love this, he rides like a true Blackhawk. I don't know how my mom and dad made it with Jeremy, Jacob and me. Now they have grands just like us that could do stunts for Hollywood in anything with a motor.

"Mase, Boss Nova, I thought I was going to be late." He pulls his helmet off and has the Blackhawk smile in place.

Pulling him over, I kiss his head. "We'd wait for you, Brother. Why didn't Jeti come?"

He rolls his eyes. "They're going to see the babies and do their nails."

Nova laughs. "Girl-time is important. We don't need to understand it to know they get back from it with smiles and appreciation for not bitching about the time away from us."

Shaking my head, I watch Nash pull his tablet. "Justice is gonna teach me to write it in my head while the tablet is in my bag but I have to do this for now. That's a good one." He types then smiles up at Nova. "I'll be ready when my old lady shows."

Jinx comes out with Cayden and Brinks following. "Brothers." The acknowledgement has me throwing chin.

We help get supplies and lunch in the truck and load Jinx's bike on the trailer. Champ jumps in the truck with Brinks while we get our pieces set. I like talking to them on the ride. Throwing shit back and forth to the truck sucks and means I'm missing shit so the pieces work. Teller, Chris and Riley meet us at the gate.

"Thanks for getting the supplies, Brothers." I throw waiting for Teller to move to my side.

He shakes his head. "You're VP, Mase."

I nod. I've been VP longer than the twins and was just reminded that Teller's been VP a fuck of a lot longer. "So are you, take your place, Brother, it's been your position since you were ten. It's an appreciation that should never get lost in our minds because we need milk on the way home or to remember to add Security to the gate."

He throws me chin and a blast of appreciation.

"Nice, Mase. I'll remember now that I've heard it." Jinx makes me smile piping up here. The Brother remembers everything.

Chris, Cayden and Nash tell Riley and the twins about Teller and Justice in the crew house. Nash was young and stayed with Taylor and Beth until he was eight. He shadowed Justice and Teller for almost a year and got that love of flying from them. Jeti picked it up too. It was crazy to see them struggling with the pull on the choppers. Justice had them in a jet for training before they went into chopper training. The simulators helped.

Turning, I think about how fuckin' lucky I was to land with Justice and Teller. It's been forever and being older just means I've seen more shit than they have. That's probably not true anymore. They see shit I'd never want to.

Turning toward the river, I follow Brinks' directions to a new area with more trees and a wider section of river. This is nice.

Thoughts of riding with my Brothers push Sarah back. I'll look at it later.

~*~*~

Jumping out of the chopper I'm glad I see my bike and smile. It was a good day with my Brothers. I can't wait for a good night with my tiny enigma of a girl. A ride with her will make it perfect.

"Thanks for bringing us, Mase. You Brothers have all the fun." Chris thinks we lucked out with Justice and Teller.

I stop and look back. "We worked to get here, Brother. It wasn't all fun," Nash answers just like I would.

I nod at Chris. "He's right. Get with us on Monday for shit we're doing. You're welcome to show at anytime. Aylen is exploring too and needs a Protector with her. If you're not distracted by the new, take the shifts for her. Jump is every night."

Aylen sees everything and knows the work we've put in to get the 'rents respect. She's from another crew and can relate so she'd be a good one to pair him with.

He nods and I see he's throwing no Indian at me. Nash takes it again. "Don't say can't to him, Chris. I'll jump with you at twelve. I got this, Mase. Go see your girl." He looks at me reading that I may be late. "We'll be there."

I throw him a *good job* walking away. I need to get my bike then dinner for Sarah. Nash is getting stronger as a reader. I'll have to shield around him.

Running down the Ops board, I'm glad to see it's been a slow day. Kristos is a good President for this Club or the bikers and Flight Crews that have merged into our Honor Rising Club.

I bypass the office and ride to my house wondering what Sarah likes to eat. We talked about everything our first night. I know she likes eggs and pork chops for breakfast. She drinks coffee and I've seen water at her house. My feet stop on the way up the stairs. She asked about my family and the east coast then cities I've been to. We laughed at the shit we've done. I was happy to talk about the shit she wouldn't do and noted opinions and reactions to shit we did do. I didn't learn much about her.

In the shower I list what I *do* know. She's Navajo. Went into foster care at thirteen when her dad died from a construction accident. She went to school for graphic design when she was seventeen. Her guidance counselor and a caseworker helped her get into the dorms in Arizona. She's been to California with her grandmother and dad but she was too young to remember. Her dad took her camping and fishing at their place near the Cheyenne reservation. She hasn't been there since he died. She works from home but I don't know what she does. She's got book shit at her house, maybe she writes. She got me talking about the group homes then fucked with my head putting her hands on me. I couldn't read her even while she touched me.

I'm amazed she made it to college early and worked for what she wanted. Group homes aren't easy and she said hers wasn't a good one. She went through the loss of her dad in a place that sucked and still made it to good. Her house is in the second town built by Alder with high end shit that he offers to buyers. It's got to be a three bedroom, but I only saw hers and the downstairs. She's got good pans and keeps real food on hand.

I stand on the back deck and pull wind to me to dry my hair. Justice does it in the shower, when I saw, I had to try it. The fuckin' Brother looks like he just waves clothes on, I can't do that one either, I can always see me moving to get them on. Since I can pull wind when I'm outside, my hair dries in two minutes. Brushing through it, I notice it's getting long again. I'll get Nash to cut it.

Movement draws my eye. "That's one way to dry your hair, Brother." Spano has me smiling.

"Yeah. It beats riding without a lid and trying to brush it when I stop. I'm not going far enough to dry it."

He walks up the stairs. "Kateri Todachine, town two."

"Who the fuck is that?" Town two is right.

He steps back. "I was on Ops. That's where your tracking showed twice when I came in. The Lead we got from Bravo, Mal, said it's a regular stop for you."

"Kateri Todachine?" I try the name out. Maybe that's her grandmother. Nunánuk's name was Kateri. It's the Indian version of Kathryn that was given to kids taken from their tribes for Christian teaching. It's not a Navajo name. I thought it was Cheyenne. Nunánuk said a Cheyenne girl called her Kateri. When the tribe got the kids back, they had all been renamed. Nunánuk liked Kateri and kept it because being known as a crazy shaman was too much for a small girl. The Shaman she was named after is '*Squannit of the little people*'. The story is a good one that shows Squannit as a generous shaman taking care of children, but Nunánuk must have held back crazier stories. She has both names in the book of ancestors. I throw appreciation to the ancestors for getting her back safely and shake my head.

Spano throws more that doesn't work for me. "It's the name listed on the house, it's paid for and she checks out as not a threat."

No one has been in the house with us. I'd have felt that. "Who the fuck checked her out?"

His hands are up again. "You frequent so she's been checked. You've done the checks on Kristos's new rounds so don't get pissed at me. I didn't ask for it but would have done the same thing if it wasn't done. It's procedure for Officers."

I nod not sharing that it's not her name and I don't know who the fuck they checked out. "I'm headed out, did you need something?"

"No, Brother. I'm meeting Kristos and Seth. I just stopped to watch the hair drying. It's cool, by the way."

I walk in the door. "Later, Brother." Pulling my hair back, I tie it low and get on my bike. *'Mucimi, did Nunánuk ever say the name of the Cheyenne girl that gave her the name?'*

'Sarah Todachine.' He has me stopping before I'm at the Colorado gate.

"Are you fuckin' serious?" My heart is going to beat right the fuck out of my chest.

'She had an Indian name but Nunánuk didn't know it. Are you okay?'

"What's Justice doing?"

Mucimi shows on the side of me and puts his hand on my arm. "Flying. You need Teller?"

Moving off the road has Mucimi suspending right with me. "Christian?"

'Stay close, Mucimi. I'll send Justice later, Mase. You got this. There's more you're not seeing. Justice will help.' Christian isn't helpful.

Fuckin' great. "I guess you're close, Mucimi. Can you get food for me? We need dinner but I don't know what she likes so barbecue plates should work. They have everything."

He's gone without looking at me. Fuckin' great. With my heart sinking, I ride out the gate and take the twenty-minute ride to her house. Mucimi has a bag on the step. He's not going to show himself. This is not good. Picking up the bag I hit the doorbell.

Sarah is surprised when she opens the door. "Mase?"

"Is your grandmother Sarah Todachine?" My eyes take in her delicate features turning blank. Those eyes guarded.

Her tiny body freezes. "How do you know that?" It is. Monotone like her *yes, sir* in the bedroom is not what I expect.

My dick twitches remembering the sound. "Is your name Kateri?"

Her nod is tentative. I've never seen nervous come out of her normally calm, cool and collected manner. I feel it now. "What is this, Mase?"

Lifting the bag, I show her. "Dinner and hopefully a chance to get to know more about you." Like why the fuck I don't get her real name.

"Why?" She's not happy.

I can't read her but I feel that. "We've been fuckin' for over a month. Don't you want to know more about me?" I sure as fuck have questions besides her name. I want to know everything about her, but I want her to want me to know it.

Her eyes show fear. What the fuck?

'*Tell her why! She's never had a boyfriend or anyone that cared.*' Mucimi has my jaw clenching.

"I want more than a call for service, Kateri."

'*Use Sarah!*' Fuckin' Mucimi.

I keep talking before she can answer. "Sarah, I want to know more about you. It's just dinner. I'm not asking for anything but the time it takes to eat." For now. I plan on changing that as soon as we finish eating. A ride will do us both good. Wind is good for settling your mind and hopefully loosening her hold on that calm, cool and collected persona so I get to know who Kateri is.

"I'm working, Mase. We agreed to the calls so I don't understand this. I have a deadline and can't do this right now." She backs up and closes the door.

That's not going to get her on my bike.

I turn and Mucimi snatches the bag. '*Your house.*'

Fuckin' great.

~*~*~

In my backyard I feel someone close and open my eyes. "Brother."

Justice never showed last night so I'm relieved to see him now. It's got to be around four in the morning. Mucimi left the food on my table and didn't answer when I called to him. For some reason, I'd rather Justice tell me bad shit. Mucimi is too sensitive and Christian too blunt.

He nods. "I needed to calm Mucimi then listen to everyone in the fuckin' MC and Princes that feels they have a right to offer opinions."

My heart pounds. "Why is everyone offering opinions on a woman they don't know?"

He sits hitting my leg so I sit beside him. Taking my forearm isn't helping my heart. It's not bad, it's one of those horrendous stories that had Mucimi looking for comfort from Brantley or my dad.

Justice nods. "Kateri's grandmother died when she was eight. Her mom is one of the missing Indians that had her at seventeen then vanished shortly after. Her grandmother moved with Crow and his tribe to land allotted by the Indian Nation here. They're not with the Pueblo's but Pueblo accepts them without all the political and tradition wars we've seen."

He's not up on Indian histories so I nod. This isn't the reason he's calming me. "It's not, Brother. When Kateri's dad died, she went into care. She made plans with her guidance counselor and had a caseworker in Arizona from a college help set it up so she could live in a dorm at seventeen. The guidance counselor called in three reports about possible abuse but was warned off by the vice principal. Kateri's foster dad was a cop and single."

I hold his arm tight grasping for anything to keep me right here listening to the rest. I nod for him with every muscle in me ready to spring but locked tight. "He's dead. Cort killed him for killing a Brother that was also a cop. That Brother's sister is Tag's old lady and carries Cort's protection for life."

This is unreal. "Her name?"

"Mucimi spent almost all night at the reservation with Christian, Aiyana and Nunánuk. She was the woman that gave Nunánuk the Kateri name. She was two years older than Nunánuk and helped with the younger kids in that fucked school kidnapping thing. Kateri's name is Kateri after Nunánuk, Sarah after her grandmother, Todachine. The cop didn't like the Indian name and called her Sarah. She uses it only for sexual encounters and you're the second she's had since she got out of school. The other is a Brother that moved east. The reason she uses Sarah..."

My head snaps up stopping him when he sees my eyes. "I get it. Tell me she wasn't used by a Brother."

He shakes his head no and tightens the hold on my arm. "No, but he wasn't looking for longer than a night. She called a couple of times over three months."

I breathe and relax trying to swallow down what feels like a hockey puck in my throat. "I can't read her at all. Even touching her, I can't read her."

He nods keeping that hold on my arm. "She's yours, Brother. She's scared, has fucked up shit in her head and no one to trust. Mucimi says Nunánuk wants you to bring her to the ancestors. Christian warned me to keep you calm and get you to move slow. She doesn't know her tribe, the Brothers or you. She *does* trust you. You've got work to put in here before she trusts you with more. If you can get her to dinner at the compound, we can help. All together, we can help."

I shake my head. "All together you'll scare the shit out of her or drive her to jump the cliff alone." I pull but he's not letting my arm go.

He jumps and I'm slammed with energy that feels like it's weighing me down. "What are you doing?" The words are barely audible.

Justice looks up and I see everyone here. "Prez, Brothers." I try to throw chin because I don't think my voice made it.

"Let him go, Justice." Prez gets me to breathing normally without the weight on or in my body as soon as Justice lets my arm go.

"Thanks, what the fuck was that?" Taking a deep breath, I feel the calm as if it's working from the inside out now.

Prez sits with us. "He's too fuckin' strong and doesn't know what that feels like. He was right to bring you here, Mase. Elizabeth has Tess with her. You need information that only Tess can give you. Take what everyone gives you and keep pushing to get your girl comfortable with the family. She's been alone for too long."

I nod. Jeremy and Jacob sit with hands on me. "I will, Prez."

He nods then is gone. Christian is smiling. "You already thought of something. Don't fuck it up. Call if you need me." He's gone.

I look at Jacob. "I thought of something that helps?"

He shrugs. "He was smiling. It beats Mucimi's tears. Christian told us about fucked up behavior modification. Look up Presidio Modelo, it was a jail in Cuba. It will help. Don't ever mention cameras and stay away from home movies."

I nod trying to remember the Presido Modelo shit. Prisoners were on their best behavior because they never knew when the guards were watching from a lighthouse looking tower in the center of a huge dome like building. There were no gates to their cells and the only floor was the walkways going around the outside. Best behavior, it's that grace I notice in her movements. She was watched on camera or felt she was when she was home.

Jeremy lets me go. "Yeah, you got it. Don't fuck it up." He's gone.

I shake my head. "Our family is crazy."

He nods without the smile I was hoping for. "We are but we're good at family. Jeremy says you're stronger than him. Keep it together and we've got a chance of helping you. If you lose it, she's gone. Don't fuckin' lose it." Jacob doesn't give warnings so this one will be taken seriously.

I nod taking it all in. Losing her isn't an option I can look at right now. This is why Justice was holding me down. I turn toward him. "Thanks, Justice. I'll get her to the compound somehow."

He nods and points. "Elizabeth is taking Tess back, it's too much, she'll be at the compound when you bring Kateri."

Fuck. Taking a deep breath I look at my Brothers. They're all throwing calm and encouragement. Since Justice said I bring Kateri, that name feels weird but I know it's right, since I'm bringing her to the compound, I guess I figure something out.

He doesn't smile but nods. "Take what you need here, Brother. Call to me."

I can only nod.

Chapter One

Four days

Mase

I'm pissed as I run the endurance course. Four fuckin' days and Kateri hasn't answered my text. When I get down the stairs, I run to a bag and hit it over and over. Teller shows holding the bag in place. He's been here too much lately. I breathe with every punch, calm my shit down and walk to the wall. Sliding down, I close my eyes and jump.

The ancestors make it easier to see I need more than pissed right now. Jacob's warning is center stage in my head. Throwing appreciation, I jump back noting Teller is gone. It takes twenty minutes for me to get to lunch, in gear, with dry hair. I think I'm getting faster. I stood under the water for fuckin' ever hoping for some advice that I can use from someone. Divine intervention from the ancestors isn't in the cards today.

Kristos is alone at the table. I look and see Michaels at the wall. I need to focus.

Kristos nods. "Brother, I'm glad you showed."

I don't look to see why. I've been shielding everyone but Justice and Teller. "Do you need something, Pres?" I could use a job.

"No. You do. Your girl was at the Utah Club yesterday. She scoped it out and left alone."

Everything in me stops. Losing my shit will lose her. How fuckin' crazy it is to feel like this runs through my head. She doesn't know she's mine. *I* don't know if she's fuckin' mine and I'm ready to blow the Club away so she never walks through the door again. I guess she's mine. With a deep breath I nod.

He goes on. "Seth is on Ops and has surveillance watching for her. If she shows tonight, you'll get the call. I'll be going with you."

That gets my attention. "Why you?"

"So you aren't blowing the Club up guaranteeing she'll never walk through the doors again. You need to keep it together, Brother. I don't have advice or plan to help you out. I can and will be close if you need me." He puts his hand out.

I take his arm feeling relieved. Divine intervention from the ancestors. "Thanks for not throwing shit at me."

He smiles nodding to the Prospect. "I figure you've got enough of that. I can't give advice on someone I've never met and didn't get the story to know enough."

We order and Brothers show while we eat. I've got nothing to add and Brothers don't ask me anything. I finish and check time. Pres stands when I do. "I'm out on a Colorado shift."

He shakes his head. "You're with me on Utah. Spano took Colorado with Anvil's Team. Seth said they're ready."

I nod and follow him out. Anvil is an Enforcer trained by Champion. They're ready. Riding with Pres will keep me focused. He's a smart Brother but I don't like my shit messing with his day. He doesn't start his bike so I look his way for why. The Team still isn't out yet.

He's looking straight ahead. "Cort called asking if I need help. I picked up something about a vision. I didn't understand until I saw Teller here earlier. Are you as strong as Justice?"

I smile for the first time in days. "No. He can hold me down without any effort. Teller can too. If I wasn't Mucimi's uncle, he would too. I'm not doing a fuckin' thing that will push her away, Pres. I never understood how you kept it together with Natalia on the chopper. I do now. Brothers lose it with the old ladies. I can see how and get that if I lose it, I lose her. I don't have the time in with her that you did but I got the warning and know losing it isn't an option we'd be able to live through."

He smiles. "I hope you mean you and your girl not the Club."

I laugh. "Does it matter?"

He gives it to me starting his bike. "I guess not. The Team is at the gate." He hits his mic on. I follow hitting mine.

"Brekan is settling." He throws out.

"Yeah. Chris is a good fit. He's young but has a draw to him. More Brothers out of training will help there."

"Yeah." We ride watching the mountains get close.

Mucimi bought the land up here because it has a big expanse of high and flat. It works for Aerial and positions the Club out of the way but right on the state lines. At first we were just a company expanding training. Now we have the Club, six towns that are growing daily, a complete base and Cort's crazy stockpile of vehicles from golf carts to fighter jets. Because of those six towns generating more to the states' revenues without pulling anything from the states' resources, we get a pass from just about everyone.

An inspector had a problem with noise or some shit too close to town one in Utah and Pres sent him packing.

The next day I had a building started for local and state inspections on everything. We have three Brothers that watch everything going up and approving the plans Alder and Paul come up with. One Brother is on Utah, one Colorado and the third is an engineer for everything. The smart car lanes got approval faster than Prez got in New England. I think it took an hour. They follow the rules without the bullshit. I sent it to Raid and Darren. Jinx has a Mason so he's good. Jack said Falcon picked his officials.

"Tell me about your girl." Pres pulls me away from how shit works to Kateri.

I know only what Justice told me. "What do you know?"

"She works from home and doesn't go out much. She's got Clubs across the country worried about you going off but doesn't seem to know it. She's got a tie to Crow."

That surprises me. "Crow? She's your family?"

"You know when I got family. I don't know her, know very little about her and haven't seen her. Why is everyone on alert?" His head shows he didn't question anyone. It's my story to tell.

I love the Brother for showing that respect. "I'm not being disrespectful but I'm not talking about this on an open mic."

'*Fair enough.*' He throws shocking the fuck out of me.

'*That is new, when did you start throwing?*'

He pulls to a lookout on the road leading down from the Club pointing at the other side. The Team pulls across the road. I like this one and hit my mic off taking in the view of the city in a valley, protected on two sides by mountains and a town a little further out and up on distant foothills. Mucimi bought everything up to the city giving us a huge buffer zone. Drones are working surveillance regularly because we can't fence the animals in or out where there are no roads.

Pres is smiling. "I threw to you?" He didn't know. Freaky is growing fast in him.

"Yeah, Pres."

His smile reaches his eyes throwing more blue into their mix. "I'll let Justice and Cort know. It's called throwing?"

I smile. "Yeah, Pres. Let me know if you start moving shit."

He shakes his head. "Knight just said reading. Christian too." His eyes are lit with amusement.

I'm glad that keeps him smiling. "At the time, my brother was scared because he just blasted you. Knight isn't always clear and reading to him may include all kinds of ability. The MC except Ricky and Elizabeth tend to lump everyone as readers. Only the Clubs know their abilities."

He nods. "Cort said we don't hide it from anyone. I can see it taking a threat away from the abilities but adding a different threat to them."

I shake my head. "That's why he sends a platoon."

He laughs. "I can see that being a deterrent. Am I practicing moving shit? Is there a freaky training I need?"

I laugh but stop when Christian shows.

The Team Lead pulls, then holsters his gun but doesn't cross the street. Cline knows freaky.

Christian rolls his eyes. He'd have us shielded. "Seth and Nash will start that soon. You're not Mase freaky, you're more like Seth. He's a reader with some pushing and throwing thought skills. Nash will help, he's always had ability and grew up without ever hiding them. Prez doesn't show all his ability as a form of defense. Do that." He's gone and I shake my head.

"Blackhawks are crazy."

He laughs. I like the carefree look on him. "That explains the alert on you." He gets off his bike and walks toward a clump of weeds around a rock. I throw fire then wind clearing the weeds so he can sit and follow. "Thanks, that's convenient. Tell me about your girl."

I tell him everything Kateri said to me, everything Justice said and the little advice I've gotten. He's pissed in a way I feel. "You don't read her?"

"Not at all. I feel her emotions but can't read her even if she's touching me."

His eyes are swirling as if the reddish color and new blue are fighting for space. It swallows up the tan color completely. I've never seen this and pull a shield then push it back. He's pissed. "CPS and a cop. It fits with what Jinx and Beacon told me. Did she move here because of a threat?"

I shrug. "I haven't talked to her since Justice told me. She hasn't answered my text." It would make sense. Why won't she answer my text then show in the Utah Club?

He hits his mic. "Seth, get us off the room and Kateri's house covered."

"You're on with just me. I have her on surveillance. You want a physical presence, Pres?"

I shake my head. Pres doesn't give me time to say anything. "She was given to the cop by CPS. What's your first thought?"

"Cover her, but there's more to it," Seth answers.

I nod. "The Presido Modelo effect. She may break seeing a physical presence."

Seth jumps in again. "That's one aspect. Another is she got money from some foundation Hannah set up and paid for her house. That's under Badass protection but was never advertised as Badass. It was money distributed from what we took from the agencies and gave to kids that were on a list as sold. It could be a coincidence, but her name and the reservation tie throw a reader warning to me. No one has said if she's a reader or ability kid. Asa is working on her name and history. I could be off, but I'm covering bases just in case. She's staying hidden in a way that's odd to watch. Maybe it's just the Presido Modelo thing, but she's here where cameras are a given."

I can picture him shrugging.

Pres nods. "Good job. Keep physical off and let me know what you find. Get Security upped in town two to yellow. Watch recognition for outsiders." That throws relief all over me.

"Roger, Pres. Utah is logging outsiders in two and three. The city has a yearly carnival going on so it's plausible. Raising the threat level has me relieved. I have twenty-six in Colorado on the tagged board and even more in Utah."

Pres nods. "Throw another Team in the highest tag populations. I'm glad you're in Ops, Brother. Is Asa with you?"

"Pulling information and running my tags for me. He's got IT working it." Seth sounds proud.

"I'm on the side." Pres walks back to his bike hitting his mic off. "Back to our towns feels right."

"Roger, Pres. You're back to open in the room." Seth didn't forget.

I follow with an uneasy feeling.

The towns are calm, but I notice more activity in centers and close to the realtor in town two. Pres notices the feel and pulls over just past the realtor. We cause a stir when we get off our bikes. Pres is going to find out why. I follow him to the realtor that's talking to a group of visitors.

"Pres, I'm glad you're here. We're running out of homes and I was just asked about the building schedule."

Pres stops and looks at me. "Condos in two weeks. New subdivisions within the month in two and three."

He nods. "Nothing in one?" The realtor asks.

Pres shakes his head. "No. Town one is for the Club, FBI and military."

"Is the Club a base?" An older woman asks.

Pres smiles. "We're Badass and our mother chapter is run by Cort Masters. He's crazy with keeping the communities safe and our Brothers working. Those Brothers are made up of Badass members, ex-FBI and military. Town one in Colorado and Utah are reserved for those Brothers."

I smile at the murmurs and dick-in-a-dish reference I hear, then turn to a pussy with an ignorance that throws alerts.

"Problem with the Brothers working?" I ask.

The pussy isn't sure what to say then throws some of what he's thinking. "We can buy outside of the town."

My smile is real. "You're welcome to buy outside of town."

Pres smiles with his nod. "Land for sale starts on the west side of the city. No Badass land is up for sale."

The older woman smiles. "So no Walmart or strip malls will be built between here and the city?"

"No. We have and are building more secluded completely green houses on the land but no strip malls on Badass land," Pres answers getting smiles back as the pussy backs away.

Looking at the Lead, I throw, '*Hold him.*' Cline wonders about him yelling so I throw again. '*He'll wait patiently.*'

Throwing wind through his head has the pussy dazed. The Lead holds the pussy's arm at the corner and calls his four over to stand guard. I throw wind at the pussy again and he almost falls over. Four holds him up asking if he's okay but isn't waiting for an answer, he watches the crowd. I love my Brothers.

Pres starts walking so I take my place beside him and watch as he schmoozes with the civilians that live here. Gawkers are gawking, they're all from away. Hearing about a trash problem I pull my tablet and look for what the holdup is.

Asa jumps in my ear. "New recycle center up. Truck delay one day. Email sent, Pres Kristos, VP Mase."

Pres looks at me so I answer. "The new recycling plant just started. You should have an email about the trucks being delayed a day. The plant is between us and Delta Rising."

A guy trying to be helpful gets Pres's attention. "The City has a dump."

Pres nods. "We recycle everything and use the material to build for Badass Innovations, the public, or the

Clubs. All solar and wind collectors are made from recycling and fund the schools and public buildings. Both Delta and Honor Rising will have vet homes and businesses running next month thanks to the recycling we collect. Giving it up to the city isn't an option. The delay is just a day."

"Pres, your package is moving." Seth stops Pres from taking another step.

He turns right around heading for the bikes. "Roger, Ops. Check your email and send questions through the website."

Teller shows on the side of me. "You need to get to the Utah Club. Stay calm, Brother."

Fuckin' great. Pres moves faster. A woman yells when Teller is just gone. She should have yelled when he showed. We screw with the Team following. I didn't see anyone pick the pussy up but don't ask.

It's an eighteen-minute ride at a hundred. I know she's already here. Pres turns to me. "Stay out of sight until you need to be seen. I'm with Teller. Cline, you're on out."

We roger and I'm at the back walking in. "Southeast table in the corner, Brothers." Seth helps me out.

Moving down the back hall, I stop and wait at the Club entrance. She's three tables away from here at the window in a Native-bohemian look that just does it for me. She's covered in a way that the colors and cut of fabric show every curve on her tiny, delectable body. I'd like to spank her ass for showing at the Club alone. Brothers watch her until Pres and Teller sit at the table closest to me.

When she moves, my eyes are riveted. Her phone shows and Teller yells, '*Phone!*'

Holding my head, I pull my phone and push. '*Fuckin' Hell*!' I yell back at him while hitting my phone on when I'm out the back door. "Mase."

"Are you busy?" Her voice is shaking.

"What's wrong, Sarah?" I use Sarah to focus her.

Her breath catches telling me it worked. "I'm in the Utah Club. It feels different, like a storm."

I push to the window and watch shock hit her and she drops her phone. A second later I'm standing at her table handing it back to her.

"Teller." I feel what she means, something is coming.

He nods and stands by Pres. My eyes never leave the two Brothers watching from the bar.

"Cline, in." I order then hear the roger but scan the room.

Pres comes toward me. "What happened? There are too many in here." His hand waves on the side of his head. Reading in here isn't easy for him.

Teller moves to the table fast. "Intent changed. I'm holding them." Teller is holding the two at the bar. My eyes take the room in while he talks. "Kateri, it's nice to meet you. I'm Teller Knight from Bravo Rising. This is the President of Honor Rising, Kristos Christiansen and you know Mase Blackhawk."

I look down and almost hug her.

She's shocked, scared and relieved. "You're a seer." The whisper with her eyes on her hands has me bending.

"Look at me, Sarah." There is no room for *no* in my command.

Her movements are automatic. "Yes, Sir."

"You trust me?"

"Yes, Sir."

I put my hand out. "Teller, get to my room, bring Pres then jump."

He throws shit to Seth for Cline to take the two but I'm gone with Kateri. She turns holding on to me so I lift her up and make it to the rock. "This is the Connecticut reservation. My tribal home."

All that moves is her neck. Her eyes bouncing everywhere have me wondering if I did the right thing.

Aiyana scares the shit out of her. Her whole body is shaking and hold on me tightens.

"Aiyana, Shaman of the Connecticut tribe and member of the Princes of Prophecy and Badass Security Council." I try for a calming tone.

Aiyana rolls her eyes. "I am never referred to as a family member."

I hold my laugh. "A revered and gifted seer from the Paleo-American tribe aligned with Knights and Blackhawks. Both families are fuckin' crazy and Aiyana fits right in with her princess attitude."

Kateri relaxes her death grip on me. "First people?"

I sit quiet as Aiyana tells her of her grandmother and Nunánuk. Kateri turns from Aiyana and looks up at me. Those big light brown eyes have no fear but questions in them. "Were you sent to me?"

I wish Teller or Mucimi were here. "I don't think so. I don't get visions like that. I've been here for almost a year at Elan Rising. Were you sent to me?"

She looks at Aiyana for an answer. "Perhaps. The ancestors are happy with your visit, Kateri. Kateri Blackhawk is close and smiling upon you this day."

"Is that what I feel? This is real and I'm not drugged or anything?"

My arm gives her a squeeze. "No drugs allowed in Badass freaky Indian shit."

Christian has her turning fast and tightening her hold on me. "Aiyana owns Native Remedies. She's all about the natural, Kateri. I'm Christian, one of Mase's Brothers. You're meant to be here, the ancestors are happy and Mase will keep you safe. Bringing you today was smart. The ancestors have written an easier path." His eyes move to mine. "There's a threat to her. She knows and moved to Badass for the protection. The Club is in a brawl and you're needed. Jump when you need to but get back now."

"Fuck! Hold on, Kateri." I jump back then push us fast. Behind the bar I see Christian wasn't kidding. "Stay here and down." A bottle flies, I duck shielding Kateri from the glass. "Teller!"

"Here!"

I move smiling. Pres is kicking the shit out of a pussy with Teller watching. "The brawl?"

"They aren't hurting anyone." He shrugs. He's not seeing it. Something is coming.

Shaking my head, I let out a war cry. Everyone stops but Pres. "Take it outside!"

The Lead starts pushing Brothers out. Teller shrugs again. Fuckin' crazy Brothers.

I shoot the ex-Brother before Pres moves in again. "Seth, I need cleanup. I still feel it off, Teller."

A shot has me moving to Pres's side. The bullet hits me in the chest on the right stealing my air. Jesus fuck. '*Shield Pres*!' I throw to Teller and anyone close.

Brothers trying to get out are pushed back in falling to the floor. Two from Flight Crews are shooting at the doorway from behind a table. They fall and I shield behind me.

Moving through bullets, I fire until the third pussy falls then roll fire at the two aiming for the bar. These aren't Brothers waves at my brain and I know I need help. Throwing another shield, I jump.

Kateri registers as I fall hearing her scream. "Mase!"

'*Teller, shield*!'

Falling on the rock that has my blood on it before I land, I yell. That fuckin' hurt. Jeremy and Justice turn me.

"Jesus. Hold on, Mase. Aiyana, Aylen, Destiny, Mucimi. Teller, get Alder to Mase!" Justice has me wincing.

Once my eyes close, I float.

~*~*~

Kateri

Staring at Mase I think he's dead. The president guy he was protecting moves, so I do, until he holds his hand out.

"Stay there, Kateri. Seth, get Teams here now. My Team is down, Security is down. The only ones standing are me and Kateri."

My eyes move from Mase and the guy to the room trying to remember his name. Kristos. Bodies are everywhere. How did we make it? Everything in me shakes. It feels like an earthquake hit my bones. I move my quaking body and kneel by Mase. His clothes are full of bullet holes. Tears blur my vision. Not Mase.

Two men rush the door and Kristos points his gun. "Seth?" He puts his gun away and has the two guys help turn Mase over. Mase said Seth too but no one else is here.

Mase is a mess. My hand goes over his mouth and I feel hope. "He's breathing."

A young blonde Indian and little boy run in and Kristos with his weird eyes looks relieved.

"Gear off, Pres Kristos," the kid says while he opens a bag. It's medical? He's medical?

"He's a Doctor. Mase jumped to the ancestors," the young blonde Indian says.

"You're related." I don't know how I know this, he doesn't look like Mase.

He nods with tears in his eyes. "Mase is my uncle. I'm Nash Blackhawk." He pulls the coat off throwing it aside and I see Mase's arm full of holes.

Sitting back, I close my eyes and pray like my grandmother taught me, picturing the circle of stones and hearing her words. The four stones in the circle are bright orange as if light is shining out of them. I don't know how that is because it's always night. The words are familiar and comfortable as I let them flow out of me. I've said them thousands of times, but today they're for Mase. The warrior that showed that bravery and ancestral gifts I've heard about but never witnessed.

Hands on me have me screaming. "It's okay, Kateri. We're bringing him to the medic room. The healers are with him in Connecticut but Alder needs to work."

Nash carries me to an ambulance with flames on it. When the gurney with Mase rolls in, I relax and move away from Nash. "Did you jump?" He asks.

"I don't know what that means. I prayed like my grandmother taught me. There's a circle of rocks."

The boy doctor gets lifted in by Kristos and moves right to Mase. When the doors close, I ask Nash, "Is Kristos a Shaman too?" Teller said President.

"No, he was healed by a Shaman that fixed his eyes. Alder, do you need help?"

The boy looks over his shoulder. "I will remove bullets at medic room. Healers waiting."

Nash nods. "You have the doc waiting?"

The boy nods listening to Mase's chest. He's really a doctor.

"He's twenty-three. A doctor, architect, genetic scientist and probably a hundred other things but most importantly, President of the Alpha-Bits. They're the little Brothers he helped rescue from labs and shit. They have a compound like this one but way bigger in between Phoenix and Bravo."

This boy is twenty-three. That's not a boy and rescuing from labs and shit is a little scary. My eyes follow Alder's every move. Confident and competent are telling traits. We stop before I can add to that.

Men are at the back door pulling the gurney. I don't know what to do, where I am or if it's safe.

"You're safe, Kateri. I'll stay with you." Nash takes my hand and talks without looking back at me. "This is Honor Rising's office. There's an infirmary at Flight but Alder has a doc waiting at this one to help him. Brothers from the Club are going to the infirmary."

"I need help. You finish medic?"

I jump at the voice just behind me. Alder is on Kristos' back.

Nash stops just past the door Mase went into. "Last month. I can help."

I see Teller in the room pulling supplies out and setting trays up when Nash pulls me in. "You can help or jump and help with the ancestors."

I am not leaving here. "I'm not a medic or doctor but know how to clean and follow directions."

"Wash up, get a mask, gloves on and wait for directions," Kristos says washing his hands.

Nash pulls me to the sink and waits his turn. I finally get washed, gloves, mask and paper johnny on and stand watching. Alder is working fast to get those bullets out. Teller, Kristos, Nash and another man are doing the same. They all have an arm or leg. Nash is getting directions as a man I don't know works on the same arm. Other than bruises, one really big and dark, Mase doesn't have holes on the trunk of his body. I hope that means that he's going to be okay. There's a lot of blood showing because of so many holes.

"His gear is plated. The double plating stops even armor piercing bullets."

My eyes jump right to Kristos. He's a seer too.

Nash bumps my arm. "Can you hold the bowl? Mucimi said he's going to be fine now." Moving the tray thing out of the way, Nash moves closer to the guy I don't know.

I take the bowl and hold it on the side of him. "Thanks. Gear plating on the arms and legs isn't double but it slows the bullets so they aren't ripping through flesh causing worse damage." Nash is trying to be comforting.

That's good but not really something I want to picture. "You're all seers?" I'm not sure what to feel. They all know what I'm thinking.

No one says anything for a few seconds. "Protectors say reader not seer. Ability different. Move people, object fast, talk in mind, vision to future or now, called ability. Not all Protector have all ability. Reader in most. I am seer to solution, no vision to future." Alder surprises me.

"Mase has all that ability? I saw him move fast." I clean where Nash was just working since the guy took the bowl and is holding it for Nash.

Teller pulls a tray closer so I move toward him. "He does, but he can't read you. Are you a reader?"

My feet stop. "I get ideas, I think. I know to stay away from people from weird feelings. You all were answering my thoughts. My dad did that." I start cleaning Mase's leg beside Teller. "Mase can't read me? I saw him appear by me. He knew to cover Kristos and flew me to a reservation."

They all make sounds hiding their laughs. I don't get it.

"Mase is a heavily gifted Protector. Readers don't read everyone and don't get every thought. Some are stronger than others. Mase can feel extreme emotion from you but not read your thoughts. It drives him crazy." Teller has me feeling relieved that my every thought isn't read.

At least not by Mase. I should be running scared. I'm afraid to leave this room right now. That means something. I wish I knew what.

Moving to Alder's side, I clean the two places around where he stitched. They talk to Alder about what they're doing or have done as I clean Mase and empty bowls. He's got to be okay. They're all calm but moving quickly. I wish I could do more than clean him up. He's a good man that doesn't deserve this.

~*~*~

"Aiyana said he'll be able to jump back later."

I turn fast watching a new guy talk to Alder. He's another good guy. I relax until he looks at me.

"Justice. I'm glad you stayed. Mase was worried. Aiyana is keeping him there for a couple of hours. He needs blood and some time."

I nod looking at the bag of blood. Alder is good.

Justice smiles. "He's one of the best."

"You're another reader?"

Nash laughs. "He's the freakiest freak and does everything. He's Lead for the Protector crew here. Teller is his second and Mucimi our Prophet."

I nod. "One in the three." My dad told me of the three being one governing body. I was too young to understand but seeing this man, I feel it all and understanding hits me hard and fast.

"You see like Alder." Justice gets my attention.

My eyes narrow. "You see what I see?"

He nods. "You shield thoughts that I wouldn't disrespect you by looking at. Seeing you focus isn't shielded. Respect is big with Badass. Every Protector you meet will show that same respect." There's something so pure and trustworthy in his look, words and demeanor.

"Thank you. There are some thoughts that shouldn't be shared." I say understanding.

"Holy fuck. Is that an Indian saying?" Kristos has me turning. He's looking at Justice.

"I've heard it at Princes but I'm not versed on all tribes. Mase would know, he went through Warrior and likes all the weird details." Justice is smiling. Why? Aren't they both Indian? I feel like they are.

Justice looks right at me. "I was a scout but had other obligations for Badass that took precedence. We didn't grow up on the reservation but have always recognized the tradition and culture of our people. Most of us were raised in the Club. Kristos has ties to the tribe but just learned of them."

I nod. "I understand. The wording is from my father. He moved us off the reservation when a friend of his died. Those words were what he said when he taught me how to block my thoughts about that man."

Kristos' weird eyes change color or the color changes position. "Tell me his name wasn't Crow."

My body freezes but my mind moves through my life quickly.

Because some thoughts don't need to be shared
Because some thoughts are too hard to believe
Because some thoughts can be deadly

I step back hitting the gurney and move my hand to Mase's arm. He'll protect me. Is that from these men?

Justice puts his hand up and everyone stops moving. "Mase would lay down his life for you. You knew Crow. He was Badass and a Mason."

We don't talk about Crow. I shake my head but he doesn't stop. "He died because of men masquerading as Masons. We're working with real Masons to clean that up. You moved here for protection knowing Badass would give that to you. You trust Aiyana's words and you trust Mase. He would never put you in harm's way. You feel it. He trusts in his Brothers. You can trust in us, Kateri. Kristos has a familial tie to Crow. The Clubs here all know of Crow and many have ties to him including Cort, the President of Phoenix Rising."

My mind zooms to my dad and Crow. *Cort will help. Find Badass.* I found them when I got out of school. I nod. "Cort wasn't in the city."

He nods. "He's President of BSC West and Phoenix Rising. He's my boss." He smiles relaxing me.

Alder runs stopping right in front of me. "Boss Crow bring Alpha-Bits to Badass. We safe, Pres Cort keep us safe. Badass help get Alpha-Bits out of labs and here to safe. Alpha-Bits trust in our Brothers, Badass. Pres Cort show us how. VP Mase show you with help." He puts his arm out. "Protectors, Officers, Brothers help."

"Thank you. How many Alpha-Bits?"

"Here, one hundred forty-three."

"Shit."

He nods and puts his hands up. "Some crazy as fucking Brothers."

I bend and smile. "I bet that's not easy to control."

He smiles looking like an angel. "Brothers help. Pres Cort crazy, little help to stop crazy."

"You knew Crow. You trusted him and Cort. I will too."

He looks at Justice, so I do. "Not all Brothers are Badass or follow Badass beliefs. Protectors in every Club and Officers in all Phoenix affiliates will work to keep you safe. Call if you need us. Feeds of all roads in the Club towns help. Make it to a road and find a way to signal surveillance. We'll send help."

That's the scariest part of living here but I understand it and nod. "Do you want me to leave now?"

"Mase has spare rooms, you can stay in one. I can send a Prospect to get you clothes or whatever you need."

"Is that a Protector?" People in my house scare the hell out of me.

Teller moves. "I'll go."

"Thank you. I have a laptop on the table and bag in the closet by the front door." They don't need the reason. He vanishes.

"Prospects can get you anything you need or want. There's an app on the phone. I'll ask Asa to get you a phone and explain the app. He's Alder's second." Kristos has me nodding and relieved.

"Thank you." I have no idea where my phone went.

~*~*~

"Natalia, Asa and Cort!" A woman yells walking through the front door. I'm up and take a step back with the table in between us.

Asa captures my attention running right toward me. I bend completely captivated by his angelic face with a mohawk and earring. I see color on him and hold my laugh in. He's even got tattoos.

56

"You must be Asa. I'm Kateri. It's nice to meet you."

"I see VP Mase then train phone and apps."

I nod and he runs. "Running is a thing with the Alpha-Bits."

Natalia is watching me and Cort's eyes follow Asa. "The messenger run. I think it should be the Bit run. I'm new so I'm not starting a war with a nut like Ranger." Natalia is new.

Cort is bigger than life. I've seen a picture of him, but it didn't prepare me for this massive man. He laughs making him look not so scary.

"You're as big as my dad's friend Reed."

He stops laughing pretty damn quick. "He was my father."

I hold the back of the chair. Was. He wasn't in the city either.

Natalia moves closer. "Do you want a drink? Sit, Kateri."

I sit needing to sit before I fall. This whole day has been sad, weird and oddly relieving.

Cort sits across from me. "You knew my dad?"

"My dad did. I was just a girl. You don't look like Reed." This is unreal.

He reaches down then puts a phone on the table. "Natalia does virtual shit and made him move and talk from a picture. They have one here at the entrance for visitors. She made me one for my son." He taps the screen and Reed is behind him.

My hands hit the table in front of me in case I pass out. Reed smiles at me talking about Badass and help to the community. When he's done, I look at Natalia.

"I used the lessons Cort gave me but that fit for the first introduction. His boy is a baby." She's smiling like this is normal. I nod.

"What was your father's name?" Cort asks putting his phone away.

"Beehaz-aanii Todachine. Everyone called him Ben T."

Cort looks beyond me. "Law."

"Yes." It's his name in Navajo.

He stands. "Crow is with my dad on the virtual here. I'm glad you're alright after the shit storm they went through. Asa will get my number on your phone. Call if you need me."

I nod, completely at a loss. Why would I ever call him? He's got to be a busy man. "Thank you."

Natalia pushes a glass of water closer. "Drink. They're a lot to process. You get used to them, but they think it's all normal."

Coming from a woman that makes dead people come alive from a picture, I'm not sure she knows normal. I'd be the first to offer up that I don't know normal so maybe she does.

Chapter Two

Mase

Feeling like I've been here for a week, I'm glad when Mucimi and Justice show.

"It's time, Brother." Justice pulls me up to standing and even in this form, I feel it's off, weak or something. "I'll come to you when I'm off, Mase. Mucimi will be there or close and Aylen will show today."

"Kateri?"

"She's sound asleep on the side of your bed. We won't wake her." He holds my arm. "Jump."

I open my eyes but don't move any other muscles. My body feels like it was steamrolled. A week with the ancestors would have been good. Mucimi's hand is on my arm working to get me back to moving right. The heat feels good. Kateri's little hand is on my other arm. They told me she was fine if a little overwhelmed with knowing common people.

Something she got from Aiyana or the ancestors helped get her an easier path Christian said. I hope that's in everything but life never works that way.

Her hand tightens on my arm for a second. I guess we'll find out.

She sits straight up fast. "What's your name?" Not the question I expected but she's an enigma.

"Mucimi, Mase's nephew."

"The cowboy. I saw your picture downstairs." She's got me holding a laugh in.

"Cowboy?" Mucimi asks.

59

"You bought a cow." She still hasn't noticed me.

"He did." Her jump makes me smile. "Kateri, I'm glad you're okay."

Bending over me, she kisses my cheek. "I'm glad *you're* okay. It's been interesting. How do you feel?" She isn't giving details and has that confidence and grace up like a shield. Calm, cool and collected. Shit.

I am not moving with her right here. "Sore. A lot of muscle was hit."

"The bruises on your chest are faded. It was almost black yesterday. All the holes are closed. Healers at the reservation fixed you. Thank you for keeping us safe. Do you need anything?" Appreciation and concern are good.

"Some water." If she goes out, I can move and see how I feel.

She turns toward the nightstand, fuckin' great.

Mucimi sends a blast of heat through me. '*I'll help you sit.*' He lifts me right up so I'm sitting.

I groan wanting to laugh but the stretch on my body, all over my fuckin' body, hurts. Suspending me up, I move myself so I'm sitting on the side of the bed with a hand on my chest.

When I open my eyes, Kateri's big light brown eyes are on me. "Mucimi was being helpful. I'm sore so I had to take over. I have abilities gifted by the ancestors. They wouldn't give them to me if my heart wasn't pure." Or ready to beat out of my fuckin' chest.

Mucimi sits on the side of me nodding. I shake my head, he's not much of a wingman.

"I saw yesterday and Aylen explained last night. She's coming back today. Do you want me to leave so you can rest and the healer people can do their thing?"

We all turn at the sound of a step. Falcon walks in surprising me. He made noise so he wouldn't scare her. "You need to stay on the compound. I'm Falcon from Bravo Rising."

Kateri steps back so her hip is against my leg. Putting my hand on her waist fuckin' stretches more muscle and skin. I grit my teeth and throw chin. Jesus.

"Pres Falcon," Mucimi acknowledges.

Falcon pulls a chair over and sits. He's trying to keep her calm. Since she stepped over to me and he didn't miss that crack in her persona, that's good.

His eyes move from her to me. "Glad you're alive, Brother. Teller is working at IT with Akai and Lukas. Justice is in Ops. You're stuck with unfreaky for a while."

I laugh then groan moving my hand to my chest. I feel every movement. Kateri relaxes turning her head toward me. She's so close but if I bend, I'm going to feel it. Tightening my hand is all I can do without groaning like a pussy.

"He's a President like Kristos and Cort?"

I answer so I'm not nodding. "Justice too but he doesn't go by Pres. Protectors are based out of Bravo."

"Everyone matters, everyone is equal here." Mucimi has my eyes moving his way. He doesn't add anything so he's answering what wasn't spoken from her.

Falcon looks at me. "You're up. Teller said they stopped you from bleeding and fixed ribs and shit but had to wait for the bullets to be removed. It sounds crazy, but worked?"

"Yeah, they'll work to fix the muscle and I'll be fine. I suspended to get this far." I smile getting a laugh from him.

"You're all unbelievable. I hope the muscle is easy. You have quite a few scars but no open wounds."

I look down feeling the pull in my neck and back but it's not too bad. "Jesus. More fuckin' scars." My arms and legs have pockmarks all over the fuckin' place. "I'm glad someone got shorts on me."

Mucimi laughs. "Aylen lifted you and Kateri covered the boxers. Teller has pink hearts on you." Fuckin' Brother.

Falcon laughs. I want to shake my head. I settle on a smile. "Jesus, where the hell did he get pink hearts?"

Kateri finds this funny drawing my eyes to that smile. "I didn't think they were yours."

"No. You're not freaked by all this freaky?" I ask feeling her calm again.

Her eyes are bright and unguarded. "Aylen was here for a while. She explained but my dad had told me some so it wasn't such a shock."

'*Aylen wants to cloak her memories. We can do it if we're all together.*' Mucimi sends a blast of heat then is gone.

Falcon laughs. "It's a good thing you're not freaked, Kateri. That's fairly normal."

She nods. "I can make some breakfast and let you talk."

I tighten my hand and let her go.

Falcon shakes his head. "Breakfast is on its way. Cort told me your dad was Ben T. I went fishing with him and Reed just off the reservation. He had a lead on a boy in the city but I never found him."

Kateri is back to guarded and inches closer to me. "My dad was in construction." Her shaky monotone voice throws alerts through me.

"Sarah, you're safe. Falcon is a President for Badass. Protectors are based out of his Club. We'd know if he wasn't straight up Badass. I can shield you or move us away if I even think there is a threat."

"Yes, Sir." She looks down. Fuck. "My dad worked for Crow. We never say his name. Reed came more than Crow did. Crow showed me how to block and brought papers for school sometimes. I helped print flyers on the computer Reed brought. There was a lot of boys on the computer but more girls. Some had two names, so I'd make flyers with both names."

She looks up with her body shaking. Tightening my hold I give her, "You're safe, Kateri. I wouldn't let anything happen to you."

"The men that took me have the computer, but I remember the faces if I see them." She's still monotone.

"Do you remember names?" Falcon asks.

"I can look for them. There were a lot of lists." She delivers with no emotion.

I do not like the monotone. All I ever got was *yes, sir*. The full sentences delivered so calm throw all kinds of alerts at me.

"Slade Nova." Falcon throws out.

My head whips toward him causing my shoulders, chest and back to protest.

Kateri looks at the wall giving my body time to settle down. "Parker Nova, eight months, Cheyenne." She sounds like she's reading it.

"Eight months?" Falcon says what I'm thinking.

"When he was taken. The old ones don't have dates, just ages." She's back to here watching Falcon but hasn't moved away from me or given up on the monotone delivery.

"Good job, Yáhsháyôn." I tighten my hand smiling at her obviously extraordinary memory and hoping to get her away from whatever is scaring the fuck out of her and putting her in that void where emotions are suppressed.

"What's *Yáhsháyôn*?" Thank fuck that comes with curious eyes and a slight smile.

Falcon laughs watching her closely. Considering he's Falcon and doesn't miss a fuckin' thing, he saw it too. "They're crazy with Mohegan like we all know it. That isn't one I've heard."

I roll my eyes glad it doesn't pull anything. "My breath. Literal is *that I breathe*. Mohegan doesn't translate to biker. We make it work."

Her giggle has me bending to kiss her head. "That's a beautiful sound," I say in Mohegan on a growl. Pushing me back up, I take a breath to settle my body. "I like the giggle."

She doesn't react but looks at Falcon. "Do you know what happened to Don-say Jeronimo?" It's her normal voice and shocks me.

"Co?" How the fuck does she know Co?

She looks up at me. "Crow called him Co. My dad called him Jeronimo. He's a Shaman but not for a tribe here. He was looking for my dad's friend Ped-non. My dad thought he died, that's why we had to move. I hope Don-say made it. He hid me before the men came."

"Aiyana!" My fuckin' heart is beating like a drum.

*'Do not scream my name or I'll have Christian blast you! What has you ready to expire? Calm yourself before you **do** expire. Where is Mucimi?'*

"Is Co alive?" I feel heat run through me, throwing calm.

'Yes. I spoke with him last week.'

"Thank fuck. He helped hide Kateri. She thought he might not have made it."

'There are many thoughts too hard to believe. Co being alive and well is not one of them. I cannot give you the rest. Relax and let the healers mend your body before you damage all I healed yesterday.'

"Thanks, Aiyana, I will. Co is a name I knew and needed that he is okay." I nod to Kateri seeing relief show in those beautiful eyes.

'He will be honored by your thoughts. Rest, I must shoot a man before he hurts a shopkeep.'

I smile at Falcon. "She was on Ops. She's got to shoot at someone to clear a shopkeeper. Did Teller tell you what she did for me?"

He shakes his head. "Your ribs and something about your chest concerned them. Alder was watching your stats."

Shit. "Do you have more questions, Kateri?"

Aylen shows looking anxiously at me. "Are you okay?"

"Just tired. I need to lean back but I'm not sure I can suspend downstairs."

Her head is already shaking. "Aiyana called to me. Suspending takes energy. She wants healers with you around the clock. Where's Mucimi? He was working on strengthening the tissue around your lung."

Falcon is up. "Kateri, can you get more pillows?"

Kateri runs. Falcon looks in the closet. I see why and smile. "There's cut plywood and wood for braces in the garage."

He walks out. Aylen smiles.

"How bad was it?" I ask her.

"She healed three places in your lung. I was working on an artery with Destiny. You need to rest and the healers need to work. Why did Mucimi leave? I wasn't due here until after lunch."

"Kateri talking sends him to an elder," I tell her in Mohegan.

Concern is all over her but she's not talking. Her shields are up and holding. The chair slides across the floor away from the bed.

"I got covered. I'll stay. I'm moving you to the chair. Pres Falcon has a whole building project in his head."

I nod and relax being moved through the air while watching Kateri's face show awe when she walks in with four pillows hiding all but her head. I'm glad she's calm with all this shit.

~*~*~

Kateri

Falcon made a frame, like a lawn chair, to raise or lower the mattress. It's pretty easy and Mase is happy. Prospects brought a hospital table so he can eat without moving much. I guess moving is a problem until he's healed.

Aylen is up with Mase. He fell asleep after he ate so she's doing the heal thing. I don't know the words she says but I feel them. I had to move so I came down to get some work done.

Mase keeps distracting me. He was hurt worse than anyone said. These people are more Indian than I am, he went to that reservation place to get healed while his body was being healed by the doctors and medics here. Aylen said he got the scar on his face shielding a boy from a bullet. He took his helmet off and put it on the boy. Who does stuff like that? Every time I look at him, I want to kiss the scar and thank him for being that person who would stop a boy from being shot. I don't think there are many people like that around. Freaky is the right word, it surprises me they all use it.

Not one has asked about me being sold. They must all know. Mase called me his breath. There is no way he knows. Who would want to touch me?

My body feels like I'm wrapped in the softest cotton warming me from the inside out. I felt it a few times now so it doesn't scare me.

An alert on my screen gets my head back to business. Two baby books and a website has me done for the day.

Sending everything out, I sit thinking about Mase. He scared me showing up without a call. I went to the Club to find someone that followed the rules knowing I didn't want to give Mase up. There's something in him like the Justice guy. I know he's safe. I know he'd never hurt me. So why the hell did I go to the Club? He called me his breath and brought me dinner. I've never had a date. Is bringing dinner a date?

I google it. Wow. Scrolling I smile. Apparently, men screw this up a lot. First date dinners at home are bad. I don't think Mase cared.

I'm smiling when the door opens. "Asa!" The little guy runs in and stops short at the table. "Miss Kateri, I see VP Mase."

I nod then watch his little mohawk bounce up and down as he runs up the stairs. He's adorable. Getting up, I look for dinner.

"Alder!"

My feet stop and I watch Alder run turning for the stairs. "Boss Kateri. I check VP Mase then meet to you?"

"Okay. Asa just ran up. Is Mase okay?"

"Asa show respect. He like VP Mase and show to him. I no get call. Regular check."

I nod. "Thank you, Little Pres."

His smile makes him look younger. I don't get to see it for long. He runs up the stairs with his little backpack bouncing and medical bag held up so it doesn't hit the step in front of him. They must all be adorable.

The freezer has quite a bit of meat in it. There is nothing but meat in it, he's a guy so I guess ice cream isn't a staple. The pantry is a walk in like mine. He's got the shelves organized. Breakfast has granola, batter mix, a container of plain oatmeal, nuts, dried berries, seeds, Raisin Bran and a box of Captain Crunch with a red tape X on it. I laugh. I guess he's not into Captain Crunch.

Lunch and snack shelves have normal food. I'm glad to see peanut butter. He likes chips in any flavor and different nuts than breakfast. Men are weird.

Hearing feet on the stairs, I step out of the pantry and wait until Asa reaches the bottom. "Bye, Asa."

He stops short, turning my way. "VP Mase say come to dinner. I come back. Later, Miss Kateri."

"Later, Asa." I think about dinner for more than me and Mase. At school I had a two-burner electric stove. I'm pretty good with boxed food. The hotel in the city was two weeks of take-out and cereal. I've only been here for a month and a half and haven't had much practice with my new pans and stove. Mase cooked pork chops, hash browns and eggs. I've never used more than two pans at once. He had four pans going like he did it all the time.

When I tasted the food, I knew he'd been cooking for a while. He says he's thirty but I don't believe that. He looks older than me but way younger than thirty. Maybe it's the Indian in him.

I'm going to need help to cook for a crowd. I google cook for a crowd. Crap. I should have started cooking yesterday. I need to know how many people are eating here. Climbing the stairs, I get the Prospect app up and hope they have time for shopping. My feet stop hearing Alder and Aylen.

"Stop. I mark wall here. Go." Alder is marking walls.

"I felt the pull here too." Aylen isn't making sense with the wall thing so I step to the door.

Aylen's hands are over Mase's chest and Alder is typing in the air watching a see-through monitor with glasses on. At a guess it's what Aylen is showing him with her hands. It's not the strangest thing I've seen here but it's strange. The inside of Mase is on a monitor.

"Boss Kateri, we map to Boss Justice."

Aylen turns without moving her hands. "Hey. Justice is good but the map will make that quicker."

Alder rolls his eyes making me smile. That's what he thinks he said. I move to Mase seeing he's asleep. "I'll be downstairs."

"Mase put an order in. The Prospects will drop the food and go unless an Officer is down there." That answers that question.

"Thanks, Aylen."

Leaving, I wonder about being here. Teller brought my bag, but Prospects came with more of my stuff while Aylen was here last night. They used the back so I didn't see all they brought until I went to change. They brought a good week's worth of clothes and all my bathroom crap. They expect me to be here for a few days.

Since I saw Mase appear outside the Club I knew I wasn't letting him go or I thought it right after I got over the shock of him appearing. I needed him and he was there.

Getting my laptop open I think it's like a dream I've always been afraid to have. He showed when I felt the storm brewing. Justice said he'd lay his life down for mine. Hearing about warriors from my grandmother and Ben T then seeing them in real life makes me wish they had the chance to see them too. I hope they see them through me.

I feel that soft cotton wrapping me up again and smile. Maybe they do.

~*~*~

Mase

Jumping back, I'm surprised Alder is still here and I'm raised to almost sitting. "Brother."

"Boss Aylen see Boss Kateri." He pauses. This isn't good. "Boss Justice here to dinner. Damage to artery wall need more heal. Heart muscle swell cause less blood flow. Boss Justice help swell to heart muscle, myocarditis, lessen and refill heart with return blood no problem. Boss Justice no help, specialist come. Myocarditis not due to bacteria, but outside pressure, bruise to heart muscle. Broken blood vessel, swell, cause same reaction myocarditis. No work, strain, tax to blood flow, or heart. Freaky move is strain to you. None. Boss Justice fix, I get test before I release you. Pres Kristos agree."

Holyfuckinshit. "I'm with you, Brother. If it gets fixed, I'm good to go?"

"If fixed, I sign release, you good to go."

"The artery?"

He nods. "Easy fix. Boss Aylen say she do before Boss Justice here. Healers work fast. Wall need strengthen no damage, thin two places."

That's something, he doesn't seem worried. "The muscles are after the heart thing?"

He shakes his head. "Blood flow priority. No blood flow, no help to muscle."

He slides off the chair. "More question?"

"No, thanks, Brother."

"Always. You jump you hurt, smart. Here you die. Boss Aiyana see heart not fill. Healers save you. Honor them here, stay to bed, let them finish."

I nod. "Still with you, Brother. I'm lucky and know it. I'm not moving further than the bathroom until you say."

He smiles. "I expect fight. Glad you quick and hear me."

I put my arm out feeling it. "Glad you're you and checked. I'm honored to be one of yours, LP. You worked to get me here, I'm not throwing that kind of gift away."

He throws me chin looking so fuckin' cute. "I feel it. I help to dinner. Boss Justice here soon." He runs making me smile.

'*Christian?*'

'*Here, Mase. How are you feeling?*'

'*Tired. Alder just left. Do I need to worry?*'

'*Let the healers heal. Alder's not wrong, Mase. They need to finish.*'

'*I'll let the healers heal. Is Mucimi up there?*'

'*Yeah. He needs time.*' He doesn't say anymore.

Fuckin' great. '*We've got time. Thanks, Brother. Kuwômôyush.*'

'*Kuwômôyush, Brother. I'm glad you're staying in bed.*'

I feel he's gone and smile. I need to follow Alder's orders and stay in bed.

My dad walks in shocking the hell out of me. "Dad." My hand goes over my heart that's beating too fast.

He smiles. "Yeah. How are you feeling?"

"Steamrolled, but I feel it, so I'm saying great."

He laughs kissing my head before he sits on the side of the bed. "I'm glad you're okay or will be soon. Hannah said Justice will be here later. He was on Ops. Nash is out too."

I nod. "Have you seen Mucimi?"

He nods. "I was at Brantley's when he called to us. Justice had just taken you back. You being hurt and your girl here keeps him unsettled. Christian said his head is spinning so healing isn't working for him."

Fuck. "I can't send her home, Dad."

He shakes his head. "No, you can't. Christian sees something there. Justice has it. He said he'd deal with Mucimi after he sees you. What can I do for you, Son?"

"I'm good, Dad. Alder is here making sure of it. Aylen is throwing calm at me. You know what? Falcon has some information from Kateri. Christian said she has a threat that she knows. I don't think she has who that threat is from but may have the information that can find it."

He nods. "I'll get with Falcon and Brantley. What makes you think she has anything to follow?"

"She asked if Co was alive, using Don-say Jeronimo. He hid her when the men came. Co knew Crow and Cort's dad Reed. Eight years ago, Co left the reservation."

"Fuck, can this get more tangled?" He's surprised.

"I don't know but something brought us here. Kristos and Nova have ties to Crow. Kateri said Nova's brother, Parker was taken at eight months and his name was Nova. When he got to Alpha, his name was Parker Sloan."

My dad sits back. "She would have been what, eleven-twelve?"

I close my eyes. "Shit that struck me from what I know, or she said:

She was sold as an early teen.

Mother went missing.

Father worked to find missing kids with Masons or at least Crow and Reed.

Falcon met her dad. I think Falcon had more to ask but wasn't sure if she could handle it.

She knew all the Some Thoughts sentences perfect.

She was named after Nunánuk and understands ancestors a little.

Crow's name was never spoken and she was hidden being told to say her dad worked construction.

She has the missing kids list in her head.

She brought back Parker Nova when Falcon asked her about Slade Nova." I open my eyes seeing he has his phone out.

He nods. "I'm sending it to Brantley. I'll see Falcon. This isn't just a little coincidence. Were you sent to her?"

I want to shrug but shake my head. "She's got a threat to her, moved here and bought a house with Badass money that went to kids sold. It went through a foundation, Badass wasn't named. She was told to trust Cort years ago. She didn't know he moved so she came here seeing something about the Club while she was in the city. It struck me as Mucimi help but he's wicked emotional around her. He said Aylen wants to cloak her memories."

"Jesus, that does sound like Mucimi help, but he can't be close to her." He types then drops his phone. "So, no ice cream, cookies or milkshake?"

I hold my chest and laugh. "Granola, nuts or fruit? I'm in bed for, at the least, another day."

He smiles standing up. "Captive audience. I'll get you a vanilla shake and bring up some of your squirrel food." He wants ice cream.

I smile. "Vanilla shake sounds perfect. Just fruit with it."

He walks out smiling. I love my dad. I look around spotting my bag and pull it to me.

"None of that, Brother." Aylen sits at the end of the bed and puts her hand on my leg. "Do your thing but no suspending shit including you."

"I didn't know it meant anything. I thought it was just me. I'll ask next time."

She's happy with that and closes her eyes chanting softly. I get through the schedule and close it down. The need to jump is strong so I follow it.

~*~*~

Opening my eyes, I laugh holding my chest with one hand and reach for Kateri's with the other. "So you've met the family."

Her eyes are lit. I love that look. "I'm told there are a few missing. They let me help make dinner. Justice will bring you down but thought you'd be better off seeing them here where they won't wear you out with hugs." She finds that funny.

"I'll thank him when he comes up." Turning to the family, I throw, "I'm fine and getting better. Thanks for showing. Thanks for climbing the stairs, Joey."

Her smile is infectious. "Sebastian carried me or I would have."

"Thanks, Sebastian."

When everyone moves closer, Kateri pulls her hand. I hold the groan in and her hand tighter. "Yáhsháyôn, I'm already holding my chest." That blush is new. She bows her head and my dick twitches.

"My breath. That's cute." Nash hits Oliver getting a laugh from Taylor.

"Glad you're okay, Mase. I'm downstairs. I love the new Club, Brother." Taylor bumps my fist then pulls Nash, Oliver and Case with him. I throw the boys chin.

Sebastian holds my leg when Joey sits on the bed. "Mom is downstairs. She was in here with Aylen and Destiny. She's making food for a week. No one can stop her. Dad has enough ice cream to feed the Club. He should have left the boys here. I'm glad you're not fighting the healers. Christian said they need to finish." Her eyes are boring into mine as if she didn't just say all that on a coffee high.

"I'm not pushing it. I've got time. Is he here?"

"No, Prez is here with Jessie and Taylor. He's proud of you for not starting an old lady war or something."

I hold my chest and smile. "No old lady wars here."

She laughs. "Did he really shoot Teller?"

I nod. "He shot like seven Brothers. It was crazy. He apologized and Teller is good. Spano said he moved the laser off him fast."

She's laughing again. Sebastian lets my leg go and puts his hand out to her. "I'll see you downstairs."

Brantley sits. "You held your chest. Aylen and Destiny aren't done?" He sees everything.

"They were doing an artery. Justice is on the swelling after dinner. Tell Mucimi *Kuwômôyush, mucimi*. I'm doing good and we have time."

He nods. "That may settle him. Do you need anything?"

"Can you get the ice cream to the Bits and food to the vets before you leave?"

Kateri squeezes my hand. "I want ice cream. All you have is meat in the freezer." Her eyes get huge making me laugh with a hand on my chest. She surprised herself with that.

I stop when she bows her head. "Sorry, Sir."

Brantley gives me a look. My jaw clenches. "Keep whatever you want, Yáhsháyôn. My Dad is crazy and probably filled the freezer in the garage with ice cream."

Brantley gives out a fake laugh. "Not full but the overflow went to the garage." He watches her.

Justice shows and Brantley stands. "I'll see you downstairs, Mase. I'm glad you're okay, Brother, Kateri." He bends and hugs me then kisses Kateri's head getting her to look up.

Justice puts his hand on my chest. "You're a lucky bastard. Mitch isn't here."

My hand goes over his when I feel the laugh coming. Kateri is smiling.

~*~*~

Justice stands. "I'm out, Brother. I'll be back in the morning."

"Thanks, Justice. Carmen still here?"

He nods looking as tired as Teller. "We're a couple of houses down from the Blackhawks. Alder has her showing Kateri something tomorrow. I swear he's going to hire only women to run his shit." They vanish.

I laugh not feeling the pain or my heart beating fast. Kateri stands.

"Stay with me, Kateri. I'm not a hundred percent, you have a threat and I need to know you're safe, Yáhsháyôn."

She's got that blush making her delicate features glow. "I need to change."

I nod. "Go change. If you're not back in ten I'm coming to find you."

Her head shakes letting me know she'll be back. "You're not supposed to be up. I'll be quick." She runs.

I snag the breeches my mom put out for me and make the trip to the bathroom. My chest feels better but everything else is still pulling my skin in every direction no matter how gently I step.

When I come out, Kateri is standing by the bed in pj pants and a tight tank. Closing my eyes has her moving. "Are you okay?"

With my teeth clenched I nod. "Yeah, get into bed, Kateri."

"Yes, Sir." She moves fast and I groan seeing her crawl across my bed. The grid on the top is too fucking close for the *yes, sir*.

Blowing out a breath, I make the bed and sit. I take the pills Brantley left from Aiyana. We buy from her so I don't know why she's sending what amounts to Tylenol here.

"Do you want the bed flat?" I don't look her way.

"No, Sir." Hearing the *Sir* again, I close my eyes.

I suspend my legs over and lay back. "Come here, Yáhsháyôn." I put my arm out. She looks nervous moving closer but not on me. "It's okay, you won't hurt me." I hope.

Once she's settled, I move my arm around her keeping my jaw clenched on the pain that wants to be heard. "Thank you for putting up with the family, Alpha-Bits and Brothers."

She looks up at me with confusion in her eyes. "I like them, Sir." The monotone sets me on edge.

My eyes close until I let my breath out. "I like them, *Mase*. You're in my bed so I know you're safe. This isn't a service call. This is me needing to see and feel you close so I can sleep. Before I fall asleep, I have questions and can answer yours."

She lifts her eyes to mine while throwing nervousness out.

"It's normal for men and women to talk. That's all we're doing." I almost smile seeing her eyebrows go up. "Do you have questions?"

Those eyebrows go higher. Confusion is all over that beautifully delicate face that haunts my sleep. "Yes, Sir."

Clamping my jaw tight, I nod for her to go on. She does. "Are you angry with me?"

"Sit up, Kateri." I move my arm before she has me in more pain.

My little one is shaking. "Fuck." I breathe deep taking her hand. "I'm not angry with you, Yáhsháyôn. I'm sorry if I made you feel that way. This isn't easy because I'm dominant and you're a sub. While sex isn't what we're doing, you're my equal. I know being here and having so much new invade your life isn't easy. Adding more shit to your plate was never something I wanted to do without you being prepared for it. I appreciate you for staying and am so proud of the strength you've shown. We call it Badass shining through. It's humbling, Yáhsháyôn. Do you have questions?"

"Am I staying until you're better?" She bows her head but has eyes on me.

"Shit." First fuckin' question. I shake my head and give her an overview of what I got from Justice tonight. "Ops ran today hunting down two vehicles that stopped at your house yesterday. The Club shooting was a diversion according to one of the pussies that lived. I wish you wouldn't have asked but I won't lie to hide it, Kateri."

She bows her head. "They're looking for me?" Monotone is where we're at again. She's safe there?

"Pres wants you on the compound to keep you safe. It works with my need to breathe so here is where that happens. Your car was taken from the Club lot. Tracking is off so techs are trying for feeds to find it. Since they know about tracking and jamming, I'm not letting you out of my sight. Alder will stamp you tomorrow."

She pulls her hand away and lifts her pant leg. "Asa stamped me." She turns her foot showing me Yáhsháyôn in a calligraphy font.

Fuckin' hell. "Baby, come closer."

She leans closer with her head down. I lift her chin so I can see her pretty blush and eyes. "I love it. Thank you, Yáhsháyôn. It's the way I feel. You're my breath, baby. I want you to feel that from me always. This is not something I've ever felt so I'm going to fuck it up. You need to tell me when I am. That's as an equal, Yáhsháyôn. Can you do that?"

She's blushing again and the deeper shade is beautiful. That is so fuckin' hot. "I'll try. I don't say Sir right now?"

"We can save that for sex. This is us talking about us and how we go on from here. An attack, me being shot, your car being stolen and house broken into is not how I pictured our first date."

She smiles. "Dinner in my house was wrong anyway."

"What?" How the fuck is food wrong? Everyone eats.

Her head drops. "Sorry, Sir."

Fuck. I lift her chin up. "Why is that wrong?"

She doesn't have her smile on but her eyes are bright. "I googled dinner for a first date. It's not good and men are warned not to push the in-home dinner." It's delivered in her normal voice softly. I smile. She googled first date.

"I won't have to worry about making that mistake again. Where do you want to go on our first date?"

She freezes and looks down.

"Yáhsháyôn, it will be better if you get a say. We're equal on a first date too."

When she looks up she has tears in her eyes. "I don't understand how this works. I never had a date."

Groaning, I push myself up and pull her over to me kissing her head. "We've got time, Kateri. You can ask Carmen, Natalia or Aylen about good dates and get ideas. You pick what will make you happy."

She pushes off me and I hold the noise effects back. "Me? Where do you want to go?"

"Wherever makes you happy." Seeing her tears, I get it. "How about we try a few things then you can decide what you like and where our first date should be?"

"I can pick what I like?" She's shocked. I feel her anxiety.

Hiding my smile, I nod. "It won't be much fun if you pick what Carmen or Natalia like. Your first date is about what you like. You being happy makes it my favorite place to be."

Her eyes squint at me. "Is that how it always works?" She found me at the Club.

Shit. "You came to the Club, you know how *that* works, that is not a date. Women show to fuck. I've taken women to Club shit but it was never more than them wanting the experience."

Her head is bowed again. I need help here. She went from sold, to escaping, to school, to here. There is no way she made a friend in college.

"Yáhsháyôn, are you angry?" I use her first question.

Her eyes find mine. "I did that to you. Why do you want to have a date with me?" Have a date? She didn't have friends.

"Because you're smart, funny, confident, interested in my Club and family, you're beautiful and understand my culture. I've never found a woman that encompasses all of my passions and has her own passions and interests. I grew up where everyone is equal. We don't look for women that drop their lives to live ours. We all fall for strong women that chase their dreams and let us come along for the ride. You've met my family and Brothers. It's just who we are."

She's got her eyes on mine but she's not seeing me. After a few seconds I feel her happy and she smiles. "They're all like that. Alder has work for me for Badass Innovations and in the ABSZ Lab somewhere on his compound." Her voice is tentative but she's giving, pushing herself back to her calm persona.

I love my little Brother. "That's great. He's always looking for help. Jordan has help in Stella and has been cranking shit out every month. Nova said next is bike building for a kids video game."

"Who is Jordan?" Back to Sarah. Jesus, I need fuckin' help here.

"President of Alpha Rising. He programs all the shit for Badass Innovations. Stella is a Prince and his and Brinks' old lady. She's another mega egghead that programs and invents shit. She's working with Natalia to make virtual everything a normal part of life."

She nods but I feel her nervousness again. "Ask what you want to know, baby."

"I'm only an artist. I can't program." She looks so serious I have to smile.

"I'm not even an artist. I can ride and shoot, read and write. We're all different and need to be different for this to work. Delta's President builds and launches fuckin' satellites. I learned to build my bike, worked in the labs while I went to school, did IT in school, then rotations in everything for the Princes, but can't build a satellite. Jordan designed the Badass satellite, Stella coded for it with Hannah and a bunch of Brothers. Justice, Jeti, Aylen, and Nash fly everything. Joey is the Princes investor, Banks the BSC and Phoenix's investor, Brekan is the President of the MC and was FBI Ops and before that a Green Beret Commander. Then there's the Alpha-Bits. You've met them. Growing up equal we learned that everyone is different and different is just different. Our part of Badass is just as important as any President or Prospect. If we were all the same, we'd never get anything done."

A tentative smile shows. "You think I can work for Alder?"

I shake my head. "I know you can. You run your own business now. You get time, money, the work and have the drive. Alder is a brilliant little Brother. I bet he knows what you can do and will teach you more while you're getting his shit done. It doesn't matter what I think. Do you think you can do this?"

Her smile comes out. "I know I can do the Badass Innovations work. I think I can do what he wants for the DNA. It sounds like he just needs illustrations for Natalia to build in virtual." Already more than I know.

I pull her face to me. "You got this, Yáhsháyôn. That's Badass shining through." Kissing her lips has her surprised. It's not the first time I've seen that surprise so it pisses me off. She sits back quick. "Let's get some sleep, Kateri."

She's looking down but pulls the sheet up. "Yes, Sir."

Grinding my teeth, I look at the light and flip it off. "Goodnight, Yáhsháyôn."

"Goodnight, Si–Mase." The voice is timid but her smile is heard.

I smile in the dark feeling like I won the lottery.

Chapter Three

Two days

Mase

My eyes open and I'm up moving slowly. I don't want to wake Kateri. With my bed breeches on I walk right out of the house. If I stay, I'm fuckin' her. It's not an option yet. Alder will show today and run his tests. It may be an option later.

Getting into position, I move slowly reaching out and stretching my muscles. The pull feels good after two fuckin' days in bed. Nothing feels like my skin is ripping at every scar. That's something. Throwing appreciation to the ancestors, the healers and my family, I focus on my movements then let my mind wander.

Kateri talks to me about everything during the day. Everything but her being sold and escaping to school. She's comfortable in my house and doesn't want to go back to hers. Seth and Asa went to her house and called her with the camera on. Asa made sure she saw everything the pussies did.

I held her through her shaking and was proud that she kept it together. I've seen tears in her eyes but haven't seen her cry yet. With everything she's been through over the last week, I should have seen tears by now. Aylen has been great with her. I'll ask her tonight. Dinner at the compound should be interesting. I hope Mucimi shows.

Feeling a presence, I open my eyes. Mucimi is in front of me in tears then hugging me tight. "*Kuwômôyush*,

Mucimi. You take your time. I'll love you the same in a week."

He tightens his hold then is gone. I smile. He's so young. I'm glad he's here. My family went back yesterday morning. I know Brantley was with him for a couple of hours. Getting back to my positions, I pick up where I left off.

Kateri. With a deep breath I run through yesterday. She has work from Alder. She's excited about different paint jobs, skins and scenery for some game. Today she's working with Natalia for DNA or some shit. Alder is going to have lines building as the tests are done. He's so fuckin' smart. I don't get all she said but the lines can be moved and sections can be pulled out to show more. I thought it was one line with one result so I didn't ask. Her excitement is felt more than shown but I caught her smiling more yesterday than ever before.

The little crew showed and helped with dinner. Kateri told Asa she doesn't know how to cook much without the box. They showed her the virtual chef and made pasta salad, corn bread and green beans with onion and bacon. She was laughing with them about the feast they let her help with when I came in with the pork loin and onions. Dinner was good with the little crew answering her questions about food and training.

Natalia offered to train her. Pres thinks she needs Natalia so she doesn't drop back to the sub mode with a Brother. Everyone has seen it and has concerns about keeping her away from the Brothers. I do too. It was her life for five or six years. How do I bring it up if she doesn't talk to me about it? I'll find a way.

Finishing my sets, I stand and stretch my back. What I wouldn't give for a good run right now. I settle for a shower and breakfast after waking my tiny enigma. Yáhsháyôn.

Walking in I smile smelling breakfast. Kateri is with the chef making sausage and waffles. Asa is cutting fruit. "Brother, Yáhsháyôn, Chef."

The chef claps while Asa and Kateri smile at me. "Ooh, you beautiful Indian, what is Yáhsháyôn?"

Asa makes me laugh answering. "My breath. VP Mase show Boss Kateri heart with name."

I kiss her head walking by. "I do, Brother. You coming to ABSZ tonight?" I fill a glass from the faucet and turn dropping it. My arms go around her. "Yáhsháyôn, what's wrong?"

She folds so I lift her and take her to the office. "You, you, sorry, Sir." She jumps to monotone.

I sit behind the desk thinking I don't want to see her cry now. "Shhh, baby. Relax, catch your breath and feel me. My arms are around you keeping you safe, my heart is shielding yours, my Brothers are close if we need them. Relax, baby."

The more I talk, the more tears fall. I try Mohegan without any luck. *'Help! She's never cried. Now she won't stop.'*

'Aylen is on her way.' Justice throws.

"Aylen is on her way. She'll help, Yáhsháyôn. We can get through everything together, baby. My Brothers can help."

Her head shakes and burrows into my chest. Fuck. Her whole body is shaking.

87

I'm so fuckin' relieved to see Aylen. "Help, please."

She nods with tears in her eyes as she puts a hand on Kateri's back. "Oh, little robin. Nothing is going to hurt you here."

Kateri stiffens against me. Aylen doesn't stop. "My grandmother is close. She says Sarah is too. The best part of ancestors is knowing they're always with us. You brought your and my grandmother close. Nunánuk says it took too long. Your grandmother is proud of her little robin for finding the strength and ingenuity to fly away from the policeman." Aylen laughs. "She's very proud. Nunánuk says she's prideful in her old age."

Kateri relaxes then she's up and pulling away from me.

I tighten my arms. "Still, Kateri. While something is hurting you, my arms are your protection, my heart your shield."

Her head is shaking, I look at Aylen getting a nod.

"Kateri, look at me." Aylen has more tears. Fuckin' hell. "Mase knows you were sold and got away. The foundation that sent money was through Badass. He doesn't know details and doesn't need them. The man who bought you is dead. It's all he needs. You are safe here, you are loved here and your protection is not just from Mase. Everyone that meets you already loves you. I know I do. Cort threw you his protection. Every Officer in Badass has your back, Kateri. You're one of Crow's so they know you're one of the good guys." Thank fuck she stopped with the tears.

"I'm not good," Kateri whispers looking down.

My arms tighten automatically. "No, you're perfect, you're mine and you're loved. Do you think your grandmother would show if you weren't? She's proud and happy, Yáhsháyôn. She's seen how strong you are, she knows how smart you are, she understands why me and my family love you. Being sold isn't anything *you* did. Some fucked up men put you there. Do not let them win, my brave, strong Yáhsháyôn. I know the woman that beat them. Don't let them win now, baby. Let that Badass shine through and fight them, Yáhsháyôn. My arms are here to protect you, my heart will shield yours, my Brothers will help."

"You don't understand." She cries and my heart feels like it's getting ripped out of my chest worse than when I was hit with the bullets.

I move us to the couch with my eyes finding Aylen. They can jump.

She nods. "He does, Kateri, and doesn't care. Jump with me to the ancestors. Your grandmother has words for you. She's asking for Aiyana's help and guidance."

Kateri nods then falls against my chest. "Thank fuck."

Alder steps in. "Boss Kateri?"

"Aylen jumped with her. Her grandmother is close."

His head turns. "Navajo to Mohegan reservation?"

I get the confusion. "Ancestors are for all. Indians understood banding together for survival. With Kateri close to me, it makes sense that her ancestors would find her through mine. She needs guidance that she can't take from me."

"She love you." Fucked up thinking must be hard for the logical Brother that never had fucked up thinking.

"She was sold young. It's hard for women to get past that with men."

He's shocked. "Human traffic?"

I nod and he cries. I move Kateri's head to my shoulder so I can hold his arm. "She's here now. We'll fix her heart and show her what family is. She's so strong, Brother. She found a way to get away and to school. She'll get through this."

He nods wiping his face. "How to help fix heart?"

"Be Alder. You already help without knowing it. I don't think she had friends so interacting with her is all she needs. She'll learn by seeing it."

"Like Alpha-Bits."

"Just like the Alpha-Bits. That's why I said you're already helping. You've lived it, you know."

He shakes his head. "No sex to Alpha-Bits."

I nod. "That's why we fix her heart. Taken like that hurts what is never seen. Showing her her value to us will help. She needs to believe she's worth everything but it's new for her. We'll get there."

"You know?"

I smile thinking of Tess, Eliza, Aubrey, Marty, Aiyana, Judy and Indie but it's not real. There are too many. "It's not the first time we've seen it. Women are so strong, Brother. We just need to protect them while they rebuild their heart. Every one of them has come out stronger. Yáhsháyôn will too." I smile and it's real. "She got away from the motherfucker that bought her and he was a cop. Her grandmother said with ingenuity."

He smiles wiping his face again. "She smart like Boss Natalia, Carmen. I happy she have Nunánuk to your ancestors."

Kateri and Aylen move. Aylen is smiling.

"Good visit?" I ask.

She nods watching Kateri. "Yes. Tess will be at dinner. Aiyana explained about cloaking memories."

I move my hand to Kateri and lift her chin. "Is that what you want?"

Her tears gut me. "Yes, Sir."

I hug her. "Then that's what we'll do, Yáhsháyôn."

Aylen stands. "I have to get to work. I'll see you at the compound. You're going to love Tess, Kateri. She's a bubbly Barbie doll. It's funny."

Kateri sits up wiping her face but doesn't look at Aylen. "Thank you for bringing me. My grandmother likes you. She always gives everyone she likes bird names." She speaks softly but it isn't monotone. I see her smile.

Aylen lifts Kateri's chin and kisses her cheek. "We're all equal here. Aiyana will get pissed if she sees you bowing your head again. It's a bad habit. Your grandmother reminds me of mine. I'm glad you have her back. Mase can take you from now on, we go every night, I'll see you there all the time." She's gone and Kateri smiles.

We need to move past this. "Are you ready for breakfast?"

She bows her head then lifts it right back up. She's nervous. "Yes, Sir. I have work today." It sounds like her void and reality are crashing together.

I stand her up taking her hand wondering where her new safe will be. "Natalia and the DNA, sounds boring as hell. Alder is doing his tests. I'll get to work out if everything checks out."

She giggles then stops it. I still, smiling and tighten my hand around hers.

She peeks up giving me a pretty little shy look. "I'm just the artist. I'm not reading reports or coding."

"Without artist, I no get my result." Alder is a decent wingman.

Kateri squeezes my hand tight. "I didn't see you, Alder."

I pull our plates from the warmer smiling. Asa is a good Brother. "He was keeping me company while you jumped. The Bits had to get to work but said they'll be here on Wednesday for breakfast. Asa will check on you at the Lab later." I point to the note he left.

Breakfast is quiet but it's not a bad quiet. Alder asks her questions then freezes before eating again.

Kateri smiles at me when he does. "He sees something important," she explains like it's new to me.

I nod and give her my run down of today. Cleaning our plates, we load the dishwasher together getting a feeling of happiness rolling off her.

We ride to the Club and walk her to the Lab. Alder is quiet while we talk. Before she goes in, he puts his hand on her arm. She moves in a turn that has his hand falling.

He doesn't react. "I test VP Mase then here to Lab."

Kateri nods with a smile. "I'll see you later, LP."

He nods once. "You will."

I kiss her lips seeing surprise. "Security will get you back to the house or I'll pick you up here. Only Protectors are on you."

She nods turning away.

When the door closes, I turn. Fuck.

"She no like Security." Alder sees everything.

"No."

"I will get Alpha-Bits to transport golf cart. She ride Alpha-Bit trail. Control to her good. Security follow."

"Thanks, Brother."

Justice is in the medic room. "Justice." I acknowledge surprised he's here.

"I came with Aylen and jumped with them. Her grandmother is a comfort. She needs to jump with you."

I nod. "It was my plan."

Alder sets up his shit on a cart and pushes it to the table. "Shirt off. Boss Justice, you camera?"

Justice nods. "Whatever you need, Brother."

Pulling my shirt off I assume the patient position.

~*~*~

Justice bumps my fist. I climb then run the grate track. Alder has checked me after every fuckin' machine and exercise. Justice is fuckin' fast. I hit the last step breathing hard. We're usually neck and neck. Today I'm behind him with my hands on my knees. Something is wrong. Justice has his hand on my back. Alder has his stethoscope on my chest. I'm glad I'm low enough for him to reach it.

"Medic room, Boss Justice," Alder orders.

I'm moving and dizzy. Jesus. Back on the table with an oxygen mask on, Justice has his hands over me and Alder is on the side with his monitor showing my guts. I close my eyes and breathe.

"Not heart. Lung."

I look at the monitor. "Got it." Justice lowers his hands so he's touching me.

I turn away from the monitor. I don't know what I'm looking at so I jump.

~*~*~

Opening my eyes, I'm surprised Pres is here. "So he's okay?"

"Boss Justice fix. Protectors together at reservation heal more tonight. I am confident Boss Mase healed. Tomorrow I test. I have meet in Lab."

Pres nods. I sit up surprising them. "Are you signing off, Alder?"

He nods. "Tomorrow. Lung is healed. Test tomorrow, I sign off."

"Can I suspend today?" The ultimate test.

His head turns. "You call problem?"

"You'd be my second call. Justice would be my first. You'd need a ride."

He smiles. "You can suspend." He puts his backpack on and runs.

I look at Pres knowing he's waiting for Alder's test. "I get it. I'd want the paper too."

He smiles. "You beat my time. What the fuck is with everyone beating my time lately?"

I laugh pulling my shirt on. "Military run endurance regularly for a hell of a lot longer than Enforcer training. Everyone hates Mounty's training, but we ran that training for years competing against our own time. I'm always tied with Justice on the endurance, so I knew right away something was wrong. Did they say what? I jumped."

"Something about your lung. You'd have to ask him. Justice was needed at Phoenix." He didn't want me waking up alone. He's a good Brother. I jumped, I wasn't asleep but he doesn't get jump.

"Thanks. I'll get it tonight. I need a shower and lunch." I stop at the locker room.

He nods. "I'll bring Natalia and Kateri. How is she doing?"

"Good. Aylen jumped with her to her grandmother this morning. It helped."

He nods not understanding but he doesn't ask. "I'll see you in the dining room."

I shower letting the hot water soak in. My muscles need it. Stepping out, I pull air and smile. I fuckin' did it.

"What the fuck? I thought it was just your hair, Brother. That's crazy." Spano isn't happy with my dry technique.

I'm still smiling. "Yeah."

"You beat Kristos' time. He's going to be pissed."

I shake my head. "He knows. It's like six seconds."

"That's faster than Nova and Brinks."

I dress fast and Spano acts insulted. "Fuck, Brother."

I throw air at him pulling my holster on. "Thanks, so you're good?"

"I have to test again tomorrow. There was a problem with my lung." At his concern I throw, "Justice fixed it. Alder said I can suspend but he's testing tomorrow to make sure."

"Too bad. Delta is running nitro at the track this afternoon. Jordan got them a truck again."

"I'm in. We can have some fun with the Brothers." I smile thinking of the kids that need braces.

He laughs. "What do we need?"

"A couple of beat-up cars. They need to run for effect."

He smiles. "I'll get them to the track. This will be fun."

I stop him with a hand on his arm. "The trust gets the money."

He shrugs. "Whatever you want, I just like winning, it's always a good cause."

'*Mase*!'

I push to Pres at the Lab. "Pres?" I look from him to Kateri's bowed head, then Natalia. Her eyes are huge with tears making a line down her cheeks.

Pres is staring hard at me. '*She's following me with a yes, sir. Is this fucking brainwashing?*'

My jaw clamps tight. '*Sort of.*' Moving to her side, I try for light. "Kateri, lets get lunch."

She looks up fast. I feel her relief then confusion from her. Putting my hand out, I'm relieved when she takes it.

"Do I follow Kristos when he says I go with him?"

I'm surprised as fuck she's asking in front of him. "Natalia is right here. If you're not comfortable, you can ask her, say no, or call me. He's a Protector and will protect you with everything in him. You don't know him well but you can trust him."

She nods. "I'll remember. Alder said Alpha-Bits will come for me. He didn't say anything about Kristos."

Natalia leans into Pres. I turn Kateri. "Alpha-Bits will bring you a golf cart and show you the Alpha-Bit trail so you can come to the office when you need or want. You hit your band for Security and they'll know to watch the trail. It's got surveillance to keep the Bits safe." I'm not hiding those cameras from her.

She smiles. "Okay. I can come here alone when I want?"

I nod. "Hit for Security when you leave the house. Drive the Alpha-Bit trail and come here from the back. Your ID will open the door and the Lab is the first door."

Her hand squeezes mine and she leans closer. "Thanks. I'll do that tomorrow."

I hug her. She's cute and over whatever just happened. We follow Pres and Natalia out. Natalia isn't over what just happened. As soon as we get in the dining room Kateri's head is down.

I breathe deep. "This is the Officers table. You sit here when you come into the dining room."

"Yes, Sir." She sits fast.

I bend to her. "Kateri, look at me." I almost let out a *fuck* when she does. "If this isn't comfortable, what do you do?"

"Ask Natalia, say no, or call you."

I wait getting nothing but a blank stare. "Do you want to leave?"

She blinks. "Are you leaving me here?" That anxiety rolling off her hits me hard.

"No, Yáhsháyôn." I see the relief in her eyes.

"I want lunch like Natalia. I want to stay if you are." Her determination in monotone is odd.

I nod and kiss her lips. "Then we'll stay."

Natalia takes her hand and talks softly getting Kateri to sit facing her. I close my eyes when I sit.

When I open them, Alder is watching with tears in his eyes.

"You do not have an easy job."

I throw chin agreeing, surprised he said all the words slow.

~*~*~

I put my hand out for Kateri. "I'm glad you like the ride. It's one of my favorite pastimes."

This isn't a smile I've seen before. There are no shadows in her eyes. "I love riding. Thank you. That will be a good first date."

I hold my laugh. "It will, Yáhsháyôn. Let's see if Spano found cars."

She laughs liking our plan. "Kateri!" Natalia has that laugh shut off quick.

"It's Natalia, baby. Destiny and Stella are with her."

Her head is down. "What if they don't like me?" Timid is new.

Stopping, I turn so I'm blocking her from Natalia and the Brothers. I lift her chin. "Aylen said they already love you. People are programmed to love from birth, Yáhsháyôn. These are my Brothers from Princes. They love everyone."

She smiles and I kiss it. "Love the smile, baby. Stella is loud and obnoxious but has the softest heart around, don't let her scare you."

She nods with that blush on her face. I'm so fuckin' glad it isn't the usual surprise. As we get closer, I throw to Stella and Destiny she's never had a friend and is nervous. Stella is shocked then pissed. Destiny handles Stella so I hand Kateri over to Natalia.

Brinks stands behind Stella and Kateri moves in between me and Natalia. "Brinks, are you racing?"

He smiles. "Jinx is. Debra is on her way with Faith."

I nod. "Kateri, this is Brinks. Him and his twin, Jinx, grew up with Cort."

Cort is the magic word. She steps up and looks up to Brinks. "You're not as big as Cort."

"No, his dad was bigger. I hoped to make Reed's height but never made it. My twin is the same height. I'm not sure he ever wanted to be Reed's height. Mase is glad we're not, he's always bitching at us to lose weight."

She smiles looking up at me. "They'd still be the same height."

I shrug. "The Princes think they were spoon fed miracle grow."

Stella takes offense. "I don't. You're all fuckin' jealous."

Natalia nods. "I think so too. It's only the guys that say it."

"They're not Samoan. My dad was big like Reed." Kateri surprises me. Big like Reed?

"You're Navajo. They aren't Samoan height." Stella and the mouth.

Kateri freezes. I bend. "Do you need a minute?"

'*He wasn't her dad. She was told to say he was by Reed and Crow.*' Destiny throws.

Jesus fuck. How much more is there to Kateri? She turns into me so my arm goes around her. "Yes, Sir."

"What the fuck?" Fuckin' Stella has Kateri holding onto me.

Destiny takes Kateri's hand while I'm walking her to a tree. "If this isn't far enough, you tell me."

"Yes, Sir. I don't want to answer questions." She looks up at me fast.

"You don't have to, Yáhsháyôn."

Destiny smiles lifting Kateri's chin up. "We don't need the details to be your friend, Kateri. You don't know a thing about me and I bet you're going to have a blast today."

Kateri laughs squeezing my hand. "She showed me a picture and we're having fun."

"They don't need much, baby. I told you Princes love everyone."

She nods. "I'm ready."

I walk her back to the women. Brinks throws me chin. He talked to Stella. Natalia takes Kateri's hand from me. "You better get to your car before Tucker takes it."

I bend to my girl. "Brinks will watch over you. Destiny and Natalia are right here for you to ask advice or what's normal. Are you okay here with your new friends?"

Her smile has me relaxing. "I want to see you race." Timid determination again.

I kiss her lips. "Then I'm racing, Yáhsháyôn." I get a nod from Stella and Destiny and push to the car.

Asa cracks me up with his little white smart car out on the track. He's three behind the clunker Spano is standing by.

"Does it run?" I ask since it's not running now.

He smiles. "Barely, but yeah."

"That's all we need."

I climb in with the Protector gear on. Spano laughs when I pull the coat off and hand it to him. Brothers think I'm fuckin' nuts. I might be.

Teller walks with us as we move up a place. "You sure you don't want me to take it?"

I laugh at him. "You gave the other car to Tucker?"

He rolls his eyes. I smile bigger. "You're shit out of luck, Brother."

Jinx jumps in the car in the next lane. I laugh at him. "You fuck!" He laughs shaking his head.

"The money goes to the trust, Brother!" I yell over the noise.

He shakes his head at me. "I just threw a grand down." He bet on their car seeing the wreck they were against. Teller falls forward laughing.

"Steady, Brother." Spano pulls him away from the car. "You may damage it before he makes the line."

Jinx and Teller laugh all the way to the starting line.

Maverick is smiling seeing the hyenas then checking over my car. "The motor is blown already, Mase."

"She's got one more ride to give, Brother. Have a little faith."

He laughs shooting straight up.

I push making the far side to complete quiet then a huge cheer. When I climb out, everyone is laughing except Justice.

"What the fuck is wrong with you?" My Brother is not happy.

I smile holding my hand up to a cheer. "Not a damn thing. Help me push the car, it's done."

Jinx pulls up laughing. "I'll help, Brother." He gets out and helps me clear the track while Justice yells about Brothers dying and him having to explain this shit to angry Indians.

When a crew pulls up with a wrecker I hug Justice. "Alder said he's confident I'm fine, Brother. Relax. I'm fine and got permission to suspend. Pushing is easy."

He shuts up and walks away. Jinx laughs and gives me a ride back to the start line.

"I need to bet on Tucker. The Brothers don't know him here."

"I'm in." Jinx has his Jinx smile on.

"I love my Brothers."

He laughs.

~*~*~

We jump together. Justice stands. "Welcome, Kateri. These are the Protectors from Princes. We have monthly dinners and jump together then. Every night we jump but not at the same time. We're a crew of eighteen but do specialized training so there's always an extra couple of Protectors hanging around. Here with the ancestors and your new place within the Protector family, you're always safe. We'll jump again later but you're nervous. The ancestors calm you like they calm us. We use them to gain calm, celebrate our accomplishments and rant at our setbacks. Anytime you're in need, you can call on us. You're ours as much as you're Mase's. We'll protect you like he does. If you have questions, you can ask any one of us and we'll answer. You can ask questions here and it won't be repeated. Your story is yours to tell. We don't need it to claim you just like Mase. The woman we know is who you've shown to us. We see your heart. It's enough for us to trust the ancestors' happiness and what we see. You can ask in front of everyone. Aylen and Hannah may have a clearer answer than I do."

I tighten my hold on Kateri's hand encouraging her to show that strength I know she possesses. I smile when she shows it. "If you cloak, do you see my memories?"

Hannah takes her hand. "No. The ancestors cloak what hurts you. We lend our physical presence to that effort. I helped with Judy and only had a picture of a wrapping Aiyana said we need to strengthen. It was ribbon like but looked soft. When we were done, it was like a cloud around the ribbon. Nothing but a memory not able to influence your now is what Aiyana said."

"Does it hurt you?"

Destiny leans forward. "Nothing we do hurts us or you. We may get tired from expending energy, but we have the ancestors, Justice and Teller. We can get energy from each other too."

Mikey nods. "I was hurt last month. They worked around the clock to make sure I was back to good. They won't stop because it might drain them. We were taught that our Brothers are always first. Whether you're a healer, pilot, IT or Security, our Brothers come first. We take care of each other so we can take care of our Clubs. It's just who we are."

Kateri nods. "You're equal."

Justice smiles. "We are. Our jobs may be different, but we're all the same on the inside. You see it now and will understand more in time. Our ancestors handed down a vision and we follow it using Badass to promote it to more. The work you'll be doing for Badass Innovations is for games promoting those Badass beliefs to kids needing something to believe in. Your help there is just as important as Jordan's idea, Natalia's coding, Alder's Alpha-Bits printing the parts, Stella's programming and Banks' ability to market it. We're all cogs in the wheel. Spreading the vision to more is our job as one." He stands raising his arms up. "We're one with our crew, Brothers and ancestors."

The sky explodes in color. We all laugh. He's a fuckin' nut. Kateri puts her arm around my back and hugs me. I throw Justice chin and kiss her head.

"I want the cloak." She's confident and determined in that.

I nod. "That's what we'll do. I'm not a healer like them but I'll be there holding your hand."

She stands when everyone else does. "That's where I need you." Her words have me lifting her up.

"Wherever, whenever you need me I'm there, Yáhsháyôn." I kiss her.

Stella hits me. "Put her down already. She's missing the ancestors' happy dance."

I put my blushing tiny enigma down so she can see the ancestors' happy dance. Fuckin' Brothers.

~*~*~

Aquyá suspends in front of us. "Why can't I be in the picture? Destiny is in it."

Luke-Rayne rolls his eyes looking my way. I shake my head. "Take the fuckin' picture. We'll do another one and I'll take the fuckin' picture."

Mucimi fixes that. "I got it."

We laugh seeing four cameras floating. I hug my nephew. "*Kuwômôyush*, Mucimi."

He points at Aquyá. "He'll get his picture."

We all laugh seeing Aquyá trying to swat a camera away from his face. I lift Kateri still laughing when Justice yells, "Jump!"

We jump. My girl is holding on in a death grip. Brinks and McCabe are kissing Stella and Hannah as they go by. Kateri laughs. Destiny and Aylen float down holding hands stretched out. Getting close to the ground, Kateri holds tighter.

I push us up and step onto a ledge. "I'd never do anything to hurt you, Yáhsháyôn. You talked to Tess forever and got that from her too. Visions don't lie, baby. In case you didn't know, *you're mine* means forever. You're the air I breathe, my motivation for fighting the wrongs of our world. The compass that guides my spirit is in you, Kateri. From the first night, you had my heart. All that is me loves all that is you."

Her lips smack mine throwing a relief that has me on my knees before I fall.

When I feel a presence, I shake my head. Justice, Destiny and Aylen are standing in front of me, they are bound and determined to stop me from getting a kiss from my girl tonight.

'*They'll bring her up. We need to talk.*' Justice isn't here to help with a kiss.

"Yáhsháyôn, Destiny and Aylen will bring you up. I need to talk to Justice."

She turns smiling. "Can we do it again?"

Aylen puts her hand out. Destiny laughs. "Girl jump. Let's go, sisters."

I pull her back and kiss her lips then watch her rise up. "Have fun, Kateri."

Her giggle answers me.

Justice pulls me down the canyon and sits. "Aiyana is worried. I wouldn't get in your shit if I didn't agree. Because the connections and cloak are so new, you need to stick to vanilla. Jared is here tomorrow. He'll get a separate room set up, so she's not confused with who you are and her place in your life."

I see her void and reality clashing but fuck. "Jesus, I'm not into pain and the whole BDSM scene, Brother. Sadism and masochism have never been anything I found even remotely acceptable."

He nods. "Bondage, dominance and discipline are. That's all she knows, Mase. It's all she's ever known. Keeping vanilla in your room and anything that could be a reminder away from the new in your room is the point. Jared has a Club in virtual. Using tools to get you in a different place, a different scene is important. Teaching her vanilla right from the start is important. She needs to learn more than the only sexual experiences she's had. Those are with her bound, gagged or watching money exchange hands for bjs from her at poker games…"

With a growl, I'm up and pushing away from him and that fuckin' picture. He pulls me to the ground. I throw shields, push him away seeing his shock and point at him. "No! Don't you say another fuckin' word!"

Teller shows taking a step toward me.

I shake my head putting my hand out holding him in place. "No, Teller. I fuckin' know what she's lived through. I read Tess, Eliza, Indie, Aubrey. I can read all of them! The only thing that made this bearable when she says *yes sir* is I didn't have to see it. Shut the fuck up! I don't need the pictures!" I bend then fall back on my ass holding my head. "I don't need the fuckin' pictures, Brother."

Mucimi holds onto me crying. "I'll take them away. We can take them away."

Justice and Teller don't move. I jump calling for my dad and Christian then fall on the rock wiping my face. Prez and Dakota kneel with me. Jeremy and Christian put hands on my back.

"I can't do this seeing it." I barely get out.

My dad sits taking my arm. "They can take it. Relax, Mase."

I float in the heat.

When I open my eyes Justice and Teller are here with Prez and my dad.

"How do you feel, Brother?" Prez asks.

"Calm. I remember hurt but not the reason."

Prez nods and looks at Justice. "Move forward, Brother. Know I fucked up and took it back. You don't need it."

I nod and smile at him. "You don't fuck up."

He shakes his head. "I did this time. So, Jared has the room tomorrow. You're in a different setting for anything but vanilla. You good with that?"

"Yeah, whatever she needs."

They all relax. I smile. "I already agreed."

My dad pulls me over smiling. "Keep covered."

I roll my eyes. "I'm a little old for the talk, Dad. Get on the grands."

After hugs we jump back. Aylen and Destiny are still jumping the cliff with Kateri and Mikey. The fire is going and I get a beer for Justice and Teller. Trask and Brinks are talking about how good the Clubs are running with the new lineups. Nash and Tucker start flying with sparklers. Kateri comes to the fire with Mikey.

"They have a new game," Mikey says sitting next to me.

Kateri doesn't know what to do so I pull her onto my legs. "Did you have fun, Yáhsháyôn?" I hand her my beer smiling at her smile.

"The best. Thank you for bringing me. Mikey said this isn't date material unless we're not at the compound."

Carmen sits with Justice laughing. "I didn't know about dating shit. They're crazy with what they come up with. Throw out an idea and they'll make a plan. Get the Alpha-Bits in there somewhere and they make it awesome."

Kateri looks at me with a big smile. I nod. "We're not really average Brothers. If you want to see mountains we suspend to the top. We went deep sea fishing and jumped in."

Teller laughs. "Cliff diving and the guide almost had a heart attack."

"Reenacting Star Wars in the desert was fuckin' funny. The guide was trying to get Nash off the top of the set." Luke-Rayne has us all laughing.

Kateri laughs looking at Teller. He must be showing her. "You're all crazy."

My arm tightens around her. "Pretty much."

"Did you tell her about the pool you built with grenades?" Brinks asks.

I laugh loving my Brothers. They tell her so I don't have to.

Chapter Four

Kateri

Mase took me to the morning training. Aylen, Destiny, Jeti, Mikey and Stella are here! I love having friends. They all hug me.

Mase stands on the mat with the men. Stella pulls me to another mat and all the girls out here do her positions. This is different than Natalia's but easy to get the hang of. I like the feeling of the repetitive movements and get lost in the feel as I breathe and move.

"Good job, Kateri. Have you learned this one?" Stella sounds proud of me.

I open my eyes embarrassed to see Mase sitting watching me. "No."

Stella moves Mikey over to me by pulling her shirt. Mikey slaps her hand. "Asking is too hard for you?"

"Show her what the movements are for. You're bigger than her so it will work."

I smile. "Everyone is bigger than me."

Mikey nods. "That's the reason you're learning the positions. We practice them so when we need it, they'll come back as a natural reaction. Think about the set we just did. Mase, can you help me out?"

Mase is up and behind Mikey a second later. He's funny until his hand is on her neck.

She moves slow. "One." She turns lifting her elbow just like we did in positions. "Two." She moves again with one hand fisted, she pushes it with the other, elbowing to his chest this time. I see the next move when Mase tries for her waist. I wince when she spins hitting his lower back with the same elbow then stomps the back of his leg with her heel. Last is his neck with the heel of her hand when he bends.

She turns to me. "The movements should be fast and you should be trying for pain with every position. This is life and death for you. Choose life."

I nod thinking of times I could have used these moves.

Luke-Rayne comes over. "That's exactly what they're for." He looks at Mase getting a nod. "Every move is to keep you safe. Move fast and hit hard. Let's try it out." He's huge and can hurt me. No! They're Protectors and are teaching me so I can be safe with people who aren't Protectors.

I look at Mikey. "You can do it. I'm not moving and Luke-Rayne is all about the training." She'll stay right here so I stay safe. I can do this.

Mase looks calm and nods so I step forward and turn. Fast and hard. My life depends on it. Luke-Rayne's hand touches my neck and I move. Every position comes to me fast and I hit up at his neck feeling his hand blocking it. "Wow." I did it!

Mikey and Mase laugh. "Good job, Yáhsháyôn. Every set you learn is a defensive move. Use them when you need them."

I nod glad I did it right.

"She's got this. Let's get breakfast. Nova and Parker should be here soon." Mikey walks away.

"Parker Nova, eight months, Cheyenne." Comes out of my mouth automatically wondering how she knows him.

Mikey stops. "Oh shit." Luke-Rayne moves in front of me. "His name was on a list she sees. Falcon has it."

I don't understand. "She said Parker *and* Nova."

"She's Nova's old lady. Parker is his brother. Nova is Slade Nova. Parker was renamed Parker Sloan. He found Nova last month." Teller walks with us explaining.

That's the name Falcon asked about. I look up at Mase. "It's new. Parker was on the list of Protectors to watch out for." He tries to clear that up but doesn't.

"Kateri is on it too."

Mase stops and looks at Teller. "Kathryn Sarah T is the name on the list. She's in Alpha. Alder fixed it sending an e-mail."

"List? I'm on a list?" Oh no.

Mase stops walking when I do. "Jeremy made the list a while ago. It was a list of people moving to the Clubs. Most are military or security focused. Some are Protectors sent to help in some way. Natalia was on the list. Solei and AJ in Bravo. The list is from visions. I don't get visions so I can't say how they see shit. Christian and Jeremy are my brothers. I follow their advice and warnings but don't see what they do."

I nod. "I'm on the list as Kathryn?" At least it isn't my name.

He nods. "Teller said you are. Alder follows it closely so he'd know. It's not anything to worry about. How Jeremy sees shit is hard to explain. I trust it because you're here. It's hard to dispute whether he's right or not when the people on the list show."

"That's true." We walk into the dining room pod and the table is full. I smile up at Mase. "I like your family."

He smiles. "I love *our* family. You're theirs like you're mine."

"Thank you." This man-heavily-gifted-warrior has given me so much in days. I've spent years trying to figure out where I fit in this world and he showed then handed me my place. I sit and a man watches me. "You're new to me."

He nods fast. "I'm Parker. We came today for a day off with Mikey and Luke-Rayne and Jeti. Quincy is watching Duke so I can go to the FBI with them." He's got something wrong with him. That excitement is of a child. Parker Nova is found and happy. I smile at that *and* he's in the city at Alpha being taken care of by Badass. I hope they all are.

The man next to him laughs. "The FBI-Badass Training Center."

I look at him closely. "You're from the city. You stopped the men from shooting at the painter's house. I lived across the street. You stayed when the police came."

Everyone stops talking. My mind jumps.

~*~*~

Mase

Fuck, she's shaking. "Kateri, move forward. Don't look back."

She squeezes my hand closing her eyes. "Yes, Sir," she whispers.

Nash gets Parker talking. Justice watches her and I feel his energy. I'm so fuckin' glad he's here.

'*That was perfect, Brother. Keep her looking forward. She's got a photographic memory so this isn't going to be easy. We know and will keep working on that cloak when she's close.'*

I nod throwing appreciation to them and the ancestors. Taking a breath, I get food on her plate. "Do you want syrup, Yáhsháyôn?"

Her eyes open. It takes her a few seconds to focus and see her plate. "Yes, thank you."

I'm relieved I didn't get a *Sir* and move the syrup in front of her. When she eats, I breathe.

We get through breakfast and on my chopper before I feel her relax. This tells me short times with larger crowds is the way to go right now.

"So, he bought everyone choppers?"

I smile clipping her harness on pushing away the fact that I'm clipping a harness on her so my dick isn't reacting to it. "Even Mucimi. He doesn't fly. Stella has a special ordered one but it's at Princes."

She laughs. "This is why they call you crazy Princes, isn't it?"

I do my checks thinking about that. "It could be but to us it isn't unusual. What do you do when you have kids that have everything, had the best life, upbringing and are trained to keep thousands of people alive and do daily? Do you send a card?" I call to the tower surprised to hear an Alpha-Bit voice answer then smile, they're everywhere, I shouldn't be surprised.

When I lift off, she answers. "I guess a card would get old."

"This crew has done so much for so many Clubs, we used to get cards. Prez has always been generous with us. Sending fifteen on vacation every few months, with Security, was expensive. He always did. That's how we saw so much of the world. He was happy we got so many Alpha-Bits and did it using our abilities to keep them safe, against huge odds," I shrug, "that he bought the crew choppers to get around to the Clubs here."

Her voice is barely audible even on the mic. This touches her. "That's very kind of him. Having so many gifted kids must be amazing to your old Club. Stella has her chopper here."

"It was thoughtful, to me anyway. Some of us suspend quickly, but we all don't. Stella doesn't have freaky ability at all. She's got Mitch ability. Mikey wasn't with us at the time or she'd have a chopper too. My chopper was in Mass, my dad was going to send a truck with Blackhawks' down, but Prez bought these so he's keeping ours in Connecticut for now. Stella needs her boards to fly so hers was flown when Justice had his plane brought down."

"Not everyone moves like you?" I like her asking questions about the crew, the family.

"No. Lisa, Jeti, Mikey, Stella, Hannah, Lukas, Kyler, Luke-Rayne and Cayden don't. Some of them move faster than others but they don't have the push ability to make that look like they just appear. Some don't have ability like others. All but Stella and Mikey are readers."

"I like your crew and family. It's been a long time since I've seen family. My grandmother died and Crow came for me. Before that we had friends on the reservation. They were our family. I didn't remember that before. I do now. It's a good memory and feeling."

That's an odd and good thing to remember. "You didn't see families at college?" I want to ask about Crow coming for her but save it. Her memory of before should be clear unless...she remembers lists and gives information about Ben T in that void. I need to ask Aiyana if someone fucked with her memories before.

"I wasn't on campus. I stayed in a garage apartment and took classes online. I had a dorm assigned but never stayed there. The professor I stayed with my first and second year said there were problems so I stayed in a big building with an insurance company, lawyers and a bank on the first floor. My rooms were nice, but I could only go out in the day when people were in the building. Crow sent me a laptop and my computer for school. He was always nice like that. It was gifts for doing good in school." Crow was dead by then. Big building sounds like Masons.

No real dad in there yet. "How did you eat and get clothes?"

"I ordered from forms. I had an electric stove there. It was nice. Men brought supplies, but I didn't have to talk to them. I waited for them to leave before I went into the computer room. It was just wires but the door had a computer on it." She quiets lost in thought. She's got that faraway look on her face.

I let her have it and think about her jumping from Crow, when her grandmother died, to college. No dad in there either. Years of a fake dad, then the man that bought her are missing. How she got to college is missing. I need to be right with her when I ask. That's not right now but will be soon.

As we get closer to Honor, she recognizes the Club. "How did you learn to drive, Yáhsháyôn?"

She smiles at me with her eyes bright, it settles something so deep I feel it in my soul. "The professor had a friend that taught me. She brought me to a café, that's what she called it. There's one right here in town three. I liked the lessons and hated getting my license. I missed the obstacle course and the lady. She gave me my first car. The one I have now was a gift for graduating. My supplies came with an envelope the day I took my last final. It had the Badass logo and the car has a sticker on it." That makes her happy.

I talk to the tower and set down on the Badass pads away from the BSC choppers. She's still smiling when I sign off.

"That's very cool, babe. What classes did you take in school besides graphic?" Keeping her distracted I take my time unclipping her harness.

"Everything. It took me five years to get the degrees in digital media and marketing, art, then graphic design. I had so many classes to take but wanted the design in there. People understand the design word more than digital media."

I don't move once she's clear of the harness. "Did you get a list of classes to take?"

She stops breathing so I kiss her lips. It surprises her for a second then she smiles. "Yes. Crow gave it to me a long time ago. He brought me a computer and it had the list on it. He told me to remember when I got older. It was important and I had to go to Arizona."

"I'm proud of you, Yáhsháyôn. You did good getting there and following Crow's directions. He had lists for a lot of the Officers that are in the West Clubs."

She puts her arms around my shoulders and leans in. "Thank you." I know she's not thanking me for my words.

I lean and kiss her lips. Wrapping her up, I stand with her face buried in my neck. "I'm glad you had a good time last night. I love my Brothers and was proud to have you by my side, Yáhsháyôn."

When I set her down she giggles and I swear it touches my heart. "Bet the other women didn't jump the cliff."

Before she takes her second step, I pull her back. "No other woman has ever gone to a compound, slept in my bed or relaxed with my family."

She's surprised. "You said you brought women out."

I nod. "No other woman caught a hold of my heart, Yáhsháyôn. I was waiting for you and knew everything I did had the potential to hurt the woman I claim. I'm never doing that intentionally. We learned young to keep sex in perspective and what having an old lady means. You saw my parents. Tess, Rich and Patches. We've seen that from birth. An old lady is special and takes her place knowing we're all honored to have her. Not one Brother has ever brought a random woman to the compound house. We have Brothers that take an old lady for as long as it lasts without being *all in*. They aren't Protectors. Blackhawks aren't all Brothers. I explained *all in* when I put my cut on you. Blackhawks wait for that life knowing it will be worth it when we find it. My dad built a cabin years before he found my mom. It has seven bedrooms. She had six foster kids. We wait for it."

Her tear-filled eyes are smiling. "Thank you for waiting. I hope I'm worth it."

I shake my head. "You're worth everything, Yáhsháyôn. I can't live without *yáhsháyôn*."

Those tears fall. "My breath," she whispers.

I nod and lift her up. "Exactly. We have a lot to talk about. We can do that after dinner. You have work and I have another battery of tests to do for Alder and Pres."

She touches her lips to the same spot on my chest when I have her in my arms. I set her down on the tarmac and close the doors.

She waits and takes my hand when I offer it. "I'm glad Alder was with you the first time. Carmen said Justice was scared. He talked to Aiyana for a long time. You've never lost a Brother?"

Brothers show through my head. "Come, Kateri, or you'll be late. We've lost too many for stupid reasons. There are times I think fighting to spread good to people isn't worth it then we find the Alpha-Bits, you, Dreng, Faith, Daniel and Lorelei. The shit people do is horrendous. Someone needs to fight for those that can't or there won't be any good people left." I swing my leg over and put my hand out.

"It's a good thing you trained for that fight. I wasn't."

"You were trained on the computer from young. That training and school you have degrees in will help in our fight for good. Crow was a smart Brother and the ancestors guided him to the right people. We'll teach what you don't know so you get that."

Her head hits my back as she squeezes my stomach. The ride is quick and without helmets, quiet. I park on the side and walk Kateri to the Lab.

Natalia is ready and pounces as soon as we walk in. "I don't know why I expected you to be late. I'm glad you're here."

Kateri takes a step and I pull her back. Her eyes are huge. I shake my head. "I'll see you at the table for lunch. Natalia has a Team. Stick with her until you're ready to leave."

She nods looking serious. "I'll hit the band and take the golf cart home."

I nod liking the word home coming from her mouth. "Before you walk away, did you miss something?" I stop that turn she was going to take.

Those eyes look up nervously. "Miss something?"

"Babe, we spent the night at the compound, ate, jumped and played with the crew. Talked about *all in* and started on those plans for a future. When I get you to work, you're okay to just walk the fuck away?"

Her head starts lowering but my finger under her chin stops that. Those big, beautiful eyes with unshed tears gut me.

"Oh, just kiss him already. He won't leave without it and he obviously hasn't told you all their crazy rules." Natalia is done with waiting.

I smile at my girl. "We'll get on that tonight."

Her brows go up. "You could bend so I don't have to jump."

Natalia gets in our space and pulls my shirt straight down. Pushing, I move her to the side so I don't have the hand of Pres's woman pulling my shirt and putting her so close to me.

"Don't make her work so hard for it and she may kiss you today." She didn't get the message so I slide her over another foot.

Kateri smiles. "I'm pulling your shirt from now on. This is a rule?"

120

I'm not smiling. "You not feeling the need for that kiss is a different conversation that we can have without Natalia tapping her foot to remind us she's here. Pres will shoot me if I freeze her or screw the toes of her boots to the floor."

Natalia stops tapping. Kateri takes a second to answer. "Can we talk about how not knowing how to do that stopped me from doing it?"

Now I smile. "Definitely, Yáhsháyôn."

She pulls my cut so I'm closer and kisses my lips. "I don't think she's moving away so I better get to work. Good luck with the tests."

I kiss her lips then Natalia's cheek. "Have fun, Yáhsháyôn. Later, ladies. I'll see you at lunch."

~*~*~

Kateri

I look at Natalia. "Is that normal?"

She smiles. "Badass is inbred in those Brothers. Kristos said all the Princes are like that. They train from young so cool isn't even noticed by them anymore. You saw Destiny and Stella yesterday. They kicked drivers out of cars and raced with nitro like they do it every day. They don't know how to be dorks. Badass has to recruit because most of the Brothers I've met are like that. With Mase...I don't know. He's got cool, Badass and Indian all rolled together. Kristos told Major, Mase was one of the strongest Protectors Cort has seen yet. Since Cort sees everything, he must know them all."

I nod thinking she talks a lot and fast. I'm glad I don't spend all day here, having people around is new and exciting, it's also exhausting. Everyone wants to talk. The reservation and riding are nice with a group. I only hear Mase riding and at the reservation, not everyone talked. We went again late last night, Justice did the chin thing and sat on a rock with Mucimi. I was surprised they didn't say anything to us then noticed Luke-Rayne and Teller walking. It was nice to see them there and not have to talk. Mase sat right behind me with his knees boxing me in and arms around me. It was nice, safe and quiet.

"Are you with me?" She's been talking about the Badass here and their own coolness being rough around the edges until you get to know them.

I nod to Natalia. "Yeah. They're cool."

She shakes her head. "I have to say, that man wears it well. Even the scars don't hide it. I think they enhance it. He's beautiful."

Finally. "Stop talking or I'm telling Kristos what you said."

She laughs walking away. "I'll stop because he's your man. Kristos knows he's my man and every woman notices Mase with his tattoos, washboards and long hair. He'd make a fortune as a model." She's right so I don't answer.

"I got the first two from your list and started on the third. Before I add too much, I wanted your input. You just said background."

She's surprised so I wait for why. "You finished two and started the third."

I just said that, so I pull my laptop out and boot it up. It's going to be a long four hours. Stella told me about the programs, satellite and servers. They're all busy so I found what I needed and used what they've already built as much as possible. Using their code, I can add images, shadows and movements of those elements as the control target changes position. I just need to know if the background she wants is traditional or an abstract.

She pulls Stella up and we get through the first two that are straight abstract that she approves and move to the third traditional. Stella likes the background so I work until lunch finishing it for them. Putting on my backpack I watch them talk about getting the logo on the metal they're using for medical.

"Paint for shade. You can etch without digging into the metal so deep. The shading can be added during print so it's not a time waster. It would give the option of color with it. I'm not sure everyone would walk around with flames, but kids and men would like the option."

They stop and look at me. Crap. "Let's keep her," Stella has me relieved.

I smile. "I definitely don't mind the work but you all don't have enough to keep me working forty a week."

Natalia shakes her head. "You didn't listen to Lorelei when she explained pay did you?"

I shake my head not looking at them. I was so happy I got the job I didn't care.

She apparently did. "You make more than a hundred grand a year."

"Wow. That still doesn't fill my work week. I need to work at least forty hours. I have new things to keep me busy now but even drawing isn't going to fill my days."

They laugh. "Hug her for me. She fits right in," Stella tells Natalia. "We get bored too. My lab is close to my house. Natalia works on computer shit at night for Alder. Our list is still never ending."

I nod and touch Natalia's back when she hugs me. "I'll keep working on your list. It's lunch."

They both move fast. Stella looks to the right. "I have to go. I'll be back after lunch."

We nod. I wave a bye to her. She's not here, she's virtual so it's weird.

Natalia walks out so I follow her. "Thanks for reminding me."

The men at the wall follow us. Natalia isn't worried. I keep their locations in my head as we walk out one door, through the courtyard then into the dining room hall. When I see Mase turn the corner I relax.

"Perfect timing," Natalia says and jumps on Kristos.

I look at Mase. "Whatever works for you, Yáhsháyôn."

I smile and pull his shirt down. He comes with it smiling. "Love the confidence in that move, baby."

I kiss him glad it wasn't wrong. With his hand on my back, I walk to the Officers table not looking around. The men in here scare me. "How was your shift?"

"Good. I just finished a background for Stella and Natalia. They're going to do what they do and I'll fill in the background so they can move on." It feels good to share my day with him. He said that's what he does at the reservation but he never said anything last night.

That smile has my insides melting. He's happy because I enjoy my work. "I bet it's not that easy but I'm glad you like the job. Do you have old shit you need to finish up so you can focus on the Badass shit?"

Shaking my head, I answer. "The publisher I worked for went under. They can't compete with the digital stores. That was the deadline I was working on when you brought dinner. I have work from an ad agency that I can do when it comes in. It's usually websites, brochures and political signs or paraphernalia. They hired a graphic artist for their cards and promo items. That was boring and monotonous so I didn't mind losing it until the publisher was closing."

"It's good you have the time without stress." He's right so I nod.

I give my order to the Prospect and ask. "How was the test?"

"Boring and repetitive. Alder signed off. I'm good to work regular shifts."

I lean into him glad he's okay. I've never met anyone like him. Maybe Reed was like him. Ben T was big but he wasn't pretty or considerate like Mase. He took care of me, but I was like an assistant. He'd buy food and bring me clothes but I served myself and did laundry or dishes if he let them pile up or was gone. Mostly he was nice. I don't think he knew much about kids. My grandmother talked and walked with me every day. She told stories and explained things I didn't understand. My dad talked about men, the missing kids and women.

I got tests for school but never went back to real school until an assessment for high school even though I did online, then college. I had to show on campus three times. It was scary. Crow said it was important. My dad never talked about school or how my day was.

He was just a guy taking care of a kid he didn't ask for. He'd have a beer by the fire when we camped and told me about the reservation he was from. It sounded like my grandmother's, but he knew about gifts and could read people like the Princes.

Mase finding me was written my grandmother said. I'm so glad it was. He's given me family and friends. I still have my job and even more to do. My grandmother is with the ancestors and I can see her there. I stopped dreaming the day I was brought to foster care. Last night, I dreamed of a table full of people that were smiling and talking, riding behind Mase and laughing with women I haven't met yet. I can't help but smile. My dream had nothing bad in it. A life that I fit into was just waiting for Mase to find me and my dreams to begin again.

Natalia and Kristos are talking but Mase isn't. When I look up, he's looking straight ahead. Seth is looking at him. Men are weird. Seth looks right at me and Mase turns. "Everything okay, Yáhsháyôn?"

I love that name. It's only mine. "Yes. I was wondering what you and Seth were talking about." I smile at his face turning blank. "I'm kidding. I was daydreaming. I just noticed you were quiet."

That blank changes to a smile. "Dreams are good. Something to look forward to. What are your plans for your next shift?"

"Sketching some scenery for BI. That's what Alder calls Badass Innovations. Zale said he'd get me drone shots of the track."

He nods. "I'm on rounds with Pres. You need to stay on the Officer's section of the compound while I'm out. The pool is..."

"I'm working a shift right after lunch. Asa showed me the Officer's section the Alpha-Bits can go on but I'm working."

He nods. "Good girl." His voice has me looking up then down.

I did good. "Thank you, Si–Mase."

He lifts my chin and leans over kissing my lips. "Jared will be upstairs working in the spare room. He's got some computer shit to do. Are you okay with him in the house?"

"Jared is Aiyana's husband?" I met him yesterday.

"He is."

I nod. "I'm okay. I can work in the patio or on the back deck."

He shakes his head. "Do you want an Alpha-Bit with you?"

"Do they do that?"

"Asa will work from anywhere and he offered an Alpha-Bit escort, transport or companion. I think in the house alone with you has to be two unless it's Asa showing. Like I said, they can work from anywhere."

I nod. "I'd like that if they're available. I can work from the deck if they're not. There are cameras outside. Your brother said I can always get help from outside the house."

He texts Asa while asking, "What brother told you that?"

"The oldest one. He was at the reservation. You said he's the most powerful seer with vision. Justice said it too."

Seth laughs. "Christian is the youngest of the older. Joey, Taylor, Brantley, Terry, then Christian, the Js and Mase. He acts older because he's seen so much."

I get the feeling he was going to say more but he looks at Mase.

"They all look young but I thought he looked younger than Brantley and Taylor."

Seth nods. "Good genes and Brantley is Mucimi's dad. He adopted a fuck ton of kids too, but Mucimi is his so he wears that proud. Taylor was military. His demons are for life."

Wow. I nod not knowing what to say. It's not my business so I can't ask for details. Our food comes so I eat before I say something stupid. I was worried about Mase and didn't pay attention to the family's conversations. I just wanted to be close and help if I could. He didn't need much help and almost none from me. I still wanted to be there just in case. When I'm done, I listen to Mase and Spano talking. He said the virtual glasses are harder than the old ones Alpha first used.

"I'm using that program for the scenery. It's the one that you wear glasses and everyone can see a different room around you?"

They look at me. "Sorry, Sir." What is wrong with me? I know better.

Mase lifts my chin. "Those are the glasses he's talking about. Here they're easier for me and Pres but not Spano, Yáhsháyôn." What? He didn't hit me.

No one is moving. I hope I'm not shown as an example from behind. "You're not angry?"

"No, baby, we need to figure out how to get them working for him." He's not angry.

I lean over to see Natalia. "The virtual glasses they use in Ops can have the board links with a background. It's added to the glasses input. The output wouldn't be touched and the rest of the room wouldn't see the change. Stella said she put a tint on her glasses so she could read the glass day or night. Her glasses didn't change color while she was wearing them when she got to the compound at night or in her lab. Those are a different program but it would work the same."

Mase nods. "Uncle Danny has his own glasses for Ops. The color is crazy if you put them on. 3D is noticeable to everyone that tries to see through them but not to the room or his IT Control. They see it the same as the boards on the wall. He's dyslexic." He really isn't angry with me.

Natalia nods. "That's a great idea for kids. I don't work on the Ops glasses and haven't seen the code. You're working from that code, Kateri?"

I nod. "Yes, Stella gave me clearance so I'm not bothering her for pieces of programming they use in everything for BI."

"Can you fix Spano's glasses so he can read the boards easier?" Kristos asks.

"If I can ask him while he's got them on I can. The code for each pair works off the server."

Kristos puts his hand up. "Stop there."

I look down before I get slapped. "Sorry, Sir." Please, please, please don't hit me here. It's going to be worse because I already messed up.

Mase lifts my chin and my eyes fill making it hard to see him. "Kateri, Pres wants you to fix Spano's glasses. Asa is in Ops for another hour. Can you do that?"

I take a breath and look down as soon as he lets my face go. Mase has never hit me unless it was on my behind during sex. "Yes, Sir." I need to please him. Two mistakes is bad.

"Jesus fuck." Seth is mad. I keep my head down before he comes this way. The crash against the wall has me jumping. I don't look up.

"I take Boss Kateri to Ops, VP Mase." That's an Alpha-Bit.

"Do you want to go with Spano to Asa and fix the glasses, Yáhsháyôn?"

I look at him to see how angry he is. Those eyes don't show anger. "Yes, Si–Mase." His look softens. He's not angry.

"Laran will go with you. Do you need me there?"

"No, Mase. Laran knows where everything is. He sent me plans so I could get around." I have to keep him happy with me. I can do this quick and go home.

"Asa will go to the house with you."

I kiss him fast and pull my backpack on as I stand up trying to be quick and not anger him or anyone else.

Laran holds my hand. "I take you to Ops, Boss Kateri."

"Thank you, Laran." I just notice how quiet it is in the cafeteria. I don't dare look around. I've always been good at keeping my eyes off men. It's a good thing to still have retained after college. Another big bang has me walking faster.

Laran keeps my hand. "You safe, Boss Kateri. Boss Spano here, big, safe to Alpha-Bits, women."

My feet slow hearing boots following us. "Thanks," I whisper.

"Laran, go by the elevator. Boss Kateri doesn't need to go through training. I'll wait for it and swipe you up then take the stairs." Spano sounds nice.

"I will use elevator, Boss Spano." Laran tightens his hand in mine.

I nod quick, relieved I don't have to see more men.

~*~*~

Mase

Seeing Seth slam half a wall down so fuckin' fast tells me how pissed he is. As soon as Kateri set foot in the hall, Pres threw his chair through the other half of the wall and walked out.

Natalia holds my arm. "He was telling me what she was thinking. She didn't want to get slapped. You don't hit her unless it's during sex. She's afraid of other men hitting her while you're sitting right here. She doesn't want to anger anyone and she thought she angered Kristos. That's how it all started. He's calling Cort to get help for her here right away. He thought burying something helped, but it didn't."

I nod. "I need help. She'll have a dog in a day or two. It's for straight protection and PTSD. Knight said something about keeping her in the now. Tess thinks Aylen will be a help. Justice was trying to cover her shifts for the week. The problem with cloaking her memories is she's got a photographic memory and her recall is excellent."

Pres sits so I look at him finishing. "As for me spanking her ass, she called me for service. Bondage, dominance and discipline are very much my thing and I gave her what she asked for. You know she controls every bit of that before we start. I am not a kid and guide everything I do with honor for me and my partner."

With his nod I go on. "I didn't even get her real name, Brother. When I did, I was told all the things she's lived through from my Brothers. Kateri hasn't told me anything and I'm not asking. I can't do this if I get details so I can't ask. We haven't had sex since I've known her name and I'm told that is vanilla unless were in a different setting. Two things there, different setting with them sending Jared to my house means she'll need that and I've never been into sadism or masochism. She'd never be hurt by me whether she asked for it or not. I can't and won't go there for anyone. Since I spilled all that, I need advice on vanilla and I'm not taking it from your old lady."

Natalia laughs then stands. "You're a good man, Mase. Gorgeous and honorable are hard to find. I'm glad she found you and not someone that makes her life worse than she's already lived through. I'll leave you to the gentle giant that can give advice on vanilla. He isn't well versed in gentle but no woman wants that so you'll be fine."

I laugh at the look on Pres's face. He shakes his head taking her kiss as she walks by. "Fuck off, Mase."

I stop laughing. "So vanilla isn't gentle or shouldn't be?"

He nods. "Aylen is getting freed up to spend a week with Kateri. She starts tomorrow. Cort is more worried about you right now because of something that happened in the canyon. You threw Justice off you and held him and Teller in place."

I look at him not seeing it. "I did?"

"You jumped and Justice was free. I don't understand jump, ancestors and Justice fucked up so you were pissed and had that power."

"Justice doesn't fuck up. Oh fuck. He said he did. That's when he said Jared would be here and I had to teach Kateri vanilla. My dad, Prez and Christian were there with Justice and Teller. I wondered why my dad and Prez were there but didn't ask. I held them both? How the fuck? Justice is stronger than Christian. Both him and Teller?"

He nods. "Right now, anything we read from Kateri isn't ours to give you. Cort's words were, *any details from when she was sold go to Justice, Cloud or Brantley*. I'm assuming that means contact names or locations not what she did."

I shake my head and try to keep the growl out of my voice. "I've read it from too many women, Brother. Don't ever give me the details. I know Darren made it through only because he knows every fuckin' Outlaw that touched Eliza is dead. He's like Falcon and would have found them but Prez made sure he rounded them all up and made it easy." I guess I didn't get it out without the fury I'm feeling at the thought of someone hurting Kateri like that.

He sits back giving me space. "Relax, Mase. We'll get information to the people we're supposed to. Here it's just me and Seth unless Mucimi shows."

I nod. "And Natalia. You throwing that to her would have her talking to Stella. Kateri is good at blocking. Right now only the strongest readers are getting anything from her. The rest of the crew doesn't know more than the basics I got. They will if Stella gets it. Jeti, Nash, fuck, even Mucimi are too young to understand how fucked up people can be. They didn't grow up in that world. Indie, Hannah, the adopted boys know because they lived it. It was cloaked years ago, but they all are Protectors. That may not work for Kateri but it's worth a shot. They don't need the details, Brother, it can only hurt them."

He nods. "I won't let that happen. I was pissed. She thought *I* was going to hit her and she had to move fast to keep you or any other man from getting angry."

I put my hand up. "Focus, Brother. Vanilla."

"Did you ever read the list?"

I roll my eyes. "Yeah, it got me knowing what women need to get off. I never used the list like a grocery list. I read the first and they worked for experience then I went to the Club. I never needed a list again and like the discipline of controlling my needs based on what my partner puts on the table for hard limits. I'm not into negotiating with women. They know what they like and don't. I know what I want and need. It's never been an issue until now."

He shakes his head. "It isn't an issue now. Vanilla is the same without the whole scene laid out. If you need it, make your own without the toys. Use shit you find in your room or house. I think vanilla is not what you do with someone that knows hard core. Show gentle when you feel it's important to convey what you're feeling. Show Mase the rest of the time. One thing that should never stop is telling her how, why, or what you're seeing. That's important to her."

"Really? How, why and what I'm seeing. I do the *what I'm seeing*. That's never hard. How and why."

He nods. "Women need more details than we do, I guess. It's worked for me. I haven't gotten complaints."

I laugh.

~*~*~

I pull into the driveway and know this is not going my way before I get to the door. Opening the door confirms I'm right. Aiyana, Knight, Jess and Prez are in my kitchen. All we're missing is Kaleb, Jessie, Pres, Uncle Danny and Tiny.

"Uncle Danny is with your dad and Jessie getting dinner from some place up by Brekan. Kate and Tess are with Kateri. Lily, Pres, Rich and your mom took a walk with Nash. Kaleb isn't here but Aaron is in the air with Andrew. They'll be at ABSZ tonight. Tiny is back in Mass holding down the fort and driving Ricky crazy." Prez surprises me.

"Aaron is coming here?"

"This is why we're never making fuckin' normal. Everything I just said and Aaron showing is what you focus on?"

I shrug. "I read fine, Prez. I know the dog is here and Knight has to do commands and explain about staying in the now. Jess likes Natalia and is still telling her stories about Club romances. Aiyana is bored and likes Kateri because she brought new ancestors. Lily is sick of you taking off and had two days to see Aylen who will be here tonight instead of tomorrow. Kate came for Kateri. Pres and Uncle Danny aren't letting her anywhere they haven't seen. Rich is here for Tess because she wanted to make the trip from ABSZ and Patches needed to get back. Nash is here because he's worried about Kateri and Mucimi. Did I miss anyone? Oh yeah. Why the fuck are you here and why are Justice and Teller meeting you at my house?"

"You didn't say anything about your mom and dad."

That's lame. "I'm their kid, recently injured and found my old lady. It's a given." I shrug.

"Fuckin' readers." He walks out the patio door with Knight and Jess laughing.

Aiyana smiles at me. "This Club is a much better place for you, Mase. I am glad you are with a reader and in an Ops facility such as this."

"Thanks. I love it here. Did Jared finish?"

"He did. Mitch sent him the old programming so you will have an easier time than with the virtual set up. I do not understand as I've only seen what Jared has built."

I nod getting that. "I'm sure it will work. The Brother is nothing if not detail oriented."

I get her smile again. "He is that."

I walk out the door and think I should have stayed with the crazy in the house. "If Nova sees you, he's shooting you, Keesog. If you fuck up here, I'll freeze you where you stand and call him with your location."

He looks shocked. "I'm your nephew."

"You fucked up and didn't own it, never apologized, never showed respect and got on a flight home. Where am *I* wrong in there? You show you're a pussy with no backbone, no honor and not a fuckin' drop of Badass and throw that at me? Did I teach you to be a pussy?"

He sits hard. "GC brought me to apologize. I'm going there tomorrow."

I shake my head and keep walking. "You may not want to mention you had to be dragged back. That will get you shot from a real Badass Brother I'd stand behind. Grow the fuck up."

I make it to Spano's back deck. He walks out with a beer in his hand. "Figured you be here after the carnival explained why it's at your house. She fixed the glasses. Laran stayed with her until people started showing. Asa was there until his shift started. He asked me to keep watch. She was good with your mom and dad there. I don't know about the rest. They showed later."

"You can see the board better?"

He nods. "Like it's on a screen in front. It took her twenty minutes. I felt like I was at an eye exam. It's the color. I don't see some when they're mixed or some shit." He never smiles.

I'm waiting for him to say his piece. "I'm glad she got it working for you."

He nods. "She's amazing like the rest. She can't protect herself like the rest, Brother. What can I do to help that? She isn't safe cowering anywhere close to dominant Brothers. It's like a fucking target."

I nod. "She's getting help with Aylen starting tomorrow. She's learning positions and knows how to use them. It takes her once to get the set. Kate is a domestic abuse advocate and with her now. She'll give me what can help when she's done. Tess was a slave and will help with what she's been through and works. I'm not sure how I can help, so knowing what you can do is waiting on the fuckin' line of people I just mentioned, unless you got advice on vanilla sex."

He gives me a look. "No fucking women I've ever met are into that. Why would you cause more damage? Vanilla is boring, no feeling, no passion. It's like that zombie state she drops into. She deserves better than that, Brother."

I'm starting to wonder if Justice is wrong. I know it's wrong for me already. Who wants to fuck with no passion? Pres said he fucked up. Maybe something is wrong with him.

"I'm not sure I can deliver that shit so I need to get Justice to clarify what vanilla is."

"He into hard core?"

I shake my head. "No, he's always used ability, when you can think of touching everywhere at once it makes women happy."

He rolls his eyes. "Fucking ability kids."

I smile loving throwing that at him. "I don't use it unless she's blindfolded and I need a third hand or we ran tandem. The thing with ability is you need to be smart with it. Fuckin' for relief isn't winning you anything. Making that fuck easier is setting you up to fail when it's time to claim your old lady. *All in* is never achieved cutting corners, Brother. We've seen *all in* our whole lives and easy is never what we grew up seeing. Our fathers showed the work they put in and we took notes. Justice isn't stupid and made sure we knew the difference between easy and effort. The kids that didn't get those lessons are paying for that right now. Easy is only easy for a while, then you're struggling to catch up. That road is a fuck of a lot harder to climb."

He nods. "How's it work with you being older than Justice and Teller?"

This question is always asked. He's asked before in Alpha. "They're older than me in every way but years. Justice had twelve on his crew originally. When every fuckin' reader had almost all the kids dying in a vision, I was added with Luke-Rayne and Tucker. Tucker is closer to their age but I was needed at Princes more and more and

Luke-Rayne was fuckin' good at his job. Prez put us with Justice's crew. They had more of a target on them than the other crews. They were already the working crew by that time. Justice and Teller together were unbelievably focused on each other and the crew. Justice took everything and not only listened but gave it to us. He figured if the adults were sharing, he needed it and if he needed it so did we. Hearing about equal our whole lives, age didn't play a part in me or Luke-Rayne's thinking. If I had the crew in New Hampshire, Justice would have been running that Club. I'm glad I only lasted six months. It was five months too long, time away from my crew and wasting time on Officers that were playing Badass. It was always my life."

"Because of the crew." He smiles.

I nod. "My brothers are Jeremy, Jacob, Christian, Terry, Brantley and Taylor. My sister is Joey, the Princes' Banks. Our family tree includes cousins Knight and Lightfoot. It doesn't get any more Badass than that, Brother. Honor is in our blood. Equal is the only way we've ever lived."

"Fucking shit. I can see it different when you explain it like that. Why don't you ever answer anyone else?"

I check time and got it to draw this out. "You've heard me answer other Brothers. Sometimes it's because I know what they're thinking and they aren't ready to hear it. Sometimes they're trying to get a foot in the door. You're genuinely interested in how we got to live in an equal world where it seems the world is against the very thought. We're raised Badass, military and Indian for a reason. *Fuck what they think and stop fuckin' with our land and water or we'll replace you* just work together. We had the perfect three and Prez used everything he had to get his point across. The BSC testing already proves it. He had it right with Justice, Teller and Mucimi.

"I'd have never worked as a lead or second. I'm a Protector to the core. I don't mind handling the VP work while being that Protector in everything. I learned every job just like the rest. I'm a Protector for ground Ops. It's the job I love. IT is easy. Flight, I got. Ops Control, if you're jammed up, I'll take it. I wasn't given abilities to sit behind a computer. I was given them to defend the Club, our Brothers, our earth and belief that everyone is equal, on the front line. I may end up in Ops eventually. That's not today and I've just been gifted more ability, so I'm needed on that front line.

"You're going to need the answers I just gave you. Nash is young. He knows the jobs I named and can fly, drive, ride anything with a motor. He'll have your schedule done and businesses running right, he doesn't have years of experience and will need a Brother watching his back. Angel is that Brother. Nash is me, fun, funny and always up for a good time. Ability is strong in him and Brothers may not get that until it's too late. Proving himself to every Brother because he's young is going to get old. Shooting your work force isn't doing you any favors. His protection needs to be understood by those Brothers that don't know he can pull air out of their lungs or roll fire through their bodies taking their last breath. He doesn't need a gun and they'd never see him coming.

"Now, I've been here ten minutes and my girl is on the move. Thanks for keeping her covered today. Glad you got your glasses fixed and thanks for the advice. Later,

Brother." I push laughing as he curses ability Brothers again.

I didn't lie but I'm sick of Brothers asking the same stupid shit over and over, they don't listen. Spano will tell them never to ask that question or they'll get the hour lecture. I'm good with that. Maybe we can spread it to the other Clubs.

My girl's beautiful eyes are red and puffy. As soon as she sees me, she moves fast. I like being the reason she's moving fast. "My arms are your protection, my heart your shield, what do you need, Yáhsháyôn?"

"You." She holds on with her body shaking. Anxiety, nervousness and shame are rolling off her.

I lift her up and carry her out to the back yard. "Close your eyes, baby." Crossing the walkway, I push and sit us on the ledge I use to see Badass working and growing when I need the reminder. "You can open now."

She does and gives a laugh then sniffles.

Moving her hair, I kiss her neck. "You have a lot of emotions running through you. I get anxious. I get nervous with so many new people showing at once. The one I don't get is shame. What I'm going to say isn't repeated or spoken. This is for you to fight your demons head on. Tess isn't the only slave we have. You see how she's guarded, loved and accepted by everyone. Tess isn't just an old lady. She's a huge part of the Badass vision because she gets visions and helps in every way she can to keep us on the right path."

She has tears and questions, so I wait. "She's not the only one?"

I shake my head. "Aubrey, the Js wife was sold from two to five when her mom who was sold during the same time, found a way to get our attention to save her daughter. Marty works in HS Ops in Mass. She's IT and fuckin' strong as hell. Aubrey is a Protector Lead for Princes. She's fuckin' good too and rarely leaves. Aiyana and Judy, my brother Terry's wife, lived through sexual abuse. Eliza was a slave taken by the Outlaws. She's the VP of Princes old lady and HS Ops lead and a Control in Ops. Fuckin' good too. Sheila was gang raped, that's Stella's mom, Eliza's partner. They don't get more Badass than Sheila.

"There are so many that understand what you're going through and how you had to deal. They don't need details, they don't need blow by blow. They lived it and know the shit you do to survive when your only options are live or die. They chose to live and live in a way that they fight alongside their Brothers to make it better for more and for them. Judy is a reader and works with Aiyana making medicine. She's not running Ops but works to get good Badass Brothers into the Clubs. Hannah and Indie are IT and Protectors, Hannah is Head IT for Champion. Faith had her eye cut out, ear cut off and lost a finger for stopping kids from getting sold through CPS. She's still fighting to find and move those kids to safe homes."

She's watching me without tears or questions.

"Yáhsháyôn, what I'm saying is we know how hard life is, we get the choices you made were to live and we have been fighting for you, hoping to find and move you and any other woman or kid to a safe place. You never got the choice. Someone stole and sold you. They didn't ask, they didn't want your opinion and they didn't give you a say. There is absolutely no room for shame in there. If you made the choice and it was wrong, I still wouldn't think it's right. You were a fuckin' kid."

I smile. "You took what Crow told you and found a way to escape and make it through school. That's a fuckin' reason and a half to be proud, baby. You beat them. You won, again no room for shame in there. Be proud of not only living but beating them. You're like Eliza, Sheila, but mostly Marty who found a way to get out, get her daughter back and make life good for more. I'm so fuckin' proud of that woman, Kateri. What you did to make it doesn't matter, you made it and made it by outsmarting a cop that thought he was above the law. You made *that* decision."

"That's what Tess said. She didn't tell me of the others."

"It's not repeated, not thought of."

She nods. "*Some thoughts*. I get it. Crow had me read it over and over like I'd forget." The way Crow showed, told her about school and said shit, makes me think he saw what was in store for her. With Christian and Jeremy, I get play out. I think Crow died sooner than he expected. My brothers don't see themselves in visions. Crow wouldn't have either.

"They remind us we can't know everything and changing every vision foretold is dangerous. Sometimes shit has to happen to good people in order for something else to happen in the future. We hate the words, *let it play out* and *it will be fine*. I swear they were invented to fuck with our heads."

She smiles. "I can see the ability kids having a problem not being able to fix what they can. Why else would you have that ability?" She's so fuckin' smart, she gets it.

"It sucks. Since I don't get visions, it's a fuckin' struggle I hate and need help walking with."

"The ancestors?" She jumped right to comfort and guidance.

My smile is for that. "Always. We learned from young where to get help when our world felt like it was crashing down around us. The ancestors, our Officers, parents, crew, we'd look for comfort and guidance to make sense of those two fuckin' phrases that are said too fuckin' often."

Her eyes go out of focus. "You think I'm one of those times?"

I shrug. "It doesn't matter, I didn't live here and can't change it. Looking at it now, I think Crow saw something and didn't live long enough to get you safe. Our job now is finding who wants you back. They may be a key to more kids or women that need a safe place. At the very least, we'd get rid of the threat to you."

"How can I help?"

"Badass shining through. I love that. We have some things to talk about before I can answer. I can say, I can't listen to details. Not being able to read you keeps me rational. I read the other women we aren't talking about. I can't hear what you lived through, Yáhsháyôn. If I lose it, I lose you. That is not an option. The warning was clear and from Jacob who has never given me a warning before. It's a warning I need to heed. Jacob is the Protector of the Three. Me losing it will hurt Prez, Christian or Jeremy besides losing you. Again, not an option. I will hold your hand, protect you with my life and shield you with my heart. That's without the details."

She sits up and straddles my legs. Fuckin' great. "I asked Tess and Kate to keep the details from you. Tess is shielding those thoughts so you never get them. She knew before I said it."

I nod. "Visions."

"What else do we need to talk about?"

I groan. Her waking up in my bed daily without me touching her is testing my control like nothing else in my life ever has. "I can't do this with you on my lap, legs spread and thighs against mine."

I see it hit her and she jumps to move off me. "This is a cliff, baby. It's a long way down."

She looks over her shoulder and leans into me. Not that I needed help but her tits against my chest have me pushing to stand. I set her down and adjust my dick so I'm not advertising my needs to the world. Being able to do that without it being seen is one of those things I'd never tell Spano just to rub it in. I pull her back to a rock and sit her on my leg feeling my gear press the life out of my dick. Jesus.

"We have another warning about you learning a different sex than what you know. Jared was setting up the spare room for scenes like we did. Our bedroom is for us without the scene. I'll get clarification on vanilla. So far, it's not clear to me what vanilla even means. Even the grands are known for their wild ways. Great grand sex has definite negative connected to it. They're all dead and I'm thinking limp dick before I can even start."

She giggles making me smile. "I can google it."

"That may help. So far, I'm uninspired. The reasoning for vanilla was a warning, but also because you drop to a sub stance that's holding you at the sound or words from dominant men. Being a Club of predominantly male Brothers, they notice that shit. Asa is keeping Alpha-Bits close so you're comfortable but also to keep you in the now. Knight brought you a dog that will do the same thing, but that protection is obvious. He does something to help with the now."

"You're scaring me. I'm losing me? Like split personality?" Those beautiful light brown eyes shouldn't have tears.

Fuck. "More like a trigger is set and you jump back. The cloaking will take time because you have a photographic memory. Your brain looks for information different than people without a photographic memory."

She nods. "Nothing about me is ever easy. I don't see everything so clearly. I thought the cloak worked."

"We just need time, the healers for the cloak and you to train your mind to stay away from thoughts that are covered for you to move forward."

"I'll work at that. Maybe Aylen can help. Kate said she's got more degrees than me." She'd be surprised how many Protectors do. Since she's willing to put that work in, I know she'll work through this.

"I bet she can, Yáhsháyôn. She can add to the cloak while she's close. She's a gifted healer. Are you ready to see what Kate advises?"

She stands then bends to kiss me. "I think I love you, Mase Blackhawk."

My arms snatch her right back to me so I can kiss her for saying the words. Teeth, tongues, hands and my dick throbbing against the plating of my gear would only stop for one reason. I growl, "Fuckin' Brothers."

"They made me! Prez and GC cornered me, then ordered me to come get you. Being the youngest fuckin' nurses!"

Kateri is shaking against me and I know she's laughing not scared. "We're on our way, Brother. I feel you. I was the youngest too. That will change. You'll be able to tell most Brothers to fuck off."

Nash smiles. "Oh, I can't wait. I'm so fuckin' over getting shit from everyone. Thanks for not giving me shit, Brother. GC said I can't come back without you."

"Brother, do you really want to go back?"

"You and Kateri look okay. Are you?"

Kateri turns toward him. "I am right now. I'll work on the losing me and Aylen can help with the other crap. Knowing it's happening scared me but knowing I have help and a whole family watching out makes that less scary."

Nash leans in. "I'm not going back to the crazy Princes and stooges. I'm out, call to me if you need me. I'm going to kiss your head. You're ours now. It's normal and our way of saying we're right here with our hands out. Don't tell anyone, but Mase is always the cool uncle so he's the favorite. We'd do anything to keep him smiling. He's way more fun smiling." He kisses her head and I push him off the cliff hearing him laugh as he falls.

"Fuckin' kids. Are you ready, Yáhsháyôn?"

"Yeah. I think Nash is my favorite."

I laugh suspending us as slow as I can back to our house. My father is pissed. I smile walking right by them all to sit with Kate and Tess. Once Kateri is sitting, I pull out a chair. My dad pulls my cut.

I turn on him. "I don't remember inviting a carnival to my house tonight. For every fuckin' Brother, I've been there, for you, I've been there. Right now, my one and only concern is Kateri and what she needs. Tell me mom wouldn't be your first priority. Find something to do while I show her what my father taught me about *all in* and what my old lady deserves. When I'm sure she's settled, has eaten and is calm, I'll see why my Brothers have gathered. Maybe you should take Keesog to see Nova. He missed the lessons of our fathers' that I never did."

Prez laughs. I shake my head and sit looking at Kate. "Do we need to move for some privacy, or can you talk here?"

She watches Brothers walk out. I smile. Aiyana sits. This is like the fuckin' day that never ends.

Aiyana throws, '*Fuckin' Badass is always best when shown.*'

I do everything I can not to laugh and look at Kate.

Chapter Five

Mase

My leg being ridden is enough to have me ready when my eyes open. "Fuckin' Hell. That's a beautiful picture to have but better memory to carry, Yáhsháyôn," I whisper so I'm not scaring the fuck out of her.

She doesn't react and thank fuck doesn't stop. Moving her hair, I smile seeing her eyes closed. My girl can't hold that calm, cool and collected in her sleep.

Skimming one hand to her ass, I add some pressure getting a whimper. She's so fuckin' sexy with her tiny body that matches a playboy bunny sticker I have on my truck. I moan softly remembering when I had her posed for me. Blindfolded, bound to a post, I pulled her head back by the hair getting the arch in her back pushing that ass out for me to fuck. Those little red heels had me on my fuckin' knees walking in. I fucked her with only those fuckin' heels on.

Shit. Vanilla or Kate said teach her something more than sex only when she's forced. I've never forced a woman and was pissed. Tess calmed me explaining how Rich and Patches taught her from the beginning and she got to choose so vanilla wasn't an option once she understood.

The beginning. Thinking vanilla isn't working for me, I slide a hand down her back slowly entering her panties to cup her ass. Her moan encourages me to take that further and slide a finger in. Her eyes open and body freezes.

"Baby, don't stop now. My woman waking me up in a way that can only be described as sexy as hell isn't leaving this bed until I get to see her come with my fingers petting her pretty kitty and her getting herself off on my leg. Move that ass, baby. You're so wet my fingers don't need much to help." I push with the palm of my hand and she gives a little growl as she takes over. "Fuckin' sexy, Yáhsháyôn."

"Sir," she whispers out.

My hand holds her ass tight against my leg. "Oh no, baby. Wrong room for that one." Pulling her with me, I lay flat and have her pussy against my dick. "Sit up, Kateri. You take what you want, showing me you get where you are and how fuckin' sexy my girl wakes me up. When you get what you want, know I'm fuckin' the shit out of you in this room while you yell my name. That name better be Mase or I'm slapping your ass until it is. Fuck vanilla."

Her eyes are huge then get bright. "I'll be a good girl, S...Mase." She changes that seeing my eyes flash a warning.

"Then move, Yáhsháyôn."

She fuckin' moves. My hands go right for her tits in the tight tank that does nothing to hide them. Her hands slap my chest.

I know it's to hold herself up but use it. "You got it, my beautiful Kateri. Your hands on me will have me fighting to control my dick."

Her hands move and I *am* fighting my dick. Focusing on her tits, I rip her tank down the middle and moan. "Gorgeous fuckin' Kateri." My mouth latching on to a nipple gets her moving faster mewling and growling like a little tiger cub. My dick likes the cub growl. With hands on her ass, I push her further on her grind stroke.

Her hands fuck with my head running through my hair and down my neck then shoulder. She's never touched more than my dick. I like those hands moving.

"S–Mase!"

My head whipping up on a growl is just in time to see why my name is on those beautiful bowed lips. I give her no time and kiss those lips while I follow her down to the bottom of the bed unbuttoning my breeches.

Her hands grab in my hair guiding me to her neck. My mouth loves every spot on my tiny enigma's body. I know right where to go while she gets control of her breath. Her back arches when I clamp down on the underside of her tit.

"Hands, baby." I watch those hands slide down her body and growl. "Fuckin' beautiful but I've seen it. Hands on me, Yáhsháyôn. I love those tiny hands pulling my hair or biting into my arms." I tear the cloth in my way and pounce on her glistening pussy. "So fuckin' ready for me."

Her hands slide through my hair until my mouth is on her, then she pulls. We are never making vanilla but her hands are on me so I give us the V-A and focus on her moving and sounds. Moving before she's off has my little cub growling and digging her claws into my biceps. Flipping her, I pull her up and hold her against my chest.

"No fuckin' way I can watch you come again. I need a condom."

"I can't get pregnant. I'm clean. Alder checked." It sounds like a beg.

I turned her so I had a chance for the condom. I lose.

"How that can push my control has to wait. My dick needs in that pretty little kitty, now." Thrusting up has me in and my girl spasming around me. Holding her down, I wait it out with a hand covering her tit and pussy. She bounces causing a moan. I don't ever lose it, but I'm losing it. "Go, baby. Get that pretty kitty purring for me."

Her hand moves under mine and we're off. What the fuck? "Hold on, baby. We're being pulled." I pause for a breath reeling from the ride.

"Ancestors," she breathes out.

"Fuck if it isn't. Kinky bastards. Pet that kitty, beautiful. I'm feeling it all wrapping around me."

She fuckin' does and I'm shocked, proud and fuckin' whacked because it's got me moving faster for her. "Feel it, Yáhsháyôn. Love holding us. They're showing it." The colors are out of this world. Crazy bastards.

"Yes, Mase!"

~*~*~

Opening my eyes, I laugh. I've heard it but they're fuckin' funny. So much for vanilla. Fuckin' ancestor watchers can never be vanilla. This has got to be the reason Princes are fuckin' crazy. Bringing a wet towel to me, I clean my beautiful girl up and dump her tattered pjs in the trash. Suspending her, I fix the mess we made of the bed and move her to the head of it. I get in and pull my tiny enigma to me. She sleeps against my chest.

'*Christian?*'

'*Here, Mase.*'

'*She can't get pregnant isn't from a shot, is it?*'

'*Sorry, Mase, no. She had the surgery before she was brought to the cop. He paid extra for it.*'

Everything in me stops. My eyes burn and throat closes as that pain stabs through my heart. They sterilized a thirteen-year-old girl to sell her. A thirteen-year-old girl. I'm up. '*Help.*'

'*Aylen will keep her sleeping. Get out. Justice is there.*'

I have only my breeches on standing at the end of the runway with my hands on my knees, hair hanging to the ground and tears on my face. Justice, Teller and Prez show here with hands on my back.

"They sterilized her at thirteen." I stand flipping my hair back and glare at the sky. "What the fuck do I do with that!?"

Prez pulls me into him. "I don't know, Brother. Find a rock to crush, a tree to down, get it out so we can deal."

I push to the hill making a path of trees and rocks on the edges of a circle. Thirteen. The thirteenth tree falls and I bend to breathe. Thirteen.

What the fuck kind of monster does that shit to a kid. Standing I push another tree. One that plans on her being long-term. I shake my head. He's lucky he's fuckin' dead.

Trees move and I watch feeling empty. Just a bystander as shit moves around me. She was thirteen. Will never have the chance to make a decision on kids. She told me she stopped dreaming. What could a thirteen-year-old girl dream when she's sold, sterilized and has no one to look for her. No hope.

My hands hit my knees again. My family is huge. We have kids dropping from everywhere needing a home. She loves her job. She's good at more than drawing and marketing. She ran code saying she didn't know it. She's learning to be around people. We made it to V-A before the kinky fuckin' ancestors decided to watch and blow my chance at vanilla.

Prez and Teller laugh. I stand and shake my head. "Get the fuck out of my head."

Prez smiles. "Soon, Brother. You have a plan. You can do this, Mase. Whatever you need we're here. I said almost those same words to two of your brothers. Blackhawks understand better than most, you listen to the warnings, find a way around it with your Brothers and ancestors then scrape out that path to happy with us in front and at your back." He points.

I turn and fall to my knees. "Thank fuck for those Brothers in front and at my back. This is her picture? Her ancestors circle."

Justice nods kneeling in front of me. "This is what I saw from her. You know your ability has grown. I heard you throwing appreciation to me and the ancestors. The gifts are always for a reason, Brother. It always works the same way. You are aware and keep Jacob's warning close. It needs to be close because the reason is going to show and I can already feel it gets worse before it's better. You called for help. As many times as you need it, Brother, we'll show. You're never alone to deal with this shit that's trying to take the legs right out from under you. Yeah?"

I nod loving my Brothers. "Yeah."

"Your thought was to Kateri not having a choice. You're right, Brother. She didn't get to make that decision. She escaped the cop. She made it to school. She found you. She is living her choices and her happy. She'll make it like the rest. It's not perfect but it can be her perfect. She has a shit load of decisions to make in her life. Remember this moment and let her make them. You can give her what no one else has, Brother." He puts his head against mine holding my neck. "Make it the best life she's ever seen."

I nod and stand. "Thanks, Brothers. I'll start now."

I push seeing Aylen crying as she lays on the side of Kateri. When she realizes I'm here, she's gone. I shake my head and lift my girl.

I think about what Prez and Justice said. I'm a Blackhawk. We have been through more shit, but we do not lay down or quit. I will not be the first Blackhawk to pussy out or give in. My girl deserves more than that from her man. I will be that man. Never again will she be left alone to deal. My arms tighten as if showing they'll protect her. I smile. Never again will she walk without her heart being shielded by mine.

Her eyes open catching my smile. Sexy little smile and bright eyes tell me she's free and feeling her calm, cool and collected.

"Beautiful Kateri, I love the sexy smile. I have some bad news, we didn't make vanilla. The ancestors are plotting against vanilla."

She giggles while I take it in.

"I think we should just do what feels right as we shoot for vanilla. It could be fun, baby. Think of all the time we'll get testing it out. We're only at V-A, we have five letters to go."

She outright laughs making me smile. "I'll like shooting for vanilla. You were surprised so the ancestors is something new?"

I shake my head. "Blessing the union is the way I heard it. They weren't blessing anything. They're twisted with kink thrown in, Yáhsháyôn. Who the fuck knew we had kinky ancestors?"

She's laughing again. I think we made V-A-N, we only have four letters to go.

~*~*~

Kateri

My day started amazing and that has not stopped yet. Four hours for Alder has his DNA program finished. It's amazing to see it work. Natalia is crazy smart with the computer. When she calls Alder up, he appears in the Lab with us. Crazy smart. I laugh getting a smile from the pensive little man.

Natalia uses the file Carmen sent to build the line from the beginning. I watch as Alder types on his keyboard picture keeping his eyes glued to the virtual line building itself from the results. The line builds again closer to him. He uses his finger to manipulate the line then it opens and shows more than I first saw. This is the breakdown he asked for. I added the pictures but didn't know this is what it would look like. The breakdown works perfect as he opens more and more.

I'm mesmerized with the artwork, but Alder is done before I can see it from the other side.

"I test." He types on his keyboard. "Boss Kateri, you go to ABC Lab. Boss Carmen do DNA to you?"

I smile loving this little guy. "I get to be the first to get results? In a heartbeat, LP. I can't believe it works the way you want it to. It does work the way you want it to, right?"

He smiles. "Work better. I expect one level. You build three. I have more work to you. Bone, marrow, artery, vein. Maybe cell, blood. I will research."

I look at Natalia who is clapping and ready to pounce on me. "You should get body and organs ready. He's going to have you building it anyway. With the drawings he'll be able to see normal against his patient. The test results will build a hologram of the patient, Kateri!"

I smile at her. "I got that. You're amazing people. There are books with organs in them."

Alder nods. "I operate to hologram organ. No breakdown to follow. I will follow. Boss Justice show picture to VP Mase. I will have picture without Boss Justice."

I see where he's going. "Okay. I see where that would be important and save lives. I'll research that and figure a way to get a breakdown that might work."

He shakes his head. "*Will* work. *Might* not save life. *Will* save life. My Alpha-Bits need information to chemical effect drugs cause. Life expectancy, counteract treatment before needed. No might."

I blink to see him. "I'll get a breakdown that will work."

He nods. "Asa here ten minute." He looks at his monitor. "Boss Spano have Team. PA Mary Enforcer."

I look at Natalia feeling my heart jump to my throat.

She smiles. "Aylen is with you. Mary is an Enforcer and PA. That's three Protectors and an Enforcer. You'll be safe." Aylen is going.

"I need to tell Mase."

She pulls my phone from the table. "Call now. Aylen is on her way. Good job, Kateri. The Alpha-Bits will be excited."

I smile thinking about what she told me. They need all the help they can get. I never thought my pictures would be that help. I hit Mase and hold my breath. When I turn, picture Alder is gone.

"Yáhsháyôn." The name has me breathing with a smile.

"Alder needs me to go to the ABSZ. The DNA line with the breakdown works. He has more work for me."

"When is this trip planned for?"

Asa, Aylen and a woman walk in. "Now. Asa, Aylen, Spano and Mary will be going with me. Before you ask, I'm okay with them and excited to see the Lab Carmen works in."

I hear his breath like he was holding it. "Have fun, Kateri. Call if you need me."

"I will, *Kuwômôyush*."

He laughs. "So fuckin' cute. *Kuwômôyush*, Yáhsháyôn."

When I look up, Aylen is smiling. "Perfect. Do you need to get anything before we go?"

I'm glad she's teaching me Mohegan and I made her proud. Natalia holds my backpack out.

"No. I should be fine with my bag. Thank you for coming with me."

Mary smiles. "Security means we're thanking you for keeping it interesting. Standing at a door is boring. We're flying today."

I like Mary. "It's nice to meet you and thanks. That feels better than me dragging you all around."

Aylen hooks her arm through mine. "Let's go, girl. Alder sent a stat message. He's a President so we need to skedaddle. I bet the chopper is waiting on us."

LP has some power here. I'm glad. President with no power is an insult to someone like Alder. He does everything everywhere from what Natalia said.

I reach back. "Wait." I back up and hug Natalia. "Thank you for doing all the work. I'm excited and didn't want you to miss that I noticed."

She laughs and pushes me back toward Aylen. "I linked pictures."

I let it go and walk beside Aylen. Asa and Spano are behind us, Mary in front. At the door Aylen lets me go and walks with Spano in front of us and Asa and Mary behind. I don't ask. I'm so excited to be going to the Lab. I saw it from Natalia's but I'm going on a trip in the chopper for work. When does that happen?

I climb in the chopper glad I didn't say it out loud. They all work and get choppered around or fly themselves. It's only new to me. It's exciting so I'm going with it. I've never been anywhere. Now I'm flying to a job thing.

~*~*~

Mase

We finish in the city and Seth rides with me to Kateri's house. Asa said surveillance picked up two in cable uniforms going in. He's sticking to Kateri and Alder pulled her to ABSZ. She's safest there so I'm breathing okay right now. We don't have cable in our towns. We have satellite television through a company Delta runs.

Getting off my bike I clock the camera at the garage. "I need a Security Team with a wand, Ops."

Pres comes right back. "Roger, VP. Six out."

They must be in town. Pulling my keys, I use the pick and walk in. *'On the light outside, fire alarm and doorbell.'* I keep walking.

Her furniture was slashed, shit thrown everywhere and bedroom annihilated. She didn't want anything from the house. Nothing personal was left so it made her decision easy. *'With nothing left in the house I don't get why they'd put cameras in. They had to know she'd be freaked the fuck out.'*

'Every room has at least two cameras, Mase. I called to Teller, he's got IT finding where they're going. They didn't know she had a place to go. No truck in the garage.' Seth throws.

Security comes in and Seth deals. I walk out to the road and call Kateri. "I have a buyer for your house, Yáhsháyôn. You want to sell?"

"Yes. Thank you. I was afraid to go back in even to put it on the market." She sounds relieved.

"You're never walking back in there, baby. I'll take care of it."

"Thank you. I have to go, Alder is running back here." I can hear her smile.

"Okay, baby."

"*Kuwômôyush*, Mase."

"*Kuwômôyush*, Yáhsháyôn."

I walk back into the house. "Seth, Security. Clear out."

"Roger, VP." Comes from everywhere.

I walk away and call Enrique. "Brother, it's Mase. I have brand new appliances. You got a home?"

He does. "I need Prospects from there to pick them up. You need light fixtures, they can take them too. It has to be someone from there and done tonight. I'll text you the address. Front door is unlocked."

He's got it handled. Cool.

"What's up, Mase?" Seth walks to me.

"It's sold. I'm off tomorrow. I need to get a machine or two here tomorrow."

He laughs. "I'll get the rental place Cline's brother opened on that. Backhoes?"

"That will work."

"Stella finds out you demolished a house with panels she'll go ape shit on you. I'll get the panels off later."

I nod. "Appliances are going to the city tonight. Leave the front door unlocked. I have to get the electric and water unhooked first thing in the morning."

He walks one way. I walk down the street calling my engineer. He's got utilities handled. Hitting my mic, I hope Pres is on. "Ops?"

"Read you, VP."

"Will you lose your shit if I throw grenades?"

He laughs. "Are they aimed at me?"

I wait until I can say it without laughing. "Never, Pres."

"Have at it, Brother."

"Thanks, tomorrow morning say, eight or so, you'll get a call."

He's laughing again. "Someone will. I'm with you."

"I could use the help. Thanks, Pres. I'm on the side." I smile turning back.

"Roger, VP."

Seth jogs toward me. "Two backhoes will be dropped tonight."

"Perfect. The electric and water is off by seven so we're set." I swing my leg over and call Joey. "Can you transfer money to Kateri's account for me? I just bought her house. Whatever she paid for it."

She needs the address so I give it. She's got it covered but wants to know if it's for the 'rents. I laugh. "That would save Pres headaches but I'm demolishing it. Cameras and bugs were just installed all through it. My family isn't in there."

She gets it. "*Kuwômôyush, Ituksq.*"

She laughs and hangs up with love. I love my sister.

Seth laughs when I start my bike. "Pres is going to flip when he finds out."

I give him a smile. "He's helping."

He laughs halfway through town.

We just get to town one when Pres clicks in. "VP, fight at Club Diaz."

Fuckin' great. I hit my mic on. "Roger, Ops." I leave the mic on and spin my bike around.

"Security is following you in," he tells me.

"Roger."

Pulling up to the bar a block into town three I shut my bike off. It took eight minutes to get here. I hope they're done.

"Do you ever ride doing less than a hundred?" Nemo asks.

I roll my eyes at him and push hearing shots from inside the candy shop next door to the bar. "Candy shop. Security, split and post at the bar."

I get rogered and see Seth coming in from the side. His gun is pointed at the woman screaming about buttons.

The kid behind the counter watches me touch my gun to the nut's head. "Drop it or I'll drop you."

She takes in a breath to yell and I drop her kicking the gun toward Seth. "Is this the only gun that fired?"

The kid nods shaking like a leaf. "I quit."

Seth calls a Security Brother in. "Status on the bar?"

"Fight, VP."

Fuckin' great. "You got this, Seth?"

"Go, Brother."

I push making the bar and duck a stool coming right at me. I push again and shoot the asshole that threw a stool my way. He bounces getting attention from a woman. Seeing a bottle being lifted, I shoot and push to the bar shooting another guy armed with a pool cue.

"Are we done?" I ask the stunned patrons.

The bartender stands up behind the bar and points to a guy built like Cort. Fuckin' giants here. "He started all this shit. He owes for the game."

I walk his way. "Pay up and get out."

He reaches for my coat and I shoot him. "Security!"

Nemo smiles. "We're here, VP. Just waiting for you to finish."

I roll my eyes. "Get what he owes to the bartender and get him handed off to the PD." I unclip his keys.

I point to the pool cue wielding idiot. "He owes for a cue. That one for a stool."

Walking out I push the fob. Nice truck. Getting closer I see the city PD sticker. "Nemo, he goes to holding. Send your third out here."

"Ops, I got a city PD sticker on the giant's truck."

"I have it being run, VP."

I open the door and see the two guns on the back rack. "This dark tint isn't legal."

"Ex-PD fired in first round with the new chief." Pres fills in details but not enough.

City PD fired. What the fuck is he doing up here? I walk around to the passenger side. "Nemo, find out who rode in the cable truck and hold them. Pres."

"I see it, Brother. The truck blocked it. Security is with cleanup just leaving the candy shop. Two are going through the trucks."

"Roger, Pres." Reaching in I open the glove compartment. Fuck.

"Tell me you don't have grenades on you, Brother." Pres is in my ear.

My jaw clamps tight as I pull Kateri's picture out.

"VP?"

I breathe. "Yeah, Pres. Do not get her to identify anyone until I'm with her."

"Not happening. You're holding the cards, Brother. We need everything before you start blowing shit up."

"Roger, Pres."

Security is pulling shit out of the trucks fast. I walk back to the bar just as two are hauled out by the second Security Team. The giant is trying to pull away from Nemo and his second. Seth appears by my side.

"Duct tape." I hold my hand out.

Seth pulls a flattened roll out of his cargos and holds it out. I push and have his mouth and arms duct taped so he isn't confused about what's happening here. "Where's his cuffs?" Ex-cop looking to hijack my girl isn't showing without cuffs.

"Here, VP." Nemo pulls two sets of metal cuffs out of his back pocket. I'm glad he's not still smiling.

"Cuff him over the ties."

When Nemo steps aside the dick swings his shoulder toward him.

I shoot him. "Shackles."

Security runs in with shackles. I wait until he's secure then suspend the giant motherfucker into every wall on the way out. Dropping him in the back of the SUV, I turn before I kill the motherfucker.

"Thanks, VP. Button Betty going to the Sheriff?"

I watch my hand knowing I need to get out of here. "She got ID?"

Seth puts his hand up to the Security Brother. "Sheriff. Get them out of here, now. She's in the second truck."

"Roger, Boss." They move fast.

Seth stands in front of me. "You ready to clear land or go through the shit cleanup brings in?"

I look at him and he steps back.

"Clearing land it is."

I shake my head. "How is the cable truck here and no one saw? IT didn't follow the fuckin' truck when it left her house?" I feel my body calming.

He looks at the truck then me. "Ops?"

"Finding out, Brother. No truck shows leaving the street. It shows pulling in the garage but never leaving."

My head whips to Seth. "Jammer. The bar lot isn't covered?"

Pres answers quick. "I'm showing you in the lot with the two trucks. I had to move the camera for that view. The black truck blocked the smaller white one on my first view. Asa got the truck coming up to the house and in the driveway. Jammer wouldn't have given that. We'd see snow, Brother."

Seth nods. How the fuck? "Ops, I'm hitting my mic off."

"Explain, VP." Pres doesn't like this.

"Just calling my brother, Pres."

"Roger."

I call Brantley and tell him what's going on. A second vehicle. He says to watch with tagging on then changes it. He's calling Web and will run it up there.

I tell Pres and get back to the office. We'd still see snow. I need how.

Ops is busy. Cort is up with Pres and Prez. I sit at an IT console and pull Brantley up. "Where are you, Brother?"

"Watching for hot. Take north, Jason has south." He types watching his screen.

I pull the feeds and watch traffic. It's a job I don't care for, but my girl is not up for grabs. Two Security SUVs tag hot. "Brant, we'd get snow with a jammer."

"Yeah. Alexia shows no hit to surveillance. I ran it when you called. You're up and no hits are logged. A hit would throw you offline. I'm pulling from the surveillance satellite and match what you're seeing. Two satellites with no hits means they aren't in. A truck pulls up and moves to the garage. Jason's got it. Hold on."

I watch their room waiting. Prez and Cort move over to see the monitor. I open the feed again from the end of the road and back it up. A guy in overalls comes out of the house. I look at the feed I just watched. "It's the camera?"

Brantley rolls over. "Yeah, one camera. He types something." A second goes by and the guy points something and types on a tablet. Fuckin' hell.

"Brantley, how are we stopping this?" Prez asks my question.

"Jason has the truck running hot, another is tagged at a bar. Watch through tagging." He throws it up and we watch the giant's pickup pull in and park. The next shows the cable truck pull in the lot and disappear. Fuckin' hell.

Brantley shuts the board down and shows in Princes Ops. "Web has IT setting alerts for the hot flashes. Alexia is moving a third satellite over and will set alerts straight to Ops for hot tags in your town ones and the compound. Keep physical Security with Kateri. Other than that, I don't know. We need the remote to know how they're taking cameras over."

"We have it. We have everything from both trucks," Pres tells him.

I shake my head. Brantley doesn't say what he's thinking. "If you get it to Web, we'll have more information."

"I'll bring it to him when I leave here." I look back at Pres getting a nod.

"Anything that's electronic should go to Web. The force-field?"

Pres answers. "The compound, Clubs and town ones."

"I'll get Hannah to push it up," Cort says.

Brantley looks away. "Jason offered to go down. Mucimi needs a job, it may work in your favor to get him on it with A7."

We all look at Cort. "I'll talk to Justice and Alder. Alder blocked a whole week unless he's needed for Ops."

Brantley nods and looks at Prez. "Thanks, Brantley. I'll let you know about Jason."

I shut the feed down.

"Seth is collecting electronics now. Ben has the faces for ID. I can't have you questioning or anywhere close when we question..." Pres stops when I nod.

"I'm out. Fire is too close to the surface and we'd lose our only lead if I incinerate the motherfucker."

Teller shows on the side of me, I roll my eyes and Cort laughs. "They're expecting you to lose it. I missed the ol' lady wars. I'm good either way."

I stand up shaking my head. "It's not an option, Boss. I can't fly, Pres."

Prez nods. "Nash is here."

Pres hits my shoulder. "See you on the sunny side, Brother."

"Yeah. I've got machines at the house for eight."

He shakes his head. "Do I need grenades?"

I shrug heading for the door. "Can't hurt. Later, Brothers."

Prez walks out with me. "Fire is too close?"

He always does that. "Yeah." I hold my hand out and show him. Fire covers it then looks like it's sucked back into my body. "I saw it at the lot. Seth did too. His head said it was in my eyes."

We make the training floor before he stops. "This is new."

"Never happened before. I'm not sure what the fuck I'm supposed to do with this. Thanking the ancestors is on hold. Fuckin' directions would be nice."

He stops walking. "What's going to calm you?"

I pull my hair back. "The ancestors but I'm fuckin' pissed at them too." How the fuck is this a gift?

He nods. "Let's start slow, Brother." He pulls me to Kateri's circle.

I sit in the middle of the four stones. It could work.

Prez sits in front of me. "Luke-Rayne is headed to ABSZ to show the pictures. He's a shield for her."

I'm relieved. "Thanks. Nash is another."

He nods, he knew. "How does the circle work?"

I point to the four stones. "Elements like the sweat lodge. Displaced tribes adjusted according to location, some adopted their hosts ceremonies, some merged the two. I'd say this is a merge of three Navajo, Cheyenne and Comanche or Naskapi." I point to the symbols on the stones. "Warrior and the great spirit are old Naskapi. I think the thunderbolts are blue for Comanche. It's a power symbol in all those tribes but blue is knowledge or prophet in Cheyenne and Paleo with that symbol. The wave in red is Navajo. It's a wind symbol like combat but we'd say stealth."

He looks from one to the next taking a minute to study them. "Does Justice know the symbols?"

"He took it from her picture. She doesn't jump but brings the picture up and meditates I think. Justice didn't make warrior training often. He was scheduled everywhere for everything else."

He nods. "Seeing this and the million fuckin' tribes we're seeing lately, I should have had him with you."

I shake my head. "There's only so much time in a day, Prez. I'm here and have no problem sharing what I know. Justice knows and has no problem asking for input."

"Yeah. He should be a President."

I laugh. "He is. Teller is his VP. We all know it. Falcon is always pushing it."

He smiles. "Another insightful Brother. How are you feeling?"

I put my hand out and watch it. "Calmer. I can't jump right now but am closer to *we get gifts we can handle*. I have Brothers that struggle with those gifts daily. I never thought I'd be one. I need a minute to put it in perspective."

He smiles and pulls me to the chopper. "Don't incinerate us on the way."

I smile. "Roger, Prez."

Sitting, I think about my girl, she was excited and told me about her Security before I said a word. She's comfortable with it. I look at Prez. "Why didn't your dad bring the dog over?"

He shakes his head smiling. "He's fuckin' crazy doesn't need to be stated here. You know. Once he saw Kateri he decided you need two dogs. Something about you running and her protection. You run a lot?"

I nod thinking about a dog that runs. "Since I got to New Mexico. The land does it for me. I run the canyon in Bravo, the forest in Elan and through the hills here. Kateri wants to explore. I was thinking of cutting her a path to hike the Badass land. Mucimi bought miles of land up here. It would be safer if she had a dog even closer to the Club. The sensors here are only close to the roads. We have so much not covered because of the terrain. I run that. It's peaceful."

"I'm glad you're happy here. It fits you better than Elan did. Did you meet with Cooper?"

Cooper. I shake my head answering, "Yeah, a week after all that shit went down. I wouldn't go unless he agreed to see the healers. Cayden said he wasn't sleeping and had to see I was alright daily. It took him three days, but he agreed and I sat down with him. We're good."

"Good. He's a good Brother but could have gotten someone killed."

"I'm glad he called Brinks for help. Brinks knew right away what was happening and stepped in. It's weird because they only know each other in passing."

He nods. "It's the military. Taylor said they feel it."

I can see that. "Brinks doesn't talk about his time in either. That fits. Justice got the healers in and Cort put Jester on Flight. Cooper is a good President and knows Jester is a failsafe. It keeps him calm."

"I didn't get how Cayden kept saying he was a good President. Your dad wanted to kill him for marking you."

I shrug. "He is and my dad is crazy. I was pissed a kid almost bought it but knew what was happening as it was happening. Kristos jumped in before I took over so it worked better for me and Cayden. Getting a rep as a challenging VP wouldn't have helped BSC."

"No, needing an explanation after your name doesn't. I'm glad it was you and Justice is Justice. Aaron or Hemy would have killed him."

I smile. "They would have been wrong, Prez. He's needed right where he is. Boonies surrounded by almost towns needs an old west sheriff. That's Cooper."

He nods. "Kristos?"

I smile. "I love the Brother. He draws people in like you, Cort, Falcon and Justice. He doesn't take shit and has a knack for seeing potential problems. Being younger than me makes him easy. He still likes to play."

He laughs. "Perfect fit. You remind me of Uncle Danny when he was younger. I'm so fuckin' glad they're slowing down."

We set down at the ABC Lab and Nash follows us out. He's worried.

Luke-Rayne is waiting by the door and pulls me into a hug. "You're settled. I'm honored you're willing to let me do this, Brother. I will not hurt her."

I hit his back. "I know. Shield for me so I'm not getting it but call if you need me. Aylen is with her."

He nods. "Does she get all this? Hannah can get here quick."

"Aylen is a Justice, Brother. She gets more than we do and sees outcome."

He's surprised and relieved. "I'll trust in my Brothers. I don't know her well and meant no disrespect, Prez."

Prez nods. "I know her but didn't see her well. We're good, Brother. I'm learning just like you are and like that you put Kateri first. It's as it should be. Let's get this done so Mase can breathe easy."

~*~*~

Kateri

Carmen took my blood and swabbed my mouth. I watch as the computer starts building. This is all so unbelievable. My art shows stretching as results show on the side.

"I like this better than the program. I uploaded all the files but seeing it build like this is better than the one-armed paper hanger I'm usually stuck with. You just cut the boring crap out of my day. Thanks, Kateri."

I shake my head wondering about a paper hanger. Why hang paper? What's one arm have to do with it? I don't think I've met the one-armed guy but I haven't really paid attention to the men roaming around. "I just made the art."

"How do you make art for the breakdown?" She clicks on an oval and three octagons show with numbers in different colors.

"It's really just one picture with a string of code Natalia added. The value for each result adds the shapes with the value in it and color assigned by that value. If there were no value it wouldn't show on the breakdown."

She looks at me like I'm an alien. "You understood that making a picture?"

"Alder gave me a file, I looked at the results and drew it out from the numbers. It's not like I didn't have the numbers. He gave them to me. Natalia did values so I just needed the shape and color parameters. She did the work. I made a shape and gave her two numbers for color and value."

She nods slowly. I look at the computer not sure why that's odd. Building a website is the same way. You need a value to retrieve the information. It's just not so repetitive. Luckily, the lab machine gives the need right to the program so I'm not doing her job for every line of results.

Mase walks in and I'm so relieved I go right to him. "I'm glad you came. Alder had to go but sent me books and his research so I'm kind of done. I was watching my results get built." I pull his shirt and kiss his lips.

He smiles walking me back to Carmen at the computer. "That's you?"

I smile proud. "The art is and I can say, yes, that mess of shapes is me."

Carmen laughs. "We can print it for your desk, Mase."

Pulling me to his side, so I'm plastered against him, he kisses my head. "I'll want it when it's done." His arm holds me still.

Carmen doesn't react so I guess we're good. I never know what's okay in work or at home. All the men hold or kiss their women at both places. I like it. Mase says I'm his old lady forever. I hope it lasts forever.

He finishes getting the particulars about the test results and tightens his arm as if testing how close we can get, causing me to look up. "You ready, Yáhsháyôn?"

"I need my bag then I am." Thinking he'll let me go, I look up again when he doesn't.

"You don't think much about your work here?" Where did he get that from?

I step to the side having to use some effort to pull away from him. "I'm proud I can help but don't see what they do. Websites use the same premise without so much repetition. I just used it different. Alder gave me the file so it was pretty easy. Natalia had to write all that repetitive code. I see where they have easier working models now, but I didn't build the model, I just made shapes. I'm glad it works for them and we're a step closer to getting what Alder needs for his Alpha-Bit's later health needs. My part really is shapes. I'll draw out whatever he needs to do his part."

He smiles looking proud. "That's Badass, baby."

Carmen laughs. "I knew you were going to say that. It's the wheel thing."

I nod because I've heard it a couple of times and I'm proud to be a spoke, but I'm not saying it.

"Get your bag, Yáhsháyôn."

I move to the chair and back quickly. Mase has me against him again with my bag in his hand before I know it.

I smile at Carmen's smile. "Thanks for showing me around and how the machines work to build results. I'll see you in the Lab with Natalia or at dinner."

She smiles. "You will. I'm a call away. Thanks for the shapes." Her eyes crinkle like she's holding in a laugh.

Mase laughs walking me out. "Carmen loves the Badass in you."

That's very sweet. "I love the Badass in her too. Every woman I've met is sort of the same. Even Tess and Jess have a backbone. You wouldn't think it because they're my size. Aiyana is just Badass."

He laughs. "She is. I think it's in our blood. Maybe you can have Carmen test for it."

When he stops I raise a brow at him. "She'd kick my butt if I make her do the boring work. She likes the other parts of her job. She's going to bring me to see the babies on Monday after dinner."

His eyes flash and I step back then think I imagined it. He's not smiling. Maybe he doesn't like kids.

Aylen takes my arm. "Mase loves kids. Blackhawks are crazy with adopting the world. I hope you're ready for that kind of crazy."

Asa laughs. "Alpha-Bit crazy like Boss Alexia and Web. Too many."

Carmen said Alexia has the babies. I smile looking back at Mase. I didn't even see Prez here. They're talking so I keep walking. "I don't have a problem with kids, but don't know about thirty. Maybe two or three."

Aylen laughs. "Be careful, that means six to a Blackhawk. Just ask Holly."

~*~*~

Mase

"She's excited to see the babies and adopt kids, Brother. Take a breath and pull it back in."

I growl, "Roger, Prez."

Luke-Rayne moves in. "Let's ride to the compound. The ride will do you good and it's familiar to Kateri."

I nod and walk away breathing deep. She stepped back like I was going to hurt her. The look in her eyes stunned me still so I didn't scare her more. Hearing her laugh settles me. I push. "Yáhsháyôn, I love to hear you laugh."

She turns fast with the smile still on her face. "I saw you talking to Prez. We're going to the compound."

I nod and look at Aylen. She steps back with Asa. "We are. Why were you afraid of me back there?"

She's surprised then confused. "I'm not afraid of you, Mase."

"You stepped back with fear in your eyes, baby."

She looks at my shoulder for a second then back at me. "It looked like your eyes flashed. I wasn't afraid of you. It was weird."

Thank fuck. "I'm having some fire issues. The kinky ancestors like to fuck with Blackhawks. Their gifts don't come with directions." I'm fuckin' relieved to see her smile.

"Fire issues? They gifted you fire?" She's ready to laugh.

This is good. "Yeah, but they didn't tell me or leave directions."

She giggles. "The ancestors are crazy. Oh my. Is there something I can do to help? No directions is no control. That can't be easy for you."

I smile pulling her close by her waistband. "I don't like losing control, so no it's not easy. If you see my eyes flash, tell me to calm my shit down."

She nods. "I will. Are you ready?"

The ride to the compound is minutes in the chopper. Seeing me settled has everyone settled. I need to find a way to calm this shit.

Spotting Dakota at the compound, I roll my eyes. "I told her what's happening. She's ready and Aylen is with her."

"I am told you need a way to calm quickly. My purpose here is to give you that, Brother. I will not entertain you with Dakota speak until you have a firm grasp on calming yourself so I am not the first Prince incinerated for pissing you off."

I laugh and hug him. "Thanks, Dakota. I think the crew will throw appreciation your way for keeping them out of the burn unit that Alder may already be building."

My girl laughs with Prez and Luke-Rayne.

Asa crosses his arms over his chest. "Burn room, not unit."

We all hold our laughs at that one. I kiss my girl and leave her with Luke-Rayne and Aylen. "Call if you need me. I'm seconds away."

Prez nods, Spano slaps my back. I pull Dakota to a canyon off the main. They're shielding the house and each other from me, but the fire is close just knowing what they're doing, so I let it go on tumbleweeds up against the canyon wall.

Feeling Dakota shield himself cuts through my anger and has me smiling then laughing when he throws a second shield a foot away. My hands on my knees soak up the flames without burning me.

"That's cool. My gear isn't even hot. How does this work, Dakota?"

"While I have seen fire thrown, I have never seen it held for as long as you hold it. You are not harnessing the fire. It is a part of you. While that is the case. I will stay shielded and give direction on throwing fire."

I shake my head. "I've had that one since I was sixteen, Brother. This builds in me. Kateri said my eyes flashed with it."

"Then I will stay shielded and explore your new gift, Brother. Focus on a tumbleweed you have not decimated and burn it without raising your hands."

I smile shaking my head. I love Dakota.

"I am greatly relieved to read that, Brother. Focus that way." He points me away from him.

I laugh and turn back to the tumbleweeds looking for a white one. "Left side pocket." I watch it with nothing happening.

"Thirteen." He throws out and I feel it.

The fire explodes catching everything on the left. "That's not good."

"Perhaps you should not attach anger to common words."

I give him a look. His hands go up in surrender. "Just saying."

I laugh. "No idea on how to control that from happening?"

We go back and forth trying for more control when I feel Kateri. "She's looking for me." I pull him back and right in the dining room.

Prez has Kateri in his arms looking shocked. "Justice! Mase, calm yourself."

I don't think I've ever disregarded his words. Today I do. I pull Kateri away from him with them all saying something.

She burrows her face into my neck. "Sorry, Sir." I hear her whisper over their yelling.

"You're okay, Yáhsháyôn. My arms will keep you protected, my heart shields yours." When she relaxes I do.

They're still yelling so I turn. Oh fuck. Water. I throw and Prez is drenched. Everyone freezes. Dakota looks at me.

I shrug. "Sorry, Prez."

"You received a few new gifts, Brother. I fear that will get much use. Kateri is not touched by the fire."

I kiss her head and see my arms. "Holy shit."

Justice shows and freezes then blows up. "You threw at Prez!"

Jesus. He's trying to hold me. I shake my head stepping back. He needs to read or fuckin' listen before he tries blasting or pinning me down.

Prez answers, "He took Kateri from me. Relax, Justice, and don't piss him off."

Aylen is glaring at her father and Justice. Luke-Rayne pulls Justice back. "Let go. It's not holding him and you're not listening."

"No one is listening!" Aylen is still glaring at Prez.

Justice looks at her then Prez. "Fuck! Sorry, Mase. I was shocked. I'll remember this lesson so it's not repeated."

I throw chin and relax. Kateri hasn't moved. I need to get her a minute and push us to the canyon. The far side is shaded so we go there. "Yáhsháyôn, are you okay?"

"Yes. I was scared then really scared when Prez lifted me. He said he'd find you, but I don't know him like Aylen." That's why Aylen was pissed at Prez.

"He'd never hurt you and probably thought he could get you to me fast. I felt you reaching out for me. Why were you scared, baby?"

"Luke-Rayne showed me a picture of a man I knew. I had to fight to remember his name and knew it was in the cloaked memories. You said not to go back there. I thought you'd be angry with me. Are you angry with me?" Fuck.

We're all fuckin' idiots. "No, Yáhsháyôn. I should have stopped that from happening. I didn't think of the cloak. It won't happen again. Those memories shouldn't be thought of. I'll make sure you're not questioned bringing them up again."

"Thank you. Are they all okay now? Everyone was yelling." She stayed right with us.

"Yeah. They're fine. We'll check in then go see the babies. Web's is up the road."

Her smile has me smiling. "Aylen said we can have dinner there. She called Alexia before everyone went crazy."

I push hugging her. "We're good about fixing shit so they should be calm now." I am.

She giggles as we sit at the table. They're calm. Prez throws me chin.

I throw it back. "We're going to Web's for dinner. Spano, you can take the chopper back. I'll catch a ride or borrow one."

He shakes his head. "I haven't seen Garren and Michael or the Bits in a while. Are you staying here tonight?"

I shake my head. "I have plans for the morning with Pres."

He laughs. "I'll ride back with you."
Nash smiles. "I'm in."
Aylen is in.
Fuckin' Brothers.
We all go to Web's

Chapter Six

Mase

Feeling Knight close, I push getting Kateri upstairs and in bed. "Yáhsháyôn, Knight is here. I'll be back to wash you. Sleep, baby."

She rolls not caring that we have company before seven, seconds after I fucked the shit out of her on the counter. The kitchen has a lot of tools that work if you take a minute to think about it. It reminds me to get downstairs which isn't easy trying to button the side of my bed pants that I wore for positions earlier. I suspend the chip clips and turkey baster to the sink and towel to the laundry room.

Knight walks in with two wolves. Jesus. Uncle Danny and old Pres come in right after. "Why don't you say your names?" That's the rule everyone else uses.

Knight shrugs. "Reader. You knew, moved your girl, cleaned up."

I nod. Pres looks around making me smile. "What happened to the husky?"

"Didn't fit."

I laugh looking at the wolves standing at the wall. "They fit?"

"Yeah. One yours, one hers. Calm you, protect her."

They're not staying if they scare the fuck out of her. Uncle Danny starts pulling food out. I look up hoping for lightning. It doesn't work so I help make breakfast.

"Where do you run?" Uncle Danny asks.

I point out the window. "From here down then up the other mountain. Our land runs up through the foothills over there to Colorado. Mucimi took a whole square. It's just not all flat."

Pres laughs. "He did good. I like this one. It's close but feels like we're in the wilderness."

I feel it. "Part was an Indian trail. When I run it, I can almost feel those that ran before me. It feels like home."

He watches me. "I can see that. You've always been a wanderer. I'm glad you found your home."

"He did. Fits better than Elan. Bravo was good. This is better. Warrior in his element," Knight says surprising me.

Pres nods. "You get along with Major's boy Little Ben said."

I nod checking time. "Yeah. He's helping me demolish a house at eight."

Uncle Danny laughs. I shrug and push to check on Kateri. Fuck, she's in the shower.

"Yáhsháyôn, I wanted to wash you but the stooges showed. They're making breakfast and Knight brought dogs." I keep wolves out of there. They're too big for wolves but Mundo is huge and that fuckin' dog is a wolf.

"I'm done. I'll come down. I never had a dog." She pulls my shirt and kisses me then runs to the closet.

I get deodorant on, brush through my hair, wash my face, gear up and carry my coat down. Unlocking the trunk, I drop grenades in my bag and put my coat over it. They have everything almost done.

"Your girl doing okay?" Pres asks.

"Yeah. I fucked up yesterday. She pushed the cloak for an ID on the motherfucker trying for her. He's ex-PD."

They all stop moving. I stop walking toward the coffee and explain. "She's okay and didn't fall, but I should have realized before I put her pushing the cloak. It will never happen again."

Uncle Danny points. "You need to jump?"

I look down and close my eyes. The reservation shows and I breathe it in, take the colors and water in.

When I open my eyes, I look at my arm. "Fuck me, it worked. Dakota is good." I throw appreciation and pour two cups then refill and get three cups down.

Asa runs in. I get him a plate, cup and fork. "Any more Bits coming?"

"Laran bring Boss Kateri to work. I ride with you and Pres Kristos."

I nod getting another plate and cup. While he gets juice, I cut fruit. "You want granola?"

He nods so I shake some in a bowl and get a small bowl for nuts.

Kateri comes down smiling. "It's always busy at breakfast."

"LB, Nash," Prez says walking in.

Kateri laughs. "They're twins!" She goes right to the wolves not caring who is here. I guess they're staying. I shake my head getting coffee on the table and more plates.

"Aylen!"

I take all the plates from the cabinet and put them on the end of the table. Asa gets utensils and Laran runs in pulling yogurt from the fridge and a spoon from the drawer. The Preses talk to Kateri about the dogs. She's in her glory so I make her a plate and spoon fruit out to the Bits and me.

"Laran, you want granola?"

He looks back from my seat, "No nuts. Two yogurt, VP Mase?"

I nod shaking out his granola. Finally, I sit. "Yáhsháyôn, come eat. They're staying."

She smiles. "I'm excited."

I nod pulling her chair out. She washes her hands and I check time again. I have fifteen minutes.

"I'm with Kateri," Aylen says snagging the granola and nuts.

The Preses sit. "I didn't know you ate that for breakfast." Prez is surprised.

I smile waiting for Aylen's answer. "I lived in the crew house, Dad. It would scare the hell out of me if you did know what I ate for breakfast. Before they left, I ate a lot with Teller, Mase was back then so Mucimi and Justice always had his favorites out. Phoenix ordered some weird granola."

They look at my plate making me laugh. "I eat like the Bits."

Asa nods. "He show Chef Gourmet granola bar recipe."

Laran turns pulling his little backpack. "Snack ten o'clock." He shows Prez his little granola bar. "You keep. I go home one to Boss Kateri."

"One for Boss Kateri," I correct him.

He nods. "That."

We laugh, he's fuckin' cute. I eat while they talk about squirrel food.

Prez has fruit, yogurt, granola and nuts on his plate but is eating the granola bar. They're all fuckin' crazy. "This is good."

Aylen and Kateri laugh. I kiss my girl. "Aylen and Laran are with you. Call if you need me."

She nods looking happy. "I have work later and clothes coming. Did you do that?"

"Joey. She was making sure it would be clothes you'd wear. *Kuwômôyush*, Yáhsháyôn." I kiss her head and push for my bag.

"*Kuwômôyush, Wikco Inskitôp.*" Love you, handsome Indian.

I turn and just look at her. That smile, those pretty light brown eyes. Mohegan coming out of those rose colored bowed lips. "More."

Her smile lights those eyes. "*Nuin, Nupômkoki, Náhsuk.*" My man, my world, husband. The blush looks beautiful on those cheeks.

I push lifting her right up. "*Tôn?*" How the fuck did she learn Mohegan so fast?

She giggles. "Aylen sent me a dictionary she made. It had conjugating in the front. *Nukumát.*" Easy.

I kiss her. Fuckin' woman is amazing. "I am all of that and glad you're feeling it, Yáhsháyôn. I'm honored you'd learn my language."

"I don't know much of mine. Yours was easy and worth it."

I kiss her again to laughing.

"VP Mase, hormones later. Pres Kristos wait." Asa isn't letting me be late.

I kiss my girl and tell her I'm proud and humbled in Mohegan. Running out behind Asa, I throw. "We'll learn Navajo together." I already know quite a bit of Navajo and Cheyenne.

They're all laughing. I don't give a fuck.

~*~*~

Kateri

"You learned Mohegan in a night?" Kate's Pres asks.

"Yes."

"Photographic memory. Pulls like Jared. Sees like Alder," Knight explains then looks at me. "Dog commands Mohegan."

Wow. "That's smart. Not many people will know it here."

He nods. "That's why. You know 'em?"

I look at Aylen not sure if they were all in her dictionary. I never had a dog so I don't know what commands I need. She nods. "Aylen says they're in the dictionary so I'll have them. I never had a dog." I smile. I have two dogs now. Mase really is my world.

Knight smiles. "Will teach you."

I blink back tears. "Thank you." I love having a family.

"Why is Mase demolishing a house?" Danny asks.

I look around. "He's demolishing a house?" He does a lot of things, but he never said anything like that.

"The pussies picked up yesterday had cameras and bugs all over the fuckin' thing. Every room, inside, outside. He isn't into chancing they get them all. He bought it and is taking it down so no one living there is ever on feeds. Appliances and fixtures went to the city for people needing them," Prez says causing my world to tilt.

No, no. He bought it to stop people from being recorded. I stand then sit. He's demolishing it for me. Aylen stands by my chair. "Let's go to the deck for a minute."

I look up at her then down and nod. "Yes, ma'am."

"*Pumshá, ayunam, quhsháwôk.*" Knight's voice is low.

I whisper, "Go along, help, fear."

Aylen puts her arm around my back and we walk.

"He's demolishing a house so no one is recorded." My voice is soft even in the quiet.

She nods pointing us to the swing. A dog sits in front of me. "He'll do anything for you, Kateri. He's a Badass Blackhawk. It's *mucimi* and he'll work every day of his life for you."

"What do I do for him? He does everything."

She rolls her eyes. "They're crazy. We need girl-time so you get this right. I'm not an old lady. I'll call them. Can you work later? Mase isn't on until this afternoon."

I nod. "I'm researching and sketching. I can do it here."

She nods typing something. I pet the dog. He bought my house. It's forever. I smile. I'll have *nupômkoki mucimi*. That feels real good.

~*~*~

Mase

Seeing the stooges and Prez, I climb down from the backhoe. Uncle Danny lifts Asa up and climbs in with him. Nash climbs up yelling it's his turn.

I shake my head walking to Prez. "Is Kateri okay?"

"The old ladies are at the house. She's fine. You didn't tell her about the house. She was surprised."

"I feel something but she's not scared. I don't know what this is."

He's surprised. "You feel her from here?"

"Yeah, Prez. She was reaching for me yesterday. Today it's different." Why isn't he telling me what the fuck is going on? "She was surprised." I try his tactic.

"Relax, Mase. She was surprised you'd demolish the house for her. She's getting that you love her."

She's getting? He rolls his eyes. "She's getting it's for life, Brother. Stop flashing the fuckin' fire and I won't be distracted by it."

I smile. "I didn't know I was." I look at my hand. No fire. I close my eyes breathing the air of my ancestors and smile. She knows she's mine *mucimi*. That's what I feel. When I open my eyes Kristos is on the side of Prez. I look at the backhoe he was in. Nash got his turn.

"You settled?" Kristos asks.

"Yeah. I'm getting coffee." I push for Dunkin' thinking about my girl, she's settled too.

When I make the site with my two trays, I laugh. Nash and Asa are racing from front to the back swinging the arm and bucket through the house. We threw grenades demolishing the center beams, all that was left are the outsides. Everyone comes over for coffee.

"Where's Uncle Steve?"

Old Pres looks at Uncle Danny to answer. "He didn't say."

"What do I need to do when you catch fire?" Pres asks with his eyes moving like hurricane radar.

I hand him his coffee, glad I didn't spit the drink I took in his face. He smiles knowing. "Tell me. You want the backhoe back, Pres?"

"No, I wanted to throw grenades. We did good. Nash can drive anything. The kid is fucking weird with machines."

"He is." I hear pride in the two words that came out. *Fuckin' proud* like my dad says.

My eye catches the white utility truck rolling down the road slow. "What the fuck is with the cable company trucks?"

Everyone turns to see. "It's like a target," Pres says. "Hold until he's close and we'll use it."

Prez laughs then takes a drink. Old Pres and Uncle Danny go on about liking we have a Dunkin' here. Nash turns the backhoe and drives toward us. It's a target for him too.

I smile. This is going to be fun. '*Now.*'

Every gun shows at the same time. Nash lifts the bucket and rolls to a stop lowering it on the utility body lifting the front of the truck up. The pussies raise their hands.

Pres laughs. "I love the fucking Brotherhood. Does your gun get hot, VP?"

Taking the steps to pull the driver out, I throw over my shoulder, "No, it doesn't touch Kateri either. Prez caught fire but she was fine." Yanking the door open, I pull the idiot out. I would have been gone long before anyone could open the door for me.

Old Pres is surprised by that. "You caught fire?"

I throw the pussy against the bed of the truck seeing his sleeve burning. My gun is still on him. "Talk or I'll let you burn."

"I can see this being effective." Uncle Danny is going to fuck with my Badass. I give him a look and he shuts up.

"Talk!"

The burning idiot jumps. "We're just recovery! The first team didn't come back. I got an address and picture. Buyers paying large. Put it oouut!"

"Who do you work for?" Pres asks like the guy's arm isn't burning.

The pussy whines then gives us a name. "Ellison! Please, put it out!"

My eyes focus hard and he's engulfed. I pull him off the truck so he falls in front of it. He screams. Shaking my head, I pull his air and move to the passenger.

He's crying before I open his door, again, I'd be long gone.

"Mase, try controlling the fire before it hits him. See how close you can get." Uncle Danny has the Preses and Nash laughing.

I breathe. "Get out, move to the front and get on your knees."

When he does, I look at Pres. "I would have walked at least ten-foot away. He put himself right by the charcoaled pussy. Question while I hold the fire."

He nods while the Preses laugh. I focus on fire close to his head then breathe. Not touching, two inches, hover just outside. His surprised yell has my eyes opening.

"Fuckin' cool as shit, Mase!" Nash likes that.

Pres starts asking questions. The pussy is scared as fuck telling him everything he knows. I can read it's everything he knows so I relax watching the flames hover around his body.

Prez catches my attention. "Is Ellison a Mason?"

"Used to be." The pussy cries.

Prez looks at Pres. "Your eyes are red without the fire. Do you have anything else?"

Pres shakes his head. He's so pissed I can feel it. I throw water and the pussy screams. I roll wind shutting him up. He falls forward, I wince when his head hits the tar. "Cline, cuff him and get cleanup moving."

It takes an hour of truck and pussy clearing before we get Brantley and Web's locations and more than we need about the guy. He's second generation. That struck me. The Preses go back and forth.

Bored, I go around the wrecker and SUVs and see Asa still working the backhoe. I didn't notice Nash move the other, but they got this cleared and have the crew that was waiting hooking up straps so they can salvage. The Bits and no waste can always be counted on.

~*~*~

Kateri

"Seren, Caelan, AJ, Chenzo, Hannah, thing one and two, Destiny, Faith."

The dogs are sitting on the side of the couch by me and don't move. I guess we're under no threat. Knight said they'd position for a threat. Aylen takes a boy from a model and sits on the arm of the couch. Everyone is hugging but only Destiny hugs me.

"Sit everyone. Kateri isn't used to so many people so close." Aylen has them listening like the dogs. She smiles at me. Crap.

"I'm Kateri, obviously. I'm not used to people close so it's a little overwhelming."

Stella helps. "Give her names so she knows who is who."

Once I meet everyone, it's not so scary. They're just like the other women. Caelan loves the dogs and sits in between them watching everything going on. Chenzo crawls around looking happy to be free. Lily, Jess and Kate have coffee and drinks, Natalia, Destiny and Stella have the chef up and get snacks made.

I hold baby Cove Blackhawk McCabe and watch everyone talk, laugh and plan a party. Aylen doesn't move with Beck Qunhôtuq McCabe. I love their names. They honor their fathers. Trask's dad wanted *his* father's name so Cove Beck was used. Hannah's dad is Brantley Blackhawk so his last name and first name meaning was used. I hope we get kids and can name them showing that honor.

Aylen leans over and kisses my head. "You will."

I look up fast to see her eyes. They're shining with her beautiful smile. We will. It's for real. I feel that soft cotton cloud wrapping me up and bringing tears to my eyes. At least they're happy now. I never cried then came here and have cried too often. I can show that happy with honor, to my new family, because Aylen said *we will*.

Stella leans down putting a big plate of cut fruit and vegetables on the table then steals Cove from me. "Suck it up, Kateri. They have your clothes and the fun part will start. The 'rents are crazy."

I'd like to know how their rating system works so I know how to avoid becoming crazy. Aylen laughs.

"Stop reading my every thought." I give her a stern look and reach for a a handful of berries.

Chenzo wants berries apparently. He hits my hand and berries are on the floor. I laugh trying to grab them before he can. It's a mad dash for berries but I win. When he pokes his bottom lip out, I hold a blackberry out. The lip goes in and he leans so he can get a taste. It squishes against his two little teeth getting juice dripping on his lip and my fingers.

"You like that, Chenzo?"

He leans in for more. "I like them too. They have a lot of good in them."

Stella reaches for the berries in front of us. "They do?"

I nod smiling at Chenzo trying to get another berry from my hand. "Yes, the stem; for an eye wash, stomach problems, the berry; lung problems and sore throat, the root; leaves in a cloth soaked with warm water help many ailments as a poultice."

"Are you a shaman?" Lily sits in the chair closest to me.

"No. My grandmother told me when I was young. She told me of all the food we ate and plants we'd see walking the new reservation. I don't remember the old so it was new to her."

Stella hits my arm. I turn nervously. Then think of Mikey. "Just asking is too hard? You need to hit me to be heard?"

She rolls her eyes. "Was *she* a shaman?"

"I don't think so or she wasn't for the new tribe. She learned young from my namesake who I know now as Kateri Blackhawk."

She shivers. "That gives me the willies. Nunánuk knew her grandmother."

"It was meant to be." Aylen sounds odd drawing everyone's eyes to her.

Destiny moves and takes baby Beck from Aylen. "What do you see?"

"Three boys chasing Mase with breeches like he always wears. They're running on a path in the woods. Get me a phone." Aylen blinks fast.

I lift Chenzo up and Kate takes him from me. Damn women. Jess hands her phone over and Destiny types. "It's open, throw."

Mase's form caught with a leg up, barefoot, breeches and nothing else but his smile and long hair blowing in the wind is being chased by three boys that are dressed the same but hair not quite so long. I laugh then cry. Three boys. Two close to the same height and one smaller.

"Your freaky is really freaky when it's mixed with egghead technology." Faith hugs me. "I'm glad they have it in them. I hope it settles you for the bash Seren and Lilly have planned."

Oh no. "The party is for me?"

"For Mase to claim you," Seren says like that makes it better.

"He already claimed me. I have his cut and the kinky ancestors blessed our union."

They all laugh but don't say the party is canceled.

"I'm not sure Mase will go for a huge party." I try.

"It's not huge. We did just his family, crew and Officers. We need someone to ask Aiyana and Dakota." AJ doesn't see that as a problem. I don't know them well enough to ask for anything.

Destiny does. "The crew and family will make sure you're happy, safe and calm. The Officers are aware and will keep watch on the crew, the old ladies will watch everyone. Nothing will get close to even annoying you on your day."

I nod and look at Aylen. "I'll blast the fuck out of anyone that stresses you out. Aiyana will roll wind and pain so they better show to me before her."

That sounds okay. "If Mase agrees."

"Let's get the clothes put up. The men will be back soon." Kate and Jess pull me up. Stella and Destiny follow. Then everyone does.

I hope that's really soon. "I'll need something to wear. All my clothes were ruined in the break-in."

"No wonder Mase called Joey. Nancy got Kutomá to approve the style so you'll love everything. She's tiny and dresses like you do. When Nancy got your picture, she called Kutomá because your style looks so similar." Kate has me relieved.

The bed is piled high with bags. How did they do that? Oh my, Mase isn't going to like how much they have here. "I don't need all this. I order clothes from native women."

Jess nods pulling my panties out of the dresser. This has got to be on the crazy rating scale. "Old ladies manufacture panties to be environmentally friendly. We knew you'd want that. Nancy has Victoria's sending a box, but you can cancel after the first so you're not getting them every three months." Every three months?

"You manufacture panties?" Maybe it's not so crazy for her to be offended by my panties. They want me to wear theirs.

They are everywhere putting clothes on hangers. I see a top I really like but it's dropped back on the bed then covered by a dress. This is a little crazy. I don't know what to do.

Stella takes my hand and wraps it around a glass. "Drink. It's a ceremony of sorts. Drink and have fun with it."

I drink having the feeling I'll need it to have fun with this.

~*~*~

Mase

BSC planning sucks. I'm not a planner so I don't know why I need to be here. Justice brought Falcon in a jet. Ranger and Cort showed in another. Web, Brantley, Brinks, Jinx, Ricky and Hemy are on screens. I'm in the middle of Dakota and Pres. Nova is even here, he walked in behind Alder and Asa.

Pres agrees with Cort on almost everything. The Brothers throw numbers and how on things they *can't* control. Luckily, Justice controls *too much* planning. Alder offers to go on Ops collecting information Web and Brantley don't find.

The most interesting thing so far has been watching reactions and Web keeps drawing my eyes.

While they're figuring out the teams for a tandem strike, I look right at him. "Your biggest concern?"

"Alder on Ops again and this is leading up to collecting women and kids that will need a home. We need homes for them."

Everyone stops. Alder is first to break the silence. "I need number. ABSZ safe. I will...offer safe compound."

Web shakes his head. "Women coming out of slavery protected by men knowing they'll take an order isn't going to work. We don't have enough women Protectors now. We have a little over twenty women Enforcers."

"I see problem." Alder looks at Cort.

I throw out, mostly out of boredom, "Aylen and Ajhil."

Alder nods. "Boss Aylen understand women...heart hurt."

I nod watching Prez's reaction. I'm glad he's seeing her as more than an Ops Control. He looks at Cort. "Aylen as Pres of a Club was for her advocacy and security training."

Cort nods. "I'm going to cover everything, Brother. You have Mass and Princes *doing* everything. With Ops Clubs, we'll need Clubs specializing in other areas. It's not like there isn't a need. If she were ready, I'd set her up now because we're planning to grow that need today."

"Jesus fuck." Ricky has us all nodding. For me that's with a smile.

Justice zaps me. '*Shield better.*'

I hold my body still and barely nod. Fuckin' Brother.

Feeling his calm hit me, I smile at him. I got it. Being a shit because I'm bored isn't going to help here. '*Why am I even here?*'

He shrugs. I roll my eyes. Falcon coughs covering a laugh.

Cort watches us because Falcon is. "You have something, Mase?"

"Nope. I'm not a planner and I'm bored. That leaves me thinking thoughts I shouldn't. Justice fixed that so I'm bored with nothing to think about."

"Since when are you not a planner? You planned Ops at Elan and New Hampshire." Prez isn't wrong.

"Look at the people in this room, Prez. I can plan what I need to get the job done. I don't do all this detail shit. That's your job, I do the Ops you plan, I don't need the plan until I'm doing the Ops." I smile at him because he sees it.

He laughs. "You're here because everyone that can calm your ass down is here."

I smile. "I would have gotten a sandwich if I knew that. I can control it now. I didn't incinerate the second pussy."

The Brothers on the boards are surprised, the Brothers in the room laugh. Except for Alder. He shakes his head.

"You incinerated a pussy?" Brantley worries over everything now the kids are grown.

"No. He was screaming so I took his breath stopping that. The fire didn't kill him."

"Jesus. I can come down, Mase. Do you need me or Christian?"

I wave old man Brantley off. "I've got Prez, Dakota, Uncle Danny, Uncle Steve, MC Pres, my Pres,

Seth, Asa, Alder, the whole fuckin' crew and the rest of the family here, calling or texting constantly. I'm covered enough for right now. Anymore and I'm hiding in the fuckin' woods with my old lady until you all forget my name."

They laugh. I didn't mean it as a joke.

"I can see where you'd feel like we're too close. If you're sure you've got control, we'll step back, Brother." Prez gets me.

"I need to test that control so I can get some breathing room."

"Thirteen," Dakota says.

Fire hovers over my hands and I breathe it in then look at him. He's not done with the test. "Ellison was a Mason that befriended a tribal elder. He picked the women and children of the new tribe to steal as he was introduced to them."

My jaw clenches as I close my eyes.

"I don't have that," Web says making the breathing easier.

Brinks has my eyes open. "How come the table didn't burn?"

I look at the table. No fire.

"He is controlling it. The fire has a purpose and he sees it is not the table or me for which I am eternally grateful."

I laugh. "You should have shielded if you were worried."

He shrugs. "Perhaps. If I did shield, Prez would not be so trusting to take that step back you are looking for. I felt you focus and connect to Ellison on thirteen."

I clench my jaw and nod. "What's with the number, I'm not saying it in case he loses it."

Alder looks up. "Burn room ready, VP Jinx."

I shake my head. I'm not answering that.

"The cop paid extra for Kateri to have surgery ensuring no kids at thirteen," Justice says walking to me and holds my shoulder.

"What the fuck!?" Cort is the loudest in there.

"Why the fuck are we planning? Give Mase the address and let him incinerate the motherfucking pussy!" Jinx is out of his seat pacing behind his table.

"Mase." It's not yelled to be heard over the crazy fuckin' Brothers. I look up at Brantley. "What do you need? The plan from BSC, his location and what I have for movement, me there. What do you need?"

"The BSC plan will work, Brant. I'll get him. We need the recovery teams, the information before it's lost, the locations of who we can find. I want to kill the motherfucker and that's not with fire, but I'm not losing the chance to get the others out."

He nods.

"A sound plan, Brother. It will not benefit Kateri to miss removing women and children out of anger." Dakota has my skin crawling.

I look at Brantley, Cort then Prez. "We need the plan."

Cort nods.

"Smart, VP Mase," Alder says watching Dakota. His skin is crawling too.

Cort is watching me. "You still confident in that control?"

"Yeah, Boss. It has a direction I can focus on."

He looks at Prez. "Go run. The old ladies are all at your house with the clothes."

I'm not going home yet.

"Two hours, Brother." Dakota is fuckin' cool as shit.

"Thanks, I'm out. Later, Brothers."

~*~*~

"You have got to be fuckin' kidding me." I jog across the walkway to my yard that is full of fuckin' Brothers from every Club. Pres's yard is full. Turning, I see and hear Brothers at the pool. They're fuckin' crazy. At least it's not a circus.

Old ladies are in the yard and with kids on the deck. Walking in I see women in the house.

Mikey sees me first. "She's upstairs changing, Aylen is at the door. They invaded slowly. I'm keeping to baby and moms in, everyone else is out."

I nod throwing appreciation then run the stairs. Aylen shakes her head. "She's fine. You said stick close so I am. You'll see she doesn't need it, but I wasn't making the call."

"What changed?"

She throws me a picture and my hand grabs the banister. Me and three boys. "Holy shit. Dakota said, *it will not benefit Kateri to miss removing women and children out of anger.*"

"Holy shit is right. You're wearing those pants. I think that will solidify that bond for her. She's already feeling it."

I nod. "I feel her happy. I haven't felt her scared at all today."

Her head angles. "Interesting. If you're in, I'm out, I need a drink."

I laugh and touch her shoulder. "Thanks, Brother, for everything. You need that drink with your dad and Cort."

She nods warily. "Fuckin' great."

I laugh walking in the room, then stop at the sight of her neck with a collar that has string like a dreamcatcher holding the top of a white dress with the dreamcatcher sewn into it. My eyes travel down to the uneven white turning to black like it was tie-dyed while gathered. The black goes to just under her knee then is slashed as if by a razor and hangs with pieces almost hitting her ankles. Her jewelry is always native so the thin braided leather with beads in white and black on her ankle doesn't surprise me. The native look it ties together does. She's beautiful in anything, but this, this tells of where that beauty comes from. Calm, cool and collected, my girl wears it well.

"A vision, Yáhsháyôn."

She nods. "I thought the same thing about you. You were running in breeches?"

"Yeah. They don't rip in the woods as easily as skin. Come here."

She does. Fuck, she's beautiful. "I haven't seen this dress. I love all your clothes, but this one is my new favorite."

She smiles looking right at me. Aylen was right. "People are here from everywhere. It was suggested that I change but not what to wear to a biker party."

I move the hair hanging over her shoulder so I can see the whole front. "This is perfect. While I want to unwrap you very slowly, I see you just finished adding that makeup that doesn't look like it's there."

She reaches back under her hair and the dress falls. I don't care about her makeup. Walking her back, I pick up the dress and lay it across the dresser as I go by.

"Shoes off. You'll need another black lacy thong." I tear it leaving her naked while I unbutton the breeches. She bends for her ankle jewelry and unties my moccasin while she's there.

I kiss her untying the other. "Shower, Yáhsháyôn. I don't need a hair tie."

She moves into the shower while I shed cloth from my body. I love the big round rain forest shower head in the center, but my girl's hair is dry. She hits the control for her and gets two sides throwing water. Seeing water rolling down her body I want in. She turns toward me.

"Two steps back." I hit the control shutting her low jets off and hit the next down. The jets hit her chest perfect. She moans and reaches a hand out. "Still, baby."

Her hand drops and she waits. I bend from the waist and kiss her leaving no spot in her mouth untouched. Her hand moves up earning a slap to her ass. "Still, baby."

Her moan has me holding a smile while I slide my hand down slowly cupping that fine ass and my mouth finds hers again. She angles towards me and earns another slap lower. My hand sliding on her wet ass feels her body shaking with need.

Standing, I adjust her shoulders so the jet at that height hits her tits. "Still, Yáhsháyôn or I'll turn that beautiful ass pink."

She moans getting my dick to jerk. It's a good thing she's the sub. Moving to the other side, I hit the control for a straight shower. I wash quickly making sure my hair is rinsed and go back to my girl that is visibly shaking under the hot jets.

Kneeling, I slide my hands all over her wet body feeling her insides convulse.

"What to do with my beautiful little Indian?" I look at the bench sliding my hands up and squeeze her nipples. She moans but doesn't answer.

"Jackhammer your pretty kitty while watching those perfect rose-colored nipples get hard. From behind where my view is this beautiful ass or ride sitting..."

"Ride sitting," she whispers while she looks down fast.

"My brave little Indian wants to ride. Ride sitting it is." Lifting her away from the jets, I hit the control and get the low jets running. Her legs wrap around me before I take a step toward the bench seat.

"So fuckin' eager, Yáhsháyôn. It's unexpected but I love seeing it." When my ass hits the seat, she slides back quick and lifts up, sliding right down my length.

"Fuckin' eager feels so fuckin' good, baby." Switching to Mohegan has her eyes on mine. "Your hands on me, eyes on me, beautiful Indian."

"Always." Again, she's got me holding a smile.

"Ride me hard, baby." With her knees on the bench, she rides like she's seated on an English saddle.

I take it making sure my hands don't stop. "Sliding my hands all over your slick body does it, baby." Sliding up, I pinch her nipples ready to takeover. It's enough for her. She moans grabbing my hair to pull up missing the beat.

"I got this." Moving my hands to her waist and ass, I slam her down hard getting a grunt and groan that has me taking notice. Her only sound is the soft moan. I like the new and try for more. "Pet, baby."

Her hand moves to a relieved moan.

"So fuckin' sexy my little Yáhsháyôn is." I don't stop battering her ass against my legs knowing we're not lasting. "Let go, beautiful."

She does on command without the yes sir again and I'm gone. "Mase!"

"So fuckin' beautiful to see and hear. *Kuwômôyush*, Yáhsháyôn, *nuinskitôp*." I get out and take a deep breath. Jesus.

"*Kuwômôyush, Nuin*."

I kiss her beautiful face. "I love being your man."

She kisses right above my heart. I love that too.

~*~*~

"Jesus, that's the girl? How the fuck do you all find these beautiful women?" Nova's shock pisses me off.

"Yeah, that's Kateri. Mikey is right beside her. You want to talk about us? Have you seen *Mikey*, Seren, AJ, Solei?"

He angles his head conceding. "Point made. She's beautiful just like you said."

Ford sits and leans over. "Where do you get the breeches?"

I stand. "They're made for me. I run in them so they made the low waist and buttons on the side. It's like the gear here. The lighter buckskin keeps my legs from getting torn up in the woods. The fringe covers the holes for airflow. They added the extra layer on the knees because I wear them around the house and brought some back for patches. I asked for straight leg so I can get my moccasins over them without the extra folds when I run."

"Do they make them for anyone?" He doesn't look it but Native runs deep in him.

I shake my head. "I'm six-four. You won't fit in my clothes, Brother. If you get them your measurements, they can make you breeches. I trained scouts going into warriors right there. They know me and know the wear and tear I put on my clothes. They don't reinforce for ceremonial breeches and moccasins. These are all I wear at home."

He nods. "The moccasins?"

I lift my foot up so he can see. "They make them for me. I can send them back when the bottom wears out. I have three pairs for running. I think they figured I'd wear them out faster in the desert."

"I wear breeches at home, they're not deerskin."

I nod. "They make me some for bed and the lodge. Tell them what you want and they can make it. For me they know me. You need to be specific and they'll make them the same every time. My bed pants have one button off center so it's not on my side. Shit like that is important. There are no elastics in their clothes, everything is organic. Buttons are bone, rock or shell."

He smiles. "I like that." He's another wanting all natural.

"Do you own jeans?" Cort asks.

"I have two pairs of Levi's Nancy sent a few years ago. I wear cargos and gear or breeches. I don't think I've worn them anywhere but your house for two parties. Justice and Teller order our clothes for work. The only thing I buy are Ts, shirts and breeches. Shirts and breeches are from Connecticut. Ts are the Club. Nancy sends boots, socks and wife beaters."

"Tell me the ol' ladies don't make your boxers." Cort looks offended by that.

I laugh. "Nancy sends them every year. I don't ask. She started when the kids moved out, I signed up and get them like clockwork. Pants when I asked. I don't ask for them anymore. After a couple of years, she'll send another two pairs."

"You don't shop at all?" MC Pres sits with Pres. All the Preses are hard to keep track of.

"I don't like shopping. I do the shit I like." I check on my girl loving that she turns toward me with her little smile.

"Shit. I hate shopping." MC Pres has me smiling. "Do you take out the trash?"

"Yeah, Pres, I do laundry and cook too. Prospects bring me food. I got measured for an hour so the tribe makes me clothes. Everything else is Nancy or work. Club Ts are from the website, or I ask Penny to make funny shit for me. She always does but how often do you see me in Ts?"

He waves his hand at me. "You're always in those cotton or gauzy shirts with no buttons."

I nod. "They're more comfortable than button down and I can wear them anywhere. You've seen me in the dress shirts." They're the same but with a banded collar.

Cort nods. "Viking is the style. I'm not a button fan either. Ts or Viking. Everything in my size is made to order."

"Fuckin' Brothers get away with more shit." MC Pres gets up and walks away like we offended him.

We laugh. "You're always poking people. Spano is pissed at how easy your life is because of air dry or some shit." Pres sees everything.

I crack up checking on Yáhsháyôn. She looks right at me and stands.

"He forgets shit like I'm working on not setting shit on fire every time I stand up. I'm out."

"Hold up, Brother. I need to talk to you." Cort stands.

"Kateri first, Brother."

He walks with me and goes to Seren when I stop at Kateri. "Ready for a walk, Yáhsháyôn?"

She nods with relief in those pretty light brown eyes. "Cort needs to talk to me. We'll walk to the circle Justice made for you. It will calm you."

She smiles. "Sounds good. Thank him for me."

I kiss her lips and take her hand stopping on the walkway for Cort. He has Caelan. "That makes a nice picture, Brother."

He smiles. "I thought the same thing. Both your hair is flying behind you."

I smile at my beautiful girl.

We walk with the dogs running in front of us. "What are the wolves names?"

I don't know so I look at Kateri. "Numuks and Kimuks."

I laugh. "Perfect, Yáhsháyôn."

Cort smiles. "What does it mean?"

I squeeze her hand to answer. "My wolf, your wolf. They're mixed dogs but I like wolf better."

"It fits. Can you send me the dictionary?"

Kateri stops and looks up at me. "It's not mine to give away."

I nod. "I have one I'll send but Aylen wouldn't have a problem with it. *Kikátohkáwôk mihkunum kitiyayôk wuci wutuaymuyin*. Nunánuk always said, '*Language holds the life force of a nation.*' We all heard it repeatedly and learned the old Mohegan language from birth. It's an honor to hear our native tongue spoken."

"Thanks, Brother. I'd like to understand and find what I pick up easy. Caelan is learning German and Swedish, he should learn Mohegan."

We come to the circle and Kateri hugs me. "Thank you. This is exactly like I've pictured it. The symbols are right too."

"We'll come back tonight and see if your stones glow. I can help that if they don't."

They laugh. Caelan wants down so Cort stands him up. He takes Kateri's hand and starts walking. I laugh at the little Brother that knows what he wants. She starts talking to Caelan about the stones as if he understands.

Cort smiles. "She's good with kids."

I nod having nothing to say about it. "You wanted to talk to me?"

He walks back to the path and turns to watch Kateri and Caelan. "Alder ran Kateri's DNA. He wants a meet with you first then her. Today he saw you control the fire. I believe his concern is how Kateri will react to whatever he says."

It sounds right. "He was upset when he found out she was a slave. Pres said she has a tie to Crow."

That surprises him. "What Pres is this? You all need to learn to use names."

That would make my life easy. "Kristos."

He's surprised again. "Do you trust that?"

"I do. He's just learning how to throw, but he knows weird shit and is always right. I know he doesn't understand jump. He's getting shit from somewhere. He feels shit too. It could be that. Dakota is here, he'd know."

"I'll ask."

Since he's done with that, I let him know, "I'd be concerned so I'd want to know first. She's been calm today and Aylen said she's more settled. Her bond was solidified by something Aylen saw. I feel that calm in her."

He looks from them to me. "You weren't here."

"I don't need to be close. I feel our connection. I knew when she was scared or reaching for me. Today she's been happy, content I guess."

"I see the difference. I'm glad she got that and you feel it. I see native in you more than the rest of the crew, maybe not Aylen. The rest are guided but you have both your feet planted in more of the culture. It's weird, but I think of Ford and Nash like that too. Do you need anything that we don't take care of?"

I smile. "Not that I can think of. I have my tepee here if I need it and I've never been much for the sweat lodge. That's a Ford thing. I jump regularly and run the land connecting to what I need. I have a blanket being made with my traditional tribe stitching and Navajo fringe and beads on the bottom. Aiyana is working on regalia for Kateri with my mom and sister."

His head angles to the side. "It's not a wedding?"

I smile. "No. She doesn't have family so there is no one to guide her through a wedding as you're thinking. The blanket ceremony will be with four elders acting on behalf of both of us. Aiyana, Dakota, my dad and Prez. Aiyana being the highest sponsor. She's a shaman and elder in the tribe."

"Rings?"

"I need those, I haven't had time to get to Phoenix. Justice said we use the jeweler there. I need native stones or material, or she isn't wearing it. I have a picture of something I saw in Connecticut." The stones I have will look nice in the ring.

"She won't wear it or you won't buy it?" He's funny.

"Does it matter? Look at her. She's always dressed like that. Even the ankle jewelry is native. I wouldn't consider buying something that's not. Rings aren't a tradition, but I want them."

He nods. "Got it. Send me the picture you have. I'll send the jeweler a heads-up. If he doesn't have it or close to it, we'll find a place that does."

"I like that. I'll send it with the dictionary."

Caelan runs our way. Kateri follows close. She's going to be a good mom. My whole life I've pictured myself with a big family. It was never a question for me. As many kids as my mom and dad, a woman that had an open heart like mom's and I would teach them of our ways with the passion and fierceness to defend our beliefs just like my dad taught me.

Holding Yáhsháyôn's hand while she holds Caelan's walking back, I smile, she's going to be a good mom.

Chapter Seven

Two days

Mase

I watch my girl's eyes follow the Bits out. The whole circuit crew showed today. Kateri was excited and helped make breakfast with them. I stood back and watched. Her every move was graceful and confident, back to looking almost choreographed to fit her space and frame. I love that confidence. I love the little smile that holds her thoughts and secrets. I love my Yáhsháyôn.

Walking up behind her, I wrap my arms around her wanting her to feel that love. "I have an hour. Do you want to walk, baby?"

"Yes. You were out early today." We walk out to the yard with the wolves running ahead. She's always up for anything.

"I was. Still made it back and made sure you were ready for your day, content and satisfied."

"You're very full of yourself today."

I laugh at the smackdown. "You loved being full of me today, so I have reason, Yáhsháyôn."

She looks up at me with that small amused smile. "Every day and I won't complain again."

"Where are you working today?"

"Your office here. I don't need to work in the Lab and get more done quicker without the distractions." She's still the lone wolf. Maybe not with her two wolves always close.

"You want an office of your own with some room for you to draw?"

She doesn't answer right away. My eyes roam over the hills. Her little hand holds mine tighter. "I would but the office building is very busy."

"It is." Turning her back, looking up the path toward the house, I point at a clearing on the rise. "I thought over there. It's right behind the house so you'd be close." The wolves run and sit by us.

"Is it safe here without the cameras? I can't just walk out and signal for help." The cloak is working, my girl who was terrified of cameras now sees the good in having them around for her safety.

"We can put sensors in the ground, cameras pointing out and you have your cuff. You're tracked and drones are all over this land."

She turns and walks down the path. The wolves running tell me she's settled. "I'd like that, thank you. I have money to pay for it."

"Joey asked about handling your money so it grows."

"She called yesterday. I thanked her for the clothes and told her to do her thing. I never worried over money but never had it working for me. She'll fix that. I like your sister. She's coming to visit next week." She throws appreciation as second nature. I like it understated and just so. Kateri is a lot like Joey. She doesn't need people so close, loves her family and friends in small doses and is content with her life, man and job.

"You have a lot in common with Joey. We don't see her much but feel her love always."

"I hope everyone feels that from me." Her voice is her normal soft with a hint of a smile telling me she likes showing that love her way.

"I know I do. You're more comfortable and confident in your place in my life and family. It's noticed and felt by all of us, Yáhsháyôn."

We round a bend and she stops to look back. "I spent a lot of time inside. I love the freedom of being out. I'm taking the Bits hiking right here when Aylen is back in a couple of days."

"We have Enforcers that will like the hike. They start tomorrow." Her hand tightens in mine. "They're women, baby. Meant for Alpha but on loan to us for a month before they go to Protector training. They will work with your scheduled shifts. Because you don't leave the compound, they can get a lot of book work done. You have a say in that schedule."

"I'll like that. I'll schedule them for our hike. The smaller Alpha-Bits are nervous around the men. They'll be able to enjoy the hike more." She looks up tightening that little hand. "So will I, thank you."

"Your heart and mind are settled."

"They are. I've never had this as an adult. I remember the feeling as a child walking with my grandmother. The cloak is firm, I won't push it again. Aylen said my awareness will keep me safe and those memories will not interfere with my happiness. I am still nervous at times and understand why but can't see the details that brought me those feelings."

"I'm glad Aylen was here for us. Do you have more memories cloaked from before?"

She doesn't stop walking while thinking about that so I don't. "I think I do. I remember walking with my grandmother so clearly but not our house or other details. I see her dress, face, the love in her eyes shining on me. Fires at night and her tucking me in are there in so many memories but so much is not clear and I've never tried to retrieve them."

"Your grandmother had ability, Crow and the man Ben T had them. Maybe you don't need what's not clear." I turn us around and start back. With a whistle the wolves bound from the trees back to us then run up the path.

"I don't. I'm happy knowing I was loved by my grandmother. I don't need more."

"You're an incredible woman, Yáhsháyôn. I'm glad you're my incredible woman. You haven't said but you're comfortable with my dominant personality even with the cloak."

She stops and looks up at me still holding my hand. "I remember when we met. I craved that dominance but had trouble justifying the need. The club we went to helped ease that worry some. Memories are cloaked so the why will always be a mystery." Her small smile says she doesn't mind. "Now I crave the dominance and don't care why. It's different than before, I love our new way but still crave the old at times. I like looking at you, you're a beautiful man with so much passion it's felt through your movements and expressions. I love touching you and feeling my touch affect you. With all that, I like giving you control to please me, showing me I'm cared for in a way only you can. I don't think we made it to vanilla and I'm glad. It sounds boring and a waste of our time together. I want heart thumping passion filled love the way it is." Her head bows. "Maybe some old when it strikes you."

I laugh lifting her up. "Whatever you want, baby. You've always controlled that. I'm glad this works. It's about as vanilla as I have in me. I'm still open to the service calls. If your hard limits changed, I need them."

She hugs me tight with her arms and legs. "I'll make a new list. I may have less now. Are you free tonight?"

I hold her tighter. "I am. Spare room in the red heels at eleven."

"Yes! I'll be there." My girl is happy and I feel that happiness run through me.

"Love you, Yáhsháyôn."

"Love you, Nupômkoki."

I love being her world.

~*~*~

My partner for the first Op today is Cayden. We work well together so I'm easy with it. Justice has Alder. Aylen is our pilot and Mag our cover. Seth and Case are our outs and Destiny and Keesog are shielding the choppers.

The crew is aware and ready to help if we need it. We shouldn't need it. Three safes in Ellison's house are our targets. Web has the rooms mapped out from drones he had Alder build. The infrared and thermal imaging should make this easy.

Justice stands. "Ready to jump, Brothers. Destiny, shield the chopper. Connect to Mucimi and he'll keep you from getting drained. Keesog, shield that chopper, you have

Dakota, connect and don't fuck it up or you're not making it back." His smile tells me he's not worried and he's teaching Keesog a lesson here.

With his rogers he stands at the door. "Seth, Case, cover from the door until we're low enough for you to jump. You ready, Alder?"

"Eyes closed, tight hold. Ready."

"Mase, Cayden, you're up, we're right behind you. Be fuckin' Badass, Brothers."

I put my arm out and Cayden takes it. Our MPs are out and I'm glad someone thought about this when I jump. Cayden is right-handed. This wouldn't work if he were a lefty. We land shooting the surprised Security guards making their round by the front door. Justice has Alder at the alarm already. The fuckin' Brother is like Houdini.

"Mase," Justice is ready to move.

Cayden puts his arm out and I take it moving us through the house. "Empty."

"Roger, first safe."

I hear a shot and look out the kitchen window. Case calls clear in front of a pussy laying half in the pool.

Cayden comes back to me at the stairs. "First clear. If you keep the pussies out, we'll stay clear."

Case looks through the window and nods. "Roger, CC." His arm goes out and I move us through the second floor.

"Second clear. We're at the safe."

"Roger, Brother. Coder is connecting," Aaron tells me.

The click comes through and I don't give him a chance to talk. "Save the speech. I know you're on, what's my first step."

"The keypad is reset to your birthday."

I type the numbers in and the lock disengages. "Fuckin' geeks got it going on."

He laughs while we pull shit. A flash of light has me holding Cayden's arm still. "Trip. Step back."

He moves, I tip the files up in the back then slide them under the wire one at a time until I can get the smaller pile out. "CC." I float the files behind me to Cayden.

There's a door to a smaller compartment inside. "Coder, the compartment?" I ask.

"No electric to it. The generators show only the alarm and safes covered. Case shut everything else down. The draw is consistent with keypads, nothing extra."

I push the little lever down slowly. "How you know that shit is a relief and fuckin' weird. No noises from it."

"Then open the fuckin' door and move already. We have more shit to do." Brantley's impatient.

I open the door and lay flat so I can see before I stick my hand in it.

"I made sure you had flexibles." My Brother is annoyed with me.

I reach in and pull a cigar box out. It fits like it was made for the compartment. "Then you'd see shit before me. It's a last-born thing, Brother. I get something first in this life."

Aaron laughs. "Open and make sure it's safe to travel, Warrior. Thanks, Coder. Alder is getting ready to move to the next. You're clear here."

I open the box slowly and breathe. Stones. They're good to travel.

"Roger, Shooter." I'm up and pull a hair tie from my pocket sliding it on the box then the box into Cayden's bag.

"Second clear." I call.

"Just1's location." Aaron isn't big on small talk.

Cayden's arm goes out and I push. Justice looks back and points. "Got them." We grab the bags and turn. I freeze. "Fresh paint and joint compound."

Justice looks at the wall. "I thought there was a faint paint smell. You can smell compound?"

I shrug and lift the hard backed chair in the corner then smash its legs into the wall rotating it in a circle. A leg breaks hitting a stud but I keep moving it until there's a round cut out.

"That was cool, Brother." Cort has me smiling.

I pull the sheetrock and the circle falls. "Wasn't that in a movie or something? Someone stuffed walls with money." I'm looking for who while Cayden is pulling the sheetrock down with his hands.

"Hold up. I can take the sheet." Justice has the wall peeling up. That's fuckin' cool.

"We're going to need more bags, Ops. I'm transporting what we have. Can I use an artillery box?"

Alder nods watching us. Cort rogers and has Pres getting a box emptied.

I lift everything here and look at Alder. "You want to stay or get transported back?"

"Chopper. I scan files to Web." He climbs on when I bend.

Standing, I tell Cayden, "I can't take you with Alder. I may need to fire."

"Go. I'll get shit ready for the next run."

"Alder."

"Ready, Warrior."

I push and step into the chopper. Destiny pulls the bags to her quickly and suspends the box to the door. "I wasn't sure about sending it to you."

"Send it now. Just ask. Everyone gets this is new."

She throws chin and the box is floating. "Stay alert, shield and help get the files scanned. I'll transport without bothering you."

She salutes me then moves a bag with her to the computer. "You okay, Zenobia?"

"I am. This isn't lasting, move, Brother." Aylen throws a warning out.

I move. "Justice?"

He turns toward me. "I feel it. Let's get what we can."

He's pulling blocks to the chest I look at another wall and pull. Cayden keeps the piles level. It's a good system. When the box is filled, I transport it to Keesog on Mag1.

"I sent a box to Justice." He's proud.

"Good job, Brother. I didn't see it. You don't have to shield your abilities. Use what you have and get it done. Our abilities are never hidden here."

He's surprised and nods. "We don't have much time. Ten minutes maybe."

I nod. "I'm glad you're alert, fuckin' perfect. Keep shielding. I'll bring the second box."

"I can scan files." He catches me before I push.

"Get Destiny to send a bag over, Brother. It will be a help."

He nods and turns to the computer. I push with a smile.

Justice has the second box half full. "Take the bags to Mag1 and we'll put this box on Zenobia's chopper. Distributing weight will save fuel."

"Roger." I lift the bags and push.

Keesog smiles when I drop bags. "I heard."

Throwing him chin I push.

Cort comes on. "You need someone with you, Warrior?"

"I'm not feeling it but won't turn it away. We have another Op."

"Ben is doing jump for you."

I smile. "Roger, Boss." I feel Prez's boost in my energy when I stop. Holy shit.

Justice smiles knowingly. "Teller is on me. We need to go."

I nod. "I'll start here and move down then out."

Justice suspends the box and smiles at Cayden. "Windsurf it, Brother."

Cayden is up for it and jumps on the box. They're gone quick with Cayden laughing.

I look at the wall. The money slavery brings in will not be going to this fuck or any member of his crew. The wall explodes in flames. I go right around the room. We didn't have time to pull them all down. Suspending out I stop and focus on the floor of every room I move through. I suspend through the first floor doing the same and push out the back door.

"Jesus," Aaron says when I look back.

Stopping at the garage I focus on heating gas then move. The explosion is deafening. I don't stop until I step in the chopper.

"Go!" Justice yells. Aylen flies like Justice does. The push has us up and away quickly.

"Good job, Zenobia. Flight plan logged." Aaron throws.

"Roger, covered, boost two."

Destiny rogers typing then goes right back to putting pages in the scanner. Justice smiles at me. He likes the just do it attitude.

I jump throwing Prez and the ancestors appreciation then help with the scanning.

~*~*~

The boards show red dots as the pages are scanned. After four hours they're still scanning. The map on the board shows dots leading from our morning target in nowhere Wyoming by the highway leading to Salt Lake and the connecting interstate running north and south. This runs through and connects to more highways into a million fuckin' reservations interlocking the whole west. Ellison is a fuckin' piece of work.

"Mase! Step back, Brother."

I step back looking at Cort. Then drop the page I'm holding and step on it. "Sorry. Did I scan it? Fuck!"

He puts his hand on my shoulder. "Relax. It was scanned."

I breathe smelling the lake, seeing the clear sky and relax. "I can't miss getting the information out of anger. It will hurt Kateri."

He nods leading me out of the meeting room. "That sounds like a lot of pressure and a warning from somewhere."

"It's not pressure unless I'm fuckin' it up. I'll learn not to fuck it up quicker."

He smiles walking into Pres's meeting room. "Did they clear the recovery teams?"

Pres turns from the board. "Nash just landed. Andrew in twenty. Kyler and Kutomá just lifted, they're on their way back. The mixed crews ran awesome. Nash did great as a Lead."

I'm glad he says it.

Cort nods then opens the door for the Prospect. "The two of you didn't make lunch. Sit before we're running again."

My eyes seeing food gets my stomach making noise for it. I sit and pull the top off smiling. He ordered from my list. Very cool. "Thanks, Boss."

"The Prospect said you have your own menu. Thank Table then give him a real name."

I nod taking a bite of my chicken and cheese sub loaded with mushroom and onion.

Pres shakes his head at me. "He modified the Alpha-Bits portion. They eat what we do with their salad, fruit or vegetables added."

Cort nods. "It works." He opens the door again and two more trays come in. He drops my dried fruit and nuts by my tray. "He said he forgot those."

"Thanks." I dump them over my salad and cottage cheese and finish my sandwich seeing the thin paper bag on Nash's tray. I point. "He'll like that. This is his favorite lunch."

"I told the Prospect to send the list to Phoenix so he can get it there. He should have said."

I shrug. "We eat everything, Boss. We've been everywhere and eat what's served. Knowing I'm here long term, I ordered the Bits' plates bigger and the kitchen accommodated."

Nash and Nova come in and I know we have a problem. "What's up, Nash?"

He shakes his head glaring at Nova. "Boss Nova lifted a file. I called to Justice and Prez. You don't need it. Boss Nova says you do."

"First, you've proven yourself at Lead. You don't call Brothers Boss then their name unless they're your Officers. Nova deserves respect for the work and experience he's put in but you're his equal just like you're my equal. Yeah?"

He drops in the right seat seeing his little bag on the tray. I keep going. "Second, if you think I don't need it, I probably don't need it. Nova is a close Brother and wouldn't want me left without information. You know my heart and will guard that with everything in you. It's a good call to ask for guidance, being pissed won't change anything but you not enjoying the lunch Cort ordered for you."

His smile shows as he picks up the bag then lid. "Thanks, Pres Cort. This one's my favorite."

Cort smiles. "Eat before you don't, Brother. I have the list going to Phoenix so you'll get it all the time."

Nova opens his coat and pulls a file out handing it to Cort. I eat my salad sure I don't need to see it. Cort flips it over on the table. He's not touching it.

Pres looks at me and smiles. He likes that. '*Straight up Badass.*' He throws.

Nash laughs. '*He is.*'

They talk about Andrew, Kyler and Kutomá's Op. Pres is glad it all went easy. Ellison doesn't have recovery teams left in Idaho, Wyoming, Colorado, New Mexico, Utah, Arizona and Nevada. Honor took Colorado and Utah so the Protectors could take multiple sites. Bravo took New Mexico.

Justice and Prez show quick with Dakota coming in behind at a stroll. I smile taking the granola bar and covering my tray. I don't look while they all look at each other and shield me. I drop my granola bar in my lower pocket, I may need a boost later.

Pres shakes his head smiling at me. I shrug. They'll do what they do. Justice breaks the silence. "He doesn't need it. If you read it, he better not get any bit of it from you. I'm saying no."

Prez nods.

Cort smiles and hands the file to Justice. "Thanks for keeping me out of the burn room. Someone needs this. I'd say that's you and Aylen."

I nod at Justice. He takes the file and is gone.

I turn to Nova. "I can't do details. I'm glad you didn't read it and appreciate the respect."

He throws chin and finishes eating. He's not offended and thinks he's missing shit, since it's shit he doesn't need, I don't fill it in.

Pres picks at his fries while Prez and Cort talk about the next Op.

Andrew and Justice come in and sit. "Did you order from here?" Andrew asks.

Cort stops and turns. "Prospect has it. He'll deliver five after set down."

I open the door smiling, the Prospect drops the two trays and takes mine back with him. "Thanks, Table. I'm ordered to give you a real name. You got a preference?"

"Mine works."

I laugh. "Maximus will get you Maxi or mus. You sure?"

His head is already shaking. "You pick."

"You always smell like food. Clove, basil, fennel, thyme, hazel, kale."

He smiles. "Thyme."

"There you go. Thanks, Thyme."

The happy Prospect moves a little quicker. "Thanks, VP. I'll get Spruce to change it on the schedule."

When I close the door, Andrew laughs. "I'd have picked clove."

Nash doesn't agree, "Basil."

I pull my laptop and get shit done while we're waiting.

~*~*~

Kateri

"Mikey."

I turn toward the door. "Hi, Mikey, it's been slow today."

She unzips her coat and drops her backpack. "Ops is running. I hate to use you, but the office is crazy and I've got work to do. I can't go into town without a whole damn team and I need some place quiet."

"You're bumping off the favorites from my list. The office is over there. Help yourself to food and drink. I'm working too."

She kisses my cheek and walks to the office with her bag leaving her coat on the chair. It's the same coat Mase wears with the gun on the back. The woman must be an ox. Mase's coat weighs a ton.

I get back to Alder's research. Once I have a few organs, I want to try it out, so I pull the code Natalia built and copy/paste the sections I need. Mikey comes out and sits watching. After a while I forget she's here and open to a hologram board. My organs build for someone named Eli. Alerts show on his liver. That's odd for a child. Using my fingers, I spread it open and see the numbers and spots showing the buildup.

"That's cool."

I jump and smile at her. "I forgot you were here. I'm just testing the pictures for Alder. I'm done for today. Four down, a hundred to go." I close it down fast not sure if she should be seeing someone's medical information.

"I'm done too. Do you program anything?"

Saving the files, I close my laptop. "I don't program. I copy and pasted Natalia's code from the DNA model. I can change the shape so it works for almost everything."

"Does the BSC pay you?"

"I work for Alder and BI. That's Badass Innovations. I don't think either are the BSC. That's the conglomerate of Clubs, right?" It's on her coat so she'd know.

"Yeah. I'm working on a board for BSC. It's loaded with a matrix that moves people within a Club, up or down based on test scores but also Officers. I need an easier way for Cort to see that. Maybe an easier way to use it. Jacob had it in circles and that didn't work for years. I just don't know what the hell I need or who to ask. Stella is always busy."

I open my laptop up and call Stella. "You're BSC. Mikey had a question and I have time. If you answer her and I can do it, I'll take the job."

She smiles. "I love the fuck out of you, Kateri. What do you have, Mikey?"

Mikey gives her the problem then what she's looking for. I get permission to work on the board then special glasses that will make working on it easier. I have to work from virtual so I'm not working on the original satellite program that's locked to three geeks. I agree to the work parameters and am told Asa will bring me glasses. Stella signs off and Mikey laughs excitedly.

"Show me the board and explain how it works. I'll look at it with the special glasses and see if I can come up with an easier way to see it. I'll need the link so I can pull it up from the virtual. I think you can send it in that chat thing. Stella set me up with one, it's just my name."

Her list pops up. "Kateri Blackhawk or Kateri?"

"Just Kateri." I'm Kateri Blackhawk. Oh my, that feels good.

She explains and shows me how the matrix works then the second page that works with Officers. The matrix is so complicated but I'm not working on the matrix. I just need a way to show results that's not a list. Circles don't work and that would be basic with the technology we already have. I think I have it and start asking questions.

"Can I show the result from the first page like this?" I show her the DNA model and pull a line out.

"Yes. That would be awesome. Can you use symbols for the test the results are showing for?"

"Yes. Can I show the full results on the side by scores?" I add a box on the side and show her what I mean. It's just the line with dominant features.

We go through all my questions and Mikey is happy. "I'll work on a way to show the second board once I have this one done. Tomorrow I'm free so I'll work just this."

I get a hug then invited to lunch. "Can I make you lunch here? I need to eat."

"I'll help and thanks. The Ops Brothers aren't all back yet and I don't know all these Brothers." She follows me to the kitchen.

"I only know the Officers. Mase said they were doing Ops and he didn't know when he'd be home. I don't want to go to the office if he's not there."

We work well together. She makes salad like I do while I make chicken salad for wraps. She puts dried fruit on the salad and cottage cheese on the table. "Do you want nuts?"

I smile. "No, that's a Mase thing. I eat it just the way you set it up."

We talk about Parker and his fish; I love him already.

As we're cleaning up her phone rings. "Shit. They're meeting in ten. I need to get to Ops. I'm on this one too." She rushes to get the plates to the dishwasher.

"Go, Mikey. I'm not on Ops and finished work for today. I got this."

With a hug and thanks, she's gone. I smile cleaning up the counter. Mikey is sweet and loves her Nova brothers. I'm glad they found each other and they're all happy.

I giggle washing the dishcloth. I'm happy too.

~*~*~

Mase

We have paper from every office that recovery team-leads for Ellison had but his base in California and this one in Rock Springs, Wyoming. The Alpha-Bit IT is crazier than Brantley's. They have average snowfall, population and that it's number ten on the safest cities in Wyoming. I skim the details thinking the people in the city don't know shit about safe if the biggest human trafficker from just west of the Great Plains is set up in the biggest building of their downtown area since before he was born.

I flip to the pictures. "You've got to be fuckin' kidding me. Is this right, Alder? He's next door to the Masonic lodge?"

Alder nods. "I put to show, not incinerate."

"Fuck! Mase, calm your fuckin' fire shit down." Andrew moves for water.

I throw water on the page and shake it out before he turns back. "Just tell me. I'll put it out."

He shakes his head dropping in his seat. "That's a gift?"

I shrug trying to read the last page. "VP Mase, read here. I will remember no page to you."

"Thanks, Brother. I'll bring my bag for the next one." I smile. "Or not. I can't burn a hologram. I'd probably melt my laptop."

He smiles waving his hand at the board.

"Five out," Aylen says.

I finish and stand. "Keesog, do the same as the last Op and we're golden. Silencers on. We're dropped in the back, low traffic. With less than twenty-five thousand people that's normal. PD will be dealing with calls so we're clear of them. Mikey and Kyler, you're on out. Andrew, Seth, you're in. Cayden, you're with me and Alder. Remember, abilities aren't hidden, you do the job with everything in you so we can move on."

I get rogers and open the door. "Zenobia, you're going to be noticed. Drop and jump."

"Roger, Warrior."

I bend. "Alder?"

He climbs on my back and gets his hands set. "Eyes closed. Tight hold. Ready."

"We need handles for you, Brother. Cayden, now." I push and land on the roof gently.

"I make to next Op." Alder makes me smile.

Cayden pulls the door open and we're going down. I hear Ellison on the phone and slow. He's already trying for insurance money on his house. Fuckin' weasel.

"IT record. Go, VP Mase," Alder whispers.

I push to, then through the door, bending with my gun trained on the little fuck. "Hang up."

He hangs his old-fashioned corded phone up and raises his hands. "How did you get up here? What is he doing?"

I lift the motherfucker up and suspend him toward me. "Not a fuckin' word or the fire you see will be the last thing you feel." It will be but I don't want him whining while we wait.

He sucks in a breath watching my hands.

Cayden pulls his computer apart and takes the memory boards. He throws a hard drive near it and pulls a laptop out of a messenger bag then hunts for more.

"LP?"

Alder's reading a calendar from the desk. "Files, all go. Map to wall. Mason meetings. Take appointment book. No phone, Warrior."

"Where's your phone?"

He looks down. I see the bulge in his pocket. "LP, it's on him."

Alder looks at me and nods running to us. "Need phone working." He pulls the phone and pats the motherfucker down. "Two phone. Gun on ankle."

Seth shows at the door and freezes. I must be the reason.

"Move, Brother." I get him going.

He takes the first two bags and the map pushing to get gone.

"LP?"

Alder points. "Cabinet one bag."

"CC?"

"LP and the bag." Cayden lifts the bag and bends.

"Go. Status." I ask the rest.

Andrew cleared the safe and is moving up. Kyler and Mikey dropped guards in the basement and are on their way up. Keesog is pulling shit to the chopper.

'Seth and Kyler, bring the file cabinet up. I'm starting from the first floor.'

They roger and I grab the fuck pushing us through the building. The basement has a big oil tank. Fuckin' perfect. Letting the fuck go, I shield and blow the tank with wind. What amounts to diesel fuel is everywhere. The pussy is yelling about the fire on his shirt. I smile pushing him back and watch as he falls into a puddle. He twists and turns thinking the diesel is all going to catch fire. He's an idiot. It needs to raise to 131° to catch but his clothes don't. I help him out heating the room as I push to the stairs. The room explodes in fire. It's fuckin' hot so I move fast to the first floor.

Setting the walls on fire from the floor up will make sure no one enters. I cover the perimeter and push to the second. I float around thinking of the motherfucker setting up in a supposed safe place and watch the flames lick up the walls. When I'm satisfied, I hit his office then push to the roof and bend for Alder. "Zenobia."

He puts his hand out testing for heat. Smiling he climbs on my back. Web yells in my ear. Cort yells back.

I take Mikey's arm and push to the chopper as it's lowering. Aylen is down for a second then rises fast.

"Good job, Brothers." I throw shaking my head to clear it.

"Breathe, Mase." Cort reminds me I'm not settled.

I bend for Alder and breathe. The ancestors clear diesel from my head. Standing, I pull wind around me and can breathe easy here.

"Thank fuck. Alder, you're fuckin' crazy." Andrew is annoying me.

"VP Mase safe to me, Boss Mikey. He no like whining. No safe to you." Alder has me smiling.

I sit and close my eyes throwing appreciation to the ancestors and my Brothers.

When I open my eyes I give it to them, "Thanks, Brothers, Ops, IT, unless you start yelling in my ear again."

Cort laughs. "You did good, Brother. You're settled?"

"I am, Boss." I hold my hands up so he can see.

"Get them home, Zenobia." Cort tells Pres we're clear and heading home.

"Roger, covered, boost two." Aylen is professional and fuckin' good.

Keesog rogers her making me smile.

The motherfucker is dead. I don't know how many women and kids we saved, but one is worth it. I think about my tiny Indian woman. I hope she had a good day. We have the Club tonight and her service call at eleven.

~*~*~

The Colorado Club is packed. The Brothers give a war cry when we walk in. Pres and Natalia are with Yáhsháyôn and me. It makes this better when Prez and Cort show right behind us. The Brothers are loud with appreciation for the Ops Controls. Keesog runs beer to us.

I snag his cut before he can take off and hug him. "I'm honored I got to see Badass shining through,

Brother. We wouldn't have made it with all we got without you."

I hold on when he jumps hugging me again. "Thanks, Uncle Mase. I felt it today."

Dakota lets out a war cry that has everyone quiet.

Prez holds up his beer. "For my part, eleven recovery teams will not be stealing women or kids. Protectors retrieved information about forty-two recoveries so far, there are more documents because there always are, but human trafficking took a major blow today. That blow was dealt by Justice's planning, Alder's stealth and Mase's internal flame for right."

Everyone laughs. Kateri tightens her hold at my waist. I shake my head with a smile on my face. Prez looks at Cort.

Cort holds his beer up. "I don't do status but my part was watching the Protectors stop fourteen recovery teams and collect files. For the second it was watching Mase keep his cool while burning with anger for the kingpin of trafficking in our part of the country. I have to tell you, Brothers, every job was done above and beyond expectations. Every position was manned perfectly and I am honored you're all so fucking Badass."

The Brothers are loud.

I look for Keesog and throw, *'I'm not the only one that noticed, good fuckin' job, Brother.'* He throws me chin with tears in his eyes.

Cort looks at Pres.

I smile when he holds his beer up. "I think this is a new tradition, major Ops in multiple locations will have status. My Brothers, you've heard. Grand totals are 37 recovery teams and 42 to reclaim. We are not done. Reclaim means reintroduce to a normal life where Badass rules and slavery is *not* an option. We'll need help and I know my Brothers won't let me down. Your Brothers worked hard, be proud, be honored and be glad we're fucking Badass."

The Club erupts. I hug my girl thanking her for lighting the fire in me so I could help today. She doesn't let go and I realize she's crying.

I push to the backdoor. "Talk to me, Yáhsháyôn. My heart is going wild here."

She takes her face out of my neck and shakes her head. "You have forty-two to reclaim, they'll be free. You all did that. You stopped the people stealing women and kids. I'm so proud and humbled by all the Clubs do, for all *you* do. Thank you for every single person you saved today."

I squeeze her while she wipes under her eyes. "Anything for my Yáhsháyôn and those women and kids. You lit the flame for that passion in me and every Team that ran today, baby. Women and kids are going to be found and given a home where they're safe and valued. Thank you."

She shakes her head. "Take me back in and put me down."

I push and set her down in front of Aylen. "Brother, you're just like Justice. I'm honored you were my pilot and saw pride in his eyes that you're one of ours. Be proud, Aylen. I am." I hug her feeling her happy.

Cayden, Seth, Mikey and Andrew all get words and hugs. When I see Alder sitting on the bar by Justice, I look at Kateri and point. She nods taking a step closer to Mikey and Aylen.

I get to Alder and stand in front of him. "Web is going to hit the fuckin' roof if he finds out you're in the Club, Brother."

He laughs. "I no tell. I honor to be partner to you, VP Mase."

I hug him. "So am I, Brother. You always floor me but today, the trust you showed when I was pissed and couldn't control it all," I shake my head and swallow hard, "thank you, for believing in me. I'm honored."

"I feel it."

I hug him again. "Love ya, LP."

He throws chin with tears in his eyes.

Andrew talks to Justice about staying for training. Justice looks at me.

'They don't run like we do, Brother. They need to trust in their Brothers. You're the best teacher I know for that. The wording was, 'your crew and who follows.' Those followers are showing.'

He hugs me. "You're fuckin' helping."

I nod. "Did you see Keesog at all today?"

He laughs slapping my back. "Thanks for that. I'm honored, Brother."

I throw him chin and push to Kateri's side.

Pres finds me. "You know Jordan is okay with changing Officers and Brothers in the Club. I'm not Jordan. You ain't fucking leaving, Brother, ever."

I smile. "I'm home, Kristos." I give him a second and go on. "Since the vision showed me finding my place by your side I've been waiting. Today is the start, Brother. We'll run fast, hard and fuckin' Badass for years. I'm honored to be here with a Brother I believe in for that ride. You're Kristos from now on because there are too many fuckin' Preses around to keep giving them adjectives. In my heart you'll always be Pres."

He hugs me hard. "I'm honored. Thanks, Mase." I hear and feel the emotion in his voice.

Cort hits my back fuckin' hard. "You make me look good, Brother. As much as I know this had to be killing you, you kept it together and did the job. I love the flare you put on everything."

I laugh and hug him before he throws another pun out. "Thanks, Boss. You make running Ops easy."

"I didn't say a fucking word. It was all you, Brother. Protectors don't need to be micromanaged. Location and Brothers at their backs is all they need. You all prove it daily. I'm honored to be the Brother at your back, Mase."

"It's because we know you're there that we run as easy as we do. You got Prez with me before I needed him. You had lunch waiting as the Brothers showed. Paired me with Cayden because he's right-handed. Taking care of us is a big part of why and how we get shit done, Brother. You make it easy. We feel it and respond in kind."

He hugs me.

Prez is smiling on the side of us. He hugs me when Cort lets me go. "At fifteen, you had my attention. Now, I'm so fuckin' proud I don't have enough words. You're home, you're happy and you're fuckin' Badass as it gets. I'm stealing from your dad, he'd be saying it anyway. Fuckin' proud, so fuckin' proud, Mase."

I hug him again because I can't talk feeling that deep.

He hits my back. "Love ya, Brother."
"Love ya, Prez."

I feel Kateri's arm go around my back when Prez lets me go. He smiles. "He was amazing again today, Kateri."

She smiles up at me. "I'm glad you said again. I told him how proud I am, but he doesn't see it. It's just a day in the life of Mase."

Everyone laughs agreeing.

~*~*~

Kateri

Mase took me to a Club close to the Delta Club the second time I called him. I was terrified but don't push the cloak to find out why. It was enlightening. I learned Mase is only into the dom-sub relationship and that's only in the bedroom. Sort of letting his sub get out all the naughty things she likes to do without the shame of wanting to do all the naughty stuff.

I'm a natural sub in the bedroom, wanting to please him and do things other people frown upon, but in my daily life, I like making my own decisions.

Mase is a dom that wants to take care with his sub and not dominate her every minute. Even before he brought dinner to my house, he'd ask about my day and look proud that I finished a project or got a new contract for work. He was genuinely interested in my life. Now I can see it as normal relationship progression, before I was terrified of him taking complete control over my life and time. I smile at the thought. He's Mase.

The other thing I learned is I had a lot of decisions to make. I called him sir and he said it was fine. I wanted to be called baby and he liked that too. We walked around the sex-club talking out all aspects of how we'd proceed. He liked the kneeling stance the subs assume, so I do that. He hated the leash on women but liked the collar and said he'd like that for me if we work out. He wouldn't bring me to the rooms upstairs because he didn't believe women need abuse and humiliation to get off and he'd never get off if he hurt a woman.

I think I fell in love with him that day, but I didn't know what love was so I never said.

While we ironed out our list of rules and limits, watching people play the role I wanted with him, I also realized Mase was a man I could trust and pretty much gave him complete control with only a few hard limits. Fisting, erotic asphyxiation, oral/anal play, electricity or fire play, any fear play, sharing and voyeurism. Mase threw them out saying nothing on it was his thing.

Our third time together proved that. He was demanding but never degrading or selfish, he got off on me getting off and spanked my behind for not following his instructions. Since I was bound, not following instructions could have gotten me hurt. I like that he cared enough to make sure I didn't get hurt and was embarrassed that I enjoyed being spanked then told how pretty the color was.

He's always telling me how good or pretty I am. Compliments are not something I've heard a lot of apparently. I like hearing them now. I like pleasing a man that treats me like I matter and I love being his next breath in and out of the bedroom.

I hear him walking this way and move back into position making sure my shoes are directly in front of my knees. My head is bowed before he takes a step in the room.

"As beautiful as that sight is, I need your attention as my equal, Yáhsháyôn." He puts his hand out and I take it standing.

"Yes, thank you, Sir." I step into the heels and he lifts me.

"My equal, Kateri. I'll spank your ass for that one later. Now, do I have your attention?" He's got my face in his hand and is holding my eyes.

"Yes, Mase."

He kisses me gently. He's not angry. "Today I realized our relationship has changed. I need you to know the old lady rules, then my rules. These are what we'd call hard limits. I also need to know if in our daily life you need more from me."

I nod not understanding all the old lady rules so this will be a help. He carries me to the stairs and sits on the landing. This is an odd place to talk but I say nothing.

He tells me of the old lady rules and I ask, "Riding behind another Brother gets him killed? Why would I and how does he die?"

His eyes crinkle on the sides. "Who said they get killed?"

"The old ladies."

He nods. "I don't ever want you on another Brother's bike. If another Brother touches you, I would consider killing him. That said, how would you feel if I pulled up and a woman was on the back of my bike?"

"I'd want to rip her hair out."

He smiles. "I'd want to set him on fire and I probably would. Another man doesn't touch what is mine.

Not all Brothers live like I do. I wouldn't touch a Brother's woman. He's my Brother and respect is earned and shown. I've got a lot of years to live and I'm not living it trying to earn respect back or a reputation down. So, no one touches what is mine and you have some responsibility in not allowing it, moving away or just telling me someone isn't listening."

"Will you kill them?" Oh my, this is worse than the old ladies said.

"I'm a reader. I can read intent and will never put you in a position that leaves you out there with Brothers that have an intent to take or hurt what is mine. Tonight, I left you with Mikey and Aylen while I talked to my Brothers. The rest of the time you were right with me. I'd never leave you alone at the Club."

That's true, he's very protective of me, which I like. I don't know the Brothers like he does so I need to trust his rules to keep me safe. "Okay. I agree to the old lady rules, if I pay my way. Joey said old ladies do half."

He nods. "I don't pay for the house because I'm an Officer. I pay for my bike to be maintained, food, gas in my truck and personal vehicle insurance. Prospect service is included for me, so I don't pay them either. Your new car will be here tomorrow, you can pay the insurance once your name change paperwork is in."

"You bought me a car?"

"An SUV so you can bring it on the dirt paths in the woods, drive in the snow and not get stuck and have enough room for the wolves. You told me you liked the hard top Wrangler. The top two best in snow are small so I picked the third which was your choice. It's not huge but I have a truck so it will work."

"Thank you. I can pay for the SUV."

He shakes his head. "You can pay for half the bills which aren't much. You can pay for anything you want that isn't a house thing. I'm going to buy what I buy and not think twice about it. Your car was stolen from the Club while you were helping take care of me. I was unconscious so I missed stopping your car from being stolen and I appreciate that you stayed and helped take care of me. I'm not fighting you over a gift I put thought into when you were *helping* me."

I nod realizing my mistake with his explanation. "I'm sorry I didn't see it as appreciation sooner. Thank you and I'll love it."

"My rules. I will decide shit without you but do that with thought or reason behind it. I want everything for you to be easy and will clear that path when I can. You should do what you love without the stress of making it to that place. If I give you a way to make happy, I'll get happy back. Ask if you don't get it. The big things that involve you will be talked about like your office. It's not mine, I have no idea what you need to be comfortable there, so it's yours to design and I'll make sure you're safe in it. The big decisions are ours. You get a say. The little shit is little shit, a car is little shit. I pay almost nothing to live here, so unless I'm jet shopping, everything is little shit."

I nod not having a problem with his reasoning and love him more for wanting me to be happy.

He goes on to his next point quickly. "An old lady is a target. I'm a Blackhawk so the target is bigger. My family name is linked to money so we're still growing that target. I've run Ops internationally stealing the Alpha-Bits from the labs they were in or from businesses they were slaves at. I'm from Princes where we ran the whole east coast and pissed off the CIA, Homeland and just about every federal branch of the military except the FBI. We ran Ops to shield readers and kids with reader ability from hate groups. Today we ran Ops against human trafficking. We've been doing it for years but today was big. We took out a whole operation and have plans to steal women and kids out of slavery. The target you now have on you is huge. I'm not a man that quits so that target is long term. After saying all that, we've lived with this our whole lives and have a proven track record of keeping our old ladies and kids safe. Badass isn't new, it isn't for the faint of heart because we don't have a problem killing anyone that threatens our families. I need you to understand your Security is important. It's not a game, it's life and death. We'll cover you, teach you how to help cover yourself and never give up if you are taken. If the old ladies talked to you, Natalia has already told you how we do that."

I just nod because they didn't tell me all the people that Badass has gunning for them.

"You need to hit for Security if you leave the house. You never go to the Clubhouses alone. You need a Team to leave the compound. You can drive yourself with a Team following or ride in a Security SUV. You let me know you're leaving the compound and let me know when you get home. That's by text. I may not answer, but I'll send an emoticon when I'm able. I run Ops regularly and can't always be close. Today I was in Wyoming twice. At the Club you heard why. The rules for old ladies are how we keep our old ladies and kids safe."

I nod again surprised he was in Wyoming, twice.

"I'm not picking clothes for you. I'm not managing your schedule. I don't expect you to cook, clean or do more than I do. I never wanted anything but an equal in an old lady. Do you need me to do something I missed in there?" He's always so direct and considerate.

"I live my life by your side and accept the Security aspect of yours." I try for simple in all he said.

He smiles. "Basically, yeah."

"I will go to training with Stella and Natalia from now on. I have nothing that I need you to do for me and I'm glad you asked. I'd like to know when you leave the state. I had no idea you were in Wyoming. Mikey ate lunch with me and I didn't know." She went to Wyoming too. That's crazy.

He nods. "I'll let you know by text and tell you when I'm back. I had lunch here at the office. Mikey can't talk about Ops. It's a way to keep details from getting out and Brothers on Ops safe." He's very reasonable.

"Do you want to change anything about the limits you set when we started?" We're done with his rules, I guess.

"No. I thought about what I originally gave you and trust you more than I believed was possible. Do you want to add anything?"

"I do." He pulls something from his breeches pocket. "A day collar that will remind us that you're mine and I have the responsibility to make sure you stay mine by showing you love, respect and honor." He holds it out for me to see.

The braided leather is thin and dainty looking but it's a rope braid that I know is not dainty in the least. The charm hanging from the center is the earth with continents and water made of gemstones. How did they do that in the size of a quarter?

"It's beautiful."

He turns it over and I cry. The symbol for wind is in the same gemstone design. He's my world and I'm his breath.

"*Kuwômôyush*, Yáhsháyôn." His voice is soft.

"*Kuwômôyush*, Nupômkoki."

He stands and puts the collar on me while I wipe my face. "Go to the spare room and wait at the door, Yáhsháyôn."

I move quickly holding my world with my fingers feeling the little bumps and ridges. I love the way he shows me love. There's a carpet in front of the door. I kneel and wait with my head bowed, shoes lined perfect to my knees and one hand on my leg, the other is still holding my world.

I hear him walking and let my world go checking that I didn't knock a shoe out of place. I try to hide my smile and excitement as he walks by me and into the room. He fiddles with something in the corner before he comes back.

Bending, he puts glasses on me. This is different. "The wrap arounds are a virtual world we can play in. It is a Club in Mass that I've never been to so we'll get to do that together."

I hear a click then voices. I don't dare look up.

"Baby."

"Thank you, Sir." I take his hand and slide the heels on. When I'm ready, he starts walking.

"We can watch, fuck with watchers in public, our room, or close the curtains and be alone. Right now, we're just looking around and deciding where I'm going to fuck you." He closes the door and walks slowly.

My breath is coming out fast, I am so excited and can't believe how many people are here. I know the room is a bedroom but it doesn't feel like it.

At the bar, a pretty blond man looks me over as if he sees me. "Are you lookin' for a partner?"

Mase looks at me so I bow my head. "I haven't decided." He turns to the bartender. "Beer."

When he turns back to me, he offers me the beer. How in the world?

"Thank you, Sir." I hide my smile and take a drink from the cold bottle. He's like a magician.

His hand goes across my stomach and he turns me so my back is to him. The hand stays right where it is and I realize I'm naked in this club. My blood runs hot, as in lava is running through my veins. Oh my.

"Let's walk, baby. Watch and stop when you're interested." His hand moves up from my stomach to my breast.

"Yes, Sir," I breathe out with my nether regions throbbing.

People are having sex everywhere. I wasn't this hot and bothered when I had clothes on at the club we walked through. Naked is definitely adding to this experience.

Turning, I see a very beautiful exotic woman put her hand on Mase's chest. He shakes his head and she moves away. I stop at the doorway to a room that has music playing. The dancers are almost naked or are naked. I take a step and moan when he pinches my nipple.

"Stop when you're interested. There is a table open." He walks and I know I'm being spanked for that one.

That's three, I think. He sits and turns me so I'm facing the room. His hand waves and a couple come over looking at me then Mase.

"Can I touch?" The man asks.

My eyes go to Mase. His eyes flash so my head bows quickly. Oh my. Four.

"I could use help holding her while I give her the spanking she deserves."

The woman slides her hand right down my front *and I feel it.* My mouth opens so I can breathe without hyperventilating. "She's very beautiful."

Mase agrees, "She is but is distracted and forgot her place here." He lifts my chin up and commands, "Turn and bend at the waist so only your head is on the table, baby."

"Yes, Sir." I do as I'm told and lay my head on the table feeling very exposed and extremely excited.

"Arms up." He commands and my arms move. He cuffs me so I'm stretched out.

Hands are touching me all over. "That's a good sub," the man says and I know his firmer hands are on my behind moving up.

How is he doing this? I should be begging him not to stop.

"Do you like people watching your pretty kitty being pet, baby?"

I asked him to find a less offensive name for my vagina and he always uses kitty. It should be insulting but I love it.

"Yes, Sir. It's very exciting."

Hands touch me *there* and I jump.

"Don't offend our new friends, baby. They're showing appreciation for your beautiful body."

"I'm sorry for offending our new friends and being disrespectful to you, Sir," I whisper out while trying to hold a moan in.

"Still, baby."

"Yes, Sir."

Hands cup my breasts and I brace my feet before I fall to my knees. I know Mase's hands as they slide on my behind, the hands on my breasts don't stop.

"Count for me, Yáhsháyôn."

I take a breath knowing what's coming. The slap jolts something in me and I moan at the pleasure the pain feels like it unveils. "One," I breathe.

~*~*~

Mase

The glasses make everything look so fuckin' real. My hand slides down her ass and dips into her pussy. She's dripping and all I've done is slap her ass. I smile thinking of another hand on her while I slap her again.

"Two." Her body shakes with need. I love seeing it.

The woman sits on the floor and I moan. Jesus fuck.

"So pretty, baby." My hand rubs her ass while I unbutton my breeches. "You like your nipples sucked while I'm spanking you, baby?"

"Yes, Sir." She's loud and more people come over to watch. I slap her ass and slide my fingers in her. "Three." She doesn't lose track.

I hold her hips up trying to follow every hand on her so she feels it. "So wet for me, baby. I need to fuck you right here."

"Please, Sir." Kateri is feeling it.

"What a good sub. I can hold her open for you." Jesus, the woman's hands look like they're on Kateri's fine ass.

I slide in trying to keep the hands on her and mouth on her tit. She moans and I'm way past ready. "Yáhsháyôn, so fuckin' ready."

The crowd talks so I let them while I fuck my girl with an audience. It doesn't take long for her body to clench.

"Hold it, baby," I breathe out in between the crowd critique.

They're getting *me* hot and I know they aren't real. A man starts fuckin' his woman right on the side of me and I'm losing it.

"Those hands and mouth on you, baby, is doing me in."

She moans and it isn't one of her soft whispered moans.

I'm gone. "Let go, baby."

She convulses around me causing my body to bend forward.

"My fuckin' good girl. One more."

"Mase!"

I move then freeze emptying into her. Holyfuckinshit. My arms wrap around her.

"Fuckin' beautiful, Yáhsháyôn." Reaching, I uncuff her and bring her to the floor with me.

With a hand across her front, I get the wrap around off her and switch it off. I slide mine off and put them on the table feeling like my energy emptied out of me. Too much at once. I'll tone it down next time.

I smile looking at my girl. No I won't. I'll give her everything, always.

Chapter Eight

Two days

Mase

Running the property in the dark with Kimuks is a new favorite. The fuckin' dog has endurance, I'll give him that. I tell him everything that goes through my head or I stay quiet and just feel the land under my feet, my body moving, my place in my world. He never complains either way. I stop at the stream running through the foothills closer to Honor's compound. Kimuks drinks but doesn't waste time or fill up. Maybe he was a marathoner in a past life. Hearing the buzz of the drones, I smile.

"Some Brothers thought Honor Rising was a pussy name. Fuckin' Brothers don't get it. Our beginning is here, Kimuks. Honor is rising and we'll all start feeling it soon. It's just the beginning and it already feels great. I'm settling with my Club, Pres, the ancestors. Home feels good, Brother. I hope you and Numuks feel it."

We're quiet coming around the south side of the compound and pass my Yáhsháyôn's circle. I need to show Pres the circle so it doesn't get disrespected by Brothers not understanding. He can tell them at Church.

Kimuks races ahead of me. "Fuckin' show off."

The laugh has me stopping fuckin' quick. "Pres?"

"Kristos, yeah, Brother. Did he beat you?"

I smile seeing him walk my way. "He did. You're up early."

He nods. "There's something here. The office feels right, home. Here it's different. There's a peace to the trees, at times I hear water, animals. I don't normally walk the paths down. I go around the compound but always feel it here."

"I feel it. Come down. I need to ask a favor while you're here. Two favors. Before we go down, Kateri needs an office and place to do her drawing. Can we use this clearing for a building for that?"

"Whatever she needs. You need Security out here."

I love my Brother. I nod and walk down the path. "I'll get it covered. The second is the circle. I was pissed and knocking trees down. Justice used a picture Kateri connected to her ancestors with and laid it out for her and for me. I don't use it but feel it. She can connect to her people here. She's been down every day since I showed her."

I stop talking and look back. He's stopped on the path. "Brother?"

His eyes find mine in the dark. "Sacred circle. The mix shows our religion, I guess. One religion, the Great spirit that guides and enforces for Mother Earth, a living being that gives us life, purpose, home."

Holy shit. Kimuks sits leaning against my leg. I look from him to Kristos waiting for more. He takes the steps and I know he isn't seeing me. He's looking at the wood around the circle, the stones just inside the wood, then four elements, four directions.

"The earth for this warrior, there can be no greater love." He turns fast. "You're teaching us, showing us, guiding us?"

And he thought he was just a reader. I smile. "Whatever you need, Brother."

He shakes his head. "Don't do that, not here. You're here for more than the Club, aren't you?"

Shit. '*Justice?*'

'*I'm up, Brother. I need two.*'

Coming into the center of the element stones I kneel. "Justice is on his way." I point him to kneel between south and east. Justice's crow lands on the stone with wind. "Show off."

He laughs becoming him. Kristos is shocked. Justice kneels between north and west. Teller shows and fills in beside me. Justice starts with a whole fuckin' lesson about the vision and great seers. I close my eyes and feel my ancestors close. I love that. When I hear Lame Deer's '*mankind is on a path of self-destruction*' words, I open my eyes and pay attention. I love the next part, '*we cannot harm any part of her without hurting ourselves.*' I smile feeling it.

Justice and Teller go on about the great leaders, great seers and great warriors.

Kristos stops Justice mid-sentence. "You're a great Leader, Mucimi a great seer, Mase a great warrior. The great means gifted?"

Justice nods. "Through every generation we've had more and more gifted. Pres, Danny and Knight at the beginning. Pres sees like Alder without reader ability, but he has it. With Prez, he was gifted Jacob, the Protector of the Three. He has a teacher in Christian, Taylor, my dads - Dakota and Jessie. Then the great Princess Aiyana."

Kristos nods. "You have more. Every kid is yours like the 'rents are Ben Knight's. Ben Knight is Ben James'. You're Ben Knight's."

I shake my head. "It's not that simple. We're all Ben Knight's and Ben James' but I'm Justice's warrior. I'm Cort's warrior, I'm your warrior, Brother. Our world is a living breathing being. Shaping mankind is not left to one. This is generations sped up." I smile. "Ten-year spans show ability that's never been seen in Indians or not all seen in one Indian."

He nods. "The fire?"

Teller answers for me. "He has all Christian's ability plus the fire, healing and Leader. Nash will be his second and stronger in ability."

"Wait. His second?"

Justice nods. "All Protectors will work for all BSC. They'll move around when and where they're needed to protect our collective beliefs."

Kristos looks over the stones. "Stopping the self-destructive path. You got bikers, readers, the FBI, Masons, genetically altered, now the push is Indians."

I shake my head. "We aren't pushing anything. Touching many different cultures and beliefs is happening naturally through seeing what we do and why we do it. It's easy for people to jump on board for a cause like modern slavery, witch hunts, growing people. Selling kids has been going on forever. Mass graves full of indigenous kids are on the news reminding us the kids are still being stolen. People are pissed now because it's hitting close to their homes, their kids. It has to stop and they'll help now."

He nods. "This isn't told to everyone. Why me?"

"You're another Leader with ability. Since Mase has been close, those abilities are showing. You don't just see like Alder anymore. Every Leader needs a second. For me Teller is my right hand, without him I am nothing, with

257

him I am more. Add Mucimi, Mase, Luke-Rayne, Nash, you get it. We're nothing without our Brothers. Badass is never alone, once Wall understood, our Indians started teaching *Be Fuckin' Badass*."

Prez sits. "It's effective."

I look down fast. "You didn't know all this before they moved?"

He sees the LS boards. Prez smiles. "I don't need everything Justice and Teller get and they have reasons I'm not challenging. I have Christian, Aiyana, Jeremy, Aubrey, you see it. We don't change every vision because we've seen what happens when we do. Aubrey was sold from two to five. She was our lesson. We're not perfect and fuck-up like everyone else. We try to keep it to a minimum." He smiles. "The board wasn't a fuck-up so much as not getting information. I could blame everyone I asked – for not understanding, or move on and use it with the knowledge Mikey has. I moved on. There are things that look different when you see the whole picture. It's a lesson we learned from Ben James that teaches us not to judge when we don't get that full picture."

Kristos looks embarrassed. "No disrespect intended. I knew you didn't understand but didn't see the reason. This is my lesson that I don't need the reason. I trust in my Brothers because I have no reason not to. I'll show that honor by learning the lessons of my father and you, Ben Knight."

"Jesus, I feel his ability growing. Maybe you shouldn't have done this here. We have a meet then I'm on Mase duty while he gets shit from Alder." Prez stands making me laugh.

"We got shower, food and explaining time. I'll be there, Prez."

He nods. "I'm eating at your house."

Kristos calls in. "I'm going to get Natalia. She's at IT today."

"The circle?" I ask before he forgets.

He stops. "I'll make it known not to fuck with it. Between my eyes and your fire, no one will fuck with it. I swear they think Spano is here to keep our shit from blowing the place sky high." He turns and jogs up the path.

Prez cracks up. "He'll get it. I did."

Justice rises and kisses his head. "Thank fuck you did. I'm out. Later." He's a bird in the wind.

Prez shakes his head. "I'm never seeing normal."

I pull him to the house hearing Teller laughing. "Normal is overrated, Prez." I let him go and walk in smiling.

~*~*~

Hemy comes in and I laugh. His shirt says, *Next!* He shrugs. "I like it. I get new shirts every time I'm here."

Cort laughs coming down the stairs. His shirt says Next! with Phoenix on the sleeve.

Aaron comes down and sits by me. He's worried about the kids leaving. I take his arm surprising him. "Thanks, Brother. Christian always wanted healer. Is he pissed at you?"

I laugh. "Nah. He's seen so much he didn't want it after all the other shit he was dealing with. It's a good line for a smile so he still uses it."

Prez gets our attention. Justice, Falcon and Teller show on the floor and he rolls his eyes. Teller and Falcon sit. Mass, Virginia and Prince Protectors and Presidents are here. I don't count the stooges.

Ricky stands looking at the kids with their excitement bubbling out and everyone quiets.

Prez throws chin and looks around. "Presidents that are fighting to right the wrongs across the country need help. They'd make it through but depleting resources and losing Brothers is unnecessary when we have the answer right here. It's taken a while to get here but we're here. It's time to once again band together and work as one. Justice."

Prez steps aside and Justice steps forward holding his hands up like he's framing his face on the top and bottom. Jacob appears in hologram form talking to Cort. Justice opens his arms and they appear above him. Jacob's voice gets louder..."*The ancestors gifted Justice with your insight and abilities as much as mine or Christian's. He is a Leader. He's always been a Leader and will continue leading his people, that's his crew and whoever follows. That doesn't have much to do with you on the surface because he's already doing that. You took him as a second, knowing his leadership and abilities need to be understood and used for the Club's purpose. It is the same as the vision's purpose.*" Justice claps his hands over his head and the hologram is gone. How fuckin' cool is that?

Everyone in the room is quiet. "That was at the reservation the day the ancestors gifted me with more crazy shit. The part that's important to you is the sentence, '*He's always been a leader and will continue to lead his people, that's his crew and whoever follows.*' Prez thought you needed all of it but that sentence is important right here." He pauses giving Prez a quick look.

"Every Prince, MC BSC West kid, as we're still called, are my crew starting today. You will all be trained, you will all work your Clubs, you will all jump nightly strengthening our bond. I'll say that again, strengthening OUR bond. There is no competition, there is no rivalry, there are no secrets. I read everyone. I know until yesterday Keesog didn't understand what being part of a BSC Protector Crew meant. I see him in visions becoming a great teacher for the BSC, training the kids being born now. Destiny has more abilities gifted and just started learning her value to us and to civilians we swore to protect when we bought into their communities. Aylen," He shakes his head, "She's got it all and will use it as a President in two years. Nash will be a VP within a year. We have the need. You have the ability. Every one of my old crew is waiting with their hands out. We need you to step up and show us how you can help. Destiny, what did you have to do to see the value you bring to the table?"

Destiny stands. "Jump with the crew. Use what I know in a more focused way. Spend time with my Brothers and see I didn't know as much as I thought I did. We're all readers. I thought I read everyone," she shakes her head, "I wasn't even close. I'm learning and see how I wasn't much help to anyone. Being that help shows me I have more to give. I'm shooting for VP, I'm no President." She smiles when the kids laugh.

"Kutomá, what have you learned?"

She stands bowing. I laugh at the clown. "I'm a Lead. I ran a Team and they made me proud. Having the connection helps build a trust I didn't know we needed. We need to jump together. It's all little stuff really, but the little stuff makes a big difference. I watched Justice's teams run the two main ops and they hardly talk. They know they can trust each other to do a job, they know they have each other's backs and show a confidence I've never seen as clearly as I do now. It's easy crap but we better learn it. Justice believed I could be a Lead and showed me that I can. I've always wanted to be a trainer. When I get home, I'm asking for it. I can train and Lead a Team. It will keep me learning for my trainees." She bows and sits.

"Keesog." Justice calls.

He stands smiling with his eyes on me. "I always jump. It was never with my Brothers. Kutomá is right. It takes no effort on our part to be the best us we can. We already are. I think Justice sees us different because he gets visions we don't. We need to be the best us while working together and helping the vision. Without a purpose we're just taking up space. I can say it because I'm probably the biggest pain in the ass around." He looks at me. "Until yesterday. I didn't do much but it's shit that everyone can't do. *I can*, I did and it felt amazing. I'm gifted with so much that doesn't mean much to me, but it should. It means everything to the women we found yesterday and the women and kids that never get taken because I sent an empty box to Justice and helped scan files. My abilities are a gift and I forgot that they need to be used for our shared purpose. I'm staying and learning everything I can, so I can be a Lead too." He throws chin to Justice and every kid takes note.

Justice smiles. "If I can get Keesog to see his worth, no argument you throw will stick."

Everyone laughs. He raises his hand. "We need to be organized to be effective. Protectors will move around when the need arises. This week it's here. We need Teams to do this. I will train you so we can see where you fit. Keesog is right, I see you differently than you do. I know Phoenix is a Leader. He's IT and should be leading there. He's got more organizational skills than I do. I need your help, Brother, and I need it fuckin' quick."

Phoenix stands. "Anything, always."

I look down breathing deep. Fuckin' sweet. Justice goes on for a minute then looks back.

Prez steps up. "Presidents, the kids will move around. You will see some take Officer positions in different Clubs. They will work regular Club jobs like they always have. Now it's with a focused purpose and a direct Lead. You are always their President, but they have more that you don't understand and need Leads that help in those areas. They will get covered when they need it. Your help will be needed. We have Brothers ready to step in. I have been known to run a Club or training when I'm needed, sometimes when I'm not. One thing that I noted yesterday, some of the Protectors are expending energy shielding their abilities. We shield nothing. They will learn to use what they have, every time they need it. We don't hold back and they can save that energy for the job." He smiles. "Ask for what you need. We'll send help. If you have questions, stay, if not, you're dismissed."

The New Hampshire President makes the floor first. I go to Ricky and hug him.

"Glad you're okay, Brother. I was worried."

I step back and nod. "Everyone was. Most don't see what's next." I smile pointing at Falcon's shirt.

He laughs. "They're fuckin' nuts. Christian said you got Keesog working."

I shake my head. "Justice put him on the Op."

He laughs. "Okay. How is your girl?"

"Good. She loves the old ladies and crew."

"Jeti loves her already. Cayden and Lukas are excited. They love the way this is working."

I nod. "They're all good kids." I'm jumped with knees in my back and an arm around my throat. Knowing it's fuckin' Keesog, I flip him, pull him closer and hold him down when he lands. I moved nothing on my body to do it knowing I got his attention. "Respect is shown always. While I am an elder in the Club, talking to a President, I am shown respect. While I'm shown that respect, your patience to wait, honor to a President and elder will be noted. Being happy and excited is as it should be. You did a good fuckin' job yesterday. Today, learn patience, honor and respect."

He nods looking terrified. I look at Ricky. He shrugs. "It's the fire."

I stand and close my eyes.

"Suffice it to say, Mase isn't putting up with disrespect." Aaron has my eyes opening. Shit, everyone is turned this way. "He's worked Ops since he was fifteen and has seen it all. Don't fuckin' piss him off, Brothers. He doesn't give a shit who your father is."

I smile. Christian flashes on the screen. "Thanks, Mase. Tell Alder he needs two rooms." He's gone and I crack up.

Jordan puts a hand out for Keesog. "You show him you learned by telling him."

Keesog turns to me as if he's a puppet. "I won't disrespect you again, Uncle Mase. This ain't the time or place for monkeying around."

I throw him chin. "It's not and I'm not the Brother you surprise with that shit."

"I saw it. Never again."

I laugh and pull him closer. "Good job, Brother."

He smiles walking to Case and Oliver.

Prez comes to me. "It's time."

I turn. Cort and Alder are at the door. I push and look back at Justice. He throws me chin. '*Call if you need me.*'

Throwing chin, I warn, then pull them to the meeting room.

Prez sits at the table smiling. Cort doesn't care and paces. I shrug. Alder pulls his little pack off and starts typing. "Pres Cort, Pres Kristos, Pres Major, Boss Nova, Parker, Boss Kateri share DNA markers."

Cort stops moving. Prez stands. I shake my head. "How?"

"Cousin, distant cousin, Pres Cort closest." Alder is hedging.

I watch Cort. "Rex? That's how Kateri knew my dad and Crow. This is some shit. How do Parker and Nova fit there?"

"Tie to Crow. Major, Jordan, Kristos?" I throw out but don't see it, it's a guess.

Prez shakes his head. "Christian."

He shows on the screen. "I got like a minute."

"Keesog is here." Prez makes me smile.

"Running Ops without Protectors isn't easy, Prez. I've got less than a minute."

265

"Go, Brother." He smiles. "Teller."

Teller shows and sits on the side of me. I don't waste time. "Kateri shares blood with Cort and Crow."

"She's Rex's granddaughter. Her grandmother hid the daughter then Kateri. She saw the daughter taken and then saw when she died. She went to Crow. He got Reed to meet Kateri and made plans to keep her safe until they checked out the story. The grandmother was killed right on the reservation. Crow knew but no body was found. He had a Mason step in and take care of Kateri. Ben T died, Crow died and Kateri was gone." He stops talking.

There's always more. Who isn't named? Heam, Brekan. "Wait, Crow and Heam were related?"

Teller looks offended. "Half-Brothers. You're going back a lot of years. Indian women had a lot of kids and they weren't all by the same man."

"Because that would be too easy." I roll my eyes at him.

He stands. "You lived with one mom and dad. How many Blackhawks can say that?"

I nod. "Point taken, Brother. My family has always been just mine. The stories are just stories when you've never lived it. I'll remember and show more respect."

He smiles. "If you weren't so fuckin' good at everything, I'd blast the fuck out of you."

"You've always got Keesog to look forward to." I watch his eyes roll and ask, "What is our biggest take away here?"

"Rex had a kid, his girl was sold, his granddaughter was sold. Reed knew, Crow knew. His granddaughter doesn't know family and isn't going to trust those ties without proof. There is no proof. Distant ties mean nothing to a slave that's got more cloaked memories than ones she can remember."

I'm up and holding his throat to the wall. "She is *not* a fuckin' slave anymore!"

Cort holds my wrist and pulls my hand back. Prez holds my head to his. "Look at who you're pissed at, Brother. He means no disrespect to you or Kateri. He was making the point that she has no ties that she can remember but bits and pieces of her grandmother. It was not to hurt you."

"Fuck!" I bend and breathe.

Warm calm hits me then I feel his hand on the back of my head. "I deserve that after giving you shit. That was a brutal way to put it. I was making the point for Cort and didn't think about how it would hit you. My intention is never to hurt my Brothers. Intentions don't help once it's out. I'm sorry, Brother. I hope that helps."

I stand still breathing heavy but hug him.

He steps back looking at my fiery arms. "This is a risk but you need it. Kateri can't push the cloaks to look for ties. You were right about there being more. That more will hurt her in ways we can't take back. There is a tie coming that will bring Rex and Kateri together. Give them that happy ending, they don't need this one or how."

There's a warning in there that I don't need to push. I nod. "Thanks and sorry, Brother."

He smiles, rises up and kisses my head then is gone. I shake my head thinking about the warning. Cort has his arms crossed over his chest. He's not happy.

I nod at him. "I can't push for more with the warning. I was pissed but Prez is right, Teller would shield me with his life. Whatever is coming is big and the how isn't important, but it will make them both happy. This news can only hurt them both. Rex is a good man and doesn't need another loss. It would be Kateri's mother and Kateri. I'm not losing her for an answer on how, Brother. They'll get the family connection in a way that doesn't need the how."

He looks down. He's feeling it.

Trying to ease that, I throw more out, "I get this is a loss to you. We'll get there but it can't be today. There is no reason you can't build a relationship with Kateri while we're waiting for what's next. Tell me how and I'll help that any way I can."

He nods. "I don't get how Brothers want what you all have. I never heard of visions before and I fucking hate the play it out shit. My reality is I have a cousin that was sold as a slave and has no one to claim her now that she's found. My only blood relative is Rex. He has no clue." He shakes his head. "She has family for her wedding and we can't tell her. She'll go through it thinking she's alone and we'll sit and watch. How is vision helping here?"

Mucimi slides in as if he's on a baseball field. "Teller's wrong. Grandmother hid Kateri with Crow when sister was stolen. File doesn't have it. Fake Masons wanted Badass off the reservation so they could get kids. Sister is Kathryn Sarah T. Died last year; her boy is three being raised for a slave in Arizona."

Cort lifts Mucimi up. "Where in Arizona?"

Mucimi closes his eyes. "Navajo Nation southwest of Canyon de Chelly. Away from the tribe. There," he points to the map on the board. "House is three boys. Two girls in Nevada with two old slaves. I can't see it."

Cort hugs him. "Thank you. I take back the vision shit." He looks at Prez and me. "We've got Ops to run."

I'm up and ready. Alder stops us all. "Pres Cort, I partner VP Mase?"

Cort nods. "We may need a doctor. Thanks, Brother."

Alder runs. "Ten minute. I change."

"Justice!" Prez yells.

I jog behind them pulling my coat off. "Teller, I need a Badass shirt and ammo." I'm in one of my shirts because I'm not scheduled for Ops today.

Justice shows. "Fuckin' hell. I'll get a Team together. We need a place for the women and girls before we bring them in. Alder's going? Fuck. Mase, you got this?" He's reading to catch up to Prez and Cort's half-made plans.

"Yeah." I hit the keypad following them into Ops.

"Nash, Aylen. Destiny, Kyler, Cayden, Case, Keesog, Kutomá. Two for cover, Mase."

"Mikey and Andrew or Heath." I throw seeing the map on the wall. IT is fuckin' good.

"Ben, are you running Ops?" Cort asks.

Oh shit. Prez smiles. "Aaron and Justice can run. I'm with you."

My eyes whip to Justice. His eyes close as he breathes. "I need another chopper and crew," I tell Justice getting his eyes open.

Prez and Cort walk out like Ops isn't being planned in three minutes. Mucimi has Luke-Rayne by the arm dragging him to stand in front of Justice. I hold my laugh.

"I need a chopper and crew, stealth and Protectors." Justice doesn't miss a beat.

Luke-Rayne is amused. "Jeti is off and you got a shit load of kids looking to prove themselves."

Justice closes his eyes and opens to all Protectors. "I have the location on three boys held in Arizona being groomed as slaves. One has a tie to Kateri. I need three crews. Nash, Jeti, Aylen, on stealth. Destiny, Kyler, Cayden, Case, Keesog, Kutomá, Mikey, Heath, Andrew, Blake, Axe, Indie, Colt. On top of the rescue planned, Prez and Cort are assisting. Their protection is assumed by every one of you. Gear up. Meet Mase, your Lead, at the chopper pads in front. You have ten. Protectors that are not on a chopper can help, we have no surveillance or plan and need IT." He rolls his eyes then nods at Phoenix coming through the door. "We need a place and plan for two women and two girls. The Preses are adding to our rescue. Assistance when we return and anything else you can think of is appreciated. Teller, when you're done, I need help, Brother."

Mucimi doesn't give Justice a second to breathe. "They're already planning it. I'm going. I can help on the chopper and shield Cort."

I pull Mucimi toward the door. I'm going to need help. "Gear up."

He turns to Justice. "Goshute. White Pine County Nevada. Cort said he's not leaving them when we'll be close."

Aaron and Ranger run in. I keep pushing Mucimi out. Luke-Rayne is laughing.

My fuckin' life is crazy, I don't feel bad, Justice's is crazier. I text Kateri that I'm on Ops in Arizona then Nevada and don't know when I'll be back. She sends me a salute. Then a heart.

~*~*~

Kateri

I open the door to Seren and Caelan. I take the little guy before she takes a step in. "I'm glad you're here. I just finished for the day and haven't decided on what to do."

She smiles. I can't believe she's not a model. "Thanks for letting us in. Cort said he's meeting me here. He didn't say when, just that I'm supposed to get here. Ranger had a chopper waiting for me." She shakes her head in a way that says she sees the crazy in that.

"Do you want a drink? I can make lunch."

She drops the bag as big as a suitcase and sits. "No. I need to talk to you before everyone gets here. The east coast people are crazy and weird."

I nod because I've seen it.

"Aiyana called me on the tablet Cort uses at the house. She asked that I get here and explain because men are crazy and think women are weak. Mind you, this was before I got the text from Cort then Ranger."

"That is weird."

"Yes, it is. Anyway, I'm supposed to tell you to keep the cloaks in place because what lies beneath is not something you should think or share, it's unbelievable and deadly or something like that. It gave me chills."

I nod and tell her the mantra,

"Because some thoughts don't need to be shared
Because some thoughts are too hard to believe
Because some thoughts can be deadly."

Her eyes are huge. "That's freaking scary. She said that. The cloak hides that and you'll be hurt if the cloak uncovers those thoughts. It's a hurt that you and Mase will never recover from. I got the feeling this was more about Mase, but I don't know why. He's pretty tame compared to the rest of them."

"I know why. Anything that hurts me can crush him. The gifts have him off balance when it comes to me."

She nods and takes my hand. "That makes sense for that part. Cort would react the same way so I get that. The next is unbelievable. You had a twin, she was taken with your mother when you were born. Your grandmother went to Crow for help. She was a seer and saw you being taken. Since Crow was known to help Indians and refugees, she went there. Your grandmother died and Crow had a Mason taking care of you. He was Indian and used your last name as a cover, I guess. She just said he took your name. He found something and called for help meeting your uncle, Reed. Reed had a twin, Rex, he's your grandfather and lives in my freaking house. This is where it's hurtful, but Aiyana said you're stronger than the men are. Your sister had a boy, he's three. She died last year but the boy is alive and needs a home, you are his closest living relative."

I hold my heart. I had a twin and she died. "Tell me they're on an Op to get him."

She smiles with tears in her pretty blue eyes making them shine like jewels. "They are. He's with two other boys being trained to be slaves."

No. I breathe feeling warm cotton surround me. "Not one more member of my family will live like that again. Who do I need to call to get stuff for three boys?"

She smiles wiping the tears from my face. "Aiyana was right. I'm glad I didn't chicken out. It's not Badass and Aiyana said I had to be fucking Badass. I found it funny because she talks so calm and proper."

I smile but it doesn't answer my question. "She does. Who do I call?"

"No one. Aiyana said the Brothers will handle everything because they think women are weak. Since they're pig headed, we're supposed to let them do the work. According to her, our job is to rein in our tempers while they act like Neanderthals."

I laugh thinking she may have something. "It's a good plan. She's been around them longer than me so I'll go with that."

"Men are crazy. While we wait for that to begin, what did you think of the clothes ritual thing?"

I shake my head. Three boys running with Mase are closer than I thought. She wants to distract me. She doesn't know how ready I am to have that family of my own, so I answer, "It's a good thing drinks are part of it. Who needs that many anything and how did it start? I'd love to know the stories behind that. Natalia knows how they all got together. They had wars during every match up."

She lifts Caelan and kisses his head. "I'm glad that's not how it works here. They're crazy enough without wars regularly. I'm married to king crazy so I know."

"Kate, Jess, Danny and Knight!"

The wolves jump up to greet the new people. We look at the door then each other. She can't hold it in, so we laugh.

~*~*~

Mase

Justice had us pick up the women and girls first since they had no guard. How he knew that wasn't asked. I'm impatient to get to the boys. Kateri's nephew is still in the hands of traffickers.

Alder hits my arm showing me the plan and layout on his hologram board. It looks like a long bunkhouse. I throw it to the Teams. Prez says Keesog has it for them. That kid has skillz. I ask for questions getting none. They're Protectors, they shouldn't have any questions.

As we get closer Mucimi is up looking out the window. *'What's wrong?'*

'There's more. I only saw the boys. There's more.' His tears fall.

I'm up and hugging him. *'We'll get them out.'*
"Ops."

"I see it, Brother. Four. Medics needed." *'Two teen girls, one boy, woman pregnant.'* Justice is tuned into Mucimi so he's got it.

I throw to the Teams. *'Women only on the women. Two teens, one pregnant woman. Destiny, you'll be needed with her. Blake, adjust to keep Preses covered.'*

Hearing the rogers, I look at Alder. "Cayden will carry your bag."

He nods and pulls it out from under his seat. *'Keesog, you'll be needed for the woman on that chopper. Do you need energy?'*

'I'm okay but think I will if I'm healing and shielding.'

274

"Ops."

'Teller has it.'

Keesog is cute. *'Thanks, I don't know how to throw and pull like Uncle Jeremy.'*

I feel for him. *'Teller will throw energy to you, we need you healing, we'll get you whatever you need to do that. Tell Teller what you need.'*

'Thanks, Uncle Mase. I'll tell him.'

"In three." Aylen gives us time. *'I can throw if Keesog needs it.'*

'On the chopper, your dad can throw.' I give her.

'Forgot about dear old dad.' She makes me laugh.

Prez doesn't sound like he's laughing. *'Old?'*

'Shit, love ya, Dad.'

The Protectors try to hide their laughing. I bend and Alder climbs on my back.

"Readied." *'Blake, we're on the other side. If you need me, throw it. Let's show them fuckin' Badass, Protectors.'*

"Roger," Blake answers.

"Shield the choppers and Preses." I look back at Alder.

"Readied." Alder likes the one word today.

Cayden opens the door and holds his arm out. I take it and jump. We're shooting within three steps. I'm glad that's all we need to get through the first door. Shots are fired from the other end but we keep moving. It looks like a stable with bays of hay.

"Stop!" Alder has me bending. He runs back a bay.

"Keep going," I say to Cayden as Colt and Destiny come in. "Colt, stick with CC, keep going."

I move to Destiny and Alder. Jesus, the pregnant woman is in a bed of hay. I'm not sure what he can get in a minute but times up. "Alder."

"Alive. Chopper, stat."

Great. "CC, I'm transporting."

Cayden answers quick. "Roger. Boy about twelve. I need, forget it, she showed."

"I'll be three." I lift the woman, that smells like she sleeps in a stable and bend for Alder. He climbs on and I push, pulling wind around us.

Keesog is waiting. "Go, I got her." He waves his hand in front of his nose.

"Wind. Figure a way to clean her. She was left in a stall like an animal."

He's disgusted by that and puts his hands over her gently. She calms before he's even bent to kiss her head. "I'll take care of her and the baby."

Alder gives me a nod.

I turn seeing the scared women from Nevada. "Help where you can. Alder is a doctor. Keesog a healer. We have more. Destiny."

She holds my arm and I push.

"CC?" I step to him.

"Colt's got the boy going to two." He points to the girls.

Mikey is getting a shackle off one. The other is on the floor trying to be small.

I take off my coat and shirt. "Give me your shirt, CC." I hand mine to Destiny and put my coat back on. "Status."

"Removing manacles. Third located by Prophet. Prez transported one to two. Masters on three packages." Blake sounds calm but I hear shots.

"Covering, searching." Axe isn't much for small talk.

"Prophet, on one, Destiny, on two, Keesog, three. Split medics. LP is on three."

I get rogered hearing a shot and Axe calls clear.

Mikey gets Cayden's shirt on her girl.

I lift the other girl with Indie. "We gotta go."

Destiny takes the girl Mikey has and we push.

"Board." I order and drop my scared girl with Destiny. Stepping out quick, I tell her, "Call if you need me."

She rogers but is already throwing calm at the girls.

We need to move. "Status."

"Masters needs a minute." Fuck. "One is short two and me on three," Blake comes back.

"One short a giant and tot." Cayden gets a chuckle.

"Two readied," Destiny answers.

"Three readied when Blake shows." Keesog sounds distracted.

I find Cort with a small boy in his arms. Blake is standing at the far end of a worse stable.

"Company in eight." Justice has to make this better.

"Two, three, lift. Two, cover."

They roger. "Boss?"

He shakes his head. I see what's playing in there. His family lived here like an animal.

I understand the rage he feels. "It's done. I can't make it gone until you are, Brother."

He nods and turns toward Blake. I throw Blake chin and push to the good side of hell. It doesn't take much to have an inferno going in here.

"Clear, Warrior." Blake gives me his status.

Suspending through, I make sure everything goes up. "Lift, one."

I push and step through the door. "Clear, Ops."

"Twelve minutes, good fuckin' job, Warrior and Teams. Get them home. Flight plans logged."

Aylen does her part, "Roger. Covered, boost two."

I bend to the boys in the seats. Blake pulls the medic bag over. "Bet you're glad to be out of that place."

I look up and Cayden hands me waters. "Thanks." I open them and hand one to each.

They have marks on their wrists and one leg. The shit people do to kids is unreal. While they drink and Blake talks to them about fixing them up, I look at the seats behind me.

Prez is helping with energy, Colt is staying close. Cort has the boy on his lap and Mucimi has his hands on him with tears on his face.

I smile at the two boys that are at least looking up now. "Blake and Cayden can fix your cuts. Tell them if you're hurt anywhere and they'll help."

They watch me then one nods. "Yes, master."

Jesus. "I'm Mase. There are no masters here but the big guy. He's Cort Masters and helps get kids safe. You can call us by name. What's your name?"

"Boy."

"Fuckin' hell." Blake has the boy leaning back scared.

That bowed head pisses me off. "You need a name that fits better than that," I tell him taking his hand and finish getting the gauze around it while throwing him calm. "My dad likes to fly. His name is Cloud. It fits him."

He keeps his head down but eyes look up at me. I give him a smile. "*Ôkatuq* is Mohegan for Cloud."

"Ôkatuq."

Cayden laughs. "I like it. You may fly for us some day. You have to be a good Brother and learn the Brotherhood rules so you can help us save the hurt kids. Can you do that, Ôkatuq?"

He nods with his eyes watching me. "I think you may be a future pilot." I didn't mean to name him, it was just an example to keep him talking. Now, I like it. The new Cloud doesn't get it but doesn't ask.

Cayden talks to the other boy but he won't look up. I throw calm to him but he's not chancing it. We've got time. I look back at Mucimi and the small boy. The boy is watching me.

I turn getting a smile from him. "Mucimi is my nephew. He's glad you're here."

The boy twists and Cort sets him down but doesn't let go. Mucimi smiles.

I put my arms out and the boy jumps to me. "Cute, little one."

He climbs up higher and touches my hair. Taking it out of my coat I pull the tie out and let it fall. His hands are petting it like a dog. I laugh and he smiles putting his head on my shoulder covered in hair. I watch the older boys while sitting on the floor.

Cort laughs drawing my eyes. He's watching the little one so I look down and laugh.

"You're going to be the stars in my Yáhsháyôn's eyes. I can see it already." I smile when he hides his face under my hair then peeks through.

Mucimi nods. "Ayakuhsak, Wápáyu and Ôkatuq."

Holy fuck. Cayden laughs.

Cort smiles. "It fits organic. Kateri will love them."

"You understood?"

"Stars, Wind, Cloud." He learned Mohegan like Kateri did.

I just sent him the fuckin' dictionary. The crew laughs.

~*~*~

We shower at the office. It started out rough but ended with the boys laughing when I blasted them all with wind to dry.

The Prospects got clothes that fit them better than the Club shirts someone packed the chopper with and I hate them all. I'm in breeches and decide they need them too.

As soon as my shirt is on, Cort hands me Ayakuhsak. Wápáyu holds my breeches as we walk. Ôkatuq walks beside me asking about everything. Blake and Cayden take him and answer his questions.

I ask Cort, "The women?"

"Alder said the pregnant one is at the medic room with Destiny and Aylen. He's checking the others at his compound. Kristos sent Mary to help."

I love my Brothers. We take the quick ride to the compound. Kateri is waiting at the door. Knight and Uncle Danny come for the bigger boys.

They're scared but go when I give them a nod. "No one will hurt you here. I'll blow them away in one breath."

They giggle nervously, getting smiles from everyone gathered. My girl is watching but not moving.

I smile getting a tearful smile back and walk to her. "Remember I said kids fall on us?"

She nods swiping her tears. I don't stop. "We have three boys that are hoping for a safe place to sleep." I turn to the boys. "Tell Kateri your names."

"Ôkatuq." The taller boy owns it looking down.

Danny puts him down and Kateri hugs him. "I know another Cloud that's going to be honored to share his name with you."

He looks up quick. "I can stay? I get to sleep in a house?" He has us all looking around. Jesus.

Kateri bends lifting his chin. "I was a slave then I was saved by Mase. He doesn't let you go once he claims you. It gets a little crazy, but it's a fun crazy here. There is food on the table. Take what you can eat and there will be more whenever you're hungry."

He hugs her and waits at the door, wiping his eyes, behind her. I look at Prez and smile. He's a good Brother already.

"You are?" She asks turning to see the second boy.

"Wápáyu, ma'am." He looks down.

She lifts his chin up. "Wápáyu is very important to all of us and deserves our respect always. Do you know wind is my favorite symbol?" She flips the world charm and shows him the wind symbol on her collar.

He shakes his head so cute. "Can I stay in the house too, ma'am?"

"Did Mase save you too?" She smiles when he's nodding before she finishes. "That means you belong. We wouldn't be very balanced without our wind."

He jumps on her making us laugh. Danny ushers the boys in.

Kateri stands. "And this is my sister's boy?" How the fuck does she know that?

"Ayakuhsak," he says and I laugh.

She takes him and leans into me. "Thank you."

I hold her loving this moment for what it is. "Got two others worried you forgot 'em." Knight gets us moving.

The boys were watching for us. Kate and Jess can't hold their interest until Kateri sits. They turn for food now that she's there.

Justice, then Teller hug me. Luke-Rayne, Tucker and Phoenix are next. Mucimi shows up with tepee poles getting Cort and Prez to help him build it for the boys. Kateri doesn't seem to care that it's in the middle of the living room.

I catch Justice before he goes. "How did she know?"

He rolls his eyes. "Aiyana called Seren and had her explain because we're all Neanderthals and think women are weak."

"Us?"

He shrugs. "Women are fuckin' crazy. Ask her. I'm not getting into it with Aiyana. I need her help and she's worse than Mitch when you piss her off."

I just nod. I haven't met a weak woman yet.

'You planned to tell Kateri about her sister on the chopper. Shielding her from the truth would serve to ease

your mind only. I saw your intent earlier and fixed it. Mucimi will return to being a help and I can take a much-needed break.'

I smile throwing everything out of my head. '*Thank you, Aiyana. Your help and guidance are always appreciated.*'

'*Kuwômôyush, congratulations on your new family.*'

Justice shakes his head. I hug him then laugh at him.

Chapter Nine

Kateri

I jump out of bed and run to the boys' room. They're in the room by ours for now.

Danny said he's making them a room over the garage that will give them all their own space as they grow. He had a crew working on it, but I never saw anyone but my new boys. The people in and out were a blur.

I love the idea that they'll be together but have their own space. I watch them sleep thinking about a twin I never met. I hope she sees that I have her boy and he's free. The soft cotton wraps me up. It's got to be her.

"I'll cherish him," I whisper feeling warm then it's gone. A hug. I smile at the whimsical thought.

Wápáyu turns over then jumps up. "Ma'am. How I serve you today?"

I'm mortified. "No serving me."

Ayakuhsak rolls and falls out of his little bed then jumps to his feet, of course, Ôkatuq wakes with that and is up like a shot. They're all standing by their beds with their heads down. Damn, I should know better.

I smile walking into the room and sit in the middle where it's open. "I am so happy you're all here, I was standing at the door thanking the great spirit and my ancestors for sending me such precious gifts. Sit with me and I'll tell you about our great adventure today before the Alpha-Bits get here and spill the beans."

They move tentatively but sit looking down. "You have to look at me so I know if you understand."

Every one of them lifts their heads up with a snap.

I shake my head feigning annoyance. "I was a slave and know you follow instructions. I'm going to give you new instructions to follow and we'll test it out today. If you pass the test, you get ice cream for your snack."

Their eyes go big. "Because I can see you, I know ice cream interests you. So our first instruction is that you always look everyone in the eye. Can you say that, so I know you'll remember it?"

They repeat it so I give them the next. "You clean up after *you* and always look out for each other in case your brother needs help." I get the big eyes and explain. "Here you're not slaves, you don't work for me, you're my family. You are brothers. We work together, learn together and play together. Sometimes it will be all of us, sometimes it will be some of us. Sometimes," I pause for effect, "it will be you with your friends or alone."

"Friends?" Ayakuhsak asks.

"Little boys or girls that treat you with respect and make you happy to have them close."

"Caelan my friend." Ayakuhsak informs us.

I nod at the smart little shining star of my new world. "Caelan is definitely your friend. He liked playing with his motorcycles with you. Seren said the one he gave you was his favorite. That means he's treating you the way he wants you to treat him. It made him happy and you happy. That's what friends do."

They all smile like they got more than a couple of words. I remember the feeling of awe when I did anything new. This is that moment for them.

"So, you help your brothers, take care of you and them and ask when you're not sure of something. Here, you are free and part of my new family. There are a lot of Blackhawks and Brothers, they love everyone, so you never have to be afraid with them. I was afraid the first time I met them, but now I love them."

Ayakuhsak's head angles trying to understand. "Birds?"

I laugh at the little Einstein. "Blackhawks are birds but that's our last name. Your name is Ayakuhsak Blackhawk. I am very proud of my name because the Blackhawks work hard to save and help kids and women that were sold. Wear your name proud, boys. It's a gift to us from Mase. He's an amazing man and doesn't give gifts like that to everyone. We'll honor him by treating him with respect and showing him appreciation for all he is and does."

"No serve to you. Serve to master Mase." Wápáyu isn't understanding this.

"If Mase heard you call him master, he would be hurt. He saved you from that so you'll never have a master again. We will love, guide and teach you, but no one owns Wápáyu, Ayakuhsak or Ôkatuq. Mase brought you here so he's sure it will never happen again. You're free and free means no master. Blackhawks are never owned, they fight for freedom for you, me and anyone they see that needs it."

Ôkatuq launches himself at me then Ayakuhsak hugs me from the other side. "Free Blackhawk."

"Yes. Ayakuhsak, you are a free Blackhawk." I reach for Wápáyu and pull him over. "Your names fit free. You can't harness the clouds, the wind or the stars just like you can't harness a Blackhawk. You'll learn to live free, I did and it's a wonderful new world. Let's get dressed and we can talk about our adventure for today."

They move fast making me smile. Mucimi shows scaring the crap out of me. "Mucimi! You need a bell."

He smiles and kisses my cheek then hands me a bag. When he disappears, I look in it and laugh.

"Mucimi brought you clothes, boys."

They don't move. "That's just how Mucimi is. Remember the Blackhawks can't be harnessed? That's what I mean. No one will ever own Mucimi Blackhawk." Ayakuhsak runs to me, Wápáyu is a second behind Ôkatuq.

The bag gets torn, the little breeches are a hit. Mucimi is too much and I'll thank him for that. Right now, I help two of the three dress in breeches and traditional shirts. They look like child Mase's. I say child because their shirts have color to them. Washed out red, blue and green streak the shirts like they were dipped from the bottom and left to dry. They are adorable.

I show them their drawers for their spare shirts and breeches watching the wonder and happiness push some of the fear in their eyes away.

"Moccasins then bandages, hair and teeth."

While the older brush their teeth, I brush Ayakuhsak's hair. "Do you want it tied, Ayakuhsak?"

Wápáyu has a low tie, Ôkatuq's hair is just at his shoulders.

"Free. Ayakuhsak Blackhawk free." He gets a tearful hug for that.

"We'll leave it down to hang free like you. If the wind gets to be too much, I can braid just the sides for you, it will help and leave the back free." Seeing broken hair at the top, I know his hair was up with bare elastics not ties.

"Let's go to the kitchen. The Alpha-Bits will be here soon."

"Kateri Blackhawk need clothes, ma'am." Wápáyu points at my pj pants.

I look at my pj clad leg and laugh. "Thank you. I'll be quick. Try to make your beds and put your pjs under your pillow. I'll be right back. I set him down and run.

~*~*~

Mase

I run with Kimuks knowing I'm cutting it close. The meet with Seth then clearing my desk took longer than I realized. I started running and noticed the sun's position a little too late. Walking through the slider, I smile at the two tiny hands stirring batter with a wooden spoon.

"Mase Blackhawk, I free Ayakuhsak Blackhawk."

Uncle Danny laughs. I smile at the Blackhawk being added. "You are Ayakuhsak Blackhawk. I'm proud to share that name with such hardworking Blackhawks."

Three Bits run in and stop. "Ayakuhsak, raise one of your hands." He does. "Wápáyu." He raises a hand and smiles. "Ôkatuq." He runs toward the Bits. "This is Laran, Allen and Mateo Ford. They are my friends and Brothers in the Club. They'll help make breakfast and are going on an adventure with you."

"We free Blackhawks." Ayakuhsak wants everyone to know their place.

Laran smiles up at me. "We free Fords." The Bits laugh then run.

Uncle Danny and Yáhsháyôn smile at me. I shrug. "When did their clothes get here? I just ordered them last night." I kiss my girl getting to the coffee pot.

"Mucimi brought these this morning. They have a change in their dressers." Kateri has love and happiness rolling off her.

"Do you want help for today? I don't know how long I'll be. Justice took California so I'm not so far."

Allen answers before Kateri can. "Alpha-Bits here today. Tomorrow I get schoolwork to Blackhawk boys. Dreng come help."

I kiss his head. "Thank you." Turning, I wait for Kateri.

She shakes her head. "I'll be fine with the Alpha-Bits and Security. We won't go far."

I give her a real kiss. "Thank you, Yáhsháyôn. I'll shower quick."

"Go, they'll be done in no time." She kisses above my heart.

I nod remembering her point of making meals if I'm home. I agree and push to the room hearing little giggles.

I freeze at Kateri's words. "See, just like the stars, wind and clouds you cannot harness a Blackhawk. Free is for the rest of your life."

"Free Blackhawk, free Ford friend." Ayakuhsak has my eyes burning.

I move quick and shower thinking about her words. She's the best person to explain this shit to them. I'm not sure I'd have gotten through the conversation without getting pissed.

I'm pushing down the stairs just as they're setting up the plates. Knight walks in getting the *free Blackhawk and free Ford friend* spiel from Ayakuhsak.

I spoon eggs to a Bit plate watching Knight's reaction. He freezes, throws chin and says, "'Bout time."

I laugh and dole out eggs kissing boys' heads as they sit. Uncle Danny stops my hand after one spoon and reaches for the fruit. He shrugs. "I won't have to work out so hard today."

I smile and put the eggs in front of Uncle Steve. "When in Rome."

My dad isn't going to believe this one. I sit and add granola and nuts to my plate.

Ayakuhsak watches so I offer him some. "Laran likes the granola but not the nuts."

Blackhawk boys all want to try it. Granola is passed and the Bits help get it on their plates. Kateri watches with a smile and tears in her eyes.

I touch her leg under the table. "I feel your happy. I'm happy too. Kristos will get you help if you need it. Call him if you need it. While you're out, the Prospects will get more food in and have some toys coming. We had a chest in the living room and basket for electronics. They'll have that. Outside toys are coming and uncle Danny will make a treehouse when he has the time. If you think of something I miss, tell him or order it."

She nods and I start eating. "Did you order enough clothes?"

"Pants for a week, shirts for two, Club Ts and bed breeches. Nancy will send the boy package for them, that's boxers, tanks, board shorts and footwear meaning socks, flip flops, sneakers and boots." I ordered more bed breeches for me too. Naked isn't going to work with kids running around.

She nods and eats.

Uncle Danny wants to help. "I'll get outside toys. Did you get targets and those pouches you all wore?"

"You'd have to ask the family. Brantley was handling electronics, Terry inside toys, Taylor outside, Joey clothes. A trampoline and springboard are needed."

"Alder order for training." Allen takes that away. "Desk, Boss Danny. I send console plan?"

They talk about the room and the Blackhawk boys watch without comment. I'm finished so I ask. "Do you want something special in your room?"

Every head shakes. I nod. "Not knowing what they're saying isn't easy. You'll have time to decide what you like and what you want to add when you know us better."

Wápáyu guts me. "No chain on wall in new room?"

I close my eyes and breathe. Uncle Steve handles it. "You free?"

Ayakuhsak makes me smile. "Free Blackhawks."

"No chains." Knight settles that.

"Mase, your arms." Uncle Danny has me breathing deeper while he explains. "He gets mad when kids get hurt. Kids are never chained here. The fire won't hurt you."

I open my eyes feeling a hand on my arm. Kateri smiles. "The fire doesn't hurt what he loves. We're all safe here. No chains because Blackhawks can't be harnessed."

I bend and kiss my girl. "Thank you."

"Fire no hurt you, Boss Kateri?" Mateo asks.

"No, I'm his. He'd never hurt me. The fire shows his anger but doesn't hurt us."

I nod, that's a good way to put it. "When I was pissed at the man that stole and sold kids, Alder climbed on my back. I had fire all over my arms. It never touched Alder."

The Bits are impressed. They already think Alder walks on water. I smile, he may. Getting up, I put my plate and cup in the dishwasher. The sight of the kids and Kateri at the table hit me. The uncles, the Bits, my new and old family.

"That's a sight that packs a hit. I'm honored seeing my family here today. I have much to share with the ancestors."

Mucimi shows on the side of me. "They know."

He makes me laugh. "Are you on my Ops Team?"

He shakes his head. "I'm on Honor Ops for pickup in Utah."

I kiss his head. "*Kuwômôyush*, Mucimi." I go right around the table kissing boys' heads. *Kuwômôyush*, Blackhawks and Fords." I smile when I get it back. "Yáhsháyôn, I need to go. Call Kristos for help if you need it. I'll text you when I leave and get back. *Kuwômôyush*, Yáhsháyôn."

"*Kuwômôyush*, Nupômkoki." Her smile is huge today. I love that.

I grab my coat and smile at the uncles. "*Kuwômôyush*, uncle stooges." I push fast hearing the kids laugh.

~*~*~

Kateri

Our hike down to the brook is better than I expected, being free doesn't take away the restraint they've grown up with. While new and exciting showed, they listened to warnings from the Alpha-Bits and never strayed to where they'd get hurt or lost. I commend them, getting smiles when I remind them of our ice cream snack if it continues.

This of course, makes the brook exploration easy. The Alpha-Bits are happily pointing out little fish and rocks.

Ôkatuq catches a frog giggling the whole time. I see our Security recording it and thank her.

Everyone has to hold the frog so we sit in a circle passing it around. They all giggle.

Ayakuhsak is the last to hold it. After a minute he drops the frog and smiles. "Free frog."

I laugh. "You're very cute. He's happy to be a free frog. You're going to make a great Blackhawk, Ayakuhsak."

"Ôkatuq hair no long." Mateo touches Ôkatuq's hair smiling. "Here you have what you like."

Ôkatuq looks to the side. "Master cut, hurt he hold tight."

Oh no. "We put the past behind us. Today you start with your new family and life. We don't go back to that old one. Every day is new and we get to live it free to be us."

He nods with tears in his eyes. He was used. I don't know how I know, but I do.

Wápáyu moves to Ôkatuq. "Boss Kateri, my hair cut like Ôkatuq so we be same Blackhawk free brothers? Ford free brothers same." He points to the Alpha-Bits.

"If that's what you want, Wápáyu. We don't cut our hair often, but it is your hair and I think honoring your new brother is a very good reason to cut it. It can grow together, like us and our family."

Ayakuhsak crawls onto Ôkatuq's lap. "I honor, you my family too. I will cut my hair."

I smile thinking that's a bit much for a three-year-old to understand, but it's weird here so I nod. "I bet Ôkatuq feels that honor. *I* will cut your hair all the same length so we have no mishaps with scissors."

The Security woman closest turns coughing. Ayakuhsak is up and running. Numuks corrals him with Kimuks at the path. I stand quickly. "Stay with your partners, come wash your hands in the brook, then we'll hike back and cut hair." He runs right back making me laugh. The boy is cute.

We stop at the circle thanking the great spirit for our happy and of course, Ayakuhsak's added, *free* adventure. I'm surprised to see Alder coming out the back door. He smiles at the boys running his way. His Alpha-Bits hug him then Wápáyu and Ôkatuq do. I hold Ayakuhsak's hand going up the stairs and the little cutie hugs Alder too.

I kiss his head getting a smile from him. "I'm glad you're here, LP. Can you really get warts from frogs?"

He laughs. "HPV virus cause warts. Humans carry virus not frog. Wart to frog myth is myth."

"Thank you. I made them wash anyway."

He's got the cutest smirk on. "Not bad to wash hands often. Keep HPV statistic low."

I laugh. "I knew there was a reason. I need to cut hair then I can show you the organs I've done. One concerned me." The boys go in not caring about boring work.

He nods looking focused. "I have electronic order from Boss Brantley. You cut hair lice?"

I slide the door closed. "No, Ôkatuq's hair was cut by his master. I believe he was used. I'll need a therapist to talk to him and Wápáyu."

He nods with tears in his eyes. "Boss Aylen cloak. Hair cut is used?"

"I'm not sure if that's a thing. He wouldn't look at us and said he was hurt. The other two are cutting their hair the same for their new life to start together."

He nods. "You good teacher. Honor to brothers important for new to see."

I agree so I nod.

He goes in and takes bags off the table. "You cut Ayakuhsak first, Alpha-Bits explain electronic."

I nod and get the little cutie ready for a haircut. "Your hair is very soft, Ayakuhsak."

He sits still for me and waits until I stop combing it before talking. "Mase Blackhawk wash hair special soap for me like him."

"Mase believes that everyone is equal. You wear clothes like him that are made special from his tribe. You eat the same food he eats. You live in a house and get a room like him and you wash with the same shampoo he uses on his hair. You're worth the same as Mase and are treated the same. It's important to see everyone as equal so you know how much you're worth to you and us."

"Mase Blackhawk mad boys hurt. He don't care we nothing?"

I put the scissors down. "You are Ayakuhsak Blackhawk and you're everything, Ayakuhsak. You saw how angry he was over chains on the wall. No one should live like that and Mase will do everything to stop kids from being hurt. He's finding homes for kids like you so they'll see how much of a gift they are for people that have love to give but no kids to give it to."

"I am gift for you?"

I laugh and cut his hair straight at his shoulders. "Such a precious boy. You are so much more, my Ayakuhsak. I was a slave and never had a dream until I met Mase. My first dream was of a family with the amazing man that saved me from a life of just existing. Now I have three boys and Mase. For someone that never dreamed of a future, having my first wish granted is a sign from the great spirit that I am worth it. I deserve to have a family and share all the love I feel with my Blackhawk boys. That includes the big one." I bend kissing his head. "You're all done. You honor your brother Ôkatuq. It's a gift to him that shows him you're all equal."

His head shakes with less hair and he giggles. "Equal and free Blackhawks."

I turn him around and he hugs me. "You are equal and free. You honor Blackhawk boys with love." This kid is unbelievable.

"Holy shit." The deep voice has me looking up.

I turn with Ayakuhsak still in my arms. "Cloud, CJ, I'm surprised, happy and excited for you to meet the Blackhawk boys. This is Ayakuhsak. Blackhawk boys, come meet some very special people." I carry him over to his new grandparents and set him down.

"Wápáyu." I touch his head. "And this very special boy is Ôkatuq. They're named by your son in honor of his family."

Cloud drops to his knees hugging them. "This is Cloud and CJ Blackhawk. They are Mase's parents."

"We equal, free and honor to you." Ayakuhsak makes me laugh as I hug a tear-stained CJ.

"Ayakuhsak is very outspoken and usually oddly insightful."

CJ laughs. "We heard. I was ready to knock some sense into my youngest boy's friggin head, but now I see he's also oddly insightful. Does this make you happy, Kateri?"

"A dream come true happy, CJ. I already love them all and it's been less than twenty-four hours." I get another hug, then she's all over the boys.

While Ayakuhsak and Ôkatuq are learning and showing their new tablets and whatever else they have, I cut Wápáyu's hair.

When I'm done, I tell him how proud I am to have such a special boy. "You saw your brother hurt and fixed it. That's honoring him and covering his pain with love. You are so special, I hope you see it, Wápáyu. I am honored I was given the chance to raise such a smart and thoughtful boy." I hug the surprised boy that is struggling to see his worth.

Walking him to the couch I'm surprised to see Mucimi. I didn't know he showed up again.

"Did you know Mucimi is Cloud and CJ's grandson too?"

Ôkatuq looks at Cloud for confirmation. Cloud laughs. "It's true. Mucimi is our grandson, your uncle Brantley's son."

Alder stands. "Boss Kateri, I have meet one hour. While boys busy, you show organ concern?"

I look at CJ. "We'll be at the table."

"We got this."

I get my laptop and turn it on then put my glasses on and flip through to the file.

"I'm sending the link to your chat. I pulled a file to build a model and had alerts on the liver. When I started building other organs, alerts showed on one leg more than the other. It's his foot not leg, sorry. Looking at the numbers, I googled the possible causes using the results I show. Uranium poisoning is all I could find. It doesn't make sense so I thought maybe the results were wrong. This is the second model I made using everything in the file and I come up with the exact same results."

I see through my glasses he's pulling apart the organs so he can see.

"How is bone density show to me?"

"The model built them using the results from the blood test. There are too many chemicals than what's normal, so I took all the results and added them in. All the information builds a realistic model based off everything you have in the file for this Eli."

He freezes. "All injection, DNA, blood test show by time?"

"Yes. Because there were multiple results and tests, they're added to the side but you can see them through the organs for the time that they show. Look at the liver first. It shows the red of now that sends the alert, but if you pick a date off the side, you notice the dotted outline on this one. It's the oldest test and shows the liver has rebuilt cells and the alert from that date is no longer an issue. I used dotted and faded color because I couldn't figure how else to do it." I take the glasses off and watch him go right to the foot I noticed with lower density. Since it's all on alert, this is what worried me.

He opens sections one right after another. "Allen."

Allen runs to us. I notice everyone watching the hologram model.

I shrug. "I made the pictures for his test results."

CJ looks at me like I'm nuts.

"It's just pictures." I turn around and pay attention to Allen and Alder.

"Progression to test," Alder says. I guess Allen understands because he starts moving body parts open.

"I will make robotic brace higher. Marrow growth issue?"

"I will start new C and D. Liver regrowth good. I call Boss Beacon. Alpha-Bit Lab here no medical stock. I order you stock, you build?"

"Tonight. Dreng here tomorrow. I send brace. Aaron, Boss Beacon help." Allen hits his head. "Pool brace. I have recycle. I make."

Wow, they're quick with this fixing shit. Alder turns to me. "I make call. Five-minute, Boss Katcri."

I nod and step back to the couch. Mucimi disappears and no one notices. Cloud is watching Alder. By the sound, it's a conference call. I can't help but look back when Alder growls.

"Akai, shoot Anton ass one second to laser. No time to play game. Eli need brace. Allen need medical stock. I show to Phoenix, *I* shoot Anton ass, take out ice cream machine. No time to this. Women move to compound?"

Asa nods his mohawk. Alder looks relieved. "Good. I get link to you. Get five IT work medical to Alpha-Bits. Hold Anton file. He last."

I bite down holding my teeth together and look at the boys who are all paying attention to Alder. I hear Asa laugh.

Alder says he's out and calls me over. "Boss Kateri."

I move back to the table. "Sorry you wait to me. Anton my Mucimi. You have more organ to build?"

"No. I built them all but don't have the results in there. I'm not a programmer so this took longer than I thought. I'm cutting and pasting the code and just add my organ parameters but it's a lot of code with the number of test results."

He smiles. "You programmer. I will get code finished. This help to Alpha-Bits vital to life expectancy. Eli first Alpha-Bit to X-ray. Result show more damage..." he stops like he's looking for the words.

"Than you expected?" I try.

He nods. "Yes. Alpha-Bits injected uranium regular phase injections. X-ray damage show poison result too much radiation small body mass. I no get result without radiation to see bone density. Marrow extraction test we need blood, possible damage more." He shakes his head. "More radiation to Alpha-Bit cause...death."

I bend. "I'm so sorry you had to go through all you did and I'm so glad you're smart enough not to X-ray everyone to get results. I'm honored to do this for you, Alder. I'll get this finished."

He shakes his head. "You built organ. I have IT to code. I explain why I need. Why I honored you help to Alpha-Bit, to me. I only number seven...survive."

My breath catches. Oh my. "I understand. If you need anything else, I'm here. This includes the marrow and blood you asked for."

He nods looking much older. "I will call with need. All Alpha-Bits thanks to you."

"I'm honored to help, Alder."

He nods. "I feel it. I have meet. Call Asa you have Alpha-Bit need. School tomorrow. Dreng get plan to Aaron, Faber. Doc here do physical to boys. He send test to me. VP Mase eat Alpha-Bit healthy meal. Keep boys to meal plan. I send vitamin. Anything, always, call to me."

Once his backpack is on I hug him. "Thank you, LP."

He throws chin and runs saying. "Later."

When I turn, everyone is watching. I have no idea what to say. Allen has tears in his eyes. Mateo is crying.

I go right to him. "It's okay. He has a way to see problems now and fix them. Did you see him get a brace going for Eli?"

He nods but still cries so I keep going. "That's crazy fast. He'll get what everyone needs when they need it. I'm new here and even I know that."

He gives me a sad smile. I hug him. "I never had a dream, Mateo. Since I've gotten here, dreams I didn't know I wanted are happening. Alder will fix it."

He nods with a better smile on. "Yeah."

"Alder always fix Brothers, Alpha-Bits, babies, building, computer, Ops, business, money, medicine. Today you help life expectancy to Alpha-Bits for injection. Seven model to perfect Alpha-Bit. More injection to Alder than all Alpha-Bits. I dream Alder find fix to Alder." Allen brings tears to my eyes. Alder is the only seven that survived.

I wipe my face. "I'll add it to the top of my dream list, Allen."

He smiles at me. "List?"

I try to smile. "I had family on it and that came true. I need another dream. Alder sticking around for as long as I am is a good one."

He smiles. "The best."

Cloud stands up. "I'm going to see if they need someone to transport stock for you, Allen."

"Thanks, Boss Cloud." Allen looks happier.

"I'm going to make lunch while you all figure out how to play on your new tablets and whatever."

Danny and Knight are leaning against the island when I stand. By the looks on their faces, they've been there for a while.

"Did good. Thanks," Knight says.

I don't know what to say so I nod.

"I ordered lunch. They'll be here in a few. Allen, can you show the kids the Alpha-Bit Vision?" Danny asks.

I look back. Allen has a big smile on. "I will." He runs for his backpack.

I smile at Danny. "The vision must be big."

He nods. "It's another Alder project. I have questions about the room and wanted to keep them busy."

"Good plan."

They laugh at me. I follow them upstairs smiling. One of the Security women follows me up. When I walk in the door, I'm glad she's here, there are men everywhere.

"Get lunch." Knight has everyone moving fast. He's good to have around.

Danny laughs. They're readers. I shrug looking at the truck in one corner. That's really cool.

"The reason I wanted them busy, I normally build the rooms to last for a few years. With kids Ôkatuq's age, he'd want privacy and probably a door sooner than the other two. Because they were picked up in what amounts to a stable with raw hay on the floor for beds, I stayed away from tiny house like rooms *in* the room. Ayakuhsak's free was stuck in my head. The trucks are open and there are no walls for them to feel closed in like stable stalls." He's a smart man. I nod trying not to think of my boys sleeping on hay just two nights ago.

"So, I can put tepees on the truck beds to get some privacy for now, it's cool and shows their culture so it would be comfortable."

I look around the room. The trucks are at three corners. I look up at the ceiling then the trucks. "Can you add the tepee like a curtain they can pull if they want it? They have round curtain things that would hold it so they can cover part, or all of the truck." The free may be a problem closing them in.

He smiles. "That would work well for now. The next is setting it up so Mase isn't rebuilding the whole room as they grow. I can put the track so it merges to a half-wall leading to a jungle gym platform set higher."

That would be really cool. "I like it. When it's time, the half-wall can be full wall."

He nods. "Since you like it, I'll do that. Lunch should be here."

I walk out with Security. She's shaking her head. "That's amazing."

It is. "I think it's a theme here. I'm new so that's a guess."

The men are laughing at me again.

Mase

Fuckin' Cort and the rings. I smile thinking about his crazy ritual. Raid said he does it to everyone. The jeweler had the stones and an artist waiting. When I showed the charm I had made, the Mason took it and ran. He drew out a matching bracelet, anklet, earrings and ring. The blue stone chips he'll use will make the diamond shimmer like water. The band in that shimmering blue, aqua and green are going to look alive. I love it all. An extra bracelet and anklet in that roped braided leather she likes, with symbols for the kids had me done with shopping. He'll make the clasps special and add natural stones to the wood. My enigma will love the roped leather pieces best.

The flight is made shorter with my mind on my little enigma. We set down and I'm glad to be home. Since this is a BSC Chopper, I'm not needed for anything. I do have a need to see the Flight Lead Officer, so I run in and jog up to Donna's office. The door is cracked open, I knock and walk in.

She stands. "VP."

I shake my head. "Sit, Donna. I came by to ask about surveillance on the camp by the city."

She nods pulling it up to a board. "Seventeen as of this morning. They're still on unincorporated city land. We had two standing at the fence at fourteen-ten. I had Security send drones to cover in ten-minute increments. They retreated back to the camp."

"Thanks. I'll let Pres know."

"Roger, VP."

I smile jogging down the hall. She's as good as Luke-Rayne said she was. The military are idiots, since we benefit from that, I can't complain.

Once I'm out the door I push to the office. Running up the stairs I see Pres walking into his office.

"Kristos, I just left Flight. The camp has seventeen as of this morning. Two strolled to the fence and left after Donna set drones every ten minutes."

He shakes his head. "I'll get it clear tomorrow. Every day there are more."

I nod. "I'm off tomorrow. I can play with them tonight."

He laughs. Cooper told him about the shit we did in Elan fuckin' with the local yahoos.

"Leave us something to do, Brother. Running BSC Ops lasts minutes with your fucking crews. Michaels and Spano are on tomorrow. I'll get it set for after BSC in the morning. Bravo is on the afternoon Ops."

I nod. "That's good. Do you need anything?"

He shakes his head. "You remoted for the Security meet, had everything I needed before I got here today, have run Ops daily." He shakes his head. "Brother, go home, to the family you decided on yesterday, so I have a chance to look that good."

I laugh saluting him then push. At the house, I hear laughing and smile walking in. I love hearing the family I decided on yesterday happy.

My dad and mom are playing with the boys and electronics. I stand still and watch.

"Mase Blackhawk!" Ayakuhsak has me laughing. He drops the tablet on the couch and runs to me.

"Ayakuhsak Blackhawk!" I yell back bending down. He jumps and I catch him. "Did you have a good adventure today?" I throw chin to my dad.

"Ôkatuq caught a frog. I make it free like me."

I laugh messing his shorter hair up. "Sounds perfect, Ayakuhsak. I'm honored you're mine."

Wápáyu is watching standing by the coffee table. I put Ayakuhsak on my shoulders and put my arm out. He runs.

"I love seeing my boys with the same hair." I kiss his head and hug him, turning so I can pull Ôkatuq into a hug.

"I honor my brother being equal."

"It sounds like you had a very good day. I'm proud you're learning to show honor to your new brothers so fast." I look for my girl. She looks happy standing at the island watching us. The boys step back so I take Ayakuhsak off my shoulders and set him down.

"I need to see my girl and hug my mom and dad then you can tell me about your day."

The Bits get them back to the couch and I kiss my mom and hit my dad's shoulder going to my girl.

"I missed that smile today, Yáhsháyôn."

"It's been right here all day."

I kiss it lifting her up. "Good day, baby?"

She holds on. "Very. I've decided on our first date. You're going to get roped into an Alpha-Bit Vision adventure after we eat our early dinner."

I don't think that's a bad idea. "So you want to go on another adventure today?"

She smiles big for me. "I'm the one doing the roping in. I should have googled demands on first dates."

I smile. "You can pay for that later. The vision has food. Eating there is half the fun."

Her smile grows with her eyes smoldering. Fuckin' woman. "So we're ready." She's won, done and drops her legs.

I shake my head smiling as I set her down. "You'll pay for that too, Yáhsháyôn." I get another sexy smile and laugh walking back to my mom.

"Thanks for coming, Mom." I give her a hug and kiss her cheek again.

"I love the boys. Kateri is friggin amazing. I'm glad I got to see today, Mase. Go change so we can go."

I laugh and turn to my dad for a hug. "She's still mom."

He hugs me smiling. "I love her for being mom and I'm honored to share my name with your boy."

"I love you, Dad, and I'm glad I get to show it."

He hugs me again and hits my back. "Go change. I'll get a flight plan."

I turn to the boys. "Allen, see if the other Bits want to go. Blackhawk boys, I'll have to hear about your day on the chopper. We have a date with a vision."

Ayakuhsak jumps around smiling. I push to get changed.

Chapter Ten

Three days

Mase

I push to Jinx' side and hold his arm steadying him. "Sorry, Brother. I just want to ask how last night went."

He stops and hugs me. "Debra slept in the bed with her even after the healers left. She can't believe she's not owned." His eye is spinning as he looks back at the memory of a seven-year-old slave from when I unchained her.

I need to get this to Justice. Everyone shouldn't be watching every Op.

"You and Debra will teach her, Brother. Hannah is right there so you've always got help."

He nods. "Thanks for bringing the boys, it helped. Sohn and Sabur called her on chat this morning. She looked calmer when Debra pushed me out the door."

I laugh. He's been lost since the boys went back to Alder's. He's wanted a kid since Beacon took Dreng. My robotic Brother is made to be a doting dad. His new girl will need that.

I start walking. "Call if you need me. She's going to make it, Brother. Just be patient. Hannah being close will help strengthen the cloak."

He smiles his Jinx smile. "She's going to make it."

I hit his back. "She is."

He stops me. "You made your mark, Brother. You've given us something different than the rest of your family and we all see it. We all feel it, Mase. That greatness your family shares needs a bigger board, Brother. You've got a long way to go and it's just starting. Love ya, Mase. I'm honored I get to see it."

I hug him hard not able to talk. He knows and throws me chin. I throw it back and watch as he goes right to Brinks and Cort. He pulls his phone to show his new girl helping make breakfast.

Aaron catches me. "Brother, what's this one about?" He's worried he's going to lose his crew.

"I didn't get the low down, but I figure an overview of what happened in the week here. It will clear up questions Presidents have."

He settles with that and sits. "This is good. Prez is harder to read lately."

I hit his shoulder and sit with Kristos two away from him. "Brother. I miss our breakfasts."

He laughs. "I do too. It will slow down. We got forty. From start to almost finished, we did good, Brother. No casualties, no injuries and we did it with little stress to the Club." He sees so much clearer now.

"Yeah." I look at Aaron and see he heard and is thinking about how it worked. He's getting it.

Justice, Cort and Prez show in a line in front of the big screen and Brothers move to sit.

When everyone is seated, Cort takes a step forward. "I think it was three weeks ago we found out Mase found a girl. A couple of days later, we found out *his ol' lady,*" he pauses as the Brothers laugh, I smile, "was part of a trafficking business that tied Masons and Indians. Their territory spanned a shit ton of states in the west. Mase's ol' lady was being hunted." He smiles that politician smile. "*Was* being hunted. We gathered information with help from Alder and his Alpha-Bit IT and sent crews of

Protectors out to collect the women and kids still being held as slaves, set to be recovered for resale, or held for sale. Our list said forty-two were out there. Today, a week after crews were deployed every-fucking-where, two are still out there and the operation is shut down. I'm sure we'll find a couple after IT goes through that paperwork again. I'm confident that BSC West can handle the two and whatever we find from here on out." He stops and holds his fist over his heart.

"I am honored to be right here. I'm usually the crazy example. I never gave a fuck. Today, I give a fuck. Protectors from everywhere dealt with an issue that we would have taken months to clear and probably would have lost some to resale and or they'd be hidden. A week, Brothers. If any President needs BSC West Protectors, Teams, or aircraft, they are yours. We will show you the same respect and hand you've given to us this week."

He looks at the Protectors and I feel his emotion. "A week and Mase can breathe easy, three Brothers have additions to their families and I can say my family has grown. Women and kids are safely recovered and will not be stolen in mass numbers because of you. Know it is with honor that I thank the Protectors for making it happen." He throws them chin and turns giving a hug to Justice.

Prez steps up thinking they need a minute. "Presidents, you have been here." He looks at the board on the side. "Or have watched. If you have a need, call your Lead Club. That's all it takes."

Justice steps up taking a deep breath. He smiles at the Protectors all sitting together. "No casualties, no injuries, no sweat."

They smile back proud. Justice looks over the Brothers then up to the boards. "No Club was stressed with Ops this week. We ran from BSC Clubs, didn't step on toes, didn't stress your schedules and didn't tax your resources. Teller and Phoenix may have been stressed, but this was our first and they're fuckin' proud and honored to have it under our belt.

"Prez will explain at BSC what calls to us will cover. Today the Protectors will be going back home knowing they'll be called again. We can be anywhere within minutes to an hour or two depending on location. Your biggest concern is housing, transportation and food. Teller or Phoenix will get shit set up and stocked and leave you the bill. We're still the kids." He shrugs while the Officers laugh.

"As *the kids*, we're learning our place. We have the ability and understand the job we've been called to do. We are honored to be of service to our Ancestors, our Clubs, our Brothers and our country." He turns and smiles at the Protectors. "We were born and bred to be Fuckin' Badass."

The kids cheer making the Brothers smile. Fuckin' cool. Protectors are flying across or walking to make it to him.

Kristos pushes me. "You need to be up there, Brother. If it weren't for you, they'd still be up and running."

That's a little much but I see Teller and Justice look my way so I stand.

Falcon stops me on the floor. "I got the Ben T tie to Masons. I'll make it quick. Dan has no record of him. He was Crow's. Todachine was taken when his partner died. He moved Kateri off the reservation and asked for help. He took her camping when people got close and looked for someone to help find kids because he didn't want to leave her. Reed brought me up there but it never went anywhere. He wasn't a trusting sort. Dan did have Crow paying through Masons for her school and to keep her covered. He doesn't have details."

I smile. "Thanks, Brother. I don't need the details. It does answer questions." I hug him and walk to my Brothers. Crow wasn't a trusting sort either. Something caused that but I don't need it. I hug Teller then Justice. Keesog stands waiting.

I smile and hug him when I let Justice go. "Fuckin' proud, Keesog."

He steps back with tears in his eyes. "Thanks, Uncle Mase."

Justice hits his shoulder. "Good job, Keesog. You've come a long way, Brother."

Keesog looks shocked. Teller laughs. "I'm glad Nova shooting you isn't why you're leaving and can honestly say I'm going to miss your ass."

Justice puts his hand up. "Protectors, you've been training this week, take everything you've learned home with you. Make us proud, Brothers. I'll see you tonight at the reservation. Choppers are here to take you to the planes. *Kuwômôyush, nunekanisak*."

Keesog helps the non-Indians out. "Love you, my Brothers. Learn the language."

I laugh as the kids take off. Holy shit what a day and it just started. Prez and Cort are getting questions from everyone so I head out.

Kristos waited for me. Very cool. "Thanks, Brother. I'm headed back."

He nods. "Figured you were. I didn't get a bill for food and shit."

We walk out to choppers lifting and wait under the portico.

"Only Prez and my family stayed at Honor. Cort or Justice would cover the kids. It was a Phoenix Op. Prez is covered anywhere he goes by Princes. Joey would pay before you'd see it. Since she's a Blackhawk, she'd cover them too. She holds all our accounts up there. Banks covers our shit down here, but it's just what we make here."

He nods. "Ben has a house and we have the two on the side of his for BSC. I had Banks issue the next to Blackhawks. Your dad knows he's welcome whenever. That house has no bill owed. Get that to Joey."

"Thanks, Kristos. It's not necessary and I'm honored you give it knowing that. My family is everything."

He smiles. "To all of us, Brother. This one is us."

We board to Nash's smile. "Pres Cort said I could move to Honor. My whole crew is coming."

I hug my excited nephew. "I'm happy you are, Brother. I'll like you being close. With the Officers moved at Phoenix, it's a relief."

He nods not caring, excitement is overflowing in him. "Mom and dad are coming to see my new house." He hugs Kristos. "Thanks, Pres Kristos. I have money to buy it. Joey said I'm good."

I laugh. The kid is cute.

Pres shakes his head. "Our new Stealth Officer gets his house free like the other Officers. I'll have your new cut at church, Brother."

Nash is going to pass the fuck out. He hugs Kristos again.

I have to peel him off. "Sit in the copilot seat and relax, Brother. I'll get us home."

Hay-bale laughs. "Thanks, VP. I'm not certified for stealth."

I look at him and smile. "Certified?" I move to sit to the crew laughing.

"Fuck no, Brother. You flew stealth last month for the first time and didn't know how to do more than keep us up. Nash, Officer means you get the job done. Push through it and fly us the fuck home." He pulls my cut not moving me much.

Nash pushes me out and stands. "Roger, Pres."

I sit by Pres smiling. "I worked in the simulator, Brother."

"You're fucking crazy. You don't fly stealth until you're certified. These choppers are fucking millions."

I smile. "Roger, Pres."

He shakes his head as we lift. "You fuck." He knows I wasn't flying us home. Cort would come kill me himself. The choppers are like twenty million.

I laugh. "Hey, did you decide on the mansion?"

He nods. "Brekan has it being renovated. My dad is going to move to his old rooms. Officers, Alpha-Bits and VIP will stay in it. I gave it to Badass."

Sweet. "That was nice, Brother."

He shrugs. "It's not like I can live in it and my dad needs a more stable home. It's covered in the force-field and up higher. The Club is the only thing close." It's like a fortress up there. The Club road is its only access.

I nod. "He must love that."

He smiles. "He does. He's got pictures there I have never seen. Natalia took pictures for me. I'm going up when it's done. Natalia was there yesterday with Jordan, they put virtual shit in it." He laughs. "My dad loves it. He bypassed learning computers and has virtual doing everything for him. He's got meets set up for their new Clubs through his virtual assistant. It's fucking crazy." He's excited and talking more than usual.

I laugh. "Major is a trip. I'm glad he's happy to be home again."

He nods. "I get family is everything now. I feel it too, Brother."

"I'm glad you do. I grew up wishing Badass could give that to everyone. I'm the only one in my family that's not adopted. I never lived through the shit my brothers and sister did, but I felt it, Brother. I hated reading shit from them so I didn't learn how to read well until I was older. They dealt with shit I never would have made it through. Seeing Brantley take kids, I felt it again. He came from bad and learned through my parents and Badass. Every kid but Mucimi is adopted." I smile. "Badass shining through. They're all Protectors."

He smiles thinking of his Badass family. "Family is everything. We need a shirt."

I laugh. "On it, Pres." I type it out to Mucimi. I want *Blackhawk's have skillz* on ours. He's on it.

We set down and Pres smiles. "It worked, Mase. Nash was fine."

I nod. "He's been flying forever. I knew he'd be fine. Stealth doesn't have a copilot. It's considered the pussy seat. He wouldn't stay in a pussy seat."

He cracks up. "I'm telling Ranger. The fucking Brother is always in the pussy seat talking like stealth means not heard."

"Close your eyes." I pull him to Ops. "I want to watch. He can't say shit to you."

He's laughing going through the door.

~*~*~

Seeing my brothers on the compound surveillance board, I leave a pissed Ranger, smiling Cort and amused Kristos. "Call if you need me, Kristos. My brothers are here together. Later, Brothers."

I'm on call but not needed so I get home. Christian, Jeremy and Jacob rarely travel together. I'm honored they'd show for me. "Brothers, I saw you pull up in Ops. I can't believe you're here together. I'm honored."

Christian hugs me. I'm stunned then get an arm on him. "That feels so fuckin' good, Christian."

Jacob and Jeremy smile watching. When Christian steps back I hug them. "Love ya, Js. How did you all get time here?"

"Aiyana and Elizabeth were running with Dakota in Ops there. Prez ran from here. Ricky got back this morning. Aiyana, Joey and Aubrey will be here tomorrow. The kids will run with Ricky."

I look at Christian and laugh. He pegs me a finger and suspends to the door. Shit.

"Sorry, Brother, but the hug and speech was a lot. I'm still shocked you're all here." I don't want him pissed. He showed and hugged me.

He throws me chin and looks at Jacob. I hold my laugh.

"The older boys need the cloak. They belong here. They'll be Protectors. Jeremy will do the cloak. The little one is a good reader already. He needs to be brought to the ancestors." Jacob looks at Jeremy getting a nod.

Christian turns and walks in. I shake my head. "Jesus." Ancestors and toddlers always equal abilities.

"You didn't know about the boy?" Jacob asks.

I nod. "I knew he could read but not the has ability shit. I don't read him well. He's wicked smart for three."

Jeremy is gone. I smile.

Jacob suspends to the door. "I'm going in. I want to meet him. Jeremy threw *like Putam*."

I'm relieved. "He's more like you. I'm honored, Brother."

He laughs suspending through the door. I follow walking in. "Mase Blackhawk!"

I laugh bending for the stars in my world. He jumps. "Our room is done. We can sleep in trucks tonight!"

"You slept in trucks last night, Ayakuhsak."

He nods. "Tonight we have tepees on our trucks."

I smile. "Tepees make a huge difference. I slept in a tepee room when we stayed on the reservation. It was very cool."

His eyes get big reminding me of Asa. Looking around I'm glad the Bits aren't here chanting for cool.

I picture the room and he smiles. "Where's your mom?"

He freezes. Shit. I close my eyes hugging him, knowing I just hurt him.

"Mom's in office."

My eyes pop open.

Ayakuhsak's watching Jeremy. "You're Dad Blackhawk. Just dad." He shakes his head and looks at me. "He don't know we're Blackhawk. Dad Blackhawk. Ayakuhsak, Wápáyu and Ôkatuq Blackhawk."

Everyone is laughing.

"I'll explain it to him, Scout." I kiss his head.

They're still laughing.

He nods and hops down running. "Mom! Dad Blackhawk is home and Brothers from ancestors. Mom! It's mergency!" He makes it to the door at the same time she does.

Her hand is holding her heart and tears are rolling down her face as she kneels in front of him. "Ayakuhsak."

Ôkatuq and Wápáyu hug her around him. Ayakuhsak doesn't care.

"Mom and dad Blackhawk. The man showed us running big and you have a girl with you," Wápáyu tells her.

My feet stop. I look back at fuckin' Christian, he couldn't warn me? A girl. I smile holding my heart in my chest. Mom, dad and a girl. Christian smiles at me. I throw him chin and get on my knees so I can hug my old lady and kids.

Mom and dad. Jesus, that feels so fuckin' good. "We're honored to be yours, Little Scouts."

I watch them all kiss Kateri's wet cheeks and smile getting kissed on the arm, ear and shoulder before they run. I guess mom and dad are only big to us.

I lift my girl to me and kiss her lips. "That was something I'll never forget."

She smiles swiping her face. I grab the dishtowel and wipe her face noticing she doesn't have makeup on.

She's still my enigma. Her dark lashes keep her looking beautiful even with tears.

"Yáhsháyôn, you're beautiful even in tears. Happy tears, mom Blackhawk, have you breathtaking." I kiss her head.

She giggles. "It's a good thing I'm that breath for you. Now that mom is just done, the rest of his words got through. Mergency?"

I smile. "My Brothers are here. They're together which is not normal. Christian isn't touched."

She nods as I stand her up. "I remember." She kisses my chest and turns. "Js. I'm glad you're here and sorry I had a freak-out you had to witness.

Christian smiles at her. "Jeremy caused it. You're good, Kateri."

She watches him. "I feel like we've met. You look and sound different than at the reservation, but I've heard your voice before."

He nods. "I talked to you while Aylen was with you."

She smiles holding my hand tight. "I thought I was joining the Badass crazy."

He smiles and it's genuine. "That's why I stopped. Aiyana had you so I stepped back." His eyes bounce to me then right back to her. '*The cloak is solid, Mase. The reservation isn't clear, but she won't push for it. She's determined not to touch it or she'll lose all this.*'

I throw him chin noticing Jeremy and Ayakuhsak. Shit. Ayakuhsak is sitting on the table while Jeremy is staring at him. Jacob is with Ôkatuq. Uncle Steve has Wápáyu.

Christian suspends closer. "Cort is coming with your grandfather. Jeremy and Jacob are here. Do you want Aylen?"

She tightens her hold on my hand. "No, she's been working and could use time for herself. We're supposed to go to the Protectors dinner tonight. They moved it because of Ops."

He nods. "They'll be here tonight. Justice isn't moving it again. The boys need to see the ancestors. It will work."

Kateri turns to me. "We need food."

I laugh. "If Justice moved it, we'll have food."

She nods. That's it. "Do you have the boys? I need to finish Mikey's hologram boards." She's cute.

"I do. Go finish, Yáhsháyôn."

She moves then stops. "Thank you, Christian, for helping when I thought they were all nuts. Living it is just like you said, I never had a dream come true and the crazy doesn't make it wrong." She smiles with those light brown eyes shining and her bowed lips wide. "It makes it perfect."

He throws her chin and she walks to the office with the grace and confidence of the Kateri Blackhawk that I love. My enigma.

Christian laughs. "She is, Brother. She's your other half. The bikes are here."

I smile and suspend out with him. Taylor pulls up with Asa and three bikes on the back of a pickup. They're fuckin' awesome. Ayakuhsak has stars, Wápáyu has wind in the Navajo symbol and Ôkatuq has clouds. All have their full name on the tank and the Badass logo is on the back fenders.

I hug Taylor then Asa. "Thank you, Brothers. They came out perfect."

Taylor smiles. "I called Asa for help or you'd have been waiting a week. It's been crazy at the Princes with the kids all here. It showed the Brothers all they do so it wasn't for nothing." He's glad Prez pulled them and proud of what they got done.

I hit his back and spin hearing the kids running. "Dad Blackhawk!" I smile at the little clown that has me wrapped. I bend and he jumps onto my chest like a little monkey. When Ôkatuq and Wápáyu get to me, they both have hands on my back and their heads leaning on my sides.

"This is Taylor Blackhawk, one of my big brothers. Taylor, this is Ôkatuq, Wápáyu and I have Ayakuhsak here."

Ayakuhsak jumps and Taylor catches him laughing. "Another Mucimi?"

I shrug lifting Ôkatuq to the truck. "Jeremy said like Putam." I lift Wápáyu and he smiles with tears in his eyes.

"Dad! It's the symbol from the circle, like mom's necklace."

I mess his hair. "Your bike is a gift with thought to honor who you are, Wápáyu."

He turns and hugs Taylor with an arm around Ayakuhsak. "Thank you, Taylor Blackhawk." He turns toward Jeremy. "Uncle Taylor." He corrects making me smile.

Taylor is touched and throws chin.

He sets Ayakuhsak on the bed and Ôkatuq hugs him. "Thank you, Uncle Taylor."

Ayakuhsak climbs on his bike. "Thank you, Uncle Taylor Blackhawk! Vroom!"

The kid has us all moving on. We get the bikes down, Ayakuhsak's with him on it. Asa takes Ayakuhsak with Christian and Jeremy. Jacob, Taylor and I give a lesson to the older boys. After an hour, they're riding the grass.

Mucimi shows and every fuckin' one of them drops their clothes on the ground and dress in gear. My brothers find this funny. I don't.

Christian comes from behind me. "You'll teach them their worth. Don't stress over this and miss the moment. They'll get it."

I nod. I can work the *no disrobing in front of strangers* into lessons. I got this.

He hits my back. "You do, Mase. You're a good father. Now put the fuckin' fire out."

Shit. I close my eyes and breathe. They don't know my brothers but trust me. That's what I take and breathe deep opening my eyes hearing Ayakuhsak's laugh.

The little shit is riding his bike in full gear with Jeremy suspending on the side of him. Fuckin' cute. Ôkatuq catches up, then slows down keeping pace with Ayakuhsak. Wápáyu doesn't miss a beat and takes Ayakuhsak's other side.

Cort rides up in front of a Security SUV. "Fucking kids." He makes me laugh.

"Ranger settle?"

He laughs walking toward the SUV. "He's pissed at Jack for not telling him. Jack didn't fly with stealth, so he didn't know until Mag told him. It's been a joke they didn't share. I think it's payback for Schmeg."

I crack up then hug Rex and Ajhil. Rex turns and helps Ant Irma out. I kiss her cheek and move back to where I can see the boys. Asa catches Ajhil and starts asking him about the homeless neighborhood.

Rex has his eyes on the boys. "Which one is my great grandson?"

Shit. I look at Cort.

"All of them." Cort has me relieved.

"Kateri doesn't know anything about her mom, Rex. More of her memory is cloaked so she can't answer questions."

He nods looking older and wicked sad. "Cortland told me. I didn't put it together. Kateri taking them all makes them all mine. I have three great grandsons." He smiles taking some of that sad out of him.

Mucimi stays with Ayakuhsak and Jeremy suspends to us. '*I got it.*' He touches Rex's head for a good minute. No one says a word. Cort brings Caelan to the bikes when they stop. I look back to Rex and smile.

He looks younger and happy is lighting his world. He walks by Jeremy calling Ant Irma to come meet his great grandsons. I laugh.

Nash shows with a box of meat. I guess we're grilling. Mateo and Allen ride up smiling.

I look for Taylor who is hugging Nash and Ôkatuq. '*I'm going to take the food to the pool.*'

He looks up and throws chin. He's got the boys.

~*~*~

Kateri

The boys, Parker, Nash and Mase are jumping off the mountain ledge. I can't believe that thought even passes through my head. Justice had us all jump it before it got dark. Every Protector from his original crew with spouses and kids, I'm glad he included Parker, all jumped so he could get a picture. It was unbelievable.

While they're doing that crazy, I'm showing Mikey what I came up with. It's more like the virtual holograms showing people in a group with the results showing on the side. It's how I've done everything else and it's worked so I stuck with it.

She goes from her laptop hologram board to mine, typing and looking at the results then the side results. I'm waiting to explain the first board but she's pretty intent on this one.

I look over to the ledge and don't see anyone floating up or flying down. Mase shows on the walkway with Ayakuhsak and Wápáyu in his arms and Ôkatuq on his back. When Nash appears with Parker, I relax and watch Mikey.

"This works perfect. The matrix is right."

I nod wondering why it wouldn't be. "I didn't touch the matrix. I don't really understand it or even how to read it. The job was getting the results in a way you could understand and see them better. The results page shows that better than this one."

She nods and looks over my shoulder. "Shit."

I look back. Prez, Cort and Taylor are coming this way. Mikey closes her laptop.

"It's okay, Mikey. Only high Officers and Protectors are here." Prez has her letting out her breath.

"She finished it today. I was excited to see how it came out."

They sit and Mikey looks at me nervously. "Can you show and explain the BSC testing results page."

I smile. "Sure. I'm going to use the glasses so they see the whole board without scrolling. Do you want to pick a Club?"

She's surprised but it's Ben who asks. "You have all the Clubs?"

"No. The satellite does. If I put the name in the link, it brings their training up. That's how I got Alpha Rising for Mikey."

Cort laughs.

Taylor is surprised. "How did you program this if you don't have all the Clubs?"

This makes me smile. "I keep telling everyone, but they don't understand what I do. I don't program anything. Someone programmed the matrix and testing to show results on a hologram board. I just took the results for the hologram board and made it look different. The pictures are what I add. Everything else just shows in the spots I add that result. So I copy and paste the result line of code for any given thing you test on your matrix and it shows on my picture."

Prez laughs. "Show us with Princes of Prophecy."

I put my glasses on and type the Princes into the link. The board builds starting from the top showing the symbols I added but no numbers. Jacob and Jeremy come over and watch. I pick someone named Josiah and his numbers show on the side with symbols by them. "He's aerial, Ops, IT, passed everything for Protector..."

"Fuckin' hell. Can I see?" Jacob asks.

I hand him the glasses. He touches someone else then jumps to the other board. They all laugh. Mikey looks at me and smiles. When Jacob takes people off, they laugh again. I don't get it.

Jeremy rolls his eyes. "Finally, they see it." His words come out slow, but he doesn't talk much so I nod.

Mikey laughs and I'm lost. Taylor wants the glasses and I'm pretty much done. "Do you need me to change anything or have something you want added, Mikey?"

"How do I get this to everyone?" Prez asks.

"It's on the virtual server. Stella sent me a file to work from and Mikey gave me the Alpha Rising name for the link. I'm not a programmer or coder so I don't know how that works with the server."

He laughs. "For years I've been asking how to get this to work. In a month, I have a working board and can understand it better because of pictures. I'll have Stella get it to where we can use it. Can I keep the glasses for now?"

I nod and jump.

Jeremy appears with Stella right on the side of me. "What the fuck? I was eating."

He points to Mikey.

Stella shakes her head at him. "You're a fuckin' nut."

I look down fast. Mikey laughs. Oh my, they really are crazy. I know the readers by the laughing.

"Can you get this to the Presidents?" Mikey asks her.

"Yeah, then I'm fuckin' eating." She sits and pulls my laptop over, types like she was born with a keyboard attached to her hands then stands. "Anything else?"

I laugh. She walks away mumbling, "Fuckin' Brothers."

I stand wanting to be done. "If you want me to add anything, let me know."

The Blackhawks are arguing over what Club to pull up. I shake my head when Justice, Teller and Christian show up.

Prez laughs. "I'll get you paid and thank you, Kateri."

"Thank you but you should know I didn't do this to be paid. I was just helping Mikey with some pictures. Stella and Alder give me plenty of work."

He smiles. "I heard about the organs. Thank you for that too, Kateri. Go see your boys. We're all set."

I nod and go. Mase has the boys sitting with Rex, my newest un-dreamed dream, Ant Irma, his mom and dad.

He stands when I come through the gate. "That was quick. You didn't have to rush, Yáhsháyôn."

I kiss his chest and pull his shirt so I can kiss his considerate lips. "I didn't rush. They're crazy so I didn't really explain. I may need you to get my laptop back."

He laughs then he's gone. My hand falls and I look down at the empty patch of dirt he was standing on.

CJ laughs. "It's not a bad crazy. Mass is friggin batshit crazy, it's a little more intense but still not bad."

I smile at her. "It's not. Just a lot in one day. I'm starting to worry that I won't see it soon and become just as crazy as they are."

She laughs. "You won't ever be as crazy as they are, but you'll accept it as normal."

"I can live with that."

Mase shows up with a plate and my laptop. "The LS board is cool, Yáhsháyôn."

CJ laughs.

I shake my head smiling. "Thank you, Nupômkoki. What's an LS board?"

"The board you made with the people. It's a Lives Saved matrix."

I just look at him. Lives saved? I eat while he explains it to CJ. They are crazy, then make a matrix to place people by lives saved. I guess if you're going to hang with crazy people, they're a good crowd to hang with.

Jeremy laughs sitting in front of me.

~*~*~

Mase

The kids swim with the Alpha-Bits giving lessons and women watching, while we sit. It feels like the first time today for me.

Cort hands me a bag. "He's making more with the different stones for the cases."

I got pictures but those stones didn't look alive in a picture. Pulling the box open, I let my breath out.

"They're alive." The picture looked flat but he said it was anything but. I go through each piece, the diamonds with that stone are beautiful.

"Raid thinks you're crazy for picking the big diamonds to crush. He thinks you should have bought the cheaper and used gold." Cort shakes his head. "I'm not sure if it was for a laugh but he's going to get it when he sees the pieces on her. Where did you get the blue she's got on the choker?" His mind said collar.

I smile. "Mitch has these shimmering stones on her wedding band. I called Jamie. They bought them from some place in California years ago. They had pieces made for her until she got tired of the blue. They're more expensive than the diamonds." I smile. Mitch wouldn't care. "He sold me a necklace they never gave her. I had two charms made."

He nods. "He must have found the same stones. It looks like a match."

I nod knowing he did. Joey gave them names of stones I was interested in when she left my card number. I didn't know Cort was springing the jeweler trip after an Op but they had the stones so it worked.

I guess swim time is over. The kids are running.

"We're jumping early, Brothers." Teller has us all moving.

Rex and Ant Irma will be back. Ajhil gets on his knees so the boys can hug their friend Caelan. The Bits take off having shit to do in the Lab and I push to hide jewelry.

I get back in time to take the boys up to change. Their bed pants and Ts look cute. Slippers are straight moccasins without reinforcements. I love Nancy.

"Are my Blackhawk boys ready to go meet the ancestors?"

They all agree by jumping around then trying to climb me.

I get them straight laughing. "Close your eyes and hold tight." I push to the back yard. "We're here." I shrug at my Brothers shaking their heads, it works.

The dogs run out the slider followed by Kateri. She's a vision. My girl comes right to me dressed in a cotton top similar to mine but long in the back and linen pants that flow around her legs. She looks like a native harem girl with her collar saying she's a one of. Jesus, she's killing me.

"Where is everyone?"

I kiss her lips. "The circle. Are we ready?"

Jeremy takes Ôkatuq and puts his arm on Taylor. Jacob takes Wápáyu and I put my arm around my beautiful girl. "Numuks, Kimuks, circle. Close your eyes and hold tight."

We push and show at the circle together. The crew laughs. We sit around the outside circle just fitting. Hannah and Trask have their boys with them. This is going to be huge. The wolves sit at the opening like sentinels making me proud.

Stella shows with Jordan and Brinks. "They wouldn't run it with the wolves."

Brinks shakes his head sitting her on his lap before moving her to the side. "The view isn't a rock wall and the night is beautiful."

She quiets and takes their hands making us all smile. Stella is Stella. Mucimi, Justice and Teller show. Mucimi makes us all move down so he can sit between Taylor and me.

Justice and Teller sit in the middle with Christian. "Hold onto your anchors and jump now," Christian says.

I breathe deep feeling the ground below me. "We're here." I say in Mohegan. My Yáhsháyôn translates.

Jacob smiles. "It's good to speak in our native tongue here. We will teach you the language. Before you've learned I'll give you English for what is said."

I tighten my hand on Kateri's seeing her bare leg from a slit all the way down the pant leg. I push it away and focus. "They'll hear English."

She nods smiling at Jacob. "Thank you, Protector of the Three and my boys."

Justice laughs. "Here we are one. One with our ancestors, earth and family."

He points at the sky. "Ancestors are not seen, can you feel them, Wápáyu."

I look at Wápáyu on Jacob's lap. "Around me?"

"The wind, Wápáyu. Ancestors are alive in the wind, the earth, the water, sun, moon, clouds and ..." he waits for it smiling at Ayakuhsak.

"*Ayakuhsak!*" My littlest scout has us laughing.

"Yes. They send healing, calm and light to us through all things, but here, they gather for us to gain knowledge, find peace and celebrate all that is with our people of the past showing us they are with us always."

"Mom Todachine lives here. She loves me with mom Blackhawk. She lives in the stars." Ayakuhsak has my arm tightening as Yáhsháyôn squeezes my hand.

Christian stands. "Yes. Your mom loves you through her sister, mom Blackhawk. You have two moms to keep you safe and happy, Ayakuhsak. There are many ancestors to help guide you and help keep you safe. In life that is your Blackhawk family. We show appreciation always to our ancestors for guiding that life because they're wise members of our family always willing to share their knowledge and help with us."

Ayakuhsak nods. Like it's settled. I shake my head.

Justice stands holding his hands out and the sky changes to night. The Protectors show to us, stop milling around and come to us sitting around our circle. Aiyana and Dakota show in the center.

"The ancestors shine upon us this night. Many tribes are banding together to show appreciation for our efforts to keep *all* people safe from harm. They welcome our new and celebrate our old." Ayanna sits and the sky explodes.

The kids clap and giggle with the Protectors. Kateri leans over to see all three boys. Their faces a mask of wonder.

"The stars, wind and clouds are where heaven starts. I give thanks to the ancestors for giving me the daily reminder of such precious gifts." She smiles up at me. "Especially my first dream."

I fuckin' love her.

Ayakuhsak scoots off my lap and hugs her. "I thank the ancestor for Blackhawk gifts." He's too fuckin' smart. I don't correct the ancestor because he's too fuckin' cute too.

She turns him and smiles at me hearing Wápáyu and Ôkatuq's thanks for Blackhawks.

~*~*~

The boys are down, the Brothers are gone, the kitchen and family room are clean. I take my girl's hand and pull without warning. In our room, I close the door and check that the intercom is on. We're good. Walking three steps in, I turn her and step back.

"How high do those slits go?"

Her eyes are smiling, if her lips do I'm spanking her ass. My hands watch her hand slide up a slit on the right. "I tacked them here. It's shorts length. With so many boys and men around, I was not comfortable with the slit to the waist."

"Jesus fuck. The slit went to the waist. Sliding my hand through to feel your skin would have made the kinky ancestors and me happier."

She smiles then sees my eyes and stops quick. I shake my head. "That's one. Shoes, pants, top off, my teasing little Indian."

I watch the top go over her head and have to hold in a groan. Her bra is nothing but a scrap of lace. My eyes find hers amused with me. I need her in the other room but I'm not stopping this.

Slipping her shoes off, she moves her hand to the side of her pants and flips a wooden toggle through a leather strap. Fuckin' sexy. Her pants fall and I hold my breath. Taking a step, I lift her pants and shirt giving them a shake to keep me breathing normally. I move her shoes to the chair and lay her clothes over the back.

Standing in front of her, I take her hand and lift it over her head seeing the scrap of lace barely hold her tit in. I spin her slowly, my eyes watching the string and stopping on her bare cheek. I'm so fucked.

I watch seeing the little triangle before it disappears showing her full ass. "My hand would have hit no resistance sliding in the side and skimming your beautiful ass, Yáhsháyôn."

She doesn't say a word. I step to the dresser and pull out the flat vibrators. Turning one on, I flip it, sliding it slowly from her neck down and over the scrap of lace making sure I catch it on her hard nipple. Moving it lower, I take my time making sure she feels it before cupping her with it flat in my palm. "The perfect purr for your pretty kitty, Yáhsháyôn."

Her breath hitches when I grind it into her. I move it to just over the triangle of lace covering her pussy and bend. Turning it so it will stick, I get it above, just to the side of that little rise inside of her that I want singing for me.

My jaw clenches seeing her stomach break out in goosebumps while attaching the other on the opposite side. I stand looking at them, they're in the right place, just edging the lace doing nothing to cover what I want. The panties are a waste of lace so I tear them off.

My arm reaches out for the pillow on the chest, throwing it on the floor, I point. "A beautiful tease, baby. I'm not into being teased tonight."

She kneels and unbuttons my breeches. Those light brown eyes look up with amusement and love in them. Mine don't like the amusement and I feel anger flash. She smiles pulling me into her mouth.

I'm so fucked.

Chapter Eleven

Mase

'*Mase*!'

I stop at Justice's cry for help. "Here. Where do you need me?"

'*ABSZ. I've got Nash bringing you, hurry, Brother.*' Teller sounds like he's barely holding on.

'*I'll get there. Christian!*' I throw to Nash and Christian. I need help over the distance to the ABSZ.

He shows on the side of me. '*Push, Jeremy!*'

I'm moved and feel the jolt right through me. I hit the ground still moving forward and fall to my knees scratching at dirt to stand.

"Justice!" My heart is ready to beat right the fuck out of my chest. I'm not feeling them.

Doc opens the door to a pod just up from us. "Here. The baby is healthy."

I push and drop to my knees seeing them. "I'm here. It's going to be okay." Pulling them both to me, I look at the woman and take in what she did. Thank fuck the baby is okay.

Justice is shaking. He was trying to heal her. "Christian, throw energy." '*Help! Energy, Justice and Teller.*' I throw to the crew and look around. '*Jeremy, find Mucimi. Get him to the reservation. Jacob, help pull Justice and Teller at the reservation.*'

He's got it. I move us away from the bed and blood. "Brothers, jump. The crew is helping. Jacob is there. Jump now!"

335

I lean their bodies on the seat of the couch and push back to the bedroom. "Why the fuck would she do this?"

Doc puts the baby wrapped in a towel on his arm. "She was passed out when I got here. Justice called me and sent Teller, but she had already lost too much blood. When her heart gave out, he yelled for you. Mucimi vanished. Brother, if she went this far, she would have found another way. I need to get the baby out of here."

'*No! She goes with you!*' Jeremy yells in my head.

"Jesus fuck. Don't yell in my fuckin' head."

"The baby goes to Joey," Christian says calmly from the doorway. "Mucimi fell trying to get to us. Jeremy got him safe, they're going to the reservation."

I try to think. "I need Alder, Cort and Falcon."

Christian is gone. I look at Doc. "What do you need for the baby right now?"

"I checked her but haven't cleaned her. She's breathing fine and has good color."

Okay that's all good shit. "Clean her here. She doesn't leave here."

Falcon walks in the room and scans.

"She tried cutting the baby out of her." Doc helps him out.

I shake my head. "He needs to clean the baby. Cort and Alder are on their way. I need help, Brother. Justice and Teller are at the reservation, Mucimi is on his way there. They tried healing her."

He looks at the dead woman and clenches his jaw. With a military pivot, he takes the baby from Doc and walks out.

I look at Doc. "Go, get her clean and recheck her."

Cort shows on the side of me. Alder is here before Cort takes a step toward the bed. "Shortest explanation. Woman tried to cut the baby out. Justice got here and called Teller and Mucimi. They tried to heal her. Teller brought Doc in but she was already dying. Justice called to me then fell, Teller was barely holding on. Mucimi fell on his way to Honor. They're all at the reservation with Jeremy, Jacob and the crew throwing energy."

"Where's Mucimi's body?" Cort always has good questions.

"Jeremy got him safe and him to the reservation. They needed energy from us to get them there. He's safe."

He nods. "She killed the baby?"

I shake my head no. "It's with Doc and Falcon getting cleaned and checked."

Alder runs. Cort looks at me. "You need to get to Justice?"

I nod. "The baby comes with me. Jeremy said it goes to Joey. Since he screamed it, there's a reason. I don't know more than what I told you. I would cremate her but Justice was shaking bad. He gave too much."

He hugs me. "Go. I got this. The baby will be right here when you get back."

I walk out and sit on the couch, then jump.

~*~*~

I jump back and open my eyes to Jeti on the chair with the baby. I hear Cort but don't see him.

"He won't let anyone else in. Him and Pres Falcon took the woman out for cleanup. The doctor left. Alder went to change, he's flying to Honor with us."

I nod. "Thanks for getting here."

"I jumped back when Dakota and Prez showed. You weren't there. When I showed, Cort said you just jumped. Are they okay?"

I nod. "Aylen helped explain shit. Aiyana, Dakota and Jeremy were throwing to them. They can't cloak it but they'll dull it for them."

She nods looking at the baby. "Alder had me give her water."

"Thank you, Jeti. Do you need to jump?"

Her tear-filled eyes find mine. I stand and walk the three steps to the chair taking the baby. "Jump. I'll wait right here, Brother. Everyone is there."

She jumps without answering. I call Kateri looking at the tiny baby, I haven't heard a cry yet.

Yáhsháyôn answers sounding relieved. Cort called her. Seren is bringing shit Alder needs from a clinic. My mom is helping her get baby shit for a few days. The boys are trying to help. She asks about the three. I love her for it.

"They're shaken but will be okay, Yáhsháyôn. Thank you for asking. Jeti showed here to help, she's shaken, I'll try to get her to the house."

"Damn, she's young to see something so horrible. I'll let your mom know. We'll take care of her." She's got that love growing as if infinity isn't far enough.

"*Kuwômôyush*, Yáhsháyôn. I'm already breathing easier. I'll be back as soon as I can."

"*Kuwômôyush*, Nupômkoki."

I breathe and open the front door. Falcon turns with his phone to his ear. Cort watches me. "Jeti needed to jump. They shouldn't be long. Aiyana, Dakota and Jeremy were dulling it."

"Cloaking?"

I shake my head. "You can't cloak Leads like Justice and Teller. They'll dull what Justice was feeling. He was exhausted on top of losing her. With energy, he'll think clearer. Teller can get more. He'll keep Justice moving forward."

Cort is confused. "They cloaked you."

I nod. "Unless I ask, they won't or can't. I'm not a Lead like Justice. I'm a Protector. I'm not making decisions on life or death for others on a scale with his. He needs to feel every decision and reaction he causes. For me, the bad guys are my target. I'm not Justice."

He nods thinking he should have known that.

I leave it alone. "Thanks for handling this. Do you need me to do anything for you, Boss?"

"No. You covered them. Jeremy dropped Mucimi at Alpha. Parker was alone at the house. He called Nova crying. He thought Mucimi was dead."

Jesus. "He must have thought it was Nova."

He nods. "I gave Nova that. He said Parker was in gear for a ride. He's settled and fine. Mikey is with Mucimi and Jeremy there, or their bodies."

I nod. "I'll talk to Jeremy. This isn't Princes." Neither are left anywhere unguarded.

Falcon shakes his head. "Leave it. He got him safe, Parker is fine and he brought them to Mikey's to jump. This isn't normal and Jeremy did the right thing. Mikey said they can't get to the ancestors exhausted or hurt." It sounds like a question.

"You're right, I'll leave it. No, they can't jump or they may not make it. I was throwing orders everywhere. Jacob was there to pull them. The crew throwing energy. Jeremy finding Mucimi, but I had Doc and the baby. Christian was transporting you here. I couldn't leave them to jump, it's Justice and Teller."

Cort puts his hand on my shoulder. "I get it. Good job, Brother."

He looks behind me, so I turn. Justice and Teller are standing.

Justice lifts Jeti and walks our way. "She needs to go to Honor."

I nod.

Teller takes her from Justice. "Nash is waiting. I'll be right back."

Justice looks tired. "I can explain what you haven't gotten here."

Falcon looks at Cort to answer. "We got what we need. Take what you need to get this settled."

Justice breathes deep. "Thanks, Mase." His eyes go to Cort. "Jumping the cliff will do it. I have a Flight in two hours."

Cort smiles like a politician. "You got enough to take me?"

Christian shows. "He does. Good job, Mase. I'll meet you at your house. Jeremy is getting Mucimi to Honor. I could use a cliff jump. That was fuckin' crazy."

I hug Justice then Teller when he appears. "Where's Nash?"

"At Alder's picking him up. He'll stay low. Go, Brother." Christian hugs me around the baby. When he steps back, I push.

Jeti is in a seat. Alder sitting next to her.

I close the door and hand the baby to Jeti as I bend in front of her. "The Mom would have tried a new way, Brother. They saved the baby. Jeremy said she's supposed to go to Joey. She was meant to be here, Brother."

She hugs the tiny, wrapped baby closer. Alder has baby felt and cans. "We make sure she safe, healthy to Joey."

Jeti nods. "Yeah. Joey would beat me with her crutch if I hurt the baby."

I breathe and get cans for Jeti then me.

~*~*~

Kateri

Christian and Jacob have the boys on the trampoline. CJ has the baby and Jeti is running for imaginary needs CJ comes up with. I'm cutting cheese, fruit and vegetables for something to feed my Blackhawk boys and family. I know Jeti is a Callahan but they're all Protectors and grew up together, that makes them all family.

I set a tray on the table on top of the ice filled lid. Cheese is on the next but we only have a few crackers. I cut the fajitas we have in quarters and fill in. The fruit is easy, yogurt dip and I'm done. I set them on ice lids and pull the list for food.

I look at CJ. She's good here. The grocer is closer to town one than two. They need town names. Mase is on Ops. I go to the deck and smile watching Ôkatuq flip through the air and bounce high.

"Christian, we need food. Mostly snack foods. Mase is on Ops. Do you think I can run while everyone is here? I have a team of Enforcers."

He shakes his head no. "You need Protectors. My dad is bored. Send him with a list. That's what my mom does when he's bored."

That would work. I look for Cloud and find him in the garage sitting on a folding chair with his elbows on his knees. "Is everything okay, Cloud?"

He puts something in his lower pocket quickly. "Yeah. I was making something for the kids. Did you need something?"

Perfect. "I do. I can't leave without a Protector Team and Mase is on Ops. We're out of snack food. I have a list."

He nods. "I'll run. Send me the list in chat."

"Thank you. The boys have been scarfing fruit down like water. I'll put my ID at the bottom. The grocer uses that number."

"I have an Honor card. Don't send your ID number out."

I nod and watch him walk out to the pickup in the driveway. I guess it's a safety thing. I send him the list and get back in.

CJ looks relieved. "I'm glad you didn't go. You need a Team even if you're with Cloud. He gets annoyed when they follow him around."

I can see that. "It's a guy thing. Sending your ID is a no-no?"

She nods. "We don't ever have to. Joey will send a card number for us. She must have credit cards for us."

I wonder why that is then get it. "The ID is billed. With so many, fraudulent charges are kept to a minimum."

She nods. "Someone at the men's store billed all kinds of stuff. They returned it for cash. Nancy sends their clothes now."

"Nancy is a busy woman."

She laughs. "She is. You're more relaxed than you were. I'm glad this is getting easier."

So am I. "I think the cloak did that. The boys getting here helped. When you have to show someone else how to be strong you don't have a choice. Here we're all safe and happy so it's pretty easy." I smile. There is always someone around.

"I'm happy for you."

The baby makes little noises. "Seren."

We look at the door and sure enough Seren is there with Prospects. "I have the stuff Alder asked for."

I stand. "He's in the office." Seren sits with Caelan. The Prospects go to the office.

"Natalia."

I look at the door. I hope Cloud hurries when I hear the feet pounding on the deck stairs.

~*~*~

Mase

I'm so glad to be setting down. It was an easy Op and took minutes but it was in Arizona, so the flight back feels long.

The little girl is stuck to Aylen. She's hurt and too fuckin' thin but won't let anyone close. The woman is scared. Aylen keeps trying to talk to her, but she's not buying it.

Nash calls five out.

I move from the door and bend in front of the woman. "We have a doctor that can see you and your girl. Once you're showered, dressed and get checked we can get you fed before they bring you to the women at the compound Aylen told you about."

"She's not mine. You think you're going to stick her with me? Is that what this is, you'll use me to take care of kids to replace me?"

What the fuck? No rescued slave we've seen has acted like this. I look at Aylen. She didn't get any of this either.

"You'll live free. You're not a slave anymore. The girl isn't yours?"

"No, she's not mine. I raised her then they wanted her not me. I'm not raising kids to replace me." She screeches at me.

Aylen takes her hand and throws calm. Thank fuck, I swear she was ready to spit in my face. The woman thinks she's going to die anyway. Fuck.

"Fuckin' hell."

I look at Seth. He's not wrong.

"Ops, I have a situation here. This woman isn't the girl's mother. This girl needs to be seen."

Pres comes right back. "Set down in front, Nash. I'll come down. Does the woman need medical?"

I give Nash a second to get his roger out then answer, "Regular with Mary. Battered but no major injuries."

"Roger."

I bend to the woman again. "We didn't know she wasn't yours. Pres will come down and straighten it out. You don't have to raise her or any other kid we find. You get a say here."

She cries. "They'll kill me if I'm no good to them. I have to keep them happy."

Shit. "No one owns you here. You have no one to keep happy but you."

She looks at Aylen hoping I'm not lying to her. Jesus. I stand and step back giving Aylen a minute.

Pres opens the door. I look at Seth. He jumps out to explain with Cayden and Mikey right behind him.

I stay at the door watching. Kristos is pissed. He climbs up and goes right to the woman. She's afraid of his eyes.

"We have a doctor waiting for the girl. You can get flown to the compound with other women we rescued. The girl needs to be seen here." He waits for an outburst.

She nods. "She's not mine. The girl that had her was killed. She didn't want them using the girl and they killed her."

Kristos nods. "Aylen will get you to the compound with the other women." He turns to Aylen and gets a nod.

When he reaches for the girl, she cries. *'Your eyes scare her. You're pissed.'* I throw.

He stands and steps back. "Mikey and Cayden are with Aylen then choppered home." *'She needs to be seen now.'*

I bend to the girl. "My name is Mase Blackhawk. You're bleeding and need to see a doctor. The best doctor around is right here. I'm going to take you to him so he can fix you up."

She looks at Kristos then me and nods. I put my hands out instead of reaching for her. She leans forward and I'm up with her.

I suspend out and wait for Kristos. "Good job, Protectors."

They throw thanks to me. Seth waits with me and the girl while Mikey and Cayden board.

Kristos climbs out. "Get her to Alder. He's still at your house."

Seth nods to me. "I got the report."

"Roger, Kristos. Thanks, Seth."

I cover the girl's eyes and push.

Alder is waiting at the door. "Office." He runs in front of us.

I'm glad no one is out here. I set her down on the gurney. It's positioned for Alder's height. He pulls the shirt then gauze we got on her head off.

"This is Alder. He's a doctor. He'll make you better."

She looks at me and her eyes roll. I hold her up not knowing where to touch. "Fuck, Alder."

He turns back from the desk of medical shit. "Get Allen, out back."

I lay her down and push. "Allen, Alder needs you."

He runs. Alder points him to gloves and Allen jumps right in. He's medical but I didn't know he did everything medical. I thought he was DNA. No, Allen is a PA and helps Alta with the braces and shit.

I have no idea what to do aside from quick first aid so I put a hand on her foot and throw healing calm. '*Jeremy, if you're close, I could use help.*'

He shows on the side of me. I step back and he kneels. "*Ki Kisuq.*"

Alder turns looking at Jeremy then me. "Yours?"

I look at Jeremy. What?

He nods. '*Your girl. She needs a cloak and healing. Aiyana is waiting.*' He moves to the couch. My dad comes to the door and watches.

Jesus fuck. "Alder, I'm going to jump with her. Can you do what you do?"

"Go, you sky need ancestors," he says in Mohegan. My dad laughs.

Jesus. I hold her leg and look at Alder. "My hand stays on her."

He nods. "You sit easy me to move around."

I sit putting my legs around the gurney wheels. He nods so I jump. Aiyana, Jeremy and Dakota are waiting. We chant. I throw what I know. They do whatever they do.

Forever or however long later, Aiyana has me jumping. "The ancestors have done well for Kisuq. Her bleeding is healed, the cloak is in place. Wash her while she sleeps."

I look at her not getting that but nod. She doesn't explain so I throw appreciation to her, Dakota, Jeremy and the ancestors, then lift the tiny girl and jump.

When I open my eyes, my hand is taped to her leg. "You taped me?"

My dad turns. "You said it stays there. I taped it so they could work."

I roll my eyes at an amused Alder and Allen. "Aiyana said to wash her while she sleeps."

Alder's look turns sad. "Odor is body fluid. No good to remind?"

My dad goes through fucks. I untape my hand and look at Alder. He nods so I lift her. Jeremy is up and follows me up the stairs and into my bathroom. We wash the girl in a couple of inches of water. Her bruises are gone. Her head has a scar that looks bad, but the healers will keep working on it when they're close. I hold her up and Jeremy washes her hair gently.

He pulls wind but I stop him. "Let me fix her hair first." He doesn't get it but waits.

I cut her hair straight across from the shortest piece just under her shoulders. "Go, I'll find..."

Mucimi stands with a bag and a smile. "Kisuq."

Every-fuckin-one knowing this is fuckin' annoying. A warning would have been good. He follows Jeremy out of the bathroom and they dress her in a cotton dress with faded pink on it. It's similar to our shirts but goes to her knees. Jeremy has tears in his eyes putting a pull-up on her. I put my hand on his back. She's got tiny moccasins with beaded fringe that he smiles at. Mucimi waves at her hair getting it all flat.

Fuckin' kids. I need to practice this shit. I always see me moving. They laugh at me. Whatever. I lift her and turn toward the door.

My dad is watching with no expression. "What are you telling Kateri?"

I breathe deep. "The truth. Alder will tell her what they did so she's alert to a possible problem."

He shakes his head then I do. "She needs the truth, Dad. I have it. Kateri is stronger than I am. She'll deal and we'll move on."

He looks at Jeremy then back to me. "Okay. We'll keep the boys busy. The baby is fine Alder said."

"Fuck. I should have asked."

He laughs. "When?"

I nod following him out. "Good point. When is Joey getting here?"

"Soon."

Fuckin' great. I carry my newest little addition out to the deck. Alder stands.

"Can you tell what you did in the office?"

He runs. I take it as a yes.

Turning, I nod to my very breath. "Yáhsháyôn, you need this."

She gives my mom the baby and walks with me looking at the little girl.

"Her name is Kisuq. The woman with her said she is three. She looks smaller than three."

"What's wrong with her?"

I wait for her to walk through the office door before I answer, "Alder will tell you. I jumped and only know her bleeding stopped and the cloak is in place."

Her eyes close and a tear falls. I kiss her cheek. "Come. Sit so you can hold her. I need a drink."

She sits and I put Sky in her arms. She puts her against her heart and looks at Alder. "I don't need how she got hurt, just what you did."

Alder nods. "No speculate. I did no Ops today."

I walk out and get a drink of whiskey. I don't need any more than I know.

It's not long before Alder comes to the kitchen. "Boss Kateri talk Boss Christian."

I lift the bottle and tip it to him. He shakes his head, so I put it away.

"No detail Sky, like Boss Kateri?"

I nod. "I can't keep finding them and come home knowing the details, Brother. Theirs hurt more or something."

He nods. "Love. You feel their hurt."

"I guess. I just can't know them. The woman today, she was fuckin' pissed. She was screeching at me thinking she was going to die anyway. It was her last stand. I don't know how they're going to get fixed, Brother."

He gets juice from the fridge. I pull a glass for him.

He pours a few ounces for both of us. "I no understand mind fix. Boss Aylen know. I not need detail. Boss Aylen help to jobs, train to free, work together bond." He shakes his head. "I no time to train. Detail hurt I no can help."

I shoot the juice back and nod. "I guess that's it. I can't help a past I didn't live and know nothing about. They'd find a way to get past it. Men are different." I shrug. I'll never be that strong and I'm not sure I should be.

He nods. "Good talk. Call to me. Next Op I go. Doctor need show today. I no fix mind. I fix body."

I smile. "You're pretty good at fixing minds too, Brother."

He smiles looking younger. "Hope to me yet. Later, Brother."

I shake my head at him but don't correct the to. "Thanks for your help again, Brother."

He throws chin. I smile as he picks his bag up and runs. I love Alder.

~*~*~

Cort sits with Caelan. "Everyone just accepts she's yours."

I look at my girl holding my girl. "Yeah. Christian said I'd have a girl. When the baby wasn't it, I was relieved I had some breathing room. I called for Jeremy to heal and he said she was *Ki Kisuq*. I was surprised but not really. It was going to happen whether I'm prepared or not."

He shakes his head. "I'm not sure I could do it. Four in days."

I smile. "Brantley was like this, he got four in two days."

"Shit. I thought I'd impress you. Here are their papers. Web will have socials and shit. Alder will get with Statler on immunization based on blood and shit. The Alpha-Bits can't be near them for that immunization shit. Alder will tell you. He requested to go back on Ops as a doctor." He shakes his head smiling. "Doc made the same request when Alder told him about your girl."

I hold my hand up. "No details. I can't help a past I didn't live and know nothing about. The details hurt. I'd never be able to do the job knowing everything. That's Justice's job."

He nods sliding the envelope closer. I drop it in my pocket without moving Ayakuhsak. "I'll show them tomorrow when it matters and they're all awake."

Kristos and Taylor sit.

"Brothers." I acknowledge.

"You need to stop taking kids in. Natalia wants four now. Boys first so they can take care of their little sister."

I laugh. He gives me a look. I keep smiling. "You'll give her whatever the fuck she wants and love every minute of it."

He shakes his head smiling. "Yeah. How come Joey never had kids?"

I look at Taylor who looks down. Fuck. "She has a broken back. Jeremy healed what he could when he was young, like I wasn't born yet young. She can't have kids without causing more damage. She won't go back in a chair so kids weren't an option. With Sebastian and her jobs now, they can do this. He'd be the one that would have to do any lifting."

He looks over at Joey with her new girl against her heart. "She's going to be a good mom."

I kiss my boy's head feeling that. She's waited long enough. Christian, Jeremy and Jacob sit.

I smile loving everyone close. "Is Terry coming?"

"For the day. He can't stay." Jacob likes that he'll be here.

"Your blanket is here and Mucimi got shirts. We're dressing the boys tomorrow. We'll be here for breakfast." Christian puts his hands out. I turn Ayakuhsak and hand him over. Jeremy puts his hand on Christian's shoulder.

"How come you can hold him?" Cort and the questions.

Christian shrugs. "He'll never be a threat. Jeremy is pulling energy for me. I can't hold him long but you got to start somewhere." He smiles kissing Ayakuhsak's head.

"Love the smile, Christian," Taylor says. He always says that, but I love it too. He doesn't smile enough.

~*~*~

I lay my tired girl down. "How was your day, Yáhsháyôn?"

She smiles. "Like riding a rollercoaster. If you keep bringing kids, we need a bigger house."

I lay beside her so I can see her beautiful eyes and smile. I missed it today. "I don't plan on bringing kids. It just happens. You need to say when it's enough."

Her eyes fill but they don't spill over. "No. I didn't plan on this, but they need us. You brought kids to other places. If they need *us,* we need to take them. I didn't expect Kisuq, but I knew as soon as I saw her in your arms that she was ours. We'll figure out room when we need it."

"You're an amazing woman, Yáhsháyôn. When Jeremy came to heal her, he said she's my Kisuq. I didn't know she'd be staying until he said it. My heart flipped and I knew. She had just passed out. I needed help then she was mine. My life gets fuckin' crazy but this is a lot to take. You haven't lived our crazy. Tell me when it's enough."

She smiles like I'm amusing her. "Kisuq won't wake up until tomorrow Jacob said. Tonight, I'm telling you

I have more room in my heart. How are you doing with four new kids and a new wife?"

I lean over and kiss my old lady and almost new wife's lips. "I have more but I'm not looking for it. It will show if there's a need. Ayakuhsak is a reader of Putam's level. That's stronger than Mucimi was but more focused. Hopefully, he won't buy cows and golf carts at five."

She laughs. "We can hope. The others?"

"Sky has ability, but no one has said. I didn't ask. We'll see soon enough. Ôkatuq and Wápáyu are Protectors. For me to be told now, they'll be readers at the very least. I don't ask. I listen and watch."

She nods. "Your parents are proud and excited." She's not asking either.

"I'm surprised my dad hasn't given me the talk again. Me claiming you doesn't mean much to him. He wants a ring on your finger before kids appear."

She shakes her head. "I did get a choice."

I nod. "It's happening your way, Yáhsháyôn. He's dealing."

"Later today it won't matter. I'm excited, Nupômkoki."

I pull her over as I lay on my back. "I will work every day for you and my family, Yáhsháyôn. You deserve to live out your days happy. I'll work to give that to you with all that is me. My arms your protection and heart your shield."

~*~*~

Kateri

I kiss his chest and hear him breathe deep. He'll be up in two hours checking on the kids then running to check the land around us. He's a true warrior like my grandmother told me about.

With everyone here, he worked from earlier than I woke up, brought his sister a baby, brought me a girl, spent an hour talking to the boys about what a girl means to our family, jumped to the ancestors with us all, spent time with his brothers and still had enough for that heart pounding passionate sex that he hands out with the most romantic words and compliments I've ever heard. I can't say I deserve more than one day filled with so much love.

I kiss his chest again thanking the ancestors for bringing him into my life. His arm tightens. "Yáhsháyôn."

I smile at the whisper. He thinks I'm his breath. I know he's my world. I live a lifetime in every second we're together. He does that effortlessly.

I smile. "I'll work for you and my new family too, Nupômkoki. You deserve it. My warrior prince that hands out dreams to everyone he meets. *Kuwômôyush*," I whisper closing my eyes.

~*~*~

Mase

    I pull on my breeches and moccasins and kiss my girl's head. "My arms are your protection and heart will shield yours, Yáhsháyôn. Call to me when you need them," I say softly.

    Making the rounds, I smile at my first stop. Ayakuhsak is at the end of Kisuq's bed with his hand on her foot. I get the little blanket from the chair and cover him. Leaving them all with a kiss, I throw appreciation to the ancestors for my family.

    Pushing, I get to the slider. Kimuks waits for me to open it. I do and we run.

    "She thinks she needs me, Brother. She doesn't see it. My fantasy became my reality the night I met her. I will fight like the Protector I was trained to be to keep her and my family safe. Family first. Her glass is mended, fierceness rebuilt around her heart and she's showing us what she can do with it. She got Alder a way to treat the Alpha-Bits without any more damage to their tiny bodies. She doesn't see it. We need her. I need her."

    He doesn't offer comments. I push us to the city fence. It's clear with no evidence a camp was here. This is good. I continue on hearing the drones and smile. My Brothers will help keep them safe. My family.

Epilogue

Mase

I get the kids up and dressed. My little Kisuq is excited. Ayakuhsak explains about free and equal Blackhawks while Ôkatuq and Wápáyu get her little moccasins on her.

I turn seeing Yáhsháyôn at the door smiling. "Baby, we were surprising you. Crazy is about to start. We'll meet up with it. This morning we're out of here."

She smiles. "What do I need?"

"Nothing, it's on the chopper. Nash is waiting." I stand in front of her. "Hold the kids to me. Close your eyes, Blackhawks." When her arms slide around me, I push.

Stepping in, I release them setting the little ones on seats. "Go, Nash. Cort knows and said keep us hidden."

"On it, VP." We lift and I get my little ones and Yáhsháyôn cans then get a pair on me. We make a half circle around Ayakuhsak and Kisuq's seats. I belt Kisuq and Kateri clips Ayakuhsak in. Breakfast is a banana, burrito, juice and milk. Ôkatuq helps dole out food. The wolves sit behind us. I fed them at the house but they're hoping for cleanup duty when we move.

Kateri is amused holding the box I have our drink bottles in with her leg against the seat leg. "Where are we going?"

"A lake Kristos told me about. It's a couple of hours alone as a family. Our second date." I smile.

She laughs leaning over and pulls my shirt for a kiss. "You're guaranteed a third date if you pull this off without batshit crazy showing up."

I laugh. "If they show, I'm done with the dates?"

"I'll have to plan them. I'll get your brothers to help. They'll make sure no one shows if they have a hand in planning it."

I shake my head. "Fuckin' women. I should have asked Christian for help."

She laughs helping Kisuq with her drink bottle. I should have gotten them smaller bottles. I'll know next time.

Wápáyu wipes Ayakuhsak up as I tell them about the lake. I kiss his head. "Thank you."

"Are we swimming, Dad?" Ôkatuq looks hopeful.

"Could be. It may be cold. I'm seeing it for the first time with you. Pres told me about it being the same color as Miss Natalia's eyes. Nash got the location from him."

"How come you're not flying us?"

I smile at Wápáyu. "I'm not certified to fly stealth. That's the kind of chopper this is. I fly Blackhawks."

"Like us! Blackhawks!" Ayakuhsak has us laughing,

Kateri holds his face and blows a kiss at him. "Just like us."

"This is a Blackhawk."

I nod to my all-seeing oldest boy. "It is. It's heavily modified. I can fly it but I'm not certified. They're expensive. To replace it means they have to build one for us. If we're short because I fucked it up, someone could end up without help when they need it. We don't ever put people in danger."

Wápáyu sits up so I wait for it. "We get them out of danger. We're Blackhawks. We always watch out for our Brothers."

I laugh. "Good job."

"I can be Blackhawks?" Kisuq has me unbelting her.

"You are our newest Blackhawk. Kisuq Blackhawk is our princess like mom Blackhawk." I kiss her head.

She's beaming at Ayakuhsak. "I'm like you."

"We take care of our girls. You're like mom. She's strong but we still take care of her. We can take care of you like mom, Kisuq Blackhawk. Grandpa Cloud said our girls are special 'cause we didn't have you before, now we have you we have to work and keep you." Ôkatuq is surprised when Kateri leans over and kisses his head.

"We're each other's gifts. I'm happy to be one of your gifts, you're all my gifts."

"Five out," Nash tells me.

I belt Kisuq back in and take Yáhsháyôn's thermos so I can close it and clean our papers up. The boys help get the bottles snapped closed and box stowed under the seat. The wolves inch closer cleaning up the floor. It works well.

We set down and I know this is perfect by the view of the lake and mountains we can see from here. The kids are excited but stay sitting. I collect cans as the blades slow and pull Nash's breakfast and bottle out setting it on the seat.

"I have backpacks ready. Get your juice bottle and put it in the side pouch." I hand Yáhsháyôn a water bottle and help Ayakuhsak get his backpack on. Asa hooked me up with two Alpha-Bit packs.

Opening the door, the view is breathtaking, crystal blue against the clear sky and mountain backdrop. Fuckin' perfect. I help Kateri down and hand her Kisuq then lift the boys down.

"Good job making sure the girls felt that, Scouts. That's exactly how you take care of your girls, they're always first."

Nash jumps down with his backpack on and burrito in his hand. "Thanks, Mase." He sits in the doorway to eat.

I throw him chin and follow my excited family to the edge of the lake.

"It's like being in the middle of a picture depicting perfection." Kateri smiles back at me for half a second. "I've never seen anything more beautiful, have you?"

I smile watching them as I pull my phone. "Turn, Blackhawks." They all turn my way. I snap the picture. "Very cool. You're good to explore. No, baby, I've never seen anything more beautiful." I set it to my screensaver and put my phone away. She's watching me when I look up. I shrug.

We walk. We get our moccasins in our bags and get our feet wet in the freezing water. We throw a ball to each other, then sticks for the wolves while running through the wet sand. We find rocks that are interesting. We laugh at each other and the wolves. We explain about family and the house to Kisuq through it all.

Nash has a blanket down in front of the chopper when we make it back. We sit and eat our granola bars then watch the sky. The kids get bored with the sky and Nash plays tag with them suspending all over the place. It keeps them entertained.

"How did I do on our second date, Yáhsháyôn?"

She smiles with her beautiful light brown eyes shining. That look is the one I'll work the rest of my life for.

She sighs and I know I'm in. "Perfect. You can plan the dates if I get to see the picture."

I laugh sitting us up and wrap my arms around her. "If it's mine it's yours, Yáhsháyôn." I pull my phone out and hand it to her.

"Oh my. It's beautiful."

I look over her shoulder wanting to see it again. "My family. I've never seen anything more beautiful."

She looks up and kisses me. "Thank you."

She turns snapping a picture of Nash suspending behind the kids. Ayakuhsak is holding Kisuq's hand looking around the front of the chopper. Ôkatuq and Wápáyu are smiling at each other right behind them.

Nash has his Blackhawk smile on ready to scare the shit out of them. I laugh when he yells, "Badass!"

They all run screaming then laughing.

~*~*~

Kateri

Mase takes us right to the circle to thank the ancestors for our successful second date. The kids have me working to keep the smile off my face while they show appreciation for rocks, sticks, granola bars, a ball, the wolves and Nash. Mase looks at me and I know he's trying not to laugh.

Nash thanks the ancestors for his time with his new Blackhawk cousins.

When we jump back, we hear music. The kids, wolves and Nash run up the path.

Mase laughs. "I think the party has started, Yáhsháyôn."

"Look at them. All in breeches looking like mini-Mases."

He pulls me faster. "Mini Blackhawks. Kisuq has breeches to match yours."

I noticed earlier thinking it was cute. She has a shirt with a blue dreamcatcher stamped on the whole right side. They're all adorable.

When we get to the walkway Nash is gone. We jog across the walkway behind the kids with the wolves keeping to their sides. I love that they keep them together and safe. People are everywhere.

"Jesus." His tone has me looking up then to where he's looking. A whole section of people have their phones out and pointed at us.

"That's a little weird but the kids are cute."

He laughs stopping. "So are you, Yáhsháyôn." He kisses me like we're alone then walks me towards the crowd.

It takes me a minute to clear my head. I'm hugged before I realize it's Ant Irma. "Child, that was a sight."

Rex hugs me then Seren. Oh my. CJ hugs me and starts walking toward the stairs. I look for the kids. Mase has Kisuq and Ayakuhsak. Asa is walking to a table with Ôkatuq and Wápáyu.

"Thank you. Is that batshit crazy?"

She laughs. "Not yet. It will be soon. I was just getting you out of the crowd. The day I married Cloud, we walked out the door to a whole carnival set up on the street.

It came with an Indian section complete with tepees, drums and a fire circle. Batshit crazy but worth every friggin second. I was not expected to hug everyone there. I'm not sure I even *saw* everyone there."

I smile. Okay. We sit on the deck watching the crowd grow. I can see missing people in this crowd. Aiyana comes out of the house in a beautiful dress. She's gone a second later.

I shake my head. "I just saw Aiyana ...for a second."

CJ stands. "It's time if Aiyana is here."

I stand not sure what it's time for. I jump holding my heart as Aiyana appears on the side of me with Kisuq.

"It is an honor to add your names to the Connecticut Mohegan tribe, Kateri. They are ready to welcome you when you visit. I must warn you that is with gifts in need of a freight truck to deliver. They are as crazy as Badass."

I laugh. "Thank you, Aiyana, for sponsoring me and the tribal welcome. I'm honored to add my family's names to the Blackhawk members."

She sighs. "One day I will be included as family."

CJ laughs.

I shake my head. "Mase said you were a revered member of Knight, Lightfoot and Blackhawks. Those words were spoken with honor evident. The names are as impressive as Baxter from what I am told. I'm new, so maybe I missed something."

She smiles with a glow around her. "It is time to stop my whining and be fuckin' Badass. I will bask in that honor as I help dress my new tribal additions." She pulls me along with her. CJ is still laughing. I think batshit crazy is starting.

When we get to the room, I know it has. Every Protector woman, Seren, Ant Irma, who didn't pass by me to get here, old ladies from the other Clubs and Joey are here.

Lisa hands me a drink.

Aylen comes out of the bathroom in regalia and smiles. She's beautiful, they're all beautiful. "I just hung your regalia up. Drink up. Every Blackhawk, Knight and Lightfoot are here. You're going to need it. Cort has all the Presidents so your great uncle Heam is out there with more cousins. You will have some sane to balance the crazy. Alder is a President so his entourage will help if they're not filling the pool with fish."

Oh my.

~*~*~

Mase

I can't believe my whole family is here. My dad is proud. I've heard it three times. Brantley has my new boy with Sebastian and his new girl. I smile seeing Trask sit with his boys.

"Audrey Hepburn said, '*I believe, every day, you should have at least one exquisite moment.*' You'll have a lot of them today. I'm giving you one you can see forever."

I smile turning to Cort. "It's already been a day of exquisite moments. I appreciate your help not letting one slip away," I tell him in Mohegan.

He laughs handing me a frame. Jesus. My family running with the mountain behind us. Everyone is smiling with hair flying back. Ayakuhsak and Kisuq holding hands in front. Ôkatuq and Wápáyu have the wolves on the side of them. Yáhsháyôn is holding my hand behind the kids. It's like we were posed so everyone is caught in the perfect position. We're all in breeches and moccasins looking timeless.

I swallow hard and hug him. "Thank you."

"It could be a hundred years ago or today. Everyone was shocked seeing the beauty in that. Your family shows the life force of a nation that's strong, proud and fucking beautiful, Brother. Congratulations."

Jesus. I hug him again. "I'm so fuckin' honored to be yours, thank you, Cort."

Justice takes the picture out of my hand. "When the fuck did you get this done?"

I laugh. "When we first got here. Someone snapped it before Aiyana stole my girls."

We all look up. Helicopters come from the path side of the yard. They're bigger than toys but not as big as the Alpha-Bits'. Nash, Alder, Asa, Mateo, Juan, Ôkatuq and Wápáyu stand in a line controlling the choppers from the path.

Floating pieces of paper have everyone excited. I laugh at my dad holding Ayakuhsak up to catch the paper. One floats and I see Ôkatuq on it. I snatch it smiling at Nash. He was watching me and throws chin. He was taking pictures of us at the lake.

'*Kateri didn't grow up learning traditions. We got the offering covered. I made a book for the sponsors.*'

I love my fuckin' Brothers.

Cort laughs looking at Kateri and Kisuq running away from the water.

"It was cold. That's a cute picture."

I spin seeing my beautiful enigma in her regalia. "A vision, Yáhsháyôn."

"So are you. I was looking at the art on your back. It's beautiful." She smiles and I kiss it. She's in a dress like Aiyana wore, the beading is different colors at the top and I know it's her Navajo colors.

"Our union shows on your dress. I feel that honor deep, Yáhsháyôn."

Her calm, cool and collected shows in her eyes and movement as she reaches for my hand. "I'm honored and feel it, Nupômkoki. Beautiful. That's why they were watching us." She has the picture I forgot I was holding. She's done with the dress commentary. She bends showing the picture to Kisuq.

Shit. She's in a mini replica of Kateri's dress. I didn't even see her.

"She was collecting pictures, Brother."

I smile at Christian. "Thanks, I thought I was losing it."

"Not yet. We're watching out for them. I have Kisuq. Brantley doesn't trust dad to stay focused. He's bitching about Joey having a kid without a ring."

I roll my eyes. Sebastian claimed her a week after their first date years ago. Christian jogs away following Kisuq. I smile seeing Jacob flying a chopper by my boys and Nash. I'll have to get the cowboys on the house feed for pictures.

My girl finishes with Natalia turning back to me with her hand out. So delicate are her movements I hold my hand out surprised that this is hitting me right now with a million fuckin' people in my yard.

"The ceremony is at the circle, dancing at Natalia's, food at the pool and here. The kids are being watched over by Presidents, old ladies and your brothers." She's got that amused smile on.

I pull her close and push. "We're here, Yáhsháyôn."

She opens her eyes and laughs. "Where exactly is this tepee located?"

She knows me so well. "High on the ledge of a mountain one over from us. The runway makes it easy to locate the Club."

She pulls my shirt. "This is one of the reasons I love you so much."

"Show me, baby."

~*~*~

Kateri

I look at my rings again. I never expected them, but the man makes everything he does the best dream a girl could ever have. They sparkle as if light is alive in the stones.

He finishes talking to Heam, my great uncle or something and smiles at me. "We need to give our gifts."

I nod walking with him to the elders by the stones. Jeremy shows with cloth wrapped bundles and waits smiling. The Blackhawk smile Mase calls it. I love the smiles. Mase takes a bundle and lets my hand go. I put my arm around his waist.

"Aiyana, I am honored and proud to call you my shaman, Brother, but mostly my family. Our ties live in our books and are written on our hearts. On top of the dress and breeches is a tie you can wear showing the world."

I hold my laugh as Aiyana unties the string quickly and opens the bundle. She laughs dropping all but the T-shirt. "I will wear it often with honor to those ties."

I laugh picking up the breeches, shirts, dress and jewelry. Mase nods for me.

I hold the jewelry up. "The jewelry was on top. The stones are a mix of Mitch Baxter's and mine, Aiyana. We thought it showed our family ties binding our lives to yours as one family."

Prez, Cloud and Dakota laugh. Aiyana holds the shirt lower and looks at the jewelry. "It is with honor that I will cherish your gifts with such thought to our combined ancestry."

I hold my laugh.

"You want to go put the T shirt on, don't you?" Mase asks with that Blackhawk smile.

Aiyana hugs us both with her headdress hitting Mase in the face as she nods. I feel her take the clothes I was holding as she disappears. The men laugh. I shake my head.

Mase takes another bundle from Jeremy and gives it to his dad. "Fuckin' proud, Dad." Jeremy laughs with Dakota and Prez. Mase isn't finished. "I hope that shows with honor to you for all the lessons I live every day of my life. *Kuwômôyush*."

I hug Cloud, barely. He's got a cuff with a dreamcatcher to match the one on the traditional shirt. It looks like it was stamped on the right chest as if it's a little logo. He apparently likes it because he's going to put it on.

Dakota is touched by the book with pictures of Destiny, Justice and Aquyá here. He has the same breeches and a shirt with Prophet on it.

The biggest bundle goes to Prez. "I never understood why you never wore the clothes. You always think they look comfortable and appreciate that they're made by natives in organic material. Stella got me an avitar of you and I had them made. The shirts say, Leader, Warrior Prince, BSC, Badass, the Prince logo and Knight. They were so honored to make your clothes they wouldn't let me pay. They have your size and will make anything you want. You are as much a part of the Connecticut Mohegan as I am. Nunánuk has always been *our* great grandmother."

Prez hugs Mase thanking him. "I will wear them with honor, thank you, Mase, Kateri." He's gone.

Jeremy laughs. "He will. Good job."

I laugh when Jeremy disappears. Holding Mase's hand I walk back thinking about connections. Prez protects the reservations up there, recognizes them and now maybe will feel more at home with them, he needs the roots. With no people or family there, I can see it being hard to feel a part of it. Not growing up on the reservation, he doesn't get that Indians welcome everyone. He'd be someone they'd all show appreciation for. I'm so glad he got that he's more a part of them than he realizes. I smile, Aiyana too.

Cloud gave the kids a dreamcatcher he made with the stone like on my ring, he'll help teach them connections. He did a great job teaching his kids. I think my smile is for life.

"What are you thinking, Yáhsháyôn?"

"About connections."

He nods. "The blanket ceremony was different for us, new, nice and had me thinking about our connections."

It was and he had the theme of connections for the gifts. He's a very thoughtful man.

"I want the kids to have the connections I do. I want to take them to Heam's, Connecticut and even Rhode Island. You grew up where Cort did. He offered to bring us to the reservation here."

~*~*~

Mase

I feel her anxiety and don't understand. Connections are important.

"I wear my heritage proudly and always have. I would like to visit but worry about being remembered. I don't have details for a reason. Our kids don't have those details for a reason."

Fuck. "You're right, Yáhsháyôn. Hearing and seeing it with us can be enough. I didn't think about the cloaks or people knowing you or your grandmother."

She squeezes my hand. "I would love to see your home and the reservations you learned from. I'd like to see Heam and his home. Here we have what is important to make this our home. I have it on good authority that we'll be happy here for a long time."

I smile at that. "Which one told you that?"

She runs into the yard pulling her hand out of mine. "A little hummingbird." Bending she scoops up Ayakuhsak and spins him around.

Hummingbird, her grandmother calls people she likes birds. She said hummingbird last night. Shit, it's already starting.

I stand and watch. The kids are back in breeches with Mucimi's Ts on.

Prez has breeches and the Knight shirt on. Uncle Steve is pissed. He wants one, the Brothers laugh.

Aiyana's neck and ankle shine with blue. She doesn't have the moccasins on but she's in breeches and the T-shirt. She has a shaman and Princess shirt but is wearing the T.

Kateri sits with the women. Kisuq runs to her with Christian standing back watching. Dean holds his waist smiling.

Holly has Joey's new girl talking to Ôkatuq. Brantley kisses her head and turns to my dad. He points at the shirt. Oh shit. He gives me a look. Terry laughs kissing Judy's head as he drops a plate. He points at me shaking his head. I started shit again his head says.

I shrug. I'm going to start more. I push and get the bundle I have for Christian and stand in front of him. "I had Stella make an avitar of you. They have your sizes. Order what you want."

He hugs me. "Thanks, Mase. You've always been my favorite."

I laugh as he takes off fast. Jeremy shows in front of me. I blank my face and thoughts. He smiles then he's gone. Fuckin' readers.

I follow my girl, the little hummingbird, to her mom feeling my heart swell with every step. They're both tiny.

My old lady and now new wife looks over her shoulder and smiles at me. "I've got them. Old ladies are on kid watch for a while. Go sit with your Brothers. Brantley looks pissed at you." She giggles.

I look over and see Taylor in his shirt with the Prince logo that says Blackhawk under it. I laugh when Jeremy sits by him head to toe in Indian wear. I kiss my girls and sit with my Brothers.

Cort is amused by the Blackhawk hissy fits. Jacob and Brantley are pissed. Christian suspends by slow, so Brantley sees him. I crack up.

Aubrey brings the baby to Sebastian and gives Jacob a look. "It's Mase. You think *today* is the one he'd forget where he comes from. Men are so weird."

I laugh. My brothers are fuckin' funny. Pres and Uncle Danny sit.

"You do shop. Little Ben said you got him a wardrobe." Pres has Uncle Danny laughing.

"Nope. Stella made avatars with measurements in graph form. I sent them up to Little Bear and he ordered clothes for me. Joey got the bill and paid it. I did deliver clothes everywhere."

He gets up and walks away. Cort and Uncle Danny laugh.

When Jacob sits with his Protector of the Three shirt on Uncle Danny asks, "What's mine say?"

I'm not giving him anything without information first. "What did they get and where is it?"

"Sex toys in your closet. Be careful opening the door."

"LP1." I answer with a smile.

He's gone.

Cort laughs. "He's going to fuck with Ben James."

I nod and shrug.

Kristos sits. "He likes poking people without poking them."

Prez sits. "He's like Uncle Danny. Don't piss him off. These are as comfortable as they look. They fit perfect, thanks, Brother."

I throw him chin and smile when bundles drop in front of the Brothers. Cort laughs opening his. When he stands, he pulls his T off and everyone watches. The Brother is huge and ripped. Jesus.

Seren gives a wolf whistle and he smiles at her having no clue we all wish Reed was our dad. Christian laughs. I shrug.

Pres sits again waiting. When Uncle Danny shows in breeches and his LP1 shirt Pres glares at him. Cort laughs when Uncle Danny sits like he didn't notice.

Christian is almost hyperventilating on the side of me.

Nash is done with his delivery service and stands by me.

I stand taking the last one. "This one was special, Pres. I need you to stand so Nash can get a picture. Brothers! One minute!" I shake the shirt out and show him.

Brothers move in while Pres switches his shirts out. He hugs me and the Brothers move closer. Nash lifts Alder up on the next table and stands with us while Alder gets a picture. He looks cute in his breeches and moccasins.

Prez throws, '*Presidents stay.*'

I take the camera. Alder jumps and runs. I move the Brothers on the edges and behind away getting laughs. I don't care. I get a picture with them all smiling.

"*The First*. Kid did good." Uncle Steve says with a smile getting everyone smiling.

I snap it. I'll send it to Elizabeth for the website.

I love my fuckin' life.

Thanks for reading Kateri and Mase Blackhawk's story. This was heart wrenching to write. I see things on the news and it ends up in a book. Mase, being Mase, tempers the horror we see in real life. I hope you felt it. While tempering that, our sexy Indian delivers a heat Kateri has no problem handling. I can't wait for what's next!

Leave a review or hit a star button for me. Thanks!

L.

Acknowledgments

Life is crazy. While it is, I'm lucky to have so many, not only dealing with that crazy but helping get the next books out.

Betas, readers, women in the chat, for encouraging, throwing ideas, making me laugh, thank you. I hope I made you proud with this one.

Jo-Kat, another that sucks you in making finding mistakes hard. I've read this one so many times, I think I can recite it. Thanks for catching all I miss.

Readers, while it's crazy, I hope you find something to smile about in this one. The Blackhawks are always good for smiles. Thanks for sticking with me and my Badass world.

Until the next one, my loyal and faithful friends.

Stay safe and strong,

L.

About the Author

L. Ann started with the Baxters and followed that with multiple series and genres. While her books feature paranormal, FBI, ex-military and Badass Bikers, L. Ann is writing about the strong women that these men need in their life to help right the world's wrongs and keep their small part of the world safe. The women are extraordinary, strong and determined to make a difference.

The men fight for right in every book. Yes, they kill people. Yes, the MC shoots at the bad guys' feet to cause them pain. Yes, some throw tampons at each other regularly.

That being said, they do these things while stopping human trafficking and experimentation, bringing their world into legitimate businesses, fighting gangs to keep drugs away from their town and kids, keep women sheltered safely while trying to stop domestic abuse. These are men that don't leave a pack, Team member or Brother behind. They don't treat women as possessions and they don't cheat. Respect takes on an honorable meaning. Women and kids are cherished. Everyone is looked out for and everyone is equal.

L. Ann has made amazing worlds, tackled the taboo subjects and made it easy to imagine living in a world where your protection comes from the vampires, shifters, freaky kids, albinos and orientals, military turned FBI and some Badass Bikers.

With readers writing about rereading the series over and over, she feels like she's told her characters' stories in a way that would make them proud.

Every book will make you laugh, every book will make you angry for the wrong that happens in the world. Every book will make you cry for the pain that a character feels. Every book gives you hope that we may just get it right yet.

Author contact links

*Connect via email: **l_ann_marie@aol.com***

*Connect with me on Facebook: **L. Ann Marie Pen Page***

*Check out my website: **http://www.lannmarie.com***

*Check out the YouTube videos: **videos***

Other books by L. Ann Marie

The Baxters
*She Found Us: myBook.to/baxtersbook1 **.99***
Our Wife: myBook.to/baxtersbook2
Our Angel: myBook.to/baxtersbook3
Jake: myBook.to/baxtersbook4
Rayne: myBook.to/baxtersbook5
The MC
*Knight: myBook.to/mcbook1 **.99***
LaPonte: myBook.to/mcbook2
LaPonte-Karr: myBook.to/mcbook3
Pres: myBook.to/mcbook4
Blackhawk: myBook.to/mcbook5
Tailley: myBook.to/mcbook6
Callahan: myBook.to/mcbook7
Brighton: myBook.to/mcbook8
Moniz: myBook.to/mcbook9
Ricky: myBook.to/mcbook10
Behind the Scenes: myBook.to/mcbook0
Princes of Prophecy
Prophet Book 1: myBook.to/princesbook1
Reader: Book 2: myBook.to/princesbook2
Leader Book 3: myBook.to/princesbook3
Enforcer Book 4: myBook.to/princesbook4
Coder Book 5: myBook.to/princesbook5
Sniper Book 6: myBook.to/princesbook6
The Protectors
Christian: myBook.to/protectorsbook1
Aiyana: myBook.to/protectorsbook2
Jacob & Jeremy: myBook.to/protectorsbook3
D.C Security: http://a.co/cSZ36kz
Stand Alone
Spying Eyes: myBook.to/spyingeyes
The Providence Series
Saber's Vida: myBook.to/providence1
Saber's Porthos: myBook.to/providence2

Saber's D'Artagnan: myBook.to/providence3
Saber's Sombra: myBook.to/providence4
Saber's Aramis: myBook.to/providence5
Saber's Athos: mybook.to/providence6
The Other World Order
Princes' Reward: mybook.to/OWO1
Fated Mates: mybook.to/OWO2
Princes' Pack: mybook.to/OWO3
The BSC Series
The Phoenix Rising Series
Master's Rise: mybook.to/phoenixseries1
Benga's Rise: mybook.to/phoenixseries2
Ranger's Rise: mybook.to/phoenixseries3
The Bravo Rising Series
Jack: Honor: mybook.to/bravohonor
Falcon: Respect: mybook.to/bravorespect
Mag: Loyalty: mybook.to/bravoloyalty
Champion Rising Series
Allegory: myBooks.to/allegory
Endue: mybook.to/endue
Conform: mybook.to/conform
Justice: Tenacity: mybook.to/Bravotenacity
Ford's Rise: mybook.to/phoenixseries4
Alpha Rising Series
Driver: Grit: https://www.amazon.com/dp/B08WVQPR83
Christiansen: City Boy:
Nova: Cred: https://www.amazon.com/dp/B0943F7YCN

Boxed Sets
Baxters Series Box : https://www.amazon.com/dp/B0776G4XZ6
MC: Boxed Set 1-4: https://www.amazon.com/dp/B078TSKH7D
MC Boxed Set + Jake: Books 5-7: https://www.amazon.com/dp/B079BLCZVF
MC Boxed Set + Rayne: Books 8,9, 0: https://www.amazon.com/dp/B079HJ778R
Princes of Prophecy Books 1-3: https://www.amazon.com/dp/B079PS6PFX
Princes of Prophecy Books 4-6: https://www.amazon.com/dp/B079PY4Z9K
The Protectors Boxed Set w/ MC10 + DC:
https://www.amazon.com/dp/B079V9L3FV
The Providence Series Boxed Set 1: https://www.amazon.com/dp/B07J5884KD
The Providence Series Boxed Set 2: https://www.amazon.com/dp/B07JB3HK11

Badass Security Council Phoenix Rising: BSC Box 1:
https://www.amazon.com/dp/B08WQ41TWD

Badass Security Council Bravo Rising: BSC Box 2:
https://www.amazon.com/dp/B08WRLRP1G

Badass Security Council Champion Rising: BSC Box 3:
https://www.amazon.com/dp/B08WVQPR83

Reading Order

It is better to read them in order so you don't miss anything. The *boxed sets* help keep them straight. I answer questions from previous books as I go along (the not easy thing). So, here is the order in which they were written.

She Found Us - Baxters
Our Wife - Baxters
Our Angel - Baxters
Knight - MC
LaPonte - MC
LaPonte-Karr - MC
Pres - MC
Blackhawk - MC
Tailley - MC
Callahan - MC
Jake - Baxters
Brighton - MC
Rayne - Baxters
Moniz - MC
Behind the Scenes - MC
Prophet - Princes of Prophecy
Reader - Princes of Prophecy
Leader - Princes of Prophecy
Enforcer - Princes of Prophecy
Coder - Princes of Prophecy
Sniper - Princes of Prophecy
Christian - The Protectors
Ricky - MC
Aiyana - The Protectors
D.C. Security - Baxters/MC/Princes
Jeremy & Jacob - The Protectors
Saber's Vida - The Providence Series
Saber's Porthos - The Providence Series
Saber's D'Artagnan - The Providence Series

Saber's Sombra - The Providence Series
Saber's Aramis - The Providence Series
Saber's Athos - The Providence Series
Spying Eyes - Standalone
Princes' Reward -The Other World Series
Fated Mates -The Other World Series
Princes' Pack - The Other World Series
Master's Rise - The Phoenix Series
Benga's Rise -The Phoenix Series
Ranger's Rise - The Phoenix Series
Jack: Honor - The Bravo Series
Falcon: Respect - The Bravo Series
Mag: Loyalty - The Bravo Series
Allegory - The Champion Series
Endue - Champion Series
Conform - Champion Series
Justice: Tenacity - Bravo Series
Ford's Rise - Phoenix Series
Driver: Grit - Alpha Series
Christiansen: City Boy - Alpha Series
Nova: Creed - Alpha Series
Blackhawk: Mase - Honor Series

Made in the USA
Coppell, TX
09 April 2022